Anna Bartlett Warner

Stories of Vinegar Hill

Anna Bartlett Warner

Stories of Vinegar Hill

ISBN/EAN: 9783337006754

Printed in Europe, USA, Canada, Australia, Japan

Cover: Foto ©Andreas Hilbeck / pixelio.de

More available books at **www.hansebooks.com**

BY THE AUTHOR OF

"SUNDAY ALL THE WEEK," "LITTLE JACK'S FOUR LESSONS,"
"ELLEN MONTGOMERY'S BOOKSHELF," ETC

Seventh Thousand.

LONDON:
JAMES NISBET & CO., 21 BERNERS STREET.
MDCCCLXXXII.

𝔅𝔞𝔩𝔩𝔞𝔫𝔱𝔶𝔫𝔢 𝔓𝔯𝔢𝔰𝔰

BALLANTYNE, HANSON AND CO.
EDINBURGH AND LONDON

CONTENTS.

THE OLD CHURCH DOOR.

A

THE OLD CHURCH DOOR.

CHAPTER I.

"Behold a sower went forth to sow."

"I HARDLY know whether I ought to say I am most sorry or glad, that I must decline your obliging offer, ma'am," said the superintendent of the little Long Meadow Sunday-school. "Fact is, we have rather more than enough teachers already."

"So few children in the place?" said Mrs Kensett.

"Ah, I don't know about that!" said the superintendent, laughing; "sometimes I think there's more than enough children, too. Not in the school, however: our classes are hardly so large as the teachers would fancy. Seems a sort of waste of time, you know, to come, week after week, for only three or four children."

"Oh, I want no larger class than that," said the lady. "I think five is almost too large."

"Think so?" said Mr Morton; "most people don't. They like more of a show."

"But the show—if there is any—should be in the work done," said Mrs Kensett.

"True," said Mr Morton; "exactly so. Are you settling in Long Meadow, ma'am?"

"Only for the summer, for change of air."

"There is no better air in the country," said Mr Morton,

with emphasis. "But that would make the arrangement of a class still more difficult. Such matters for a short time always are. The new teacher brings new ways, and the other classes are unsettled. Else I am sure we should be most happy. If indeed we had more children. But it's a small place—a very small place. And as you are an invalid, perhaps rest will be better than work."

"I rest better with some work," said Mrs Kensett. "But I never thought of disturbing your settled classes. Do all the village children come to your school, sir?"

"Really," said Mr Morton, "I hardly know! Yes—upon reflection, I think they do,—about all. There are the tavern children—some half dozen—of course do not come; and one or two more that I think of."

"Are there any families living quite outside the village?" said Mrs Kensett.

"There are some," said Mr Morton, "how many I can't say —speaking of those that do not belong in any way to the society. A poor scattering set, for the most part, hid away among the bushes on Vinegar Hill. I believe the bell is warning us all to our places, Mrs Kensett,—shall I have the pleasure of giving you a seat?"

And up the white church steps went Mr Morton, bland and benign; while Mrs Kensett followed him softly along the little aisle, pondering his words—

"Hid away among the bushes on Vinegar Hill!"

In every pause of the service they came back to her, with some such refrain as this :—"He came to seek and to save." "Go ye into the highways and hedges, and compel them to come in." And then she pictured to herself the motley crowd thus gathered, and the servants returning with their glad answer: 'Lord, it is done as Thou hast commanded, and yet there is room." Room?—she looked round the little church- even there, in God's house on earth, there was room enough and to spare. Where were the people that should have filled those empty seats?—and again her heart echoed back the words: "Hid away among the bushes on Vinegar Hill."

" There's room within the Church, redeem'd
With blood of Christ divine ;
Room in the white-robed throng convened
For that dear soul of thine.

" There 's room in heaven among the choir,
And harps, and crowns of gold,
And glorious palms of victory there,
And joys that ne'er were told."

The service was over, the people dismissed to their homes; and in the clear light of the summer afternoon they went singly or in little clusters along the green village roads. Some few wheeled off in open waggons to homes a half dozen miles back in the country ; a yet smaller number were the happy owners and users of a close carriage, and saw as little as possible of the clover blossoms on their way home. Undistilled clover fragrance was, after all, rather a common thing ; and even new-mown hay must be bottled and labelled before they could find out its sweetness.

But clearly none of all these passers-by came from Vinegar Hill—not one of all that whole congregation had ever been an outcast "hid away among the bushes." Mrs Kensett lingered in her walk, gazing wistfully over the green land-scape.

On every side the ground broke into a lovely mingling of hill and valley, with here a dark spot of lake, set in the woods, and there the foaming thread of a tumbling brook ; the white church itself standing midway on one long slope ; and clustering below it, more or less near, the village houses led down to the broad green valley which gave the place its name of Long Meadow. All fair, all glowing with June light.

" Can you tell me, sir, which is Vinegar Hill ? " inquired Mrs Kensett, as a belated farmer came plodding by. He stopped and looked at her.

" Vinegar Hill ? Why !—Beant agoing there, be you ? "

" Not to-night."

" Well, I wouldn't, 'cause it 's an ugly place. Worst hole in the township. I wouldn't take evidence from Vinegar

Hill, now," said the farmer, striking the heel of his boot against a stone with great emphasis, "not as to which way my cow'd gone. Might be sure I'd find her in just t'other direction."

"But in what direction is the hill itself?"

"Vinegar Hill? why, it's there, back o' the church. Slid off from the back door, sometime, likely, and went a good way afore it stopped."

"What, that low green hill that seems all bushes?" said Mrs Kensett.

"Ay, but it ain't all bushes, more's the pity," said the farmer, shading his eyes with his hand as he looked. "There's houses enough there—too many; and rascals to fill one jail, and some to spare. Yes, that's Vinegar Hill, and a sour spot it is. Take more'n one church to sweeten it."

"And how many church members—if they worked faithfully, with God's blessing?" asked Mrs Kensett, with one of her winning smiles.

The farmer stared, then broke into a puzzled laugh.

"Well, I couldn't rightly say," he answered; "fact is, I ain't much in that line o' business, but it's an ugly spot. So, as I said, I wouldn't go nigh there. Good-night to ye!" and he strode on.

It was early yet; the proud summer day bent its head but slightly, glancing over meadow and hill; and the long sunbeams held the ground against all claims of the white-faced moon, waiting so patiently to take her place. Mrs Kensett sat down on a gray stone by the wayside, to look and think. The whole scene was wondrously peaceful, with something of that sweet, calm hush, which seems to have lingered about this seventh portion of time, ever since "God blessed the seventh day, and hallowed it." Hardly a sound stirred the air, though every green swell of land was dotted with houses and full of life, with windows gleaming in the sunshine, or even—in some deep woodland nook—glimmering and twinkling with an early candle : the Sabbath rest was upon all. Only as Mrs Kensett turned towards Vinegar Hill, she felt the difference. It looked peaceful enough with its close green covering that was neither forest nor undergrowth, but a scrub of thickset bushes : and a tinkle of cowbells moving slowly along from point to point, and a light hazy smoke that floated over the tops of the bushes, were the only signs of life. But as the sunbeams withdrew to higher ground, and twilight filled the valleys, there came up from Vinegar Hill a confused murmur—not sportive, not rejoicing, not even like the wholesome hum of business—but wild, lawless, and harsh.

Mrs Kensett rose quickly and walked away. At first towards home—then turned, and began slowly to mount the church hill once more ; saying softly to herself—"to seek and to save." And as she went, a half dozen children came stealing up on the other side, from out the thickets of Vinegar Hill, and began with great spirit to play ball against the side of the church, and marbles on its old steps.

So busy were they with their games, so intent upon the ball and the marbles, that not one of them saw a little lady cross the stile of the church fence and come towards them. Not one knew she was near, until they heard a sweet voice asking—

"Which of you little ones has been here before to-day ? "

They all stopped and looked at her.

" Hi ! " said one of the boys expressively, giving his ball a toss straight up in the air, and catching it again with great exactness.

" Come all the way up a purpose to ask ! " said another mockingly ; " and nobody don't know nothin't all about it no more 'n she don't !—Oh dear ! "

Gently Mrs Kensett repeated her question—

" How many of you have been here before to-day ? "

" Well, I haven't, for one," said a little boy.

" Can't see whose business it is, nother," said he with the ball, playing one hand against the other with most impartial skill.

" Might know we hadn't none on us been here," said a third boy. " Can't play ball agin a meetin' house full o' people. Guess there'd be a precious row if we did."

"We always does wait till they's all gone," said the little boy.

"Do none of you come when the church is open, and go in with the people?" asked Mrs Kensett.

"Not us!" said the big boy, Sam Dodd by name. "Guess we know some better 'n that."

"'Tain't for us, you know," said little Jemmy Lucas; "we's too poor."

"Poor!" echoed the other; "yes, Jemmy *he's* poor enough, for most things. My father ain't."

"What are you all going to do when you go home to-night?" said Mrs Kensett.

"Get supper."

"Is that all?"

"Enough, too," said Peter Limp, "when it's a good one. Jemmy Lucas 'll like enough get a poundin'—but the rest of us don't care about that, ye see. It varies the performances, but it ain't interestin'."

"Do none of you say your prayers before you go to bed?" asked Mrs Kensett. But nobody answered.

"Come," she said, "sit down here on the steps with me, and I 'll tell you a story."

"A real story?" said Jemmy Lucas.

"A real, true story. But tell me first, where do you all live?"

With one voice they answered—

"On Vinegar Hill."

"What, all of you?'

"Every one."

"What sort of a place is Vinegar Hill? I can see nothing but bushes."

"There's lots of other things there, you may depend," said Peter Limp, nodding his head. "More 'n ever *you* see, I *guess*."

"Is it a nice place?"

"That's according as people thinks," said Sam Dodd, with a short laugh. "Suits me well enough."

"Mother says she didn't use to bear it," said Jemmy Lucas.

"Well, let's hear the story anyway," said Peter Limp, curling himself down on the steps. "Nobody needn't to worry over Vinegar Hill. *I* say, let's have the story." And down they all sat, grouping themselves around the stranger lady in various attitudes of carelessness or attention ; ready to get all the fun and do all the mischief they possibly could.

CHAPTER II.

"My story," began Mrs Kensett, "is about the great King over all the earth."

"I say!" broke in Sam Dodd, "guess *that's* a mistake. One king don't have it all."

"There's lots o' kings," said Peter Limp.

A little hollow cough sounded so near Mrs Kensett, that she started and looked round, but there was nothing to be seen except the boys, and she went on.

"Yes, there are many kings. I suppose you can all tell me what a king is?"

"He's an awful rich man, that wears a gold crown," said Jemmy Lucas.

"And has horses and servants and things, don't he?" said Peter Limp, "and don't never do nothin' he ain't a mind to, and eats goodies just all the time."

"And makes other folks stand round," said Sam Dodd ; "and cuts their heads off if they don't mind."

"And he sits 'way up on a throne too," said little Jemmy Lucas ; "a great high place, all over di'monds."

"True," said Mrs Kensett ; "there are kings who do almost all these things. But why do they wear a crown, and sit on a throne?"

"Why, to show how grand they are," said Sam Dodd ; "and to let folks see they'd better look out."

"Then a king rules over people?"

" Yes, ma'am."

" Over everybody ?—or only a part of the world ? "

" Can't be everybody," said Sam Dodd, musing, " 'cause there's none of 'em here. And besides, if there was a lot o' kings tryin' to rule over everybody, *some* on 'em would get to fightin'."

" Yes," said the lady, "and so each king that is in the world has a certain place or part of it, called his kingdom, where he rules ; and all the people that dwell there, are called his subjects. These are the kingdoms of this world."

Again the cough sounded, and Mrs Kensett looked round.

"Who is that coughing ? " she said.

"Nothing but Molly," said Peter Limp.

" And who is Molly ? "

" Molly ?—that's one of our girls to home, Molly Limp,— you can tell her noise 'most anywhere. She's hidin' round here some place, for the story."

" But why don't she come and sit on the steps with the rest ? " said Mrs Kensett.

" Guess likely she's afeard," said Peter. " She does be as skeary as a woodchuck, mostly. I'll start her home ! "

"No, no ! " said Mrs Kensett ; " don't send her home. Bring her here."

" Well," said Peter, " I can do that too, if that'll suit."

And forthwith he darted round the corner of the church, and having captured the small sun-bonnet that was hiding there, brought it back—all limp and frightened—to the steps at Mrs Kensett's feet.

" Here she is ! " he said,—" about as poor a sample of a girl as they often get down to the museum. Now, you Moll ! you just take your finger out o' your mouth, and look at the lady. And as you ain't got to look at nothin' else, you won't care about that 'ere old sun-bonnet, I don't think. Here goes ! "—

And away sped the bonnet up into the tangled branches of an old oak tree, that threw its flickering shadow across the steps.

Poor little Molly, thus robbed of all her defences, sat frightened, trembling, and ready to cry, looking at anything but the lady. A wan, elfish child, with long, matted hair encumbering her face, and dark, shining eyes, that gleamed out as from a thicket. Her frock was soiled, and fringed with tatters, her little hands and feet were covered with grimy dust. Mrs Kensett watched her silently at first, then laid her own soft white hand upon the little begrimmed ones that lay trembling in Molly's lap. The child started, glanced up at the lady—glanced again,—and then, with a bit of a stray smile breaking over her face, Molly clasped her fingers tight round the stranger's hand, and prepared to listen ; her attention only disturbed, now and then, by that racking cough.

"The kingdoms of this world," said Mrs Kensett, "have each their king. But high over all these reigns One alone,— far greater in power, far grander in glory ; 'the King of the whole earth shall He be called.' He rules by His power for ever, even over the greatest of other kings ; He puts one on the throne, and pulls down another. He makes one poor and another rich ; He kills and He makes alive."

"Must be awful strong," said Peter Limp.

"Yes, He is mightier than all the people in all the world. Now, other rulers often ill-treat their subjects, but this great King loves every one of His. He wants them to be good, He wants them to be happy, He wants to give them great riches, and to put on them a most glorious dress ; and He has sent every one of them an invitation to a great feast, that He will give one day in His kingdom."

"I guess I wish He ruled over me," said little Jemmy Lucas. "He wouldn't have to ask twice, I can tell Him."

"I s'pose they 're all goin' ?" said Peter Limp.

"You may bet that," said Sam Dodd ; "folks ain't such fools."

"Some of them are going," said Mrs Kensett ; "and some have refused, and some have not got their invitation. I think you have never got yours, you children,—for the King has asked every one of you to His feast, too."

"Well, I should say *that* was a story as is commonly called by a shorter name," said Sam Dodd.

"I don't wonder you think so, at first," said Mrs Kensett, "but it is quite true. I came here to-day to tell you about it."

"Be civil, Sam, can't ye?" said Peter Limp. "None o' your sarce, now. I wants to hear what she 'll say."

"Say on," answered Sam, tossing his ball up and down. "It 'll be a cur'ous one, anyhow."

"Oh, it 's a book story!" cried Jemmy Lucas, as Mrs Kensett took a small volume from her pocket.

"Yes, it is a book story; but every word of this book is perfectly true. So now listen. 'The kingdom of heaven is like unto a certain king, which made a marriage for his son.' Every king on earth, as I told you, has a certain place or part of the world where he rules; he is lord over all the people that dwell there. But our story tells of another kingdom,—what is that?"

"The kingdom of heaven," said little Molly, speaking up for the first time.

"You hush," said Peter Limp. "Who wants you to be talkin', young one? Shut up, and behave."

"I want her to talk," said Mrs Kensett, with a kind look at little Molly, "I want you all to ask questions and answer mine; and Molly has answered right. The kingdom of heaven,—who rules over that?"

"I don't know—nor don't care," said Sam Dodd, tossing his ball. "Kings ain't much count, anyhow."

"The kings who reign over a country or a single city," said Mrs Kensett, "need not be much thought of by the people who live elsewhere; they have little to do with each other. But the kingdom of heaven belongs to a Sovereign who rules over the whole earth too, the glorious One I told you of just now. He is King of kings, and Lord of lords. What is His name? do you know?"

"Well, *I* don't," said Sam Dodd. "Guess all this here 's a big part o' the story, ain't it?"

"It is a *true* part," said the lady, gently. "But do none

of you know even the name of the great King of heaven and earth ?"

"Guess not," said Jemmy Lucas, shaking his head ;—"you see there ain't much as we does know."

"I am afraid you hear His name so often, that you forget what it means," said Mrs Kensett. "I am afraid you speak it carelessly a great many times every day. Think."

"Do you mean God, ma'am ?" said little Molly, in her husky voice.

"Yes, I mean God," said Mrs Kensett ; "'God who made heaven and earth, the sea and all that in them is,'—that great King who dwells in a brightness of glory, that is 'as the sun shining in His strength.'"

"Never heard Him called a King afore," said Sam Dodd, carelessly. "Heard His name often enough—you're about right there."

"Well, whenever you hear it again," said Mrs Kensett, "remember that He is far, far greater than all other kings. He has full power over every king and every subject—over every man, woman, and child—in the whole world. He made them all,—you, and me, and all the rest ; and He could take away our lives in a moment, if He chose. He made the world, and can destroy it again. Take care how you ever speak His name lightly, for He is 'a great Lord, a mighty and a terrible.'"

"Then don't He like to have 'em speak His name so ?" said little Molly.

"No, my child, it displeases Him very much."

"They do it all the time down to father's," said the little girl, thoughtfully.

"'Tain't none o' your business if they do," said Sam Dodd, sharply. "If there was such ugly little pitchers round our house, I'd cut their ears off, straight !"

"I can hardly begin to tell you how great God is," said Mrs Kensett, holding little Molly's fingers closer in her own. "Other kings reign for a few years, and then die, but the Lord is 'King for ever and ever.' He is the King of glory, and His kingdom is an everlasting kingdom."

"What sort of a throne does He have?" asked Jemmy Lucas.

"The Bible says that it is 'a glorious high throne,'—'high and lifted up:' it tells of 'a rainbow round the throne,' of a light that would blind our eyes to look upon. For 'the Lord has prepared His throne in the heavens, and His kingdom ruleth over all:' He is crowned with glory and honour."

"That sounds mighty fine," said Peter Limp. "Never heerd a word on it before."

"Is it all very true, ma'am?" said little Mary, timidly.

"*You* ain't got much to do with it, if it is," said Sam Dodd; "kings don't bother their heads along o' such concerns as *you*."

The child broke into one of her heavy coughs, then turned her eyes towards her friend, and waited for an answer. Mrs Kensett folded the thin hands in hers, clasping them softly. "It is true, every word of it," she repeated. "But what you say, Sam, is a complete mistake. The kings of this world do not always think much about their subjects, but the great King of heaven and earth never forgets for a moment even the least and poorest of His. He sees everything you do; He hears everything you say; He knows everything you think."

"I say, I don't like that," said Peter Limp, doubtfully; "I guess I ain't agoin' to believe it, nother."

"It is so, whether you like it or not," said Mrs Kensett, "because He is God. The Bible says that His eyes are in every place, beholding the evil and the good. Even the darkness hideth not from Him."

"I should like it if He'd take care of me in the dark," said Molly.

"But I guess He don't see down in our woods, does He?" said Jemmy Lucas. "The bushes is real thick."

"That makes no difference with God," said Mrs Kensett. "He can see through the bushes as easily as you can through a window, and you cannot whisper so low that He will not hear. 'Can any hide himself in secret places, that I shall not see him? saith the Lord. Do not I fill heaven and earth? saith the Lord.' This is what I want you to remember, that God is everywhere. Think of this, Molly, when you are in the dark, and ask God to take care of you. Think of it, boys, when you are hid away in the bushes, and ask Him to keep you from displeasing Him in any way. For when God sees people do wrong, it offends Him very much. Now let us kneel down here together, and ask Him to bless us and help us, that we may never offend Him any more."

In wondering curiosity the little outcasts looked on, as the strange lady knelt there in the old porch and spoke such wonderful words. Words of entreaty that God would bless these children; that He would make them all His own; that He would make their little dark hearts all clean and new in the blood of the Lord Jesus—not one of the children had ever heard anything like it before. Even Sam Dodd stood silent and still by her side when she rose up. The night was falling fast now.

"I must go," said Mrs Kensett, "I have a long walk home. When shall we go on with our Bible story about the great King?"

"We does play ball here, most nights," suggested Jemmy Lucas.

"Do you? then I will try and come 'most nights' too. Good-bye!"

And down the winding path the little lady went in the gathering twilight, while all the children scampered back to Vinegar Hill.

CHAPTER III.

So when the next afternoon began to stretch long shadows across the valleys, and to light up the hills with that special glory that comes towards the close of the day, Mrs Kensett set out again for the chosen meeting-place at the old church door. It looked all deserted as yet, and for a while she sat there quite alone—then one by one her little troop came in sight.

It was a sorrowful thing to watch the motions of these Vinegar Hill children, to see how in everything they acted and looked like little outcasts. They did not walk boldly up to the church as the village children would have done ; following the path, and delighting in the sunshine, and stopping to pick daisies by the way ; but came stealing up like wild rabbits, taking the cover of every bush, and seeming to dodge those golden rays that filled the world with glory.

Mrs Kensett watched them from the corner of the church, but quick as her eye was, it could not always tell how they got from one point to another. A wild looking little head would peer out of one clump of bushes, as if on the alert for enemies, and then, in some mysterious way, it was suddenly transferred to a bush still nearer the church, showing itself there ; so making approaches by zigzag degrees. Only little Molly was not strong enough, or not wild enough for such antics, and crept slowly and steadily up to the church. Mrs Kensett looked, and tried to keep track of the youngsters, but for a while—except Molly—she could not see one, and then with a rush they were all upon her, their brown faces gleaming with lawless fun. Then her start of surprise called forth such a whoop and halloo and outburst of delight, that Mrs Kensett felt half stunned, and had to steady her nerves with a thought of the next words of her story : "He sent forth His servants to call them that were bidden." Bidden to the feast as well as she. Oh, to persuade them to come !

"So here you are," she said, holding out her hand to Molly ; "I wonder who can tell me what we talked about yesterday ?"

"About the king," said Molly.

"It wasn't, either, said Jemmy Lucas. "It was about God's being a king. I told my mother, and she said she'd heard that once herself, a great while ago."

"Our story," said Mrs Kensett, "begins, you remember,

in this way : 'The kingdom of heaven is like unto a certain king which made a marriage for his son.'"

"The folks had one here a spell ago," said Peter Limp. "My ! how they did go on !"

"They was all dressed up, you know, more'n common," said Jemmy Lucas ; "and then they went back to the house, and the way the dishes chinked beat all."

"Well, when there is a marriage in a king's house," said Mrs Kensett, "they prepare more splendid things than I can tell you. There is a great feast got ready, with every good thing you can think of ; and many of the dishes are of gold and silver. And there is the sweetest music that men can make ; and throngs of people are invited ; and they come dressed in the richest and gayest way, because it is a very great occasion."

"I guess the folks feel great that go," said Jemmy Lucas.

"I suppose they do," said Mrs Kensett ; "whoever goes to the king's house at such a time, will see many splendid things. But God, the great King of all, has prepared things which are so glorious that they would make you forget these others in a minute ; and He has told us of a time and a place where they may be seen. You see He tells us this story to show how He feels towards us, and what He will do for us ; and also how a great many of us feel towards Him ; for just as earthly kings make a feast, and invite guests, so does God invite us to the wonders and glories which He has prepared in His kingdom."

"Guess likely most folks don't hear Him," said Sam Dodd.

"How does He tell 'em, ma'am ?" said little Molly.

"Why, in the same sort of way that other kings tell their wishes to their subjects," said Mrs Kensett ; "He sends word by His particular servants."

"What sort of a place is it, anyhow ?" asked Peter Limp.

"A more glorious and wonderful place than anybody can ever imagine," said Mrs Kensett. "An earthly king may have gold dishes on his table, and wear pearls on his dress ; but the very streets of the heavenly city are paved with gold, and the foundations are laid in precious stones of all colours.

and every gate is of one pearl. And the brilliancy that shines there is so great, that the city has no need of the sun; for 'the glory of God doth lighten it.'"

"I'd like to see it for once," said Jemmy Lucas.

"How would you like to live there?" said Mrs Kensett. Sam Dodd laughed scornfully.

"Why don't you ask him how he'd like to live in Squire Townsend's big house and garden?" he said.

"And the cherry orchard," said Peter Limp.

"Why, there would be very little sense in such a question,' said Mrs Kensett; "for Squire Townsend is only a man, and would never think of sharing his fine house with any one else. Even if he let you come there for a little while and take supper with him, he would send you away again. But all who accept the Lord's invitation to His heavenly kingdom, may dwell and rejoice there for ever."

"Well," said Jemmy Lucas, "I guess it ain't civil to say I don't believe it, but it sounds pretty queer."

"Do you know," said Mrs Kensett, "at first I could not believe it either; I could not think such glorious news could be true. But then I found that it was written in the Bible, which is the word of God, and not one of His words ever makes the least mistake.

"Now this earthly king of whom our story tells, made ready his feast; and when everything was done he 'sent forth his servants to call them that were bidden to the wedding.'"

"That's plain enough," said Sam Dodd; "but who does t'other one send, I should like to know?"

"His servants. Just as the king did in the story."

"Well, none of 'em ever came in *my* way," said Sam Dodd, "that's pretty plain."

"Yes," said Mrs Kensett, "one of them comes to you now; I am His servant."

"But you ain't a servant," said little Molly, wonderingly. "You 'se a lady."

"The servants of God, my dear," said Mrs Kensett, "may be called among men by a great many different names. They may be kings themselves, or they may be poor unknown servants, or little children like you. Anybody can be a servant of God."

"What do they have to do, ma'am?" said Jemmy Lucas.

"Whatever the Lord tells them," answered the lady. "Sometimes it is one thing, sometimes another. But always, every day, whatever their other work may be, He bids them tell the truth, and to speak no bad words, and to help and comfort other people, and to do nothing to other people which they would not like those same people to do to them."

"Ain't many of 'em down our way, then," said Peter Limp, with a low whistle. "I say, that ain't much like our sort o' folks, Sam?"

"Who cares?" answered Sam Dodd, scornfully; "what's the use?"

"Why," said Mrs Kensett, "the use is that if we are the true servants of God, He will make us happy every day here, and will take care of us, and bring us to live in His glorious kingdom for ever when we die."

"That would do for me then," said little Molly. "They does all say I 'm goin' to die."

"Do for you!" said Sam Dodd, giving the child an impatient push. "You 'd look well, stuck up in anybody's kingdom, you would! Guess you 'd get turned out faster'n you'd sneaked in."

"Listen," said Mrs Kensett, with a kind smile at the bright, anxious eyes that sought an answer to every question in her face: "God loves you all, every one; and He wants you every one to be His servants. There is no one too small, or too poor, or too weak, to serve Him. Ask Him to help you, ask Him to teach you how, for the sake of the Lord Jesus, and He will surely hear."

She knelt down again, with the children round her, in the porch of the old church; but when the prayer was ended, it might be seen that Sam Dodd had silently crept away.

CHAPTER IV.

WHAT strange things there are in this world of ours! what strange contrasts and combinations! to which we are yet so used, that we half the time forget their strangeness. So here, on this June evening, a little handful of waifs and strays came trooping into the old porch, to hear how the great King had invited every one of them to His kingdom and glory.

"O Lord, I will praise Thy name, for Thou hast done wonderful things!"

"You remember, children," so Mrs Kensett began, "that the king had made a marriage for his son. A great entertainment, with everything that was beautiful, and pleasant, and grand, which the king's wealth and power could furnish."

"I know!" said Jemmy Lucas. "I've seen 'em get married, here in this very church—the rich folks; and it does seem as if the whole church couldn't but just hold 'em, they's so grand. They flings flowers down on the steps, and they walks along right over 'em. And they's all white and coloured, like it 'most puts your eyes out, only to look at 'em."

"And then they goes home, you know," said Peter Limp, 'and eats as if they hadn't never had anythin' to eat afore, and didn't expect to again. Guess I haven't been outside and heard the dishes! And such singin' and dancin'!"

"Well," said Mrs Kensett, "a king's feast is much greater even than these; but what the great King has prepared, and what the glory of that day will be,—

'When all the saints get home,'

no one can even think.

"It says in our story, that the king sent forth his servants to call them that were bidden to the wedding. I suppose they had had a sort of general invitation before, and now the servants went to remind them; but they would not come.

And the king was so kind and patient with them, that he sent other servants, who could give his message better, maybe—saying, 'Behold, I have prepared my dinner; my oxen and my fatlings are ready; come unto the marriage.'"

"And then I s'pose they all hurried off, right away," said Jemmy Lucas.

"No," said the lady, "'they made light of it,' treated the whole matter as if it were a jest; 'and went their ways, one to his farm, and another to his merchandise.' The whole matter was too much of a trifle to interrupt their business, even for an hour."

"After the king sent to them, and all!" said Peter Limp.

"Yes, after all that. So some of them did. 'And the remnant'—the others—'took his servants, and entreated them spitefully, and slew them.'"

"The good king's servants!" cried Molly.

"I'd think they durstn't do it," said Peter Limp.

"Don't you know that bad men will dare do almost anything?" said Mrs Kensett. "And perhaps they thought the king's palace was so far away, that he would never know what they had done. But he knew everything."

"And didn't they want to go to the feast, ma'am?" said Jemmy Lucas. "That part of the story don't sound true."

"They were wicked people," said Mrs Kensett, "and the king was very good; and so they did not care for his favour. And to go to his feast, they must wash their hands, and change their dress, and give up all their bad ways; so they would not come. Some would have liked it well enough, but they had a great deal of business on hand, and so they 'went their ways, one to his farm, and another to his merchandise;' while the others killed the king's servants for only bringing them his gracious invitation."

"And they didn't really want to go and see the king?" said little Molly, with her wondering look.

"They did not want to go in the king's way, and at the king's bidding," said Mrs Kensett; "it must be when *they* were ready—not when he was. When all their business was finished up, and they could find nothing pleasant to do, *then* maybe they would think of the king's invitation."

"That wasn't very respectful," said Jemmy Lucas.

"No indeed.   But some hated the king himself : 'the remnant took his servants' (that is, those who brought the message), 'and spitefully entreated them.'   These were some who knew that they had displeased the king, and never meant to obey him at all.   And this is just the way with the invitation which God, the great King of all, gives to the people in this world.   He invites them, He sends word by His servants that all things are ready ; He entreats —yes, commands them to come.   There are glorious dwellings prepared in heaven, there is a wonderful feast laid there ; but some people say they are too busy to think of it, and others are angry with those who bring the invitation.   Many a servant of the Lord has been killed by wicked men, for just delivering his Master's message."

"Ma'am," said little Molly, "didn't *anybody* go ?"

"When the king knew how his servants had been treated," said Mrs Kensett, "he was very angry ; 'and he sent forth his armies and destroyed those murderers, and burned up their city.'   And then he sent out his servants once more, bidding them go everywhere to bring back guests to the wedding.   Into the poor, tumble-down houses, and along the wild lanes and the crowded streets they went, and gathered in 'the poor, and the maimed, and the halt, and the blind' —all sorts, 'both bad and good.'   But in that great kingdom, and at that great feast, there was 'room enough and to spare.'   And one of the servants came to the king, saying: 'Lord, it is done as thou hast commanded, and yet there is room.'"

"Why, there must have been room for everybody, I should think !" said Jemmy Lucas.

"Just so," said Mrs Kensett ; "there was room for everybody."

"It was such a great feast !" said little Molly, folding her hands, with a sigh.

"And such a good king," said Mrs Kensett.   "So when

the servant said this, he answered : 'Go out into the highways and hedges, and compel them to come in, that my
house may be filled.' Even the commonest beggar might
come; and those who had been overlooked before; and
those who lay starving by the wayside, having no home.
And 'go quickly,' he had told his servants,—lose no time ;
for some of these people were old, and some were hungry,
and many might die and not even know that the king had
invited them."

"T'other people was just the biggest fools !" said Peter
Limp.

"Well, they didn't need to go, if they wasn't a mind to,"
said Sam Dodd, roughly.

"No," said Mrs Kensett, "not if they did not choose. If
people do not wish to have God for their Friend, to have
Him to love them and take care of them; if they have no
wish to live for ever in His glorious kingdom, they need
not."

"The king was wonderful good, no mistake," said Jemmy
Lucas ; "and of course the people had oughter go, when he
sent for them ; but I don't guess they liked it much, neither."

" Why not ?" said Mrs Kensett.

" 'Tain't so pleasant as you'd think, ma'am, to go 'mong
folks when you be's all pieces and patches," said Jemmy
Lucas, glancing down at his own trousers, though, to say
truth, patches were not the worst thing there.

" Lady," said little Molly, " did they go just as they was ?"

" Ah," said Mrs Kensett, her eyes glittering with the
bright drops that flushed up into them, " the gracious king
took care of that ! He knew how these poor beggars would
feel. He knew how their rags would look at his shining
court. He knew how their soiled and weary feet would
stumble and trip, and never be able to tread his golden
pavement. So he opened for them a fountain where they
might wash the stains away ; and as each one came, there
was given to him a new robe, ' white and clean,'—' a raiment
of needlework,' with the king's own glory wrought thereon,
which the king himself had prepared for every one."

Little Molly Limp had been looking up and listening with the intensest eagerness; but now her head dropped, and she broke into a passion of quiet sobbing, weeping such tears of longing, and need, and hopelessness, as were inexpressibly touching. But Peter was roused to much indignation.

"There!" he said, "guess *that* just comes o' bringin' young ones where they ain't got no manner o' business. Hot water enough to drown a cat as has got its eyes open! You, Moll! shut up! 'Tain't none o' *your* concern what kings and folks does."

"Such a muss!" said Sam Dodd, contemptuously.

But Mrs Kensett got hold of the little hand, and stroked it softly.

"Why, Molly," she said, "it is all true; and you should not cry about it, unless for joy. For all this—ah, and much more—will God do for you and for me and for every one of us, if we will let Him. He has invited us to come; He has commanded us to come; and now we must beg Him to bring us and lead us, because He is strong and we are very weak."

Sam Dodd whistled and snapped his fingers, and turned away; but the rest knelt down with their teacher, while she prayed the Good Shepherd of the sheep to gather with His arm all these little stray ones, so lost, so forlorn; and then, bidding the children never forget the King's invitation, even for an hour, she said good-night, and went her way.

CHAPTER V.

THE next afternoon was rainy, and the next, but when yet another had come softly round, the sun shone out bright and strong, and the birds sang with all their hearts. The children, too, played with all theirs, down in the village; wherever there was a dry step for marbles, or a bit of green grass for somersets and daisies, or an extra-sized mud-puddle for sailing boats. Dolls went dry-shod over the muddy roads; and kittens shook their soft paws disapprovingly, at the touch; and little girls held up their short frocks, already two feet above danger. As for the boys and the dogs, they careered hither and thither, despising trifles, and came home to tea "a sight."

But it was not tea-time yet, and the Vinegar Hill children had come stealing up as usual to their favourite playground, and were playing ball with great zeal and spirit, looking round the while for "the lady." But she did not come.

"Guess she's got tired likely," said Peter Limp; "sort o' tired of us, you know."

"I'd like to hear all the rest o' the story, though," said Jemmy Lucas. And little Molly crept down to the stile, and sat there to wait and watch with tearful eyes. Then presently came running back in great haste and glee.

"She's a-comin'! she's a-comin'! 'way down there at the foot of the hill."

"What if she is?" said Sam Dodd, roughly. "She's a spoil-sport, that's what she is, and I just wish she was further."

"Why, don't you want to hear about the king?" said Jemmy Lucas.

"No! and I don't mean to, neither," said Sam Dodd. "What does she know about kings? I say, I'm off."

"But it ain't her, after all," said Peter Limp, coming down from a branch of the oak tree to which he had swung himself up for a better view. "It ain't her, but another woman. What's *she* after, I wonder?"

The children all stopped their play to look, as the woman came on, across the stile and up to the steps. A neat, pleasant-faced person, and rather old.

"Be you the little folks from Vinegar Hill?" she asked, catching her breath a little after the long ascent.

"I rather suspect we are," said Sam Dodd. "If that's all you've got on your mind, you can go to bed easy."

"Thank you, it's not all," said the woman, her face looking just as pleasant as ever. "I've got two or three things more. My mistress,—that's Mrs Kensett, children; she that's been teachin' of you here,—she's not well to-day, and couldn't venture out. And maybe it won't do for her to-morrow, just the same. So she wants you all to come down to her house to tea, and she can talk to you there, better and safer than in this atmospheric place."

"Why, I'm willing she should keep sick all the time, if that's the game," said Peter Limp. "Hoorah!—goin' out to tea and biscuits!"

"Does she want me too?" said little Molly, touching her shy fingers to the woman's shawl.

"No, she don't," said Peter. "Babies not invited, nor chickens, nor garden stuff gen'rally."

"Are you Molly?" said the woman, bending her pleasant eyes upon the child. "Then you're invited first of all. 'Molly must be sure to come,' Mrs Kensett said, 'because she's sick and weak.'"

The child gave a little bound in her gladness of heart, and Jemmy Lucas went head over heels down the steps, and heels over head up again, in a way that was quite miraculous. Sam Dodd alone looked sullen and sour.

"Well," he said, "got through? 'Cause we *ain't*,—and we're in a hurry."

"She's got one thing more to say, you know," said Jemmy Lucas.

"And if your time's so very valu'ble, Sam, don't wait," said Peter Limp.

"How they go on!" said the woman, speaking to herself, but quite out loud, and looking round upon the wild little group as if she had been in a menagerie of strange creatures. "What sort of a road *do* you suppose, now, such intellectuals travel? Well, I shan't take much of anybody's time, little boy, though there *is* one thing more I had to say."

"Why don't you say it, then?" asked Sam Dodd, gruffly. "Nobody ain't a hinderin' of you."

"It's not so easy for anybody to do that—when I've made up my mind to speak," said the woman, nodding her head with a good-natured smile. "But this is the thing.

T'other day when my mistress was here, talking to you children, she dropped her pencil,—has any of you seen it?"

"What sort of a pencil?" said Sam Dodd, lounging round one of the white pillars of the porch. "Loads of folks has pencils,—and loses 'em."

"Oh, was it the beautiful one that sparkled at the end?" cried Jemmy Lucas.

"Sam!" exclaimed little Molly, "I said it was like that! —don't you know? And you said it wasn't!" But Molly, as the last eager words were spoken, turned pale, and cowered where she stood. The woman saw this, and turned quick about; yet saw only Sam Dodd lounging round his pillar as before.

"We'll all look, ma'am," said Peter Limp, "but we hasn't none of us seen it."

"Except in the lady's hand," corrected Jemmy Lucas.

And forthwith, and with evident goodwill, the little waifs began the search—in every crack and cranny of the old porch, and down the path, and among the thick grass. Even Sam Dodd left his pillar, and pushed the grass right and left with his foot, and turned aside the tufts of clover. Only Molly, of all the group, stood still; her eyes following Sam's every motion, her face white and troubled. Of all this the woman took good note.

"Poor little one," she said, patting Molly kindly on the shoulder, "what are you shivering about, this June weather? This world's a kind o' hard place for such as you. Come here, boys; I'll read to you a bit before I go, and then you can look as much as you want to."

"Oh, she's got a book in her pocket, too!" said Jemmy Lucas. The woman smiled and nodded at him, then opened her book and read—

"And I saw a great white throne, and Him that sat on it, from whose face the earth and the heaven fled away; and there was found no place for them. And I saw the dead, small and great, stand before God; and the books were opened; and another book was opened, which is the book of life ; and the dead were judged out of those things which were written in the books, according to their works."

" What was in those books, ma'am ?" asked Jemmy Lucas.

" All the things that you, and I, and everybody else in the world has done," said the woman. . " And you see, maybe my mistress won't ever know now, for a while, what's become of her pencil ; but *then* she'll know, for it 's all down in the books."

" Ma'am," said little Molly, in almost a whisper, " who'll sit on the white throne ? "

And the woman answered : " The great King of heaven and earth."

" And will the heaven and earth run away because they are afraid ? " asked Jemmy Lucas.

" Yes," said the woman, " but they can't go far. Good-bye ! " and with that she rose up and went steadily down the little path, and was soon out of sight.

The children watched her, then went down on hands and knees again in the grass ; and Molly stole softly away through the bushes towards Vinegar Hill. But as she went, Sam Dodd came behind her with a bound.

" You Molly Limp ! " he said, laying a firm grip on the child's shoulder, " if you don't quit lookin' at me, and mind your own business, I'll put you where you'll have enough to see and plenty of time to see it. I'll fling you up into the sky so high you won't never come down. D'ye hear ? There you'll hang, and the stars'll come rollin' round you to burn you up." And giving the frightened child a fierce push which took her quite off her feet and sent her headlong down the hill, Sam Dodd put his hands in his pockets, and dived in among the bushes out of sight.

CHAPTER VI.

IT was rather a strange-looking little group that found its way next day to Mrs Kensett's door ; and the village people looked and wondered. Not that such children were a particularly uncommon sight in the village. Sam Dodd and his compeers were much in the habit of surveying by day the apple-trees and melon patches which they meant to visit by night ; while a travelling show of any kind was pretty sure to call out the Vinegar Hill population in force. But to see a little knot of the young outcasts together, walking quietly along the broad village street, *that* was a wonder. They looked like themselves still,—out at elbows and out at toes, and somewhat brimless in the matter of hats ; but upon some of the faces and some of the hands were strange tokens that the boys had broken caste, and made an attempt at least to show what colour they were by nature.

"Bad sign !" as the worthy farmer remarked to himself, —he to whom Mrs Kensett had applied for directions that first Sunday,—"those young vagabonds are plotting some-thin' a little above the extra."

But an inquiry as to "what was on foot now ?" brought no more satisfaction than an extremely irreverent—

"Hullo ! old plough-tail, guess 'tain't none o' *your* business,"—and the good farmer went his way, resolving to put an extra lock on his garden before the sun should set.

Otherwise, if not spoken to, the children went on quietly enough,—even a little shyly for them,—until they came to the little white fence and gate, with its enclosure of sweet flowers, where Mrs Kensett lived. There the shyness reached its full development ; and they hung about the gate, and peeped through the fence, and did everything but go in, until the lady herself saw them from the window, and came out to fetch them.

Were you ever in possession of some new pleasure which seemed (as we say) "too good to be true ?" So that the very sweetness of it made the whole thing seem quite fabu-

lous and like a dream ? Just in such fashion felt the little
waifs from Vinegar Hill, as they entered Mrs Kensett's
parlour. For the rough words and scowling looks in the
village street they were ready enough ; all *that* was part of
their daily life, and gave them no manner of concern. But
the lady's bright smile and kind tones of welcome ; the clean
room with its white matting and curtains ; the pictures on
the wall, the books on the table, the roses pressing their
sweet faces in at the open window,—all these were utterly
bewildering. Peter Limp hung back, and stood on one foot,
and twisted his old hat into what was a new shape even for
it. Jemmy Lucas got no further than to open eyes and
mouth to their most wondering extent ; and little Molly's
face settled into an expression of rapt happiness and delight.

"But where are the rest ?" inquired Mrs Kensett, as she
watched the three who had come.

"Oh, they's went about other business," explained Jemmy
Lucas. "Jem Crook said *he'd* a sight rather go a-shootin'.
He could get supper enough at home, he said."

"And Tim Wiggins was a-cuttin' of the bushes down in
the holler," said Peter Limp. "They's going to try for a
garding."

"And where is Sam ?"

Little Molly started and flushed.

"I didn't hear him say nothin' about it, ma'am," she said,
trembling.

"I did hear him say consid'rable," remarked Peter Limp.
"But guess likely the lady wouldn't care about hearin' of it
over. Rather tall talkin', it was, to tell her."

"Sam Dodd's as growly as an old cat !" said Jemmy
Lucas. "He just swore at me, up and down, for only
askin' him if he wasn't a-comin'."

"He's no great loss, anyhow," said Peter Limp. "Guess
most of us can live through the want of him, if the lady
can."

"Ah," said Mrs Kensett, sadly, "I'm afraid I know why
Sam would not come ! I think I do not need to be told."

"O lady!" cried out little Molly; and then she stopped and looked frightened.

"Never mind Sam, now," said her friend, kindly. "Put your hats down out in the hall, and then come and sit by me, all of you, and we will have a talk before tea."

Down on the soft carpet, on the little foot cushions, or on the edge of a chair, so sat the children; twisted, curled, hanging about, like the knotty growth of a perverse apple-tree, but without its quiet repose. More restless than the smallest twig or the flightiest leaf on the tree, they went from seat to seat, and from one position to another. But the eyes were bright and the faces eager, waiting for the promised talk.

"'And who is sufficient for these things?'" Mrs Kensett thought, as she looked at them; then remembered, "Ye are complete in Him."

"You see how it was, children," she began; "just as with those boys whom I asked to come to tea, so with the people that were bidden to the king's feast. 'They went their ways —one to his farm, another to his merchandise,'—each one choosing something else instead of the invitation, and going off to seek his own pleasure or business in other ways. And others still hated the king, and were angry with those who even mentioned his name.

"Did all the other folks come, ma'am?" said Molly; "the poor folks, out o' the hedges?"

"The servants," said Mrs Kensett, "followed exactly their master's command; not seeking first the great or the wise, or the rich people, but telling everybody they met the king's message of grace. If they met a rich man, they told him; but if it was a beggar, they told him too, no matter how ragged or sick or ugly he might be. 'They gathered as many as they found.'"

"Well, I *should* ha' thought the beggars would be afraid to go," said Peter Limp; "afraid o' bein' trapped, like, and ashamed o' what they didn't have on. That's how I should feel. And I ain't so ragged nother, but I ain't so fine."

"Is that how you *do* feel?" said Mrs Kensett. "For the

great King invites you to-day, to come and be one of His
children.   Will you go ?"

"Go?" said Peter Limp.   "Guess there ain't no king as
would care much about seein' me nowheres."

"This King does," said Mrs Kensett.   "He loves you
every one, and wants you every one in His kingdom.

> 'There's room around thy Father's board
> For thee and thousands more!'"

"Is that all of it, ma'am?" said little Molly, as the lady
paused and looked at the children with her loving eyes.

"All of the hymn?" she said.   "Oh no; you shall hear
the rest.

> 'Come, sinners, to the gospel feast,
> Oh come without delay,
> For there is room in Jesus' breast
> For all who will obey.
>
> 'There's room in God's eternal love
> To save thy precious soul ;
> Room in the Spirit's grace above
> To heal and make thee whole.
>
> 'There's room within the church redeem'd
> With blood of Christ divine ;
> Room in the white-robed throng convened,
> For that dear soul of thine.
>
> 'There's room in heaven among the choir,
> And harps, and crowns of gold,
> And glorious palms of victory there,
> And joys that ne'er were told.
>
> 'There's room around thy Father's board
> For thee and thousands more,
> Oh come and welcome to the Lord ;
> Yea, come this very hour.'"

"That's just what the servants told the king," remarked
Jemmy Lucas; "after they'd got so many people there,—
there was more room yet."

"Yes, and so it will always be, as long as the world lasts,"
said Mrs Kensett.   "Every day people are hearing the

message, and going to the King, 'and yet there is room.' There will always be a place for every one that comes."

"But how's we to go?" said Peter Limp. "That's what I don't see."

"How did you come here?"

"Why! we just set out and comed," replied Peter, with open eyes.

"Well, first of all, you accepted my invitation; you determined that you *would* come."

"Yes, ma'am."

"And then you set out, as you say, and took the road, which you had been told led to my house."

"Yes! How did ye know?" said Peter.

"And then, when you were in the road, you kept in it; you did not take the highway which crosses down towards the great city, nor the little by-lane which turns back to Vinegar Hill, nor even the pretty path which runs away up to your old playground by the church."

"No," said Peter, with a laugh, "in course we didn't. That warn't the way to get here."

"You wouldn't ha' seen us in some time if we had," said Jemmy Lucas.

"Well," said Mrs Kensett, "it is exactly so with going to the great King. You must resolve to go, in the first place, and you mustn't let either business or pleasure come in the way."

"Neither bushes nor shootin'," said Peter Limp, nodding his head. "I see!"

"And then," said Mrs Kensett, "you must choose the right road, and you must set out, and keep on."

"And then we'll be there!" said Jemmy Lucas. "Well, don't that sound easy, now!"

"And will the King take us to the feast, right away, ma'am?" said little Molly.

"When the servants in the story found guests for the feast," said Mrs Kensett, "you must not suppose that they were all together. Some were very near, and had but a short way to the king's house, while others must take a long

c

journey to get there. But that did not matter, so that they all arrived safe."

"And is it a long way we must go?" said Molly.

"We do not know yet, little one," said her friend, gently; "but our King knows, and He will take care of all that. The thing we have to do is to walk in His ways, and be ready. I suppose the people in the story set out for the king's house just as soon as the servants called them. Wherever they were, and whatever they were doing, they set out at once."

"They wouldn't like to wait when the king had sent for them," said Molly.

"No, indeed. And so, if we mean to accept this invitation of our God and King, if we want to dwell with Him in His kingdom, we should set out at once. There is not a minute to lose."

"But how's we to know how?" said Jemmy Lucas.

"You must beg of Him first to teach you," said Mrs Kensett; "you must ask Him to lead and bring you, as I said before. And then remember, that every bad thing, every wicked word and action, every naughty thought, are all out of the King's highway. For the road to Him is marked out with gentle words, and kind looks, and right actions; and love and patience are like a hedge-row on either side."

"How's that, now?" said Peter Limp. "'Pears as if I understood—and yet I don't, neither."

"When you were coming here this afternoon," said Mrs Kensett, "if you had seen a very muddy lane, full of dirty houses and scolding people, would you have thought that was the way to my house?"

"Guess we'd ha' known better than that," said Peter Limp.

"Why not?" said the lady.

"'Cause you's so clean and pretty, you know," said Jemmy Lucas. "Why, I don't s'pose you could live a minute where folks was fightin'."

"Well," said Mrs Kensett, "never forget that everything

good leads to God, but everything bad leads right away from Him. Pray to Him to keep you in the right way."

Then Mrs Kensett rose up, and saying that they had talked long enough for once, and that she would tell them more another time, she took little Molly by the hand, and led the way into the garden.

CHAPTER VII.

Now the garden of this old house where Mrs Kensett spent the summer, would not have pleased any regular gardener that ever I saw. For it was old-fashioned, and had old-fashioned flowers; and some of the walks were bordered with currant bushes, and some with sweet balm; and there was not a geranium, nor a fuchsia, nor a heliotrope to be seen. Great damask roses were there with crimson cheeks; but they had no name in the gay world, and were only "roses"—nothing more. And a fair white cousin of the damask roses went twining about all over the fence, breathing sweetness upon everybody who went by, but nobody knew who she was. People only said, "Oh, what a sweet rose!" They never imagined for a moment that she might be the aunt of "Clara Sylvain," or the grandmother of "Mme Bosanquet." So many roses, as well as people, live unknown in the world.

Then there were lilies,—not the Japanese foreigners, gay with spots and grand with hard names; but just "lilies," white and unspotted, lifting their pure heads far above the brown earth. And there were pinks, fringed and fragrant; and bitter southernwood, and spicy lavender, and rosemary, and rue, and thyme. A little garden society where everybody was nameless or forgotten or laid aside. And the old walls had echoed with steps and voices that were long since beyond the world's hearing; and the old fruit-trees

had showered down their wealth for more than one gene-
ration.

So up and down here went the children,—the little
strays from Vinegar Hill,—jumping, careering, or lost in
quiet admiration before some old-fashioned tuft of bloom.
For even the quietest people are generally imposing to *somebody;* and the old sweet-williams were just as wonderful to
these children, as "Henderson's Perfection" or "Hunt's
Auricula-flowered" would be to me. And a rose is a rose,
after all.

But the crowning wonder of the whole was at the farther
end ; for there, snugly hidden within an arbour, stood the
tea-table, with the shadows of the vine leaves playing
hide-and-seek upon its white cloth. And on the table
were such stores of good things; such piles of fruit and
cakes and biscuits, such pitchers of milk, such supply of
bread and butter ; that it was quite impossible to think of
anything else for a single moment after that. The little
outcasts thought they were in a dream.

It was very real, though, when it came to eating the good
things,—plates were cleared and cups emptied in a way that
was not in the least dreamy and unsubstantial ; and it
would have been hard to tell which enjoyed the fun most—
Mrs Kensett or the children.

"But, I say !" inquired Peter Limp, pausing midway in a
plate of strawberries, "who got all these here notions together ? it must ha' took a sight o' money !"

"Why, *she* did, in course," said Jemmy Lucas.

"Then," said little Molly, "she's like the king."

"Guess she is, that's a fact," said Peter Limp ; "only
we didn't want quite so much coaxin' as t'other folks. My !
wasn't Sam Dodd the biggest goose that ever walked ?"

"I think he was afraid to come," said Mrs Kensett.
"Sam thought I was angry with him about something."

"Was you ?" asked little Molly, earnestly.

"No," said Mrs Kensett, "not angry, only sorry."

Then Molly crept up close to her friend's side, and whispered—

"I know why he didn't come, but I can't tell."

"No, don't tell," said Mrs Kensett, softly; "and I shall not tell, either. Let us talk about the great King who has invited us all to His kingdom and glory. Run up and down the garden, children, and bring me the prettiest things you can find, or the most curious things, or indeed anything you like, and see what they will tell us about Him. For He made them all."

"What, the hull o' the things?" said Peter Limp.

"Every one."

"Well, I'd just like to know how, that's all," said Jemmy Lucas; "but I don't guess you know that?"

"I do about some of the things," said Mrs Kensett; "you go find them, and then we will see."

So the children rushed away; jumping over the bushes rolling like a cartwheel along the walks, and turning head over heels with great glee on every spot of green grass.

"This here's a place!" said Peter Limp, admiringly. "Guess I wouldn't mind livin' here most of the time."

"I don't s'pose heaven's much prettier!" said little Molly, stroking the red cheeks of a damask rose.

"It's got to be some bigger," said Jemmy Lucas, "or there wouldn't be nigh room enough for everybody."

"Well, I wouldn't care if 'twasn't so mighty big," said Peter Limp, rolling over and over upon the soft grass. "Some folks is just as well out as in, to my thinkin'. Sam Dodd, now—guess I could get along quite a spell without seein' him."

"But if there wasn't room for everybody, t'other folks might get in first and crowd you out," said Jemmy Lucas.

"Trust 'em for that!" said Peter.

"But just s'pose'n it should get full, and we's be too late!" said Molly—and with that her small face wrinkled up and looked very dismal indeed.

"Wish you was there this minute! blessed if I don't," said Peter Limp. "I say, you Moll! I just ain't agoin' to have you bawlin' here, scaring' the birds. Take yerself off to the lady, and find out if she knows how *you* was made, for I'm a king myself if *I* do."

Molly shrank, as she always did from a quick word; and gathering up a quantity of the crimson wind-scattered rose leaves, she trotted off back to where Mrs Kensett sat, near the table. And the tide of thoughts having now turned in that direction, Jemmy Lucas picked up a white clam shell from the strawberry bed and followed Molly; while Peter Limp, having secured a large toad and put him in his pocket with a knowing wink, came after—as grave as a judge.

Coming up first, with her hands full of the crimson leaves, Molly poured them out in the lady's lap, and then seemed to think they asked their own questions, for she said not a word, except, indeed, with her eyes.

"Oh, you want to know about the roses?" said Mrs Kensett, burying her hand in the soft heap. "But run and pick me a whole rose, Molly, and then you can hold it while I talk about it.

"You see," she said, as the little girl came back with the flower, "the Bible says that in the beginning God created the heavens and the earth. There wasn't one of these things that we see—not a flower, not a tree, not a stone, not a star—and God made them all."

"That's queer, too," said Peter Limp. "Like to know what He had to work with!"

"He had His own wonderful power, and that was all," said Mrs Kensett. "Men, you know, take something and make something else out of it. The baker makes bread from flour, and the miller makes flour from grain, and the tailor makes coats out of cloth. But when there was nothing to make anything of, in the beginning, then God made the earth and the heavens. And at first the earth did not look as it does now, but the waters were all over it like a flood; and it was quite dark."

"Didn't He make the sun then, the first thing, so that He could see to work?" said Jemmy Lucas.

"Not for that," said Mrs Kensett; "God can see in what we call darkness, just as well as in what we call light. And at first He did not make the sun, only commanded that it should be light: and it was so. And then He made the sky, and then He gathered the waters away from off the face of the earth, and let the dry land appear."

"Well, what did He do with the water, after He'd tooken it up?" said Peter Limp.

"Why, He left it in the seas and the rivers and the brooks," said the lady.

"Had all the trees been kivered up?" said Jemmy Lucas.

"Why, it must ha' made the grass too muddy for any livin' cow to eat!" said Peter Limp.

"Oh, there were no cows," said Mrs Kensett; "and there was no grass, and no trees. Nothing but brown earth and blue water, and overhead the blue sky and white clouds, for those were all that God had yet made. But when the earth was dry, God said: 'Let the earth bring forth grass, the herb yielding seed, and the fruit-tree yielding fruit after his kind, whose seed is in itself, upon the earth: and it was so.' At His command the grass sprang up, and the flowers bloomed, and the fruit-trees set their fruit."

"Does He tell 'em to do it now?" said Molly, looking down at the red rose leaves.

"Yes, it is all by His power and His command still. The weakest little flower by the road-side is in God's care, and the tallest tree gets all its strength from Him."

"But I say," said Jemmy Lucas, pulling out his shell, "how did He make *this* here concern?"

"What, the clam shells?" said Mrs Kensett. "You know a queer little fish lives in them, but do you know where *they* live?"

"In the deep, deep sea," said Jemmy Lucas: "my mother says so. Why, she used to once sail round in a boat and pick 'em up. And the water's as salt as anything."

"Well," said Mrs Kensett, "after God had gathered the sea-water together into its place, so that the dry land appeared; and when He had covered the earth with grass and trees and flowers; then next of all He made the sun and the moon and the stars, and placed them up in the sky to give light upon the earth, and to divide the day from the night."

"How did they know when night come, afore that?" asked Peter Limp. "The chickens theirselves couldn't ha' telled when to go to bed if there warn't no sun-down."

"Ah, but there were no chickens then," said Mrs Kensett, "and no people: God had not made them yet. That came next. When the sun was shining by day and the moon by night, then God said: 'Let the waters bring forth abundantly the moving creature that hath life, and fowl that may fly above the earth in the open firmament of heaven.'"

"Clams, and such?" said Jemmy Lucas.

"Yes, and chickens and birds. 'God created great whales, and every living creature that moveth, which the waters brought forth abundantly, after their kind, and every winged fowl after his kind.'"

And with that Peter Limp pulled out his imprisoned toad, and triumphantly flung him into the heap of rose leaves in the lady's lap.

"What d'ye say now?" he inquired. "Guess *he* warn't one o' 'em. 'Tain't a bull-frog, ye see,—him's a toad."

Mrs Kensett saw that, very clearly! And (strange as it may seem) she was not particularly fond of toads; and had received the intruder with a very unpleasant little thrill of the nerves. However, she had too much presence of mind to let that appear.

"Put him down on the ground, Peter," she said. "That is where he belongs—not on my lap. No, the toads were not made with the fishes, nor with the birds, but with man. Five days, five portions of time, had passed by; each one seeing some new wonder, some new treasure added to the earth; and yet there were no animals walking upon the dry land, and no man to enjoy it all. Then when the sixth day came, God said: 'Let the earth bring forth abundantly,'— before it had been the waters, but now the earth,—'cattle, and creeping things, and beast of the earth, after his kind: and it was so.' And then, Peter, the toads were made."

"And the men too?" said Jemmy Lucas.

"Yes; man was made last of all."

"Well, if there warn't nobody at all in those days," said

Peter Limp, "guess I'd just like to know who telled about it!"

"Why, the Lord himself," said Mrs Kensett; "nobody could know so well as He who did it all. Afterwards, when there were men on the earth, God told them about it, and bade them write His words down. So that is the way we come to have the Bible. God told different people what to write,—things that He knew, things that He had done, things that He would do, as well as things which they themselves had seen and known; and so we call the Bible God's book, —the word of God."

It was growing late now; the sun had dropped down behind the hills, and the twilight was wrapping its soft curtains round the sleepy little birds and the weary flowers. So Mrs Kensett led her little troop back into the house, where they picked up their ragged hats, and with a rush went out of the garden gate and away towards Vinegar Hill.

CHAPTER VIII.

"'But they made light of it!'" thought Mrs Kensett to herself, as she sat waiting for her little scholars the next fine evening. The very brightness of June weather had succeeded the days of rain, and the birds sang in the full joy of their hearts, as if there had never been another June day in the world. Yet through all the universal music, those words seemed to ring in the lady's heart: "They made light of it," "they would not come." Her face drooped on her hands, in earnest pleading.

Presently a little footstep came pattering round the church, and Molly Limp crept close to her friend's side, and looked at her with wistful eyes.

"O Molly," broke out Mrs Kensett, taking the little girl's hand in her own, "I was thinking, child, what shall I do if you all refuse the Lord's gracious invitation? There is no one so good, there is no one so lovely as He,—how is it that you do not love Him?—all of you," she added, for the others were gathering round. And human eyes so full of pity had never looked on those children before.

"I love *you*," said little Molly Limp.

"Well, we's don't know much about Him, you see, ma'am," said Jemmy Lucas.

"But think of this one thing which you do know," said Mrs Kensett. "The Lord invites you to be His children; He will give you a place in His heavenly kingdom, a seat at His heavenly feast, if you will only come."

"Queer stories you tell, I must say," remarked Sam Dodd, whose dark face had suddenly appeared over the heads of the little group; "who knows they're true, to begin with?"

"Why, I know, and so do a great many other people," said Mrs Kensett. "They are all written in God's book of truth."

"Well, *I'll* go," said little Molly, "only you see I don't know where heaven is."

"Why, it's up in the sky, you goose!" said Peter Limp, "and how anybody's to get there I'd just like to hear somebody tell."

"The Lord will take all His children there when they die,' said Mrs Kensett.

"But I thought you said now," said Jemmy Lucas.

"No, don't you remember I told you yesterday that some people would have a long journey before they got there? And some only a short one. All we have to do is to set out at once, and then whenever the end comes the King will receive us. How long would you wait, if an earthly king had sent for you to come and live in his palace?"

"Why, yesterday," put in Jemmy Lucas, "when we was just a-goin' down to see you, ma'am, we was a-gettin' ready all day! Guess I washed my hands a matter o' six times — shouldn't wonder."

"And Molly, she just kep' her sun-bonnet on the whole

while," said Peter Limp. "Warn't much gettin' ready she could do, but she done that, first rate."

"And just so I want you to prepare for the heavenly city, —do every little thing you can think of to help on the way, and set out at once. For this is what God tells us to do. We must seek to please Him ; we must obey Him ; we must think of Him as our King who rules over us, as our Heavenly Father who loves us ; we must love Him, and pray to Him, begging Him to lead us, that we may not lose our way, and to hold us up that we may not stumble, and to bring us safe to His glorious kingdom."

"But I'd like to get there all at once !" said little Molly, with a disappointed face.

" We must stay in this world till the Lord takes us away," said Mrs Kensett, holding the child's little, thin hand in a warm, soft clasp ; "and He knows just the best time for that. But when we have set out for heaven, Molly, the world will not seem like the same place that it did before. Because if we love God, and know that He loves us, that will make us happy all the day long. When we are in trouble He will take care of us, and when we are in pain He will comfort us. And the thought of our glorious home in heaven will make us patient, even though our home here be very poor."

" I don't mind *that* so much," said Molly, wistfully, "but I does ache so sometimes ! Will He help that ?"

"Oh yes, He will help the pain, or He will help His little child to bear it," said her friend. " God never leaves His children alone for a moment ; so whether they live or die, they are safe and happy in His care. And in heaven 'there shall be no more sorrow nor crying ; neither shall there be any more pain.'"

" Well, Sam," said Peter Limp, nudging the elder boy, who—half whistling, half listening—sat tossing his ball up and down,—" feel to set right off ? Sounds kinder good, don't it."

" That's accordin' as you look at things," said Sam, gruffly. " Never did like to do as I was bid, myself, and the notion ain't took me yet."

"Guess *I* don't know 'zactly what I be 's bid," said Peter, with a puzzled look. "And I don't see how 's a feller to tell."

"The Bible will tell," said Mrs Kensett. "And if you ask God, He will teach you."

"Like enough!" said Sam, giving his ball a contemptuous toss. "But Bibles don't grow on Vinegar Hill, *I* guess. And as to askin', like to know where I'd find a chance ?"

"Well, there ain't much chance, you see, ma'am," explained Jemmy Lucas. "They 's allers drinkin', up there. And they 's allers swearin' down to Limp's. And we 's so mortal poor. Guess you wouldn't like Vinegar Hill much, ma'am."

Mrs Kensett paused, looking round upon the children with eyes that made them all gaze at her.

"Children," she began, "listen. No matter who you are, God commands you to serve Him. And no matter where you live, you can always pray to Him in your hearts. There is no one too weak for Him to help, there is no one too poor to be His child. But then they must seek Him with all their hearts. As for the Bibles, I'll bring some with me sometime when I come, if you will promise to read them. You remember what I told you the Bible is ?"

"Things that God has done," said Jemmy Lucas.

"No," said Molly, "it's what He told the folks to write about 'em. But *I* can't read 'em, ma'am," she said, wistfully.

"But *I* can," said Jemmy Lucas. "And I can read to her, too."

"And your father can sell it for rum, too," said Sam Dodd. "That 'll be one of the things that 'll be done, pretty quick."

"No, he won't, neither," said Jemmy Lucas. "See if I don't keep it safe. And if he does, it 'll be *your* father as takes it, Sam Dodd !"

Sam gave a contemptuous laugh, swinging himself round the porch posts, and keeping carefully on the outskirts of the party, as he had done all along.

"Don't make much odds," he said ; "such beggars as you

ain't got enough to make it hardly worth while to keep what they *have* got!"

"Jemmy!" said Mrs Kensett, laying her hand upon the little boy's lips, and keeping back the angry words that were all ready to spring forth, "hush! you mustn't answer Sam when he speaks so: that does not please the Lord. And the best of all the things that you will find in your Bible, will be how to please Him. Remember, the way to His kingdom is not a road where people speak angry words or do naughty actions; that would be like taking the muddiest lane you could find to reach my house. God says, 'Love your enemies,' 'Do good to them that curse you.' He says, 'Swear not at all.' He says, 'Overcome evil with good.'"

"But you see, ma'am, it's part true," said the little boy, bursting into tears, as Sam Dodd—with another ringing laugh—bounded away down the hill. "We's just so poor as he says."

"And old Dodd just does it too!" said Peter Limp. "It's good Lucas can't sell Jemmy! Guess he would!"

"Poor little Jemmy," said the lady, laying a gentle hand on the boy's head. "But if Jemmy is not rich now, he can learn how to be rich by and by; and if his father here grieves him sometimes, he has all the more need to learn to know and love his Father who is in heaven. And the Bible will teach him all that. And soon he shall have one, if I live."

CHAPTER IX.

WHETHER the sweetness of the day had crept down even into the bushes on Vinegar Hill, alluring out the little wild creatures that dwelt there in the shade; whether the thought of the new Bibles was the attractive power,—certain it is, that for a good hour before Mrs Kensett left her house, the next afternoon, the children were all ready for her at the church. They did not lose their time, however. Ball and marbles went on with the utmost vigour; and if little Molly Limp's old sun-bonnet survived its many flying jumps into the tree branches, that could only be because it had passed the point where sun-bonnets can improve or grow worse. Molly herself sat very still, watching the winding path that led up from the village; and was almost as little affected by Sam Dodd's teasing work as was the old sun-bonnet. For Sam was there, despite his scorn of Bibles—playing, and hanging about, and plaguing all the smaller children. But it might be noticed that to-day, as yesterday, he kept himself on the outside of the circle, far away from Mrs Kensett, and at the end of the porch towards Vinegar Hill.

So at last the lady came up through the late sunshine, and took her place among the children; only Sam Dodd seemed careful to keep beyond her reach. She did not notice this, however, but began her talk just as usual.

"Children," she said, "we come to the last part of my story to-day, and it is the most important of all. Now tell me first what you remember about the rest of it."

"There's a great King," said little Molly, while the rest considered; "and He's asked us all to come."

"And you know," said Jemmy Lucas, "there ain't anythin' in the bull world so grand as His feast 'll be."

"And we've got to take the road that ain't muddy," said Peter Limp. "So as we won't stick fast, like—and get all dirt."

"'Cause in course the King would have a good road to His house," said Jemmy Lucas.

"So good a King," said Mrs Kensett. "But what do you mean by a good road?"

"Why, a road where there ain't nothin' bad," said Jemmy Lucas; "you know you's said the mud was like swearin' and fightin' and tellin' lies."

"S'posin' folks lives in mud—up to their eyes?" said Sam Dodd, with one of his sneering laughs, "what then?"

"If they live in the mud, and can't live anywhere else," said Mrs Kensett, "then they must walk softly, on tiptoe;

and the girls must hold up their dresses, and the boys must roll up their trousers. And they must step on every little stone and stick they can find, to raise them up. And they must pray to the great King to make the place better, and, most of all, to hold them up from falling, and to give them a dress to which the mud will not stick. People who live in the mud, Sam, may always make a clean way through it, with God's help."

"I'm goin' to tell mother every word!" said Jemmy Lucas. "That's just what she's allers a-callin' Vinegar Hill —it's a mud-hole, she says."

"And you said, ma'am," put in little Molly, softly, "that we was to set out right away, and the King wouldn't mind how we was dressed."

"No, not when you set out," said Mrs Kensett. "I didn't tell you to wear a new sun-bonnet, Molly, when you came to my house; and I let the boys come in their old jackets."

"Guess likely we couldn't do no other," said Peter Limp. "Shouldn't never ha' comed, likely, if we'd waited to dress up."

"No," said Mrs Kensett, "I knew that, and so God knows it about us. When the great king sent his servants to all the people by the wayside and under the hedges, he knew they must come just as they were. The beggars had nothing but rags; and those that were lame must come upon crutches, and the blind ones must feel their way along."

"Queer lookin' set he must ha' had, I say," remarked Sam Dodd.

"Yes, when they set out," said Mrs Kensett. "But suppose, children, that when you came to me, the other night, I had meant to keep you always, to have you live with me, and be my children?"

"Then guess likely we'd oughter been dressed up fine," said Peter Limp.

"And so we couldn't ha' come," said Jemmy Lucas.

"You see, ma'am, I hadn't nothin'!" said little Molly, with her pitiful look.

"Well," said Mrs Kensett, "suppose I had sent you this

message: ' I know you have no clean clothes, children ; but
set out just as you are, come straight to me, and I will give
you a new beautiful dress fit for my children to wear in my
house.' Then what ?"

" *I* shouldn't want none o' your old dresses, I know that,"
said Sam Dodd. "I'm rich enough to get my own things ;
and they're good enough for me, if they ain't for you."

" Ah, but our own things can never be good enough to
wear at the King's feast," said Mrs Kensett, " not if we wash
them ever so often, and mend them ever so well. In the
shining splendour of His kingdom they would be but rags
still. And therefore, in His great love, He offers us each a
complete new dress."

" Why, must all the folks be dressed alike ?" said Jemmy
Lucas.

" In one way they must be," said Mrs Kensett ; " they
must all wear something in which they shall be fit for the
King's presence."

" Comes awful hard on poor folks, don't it now ?" said
Peter Limp, shaking his head.

" But then He'll give 'em all they want !" said little Molly,
with sparkling eyes.

" Yes," said Mrs Kensett, " He will give them all they
want—*if* they want it. But if people scorn it, as Sam does,
the King will let them take care of themselves. That happens sometimes. So it was in the story: 'When the king
came in to see the guests, he saw there a man which had not
on a wedding garment.' All the others had put on the shining dress which the king had provided for them, but this
man chose to present himself in his own old clothes. Just
so will it be in the kingdom of God : He will look to see
whether those who come are fit to dwell in His presence."

" Well, what sort of a dress did he give 'em ?" asked
Jemmy Lucas.

" You know," said Mrs Kensett, " the guests were gathered
out of the highway. They were toiling there, it may be, at
some hard labour ; or they were lying there idly in some
misery, when the king's servants came: all rags, and dis-

eases, and dirt. I dare say the servants wondered how their master could invite such creatures to his feast. And so the Lord's gracious invitation finds us, children, some in sickness and sorrow, some at work ; and not one of us fit to stand before Him a moment. Well, the king found that most of these poor people had done what they could to get ready, they had washed their old clothes in his fountain, and they had tried hard to keep out of the mud, and they had put on the glorious robes which he had provided. But one man had ventured into the royal presence in all his soil and in all his rags, just as the servants found him in the highway. The others were all white and shining, but he sat there wrapped in an old tattered cloak."

"I shouldn't think he'd have dared !" said Molly.

"Guess likely the king was angry enough," said her brother Peter.

"There are some people in the world now, who are just like this man," said Mrs Kensett ; "they think they are good enough for heaven just as they are. They need not set out to serve God ; they need not get ready to stand before Him. If they are not *quite* what they ought to be, why, they think the great King of heaven and earth will never notice such a trifle. But, children, He sees *everything*. There seems to have been but one unwashed guest at the feast, yet the king saw him."

"But I thought you was like the king?" said little Molly, "and you's said we might come just as we was."

"Yes, for one afternoon," said Mrs Kensett. "But suppose, as I said, that when you came, I had meant to keep you to live with me always ?"

"Oh, in course *that* would be different," said Peter Limp.

"Guess likely we'd ha' had to slick up, then."

"But we's couldn't !" said Jemmy Lucas.

"And if I knew that, and if I was rich enough, then I should have given you each a new, clean dress."

"And if we was stuck up, like, and wouldn't put it on, then you wouldn't ha' kep' us," said Jemmy Lucas. "I see ! That's fair !"

D

"Well, what did t'other king say to the man?" put in Sam Dodd, flinging an old pine cone right at the head of Jemmy Lucas.

"You, Sam Dodd! quit that!" said the little boy. "Reckon he'd be mad enough with you, wherever you was."

"He said," answered Mrs Kensett: "'Friend, how camest thou hither, not having on a wedding garment?'"

"Why, that sounds real peaceable," said Peter Limp.

"The king waited to hear the man's excuse. But 'he was speechless,' he had none to give. Children, all the people in the world will stand together before God, one day; and then, if you are not ready for His glorious kingdom, what will you answer when the Lord asks you why?"

"Why shouldn't I be ready, I'd like to know?" said Sam Dodd, sullenly.

"God is perfectly holy, and you are a sinner," said Mrs Kensett; "God is perfectly just, and you have disobeyed Him a thousand times."

"Guess I'd tell Him I couldn't sort o' help it," said Peter Limp.

"Would that be true?" said the lady. "Cannot you help speaking bad words? cannot you help doing wicked things? Remember, there is no use in telling God a lie."

"Well, I can't get ready," said little Molly, sobbing; "so I guess the King will be angry with me. I don't know how, and I've nothin' to put on but this old frock."

"Little Molly, little Molly!" said her friend, tenderly, "do you know that the Lord knows that? He knew it when He invited you to come. A great while ago He saw that none of the people in this world were fit to stand in His presence: neither you nor I, nor anybody else, have anything of our own that we could wear. He knows all the bad thoughts that are in our hearts, and all the naughty words that are on our tongues: He knows that we are sinners, and can never be anything but sinners without His help. Yet He bids us come."

"I can't go, though," said Molly; "He'd be angry."

"Ah, but the king was not angry with the poor, ragged

people who came," said Mrs Kensett ; " but only with those who stayed away, and with the one who refused to have a new dress. For see how God has loved us. He knew we could never make ourselves fair and clean ; He knew we could never change our wicked hearts; and He therefore opened a fountain where we may wash, and bought for us each a new white robe."

Little Molly dried her eyes with her hand, and looked up wistfully.

" How 's we to get it, though ?" said Peter Limp. " That 's what I don't see."

" Just as you would in the other case," said Mrs Kensett ; " come and receive it, as you would if I had prepared one for you at my house. Set out to seek the Lord and His kingdom, and beg Him to give you all that you need, for Jesus' sake."

" Well, if this *ain't* a story !" said Sam Dodd, whistling.

" It 's cur'ous enough," said Peter Limp, " but you ain't got no business to say that to the lady"

" Ma'am," said little Molly, " has God bought **my frock** too ?"

" Ah, yes !" said Mrs Kensett, with her loving eyes full of gladness, " it is all bought and paid for, Molly—for you and for me, and for all the rest ! So may the Lord bring us all to wear it in His kingdom, for our Lord Jesus' sake !"

CHAPTER X.

" I 'm off !" said Sam Dodd, as he saw the lady approaching. " I 'll give her the start, and let her get to the pine tree yonder, and then see if I don't cut across to Vinegar Hill afore she can go the other ten feet. *She* 'll never walk herself into a fortin'."

" Why, her 's sick—don't you know ?" said Jemmy Lucas.

" Better stay to home, then, and let well folks alone," said

Sam Dodd, scowling. "If she had any airthly thing to do, now, she wouldn't be so mortal fond o' us. Ain't had a regular smashin' turn o' ball since she come, we ain't."

"She's got the books!" cried little Molly.

"Much good they'll be to you!" said Sam Dodd, giving Molly's head a sharp fillip; "*you* don't know whether B means a bat or a bumble-bee."

"Well, *I* do," said Jemmy Lucas, "and it don't mean nary one on 'em. And I'll read to Molly, too, Sam Dodd."

"Read away!" said Sam. "It'll be comfortable for her to have a book for you to read in, then, 'cause yer own won't stay home—not two days."

"Guess I'd just thank yer to let my sister alone, too," said Peter Limp.

"O sugar and molasses!" said Sam. "But you see I don't care about your thankin' me, not the crack of a whip. I'm one o' those folks as does things without lookin' for no thanks. Here comes yer schoolmarm, little chaps, so just hand her over my love, and say as I couldn't possibly wait."

And Sam Dodd swung himself round the pillar, and down upon the grass, and then rolled himself to the foot of the slope towards Vinegar Hill, at a rate that nearly made his promise good.

"Where's him a-goin' now, I wonder?" said Peter Limp, looking after Sam with some envy and longing. "Guess I might run and see, and be back in time, likely."

"Oh, you wouldn't go away *now*, Peter?" said little Molly; "why, she's got the books!" And Peter yielded to that side of the question, and forgot Sam.

"Little people," said Mrs Kensett, as she took her seat, and setting her basket before her, "you see I have brought your Bibles. But before I let you have them, I want to see if you know and remember what the Bible is, and what it tells."

"You's said it was all true," said Jemmy Lucas.

"And God telled the folks what they was to write," said little Molly. "About things He'd done, you know."

"And about the great feast," said Peter Limp.

"Yes, so it is God's Word. It tells, too, how we can get to His heavenly kingdom: what way we must go, what dress we must wear. It tells how nobody can make himself fit for the King's presence; and how He opened for us a fountain, and purchased for each of us a robe. It tells also what price was paid for all this."

"Must ha' cost a heap!" said Peter Limp.

"Yes, more than you can imagine," said Mrs Kensett. "In the beginning, when God made all things, He saw that each, as He made it, was very good. The flowers were good, blooming out in the fairest colours, and breathing the sweetest scents; and the trees were good, taking the right shape, and bearing the best fruit; the birds built their nests just right, and sang their songs without a single false note. The beasts, also, were all good and perfect according to their kind, living and working and playing, as they were meant to do. And when the first man and the first woman were made, they were perfect too. 'God saw everything that He had made, and, behold, it was very good.'"

"Warn't there *no* bad people?" asked Jemmy Lucas.

"Not one. But after a while the man and the woman disobeyed God, and then they became sinners, and when sin had once come into their hearts, there it stayed; and all their children were sinners, and all the people in the world since then have been sinners too."

"They was wicked, like," said Peter Limp.

"Yes, it was as if some beautiful dress which God had given them was all tattered and rent, and the colours all faded out, and the clean, fresh stuff had become soiled, and muddy, and foul. It was just like that, children, only very much worse; for a soiled dress can be washed, but who can make the heart clean, when once sin is there?"

"Folks is pretty bad, sure enough," said Jemmy Lucas; "they's *horrid* bad down our way; why, you couldn't begin to guess!"

"Well, who could make them all good?" said Mrs Kensett; "who could make them stop speaking bad words, and stealing, and fighting?"

"Tell you what," said Peter Limp, "you's just asked the biggest sort of a poser! Why, I don't s'pose as the hull world could do it—not if they was every one on 'em sheriffs!"

"Well, suppose the people themselves wanted to be good?" said Mrs Kensett.

"They might try," said Peter, reflectively. "*That* couldn't hurt 'em."

"Suppose they tried, then," said the lady. "Suppose every one mended up his clothes, and washed them as well as he could,—would he be fit then to stand before the King?"

But the boys laughed derisively.

"Guess likely you don't know much about the folks down yonder!" said Peter Limp. "Some o' *them* clothes is past washin'."

"But, ma'am," said little Molly, "you's said the King would give 'em a dress, every one."

"Ah, that is it!" said Mrs Kensett; "but for that, not one of us could ever live in His kingdom. For, children, though my dress may look clean and whole to you, I know it is not fit to wear in the presence of the great King. If I ventured before Him in any dress of my own, all He could do would be to send me from His presence."

"What did the king do with t'other feller?" said Jemmy Lucas.

"Just that," said Mrs Kensett. "'Then said the king to the servants, Bind him hand and foot, and take him away, and cast him into outer darkness.'"

"He was just a big fool," said Peter Limp; "why couldn't he have took what the king give him? Didn't cost *him* nothin'."

"I suppose he was too proud," said Mrs Kensett: "he would have liked better to buy it for himself. Or else he thought if he took the dress, he must enter the king's service, and he did not want to do that. Children, God knew that we were not fit to come into His presence: He knew that we could never make ourselves fit. There was sin in our hearts, and not one of us was strong enough to take it out. And God hates sin, and He could not have one bit of it in His heavenly kingdom.''

"Like as t'other king couldn't stand the rags and mud," said Jemmy Lucas.

"Yes, just so ; God must send us all away, and it is death to be driven from His presence. And there was no man that could help. Then the Son of God, our Lord Jesus Christ, said, 'Lo, I come!' He who was perfectly holy, came and opened a fountain where we might wash and be clean ; and that fountain was His own blood. With His own life He bought the new robe which God offers to each one of us. I told you it cost a great deal."

"But what made Him die ?" said Jemmy Lucas.

"God was angry with us all for disobeying Him; He would have punished us all; and then Jesus came and bore our punishment ; He died for us. He took a man's shape, and was put to death here in the world ; and now He is in heaven, to do all things that we need. For His sake God will send His Holy Spirit to take the evil out of our hearts, to help us to serve and love Him ; for His sake God will blot all our sins out of His book, and will count us right-eous only for His sake. As if we were to wash our poor clothes in some glorious fountain, and hide them all with a white, shining robe belonging to the King."

"I 'd like that," said Jemmy Lucas, "only I don't know how."

"You know how the men did in the story,—they took what the king gave them, feeling sure they had nothing, and could get nothing of their own."

"I 'd take it, ma'am," said little Molly. "But then I can't tell the King, and He don't know."

"Oh yes, He does ! He knows every word you think ; He hears every word you say," said Mrs Kensett. "Tell Him you want it, Molly ; tell Him you want to be forgiven, and to be a pure and holy child ; tell Him you want to dwell in His kingdom. Tell our dear King Jesus just what you want, and He will give it to you ; He will teach you to understand it all. You may ask anything of the Lord, for Jesus' sake."

She took the little Bibles out of her basket, giving a blue one to Molly, and a red one to Jemmy Lucas, and a green one to Peter Limp. How beautiful they looked, with their new, fresh covers, and the gilt edges glittered in the sunlight wonderfully.

"Read them, study them, love them, children," she said; "they will tell you about Jesus; they will teach you how to do His will; they will show how His love made Him come and die for you. Read them, and pray every day that the Lord would bring you safe to His heavenly kingdom for Jesus' sake. Never forget how He loves you; never forget that He knows everything you do, and hears every word you say. Never forget that He hates sin. He can do everything; in all your need, in all your trouble, in all your fear, pray to Him."

Slowly Mrs Kensett went down the little path, though the sun had set, and the twilight was deepening fast; but wild little feet, and swift pattering steps, hurried in among the bushes on Vinegar Hill.

"THE SEED IS THE WORD."

THE FOWLS OF THE AIR.

THE FOWLS OF THE AIR.

CHAPTER I.

THOSE of you who have read "The Old Church Door," will doubtless remember Mrs Kensett, the kind lady who, like her Master, "went about doing good;" sowing words of truth and life wherever and whenever she could find a chance. And you may perhaps like to know what became of all the good seed which she scattered broadcast. For it is one thing to plant in a trim little garden-bed, smooth and fenced in, easy to watch and water and weed; and quite another to sow in the broad, open field, where you can but fling the seed right and left, and then leave it to the sunshine and the rain of heaven. In those Eastern lands where this story of the sower was written, the fields are not even enclosed, but stretch on and on, in a sort of boundless way, till it seems, indeed, as if the field were the world. Rocks start up in the midst of it, and thorn-bushes strive for the possession of the good ground, and right through the field runs the highway, with its line of hard and waste soil. The seed falls there, as the sower walks up and down—good seed, fit to yield a glorious harvest; but it does not grow. "The fowls of the air come and gather it up."

Did any of you children ever see a scarecrow?—a tall, ugly figure, made up of an old bonnet, and a ragged coat, and a long stick—or some such fine materials—and set up in a cornfield to wave to and fro in the summer wind. Did you ever see a real man in such a field, hiding behind the fence bushes with his gun? Well, he was there to shoot "the fowls of the air;" and the tall, make-believe figure was to scare them away; and perhaps some of you boys have earned ten cents, now and then, by keeping watch over the field, in place of the gun or the scarecrow. For, when the farmer has sowed good seed in his field, he knows well that if those black fowls of the air come swooping down, there will be hardly a grain left.

Just so when we have heard good words of truth : when some one has been telling us of God, and how to serve and to love Him, then comes the devil, and sends a host of wicked thoughts, and wicked feelings, and wicked imaginations ; and unless they are resisted and driven off, not one of the good seeds will grow.

Ah, it is easy to watch the fenced field or the garden ; easy for kind parents and teachers to help the happy little children to remember, and try, and persevere ; but for those wild, wayside places, trodden underfoot, untilled, uncared for, those little waifs and strays who have not a kind friend in the world, what shall guard the truth in their hearts if perchance they hear it? Who shall help *them* to resist the devil? Why, their homes are the constant abiding-place of the fowls of the air.

Sam Dodd had very little idea that any good seed had fallen on *his* heart, that first day when Mrs Kensett sat and talked to the children ; and still less, perhaps, did he know the extremely "wayside" condition his heart was in : how open and exposed it was to those "fowls of the air," that are ever busy in all waste places. His mind full of evil thoughts, his lips full of evil words ; every good thing that tried to lodge there was generally caught away in a moment. No kind parent watched with his long gun of punishment ; no fear even of the law waved its ugly shape in the wind ; and as for watching himself to drive the birds away, that was the last thing Sam had ever heard of. Everybody seemed to like them where he lived ; it was thought good fun to entice them down, and see them do their work.

O those "fowls of the air!" how busy they were that day! And they took all manner of shapes, as they swooped down to gather up the seed Mrs Kensett had sown.

The first grain of good which lay on Sam's heart for a while was a little bit of a thought how good it was of the King to send him an invitation to His feast. All the way down the hill that night Sam kept thinking of it; and when he burst in, noisily as ever, at the door of his wretched home, he thought of it more than ever. Yes, it was a very wretched home, though perhaps not just the sort of one you imagine. There are a great many kinds of wretched homes, and this was one of the worst.

In the first place, however, which was all good as far as it went, the house was the largest and best built of all the houses on Vinegar Hill. It was painted red, with green doors and window shutters; and all across the front was a sort of long porch or piazza, with a wooden bench that stretched from end to end. Round the door were some half-dozen hitching-posts, and a wide open shed farther off told of accommodation in bad weather. But to-night, in the soft June twilight, there were several teams and saddle-horses fastened to the posts by the door. And now, close at hand, one could hear plain enough some of the sounds which, even softened by distance, had made Mrs Kensett feel sick at heart—loud oaths, and stormy contention, and many a drunken laugh.

None of these stopped Sam: he was too well used to them all. He burst in, as I said, with a whoop and a halloo, among a posse of men that were sitting in the back room. Ah, me! you would never have guessed in there that it was June. Could roses grow in a world where such scents were possible? Could birds sing on an evening when the air carried such sounds? The room was so dark with the smoke of a dozen pipes that the very candles burned dim, and so foul with the fumes of whisky that you could hardly draw your breath; and not a word nor a laugh that would not make you shiver. There sat poor Tim Lucas, offering his shoes for another drink, and too far gone to remember that he had parted with them already. There sat many another, from the Hill and the village, some richer, some poorer, but all sold into the chains of Satan, and led captive at his will.

James Dodd, Sam's father, kept a steady head through it all; watching his miserable guests; urging them on, now with ridicule, now with praise; taking every sort of payment for his draughts of poison; and putting Tim Lucas's shoes in his closet, with as little remorse as he put Walter Crook's money in his till.

I told you a little grain of good, a little thought of right, had lodged in Sam's heart. He did not know it; and wondered to himself now, as he went in, what made the room look so much darker and uglier than ever before. He had seen it in that state a thousand times. But how ugly it did all look, to be sure! And Sam thought curiously of Mrs Kensett's description of the King's feast. Everybody was asked,—so she had said: and some people were going,—she said that too; and Sam thought to himself, as he had before, that no one could be such a fool as to stay away. But then he was asked too! so she had declared, and yet he was not going; he did not feel so. Sam found the subject quite too large for that smoky room: he took up a bit of stick, and, going out to the door-step, sat down and began to whittle.

"Why, in course!" he broke out after a while, "that's just where it is. I *ain't* a-goin', so it stands to reason I ain't asked." And Sam threw off the light shavings with greater exactness than ever.

"Wonder if He does see down here now?" the boy began again, as a storm of foul words burst forth through the open windows. "Or hear what's goin' on? I know I wouldn't listen, if I was Him, if I didn't like it no better than *she* says He don't. What 'ud a king want with the like o' us?" Sam went on, contemptuously. "Why, if even the gov'nor knew where half o' them fellers was, they'd every one on 'em be took up afore you could count ten.

'Twouldn't be much loss, you know, to nobody else, but still it ain't exactly the kind o' invitations she was a-tellin' of. Feastin' of 'em too! My! ain't some folks just the easiest gulled! Did sound kinder pleasant, though," said Sam, relenting a little. "I say, I shouldn't mind goin'—not if it *was* true. Wonder who telled her? Them 'ere slicked-up folks allers does make believe they knows more'n common.

"They ain't a-talkin' so *very* low just now. Guess if He *can* hear whispers, it's likely He heard *that*," said Sam, with another glance into the noisy room. "We was to think of it when we was hid away in the bushes. Guess as how I'll get a little farther off."

And Sam rose up from the stone step, and lounged away into the dark thicket that lay all round the house.

"Sam! Sam Dodd! be's that you?" called a stealthy voice from out the bushes.

"O' course," said Sam, gruffly. "What wickedness is you up to now, Tim Wiggins?"

"Wickedness!" said the boy, mockingly, and sidling up to Sam. "That's a sort o' new-fashioned word out o' *your* mouth, ain't it, Sam Dodd? Wouldn't wonder, now, if you warn't a-thinkin' o' what the old woman said, up to the church. Oh dear!"

"None o' your business, anyhow," said Sam, fiercely. "I ain't, nuther, and that's more."

"Dear me!" said the other boy. "He's sure o' that!"

"Sure as you are to have your head knocked off, if you don't behave," said Sam Dodd. "What's to pay in the bushes to-night? Is't you after the sheriff, or the sheriff after you? 'Cause I'll bear a hand, if *that's* it."

"Nary one," said the boy, linking his arm in Sam's. "Come now, keep a cool tongue, can't ye? I'm just gettin' a small job ready for him, that's all."

"Oh, is that all?" said Sam. "I shouldn't call you much of a job, any day, Tim."

"'Tain't me, you fool," said the other. "It's Farmer

Graves's chickens. Them 'ere young fat ones as he sets such count on."

"What, the ones in the boxes?" said Sam. "*They're* all safe enough. Why, his wife's got 'em set round right under her bedroom winder."

"So as she could hear 'em if they cried in the night," said Tim Wiggins. "Guess *I* knows where they be. And whether they're fat, too. Why, I've felt o' them chickens once a week reg'lar ever sen' they came out o' the shell."

"And they're fat now, are they?" said Sam.

"A 1," answered the other. "There's a dozen on 'em, Sam, just six a-piece."

"Supposin' I take 'em?" said Sam.

"Supposin' you ain't turned chicken yerself, to make the thirteenth," said Tim Wiggins. "Why, I say that talk up yonder to the church made *me* so hungry I couldn't hardly wait."

"Feared you don't get much to eat down your way," said Sam, coolly. "*I* ain't forgot my dinner yet. Hows'ever, I don't often make objections to a chicken supper. But I tell you what, Tim Wiggins, old Graves keeps a gun."

"Let him keep it! he's welcome," said the other, with a sneer. "Guess *I* ain't green enough to stand out in the moonlight to be shot. He can blaze away just as powerful as he's a mind ter. Won't hurt me none, nor the dear little chickens he's so fond of. They'll hev' their feelin's all locked up and packed away, afore that old gun's loaded. But I say, Sam, be you a-goin'? or ain't you quite got through meditatin' yet?"

For all answer to which Sam knocked off his companion's hat, and then engaged him in a rousing scuffle; which being well over, with a wild, whooping halloo, the two boys dashed away into the night, and the echoes of Vinegar Hill sank down once more, and were still.

CHAPTER II.

UNDER cover of the night, now, the two boys stole on, softly as two cushion-shod cats; hushing their voices when once beyond the bounds of Vinegar Hill, and keeping in the shadow of fences, barns, trees, and hedges, wherever they could be found. For although the moon rose late this night, yet already there came up a warning glory of her approach, chasing and rebuking the works of darkness.

Silently the boys crept along, but swiftly too; moving with so exactly the same impulse, turning and winding and stooping at so exactly the same points, that one might fancy not only that each knew the way, but that they had often travelled it before together. Ah, where had not those two boys been together, under cover of the night?

"I say," whispered Tim Wiggins, as they reached the farm, "they's up yet!"

"Old woman's give him a better supper'n common, bein' as it's Sunday," growled Sam. "Moon's comin' up, too, and that's more."

"Let her come," said Tim Wiggins. "'Tain't the first time I've seen her white phiz, by several. It's too confounded dark round where the coops is, t'other side, to see much—if there was twenty moons."

"Guess you'll find one'll make it light enough to do *your* business," said Sam Dodd. "Old Graves ain't perticklar about seein' the hull of a bush afore he lets fly."

"I just wish you was home and abed, tucked in!" said Tim Wiggins, impatiently. "'*Tis* kinder late for babies to be out. Moonlight's ketchin', too, I've heerd tell."

"You mind yer own business, Tim Wiggins," said Sam, fiercely, "'cause if I have to take it in hand, it'll be so well done that there won't be nothin' left for you to do never arterwards."

"Oh dear!" sneered Tim. "There! the light's out! and it won't take 'em two seconds to get asleep, 'cause they ain't

E

more'n half awake none o' the time. Now, Sam, for supper!"

Sam made no answer. But as they crept softly round the house, making a careful examination on all sides, there came over him again the thought of the afternoon's talk— of the words of the lady's prayer. The feast which the King had made,—what a thing that would be!

And what did He think of this way people took to get a feast for themselves? "He sees you, boys, wherever you are,"—so the lady had said. Sam shivered a little, and felt for a minute as if there were, indeed, "twenty moons."

Everything was very quiet within doors; the silence almost seemed to make Tim's words good; and without there was nothing louder than the soft hum of summer insects, and the cry of the night-hawk, and the distant rush and murmur of a little brook. The leaves waved gently in their June freshness; the blades of grass held their dewy crowns erect; the shadows changed and softened every moment with the coming light of the moon. The dark outline of the chicken-coops could but just be seen. But with one glimpse of them, Sam Dodd was himself again.

"Tell you what," he whispered, "let's take 'em up, coops and all, down into the woods yonder."

"Won't do," said Tim. "Coops might be weightier'n we thought,—and you kin shake chickens awake in a jiffy. Or they's might be fast to the ground with stakes. Just you hold the bag, Sam, and I'll choke 'em so easy they'll all think they's dreamin' o' biled pertaters."

Down on the grass knelt Sam, holding the bag wide open, while Tim—having with great care pulled up the one movable slat of the coop—put in his hand and began the work. With infinite skill he contrived to seize each chicken by the neck, holding it so tight, that not an outcry could be made, until with a dexterous twist, he put outcries quite out of the question. One coop was emptied, and another; but in the third, an adventurous young cockerel, having caught one gleam of the moonlight, opened his mouth and hal looed.

"Blast him," muttered Tim Wiggins, savagely, "our fun's up. I'll stop *his* noise, though."

But the young cock, throttled midway in another jubilee crow, broke down in so extraordinary a manner, with such a very alarming blast of his trumpet, that the boys caught up their bag and darted round the house, then stopped to listen.

Slowly up went the window, creaking and rattling as if that were an exercise to which it was not well fitted. Then silence again.

"Well, I'm sure I *did* hear a noise among the chickens," said the voice of Mrs Graves.

"Just the moon," said the farmer, sleepily. "Always do feel called upon to crow when the moon comes up—whether it's three o'clock, or two o'clock, or eleven o'clock. Don't make no sort o' odds."

"But they're not crowing," said Mrs Graves.

"Ain't no breed o' chickens as crows *all* the time," said the farmer. "Not so fur's I know. And I'm sure that's a blessing."

"Well, it didn't sound like a crow, one bit," said Mrs Graves. "It was a scream. I wouldn't wonder if that brown mink was there again."

"Couldn't get in, if he was," said the farmer; "I fastened up them coops myself, and didn't leave door-room enough for a weasel, not to say a mink."

"Why don't they crow again, then?" said his wife, straining her eyes and ears to make out something from the dark silence.

"Moon's an old story, now," said Mr Graves, yawning. "Might keep on till daylight, if it warn't."

"What's that down among the bushes?" said the sharp-eyed little woman, leaning out of the window. "I do believe, Ahab, it's that mink! Shoo! shoo! get out!" And Mrs Graves clapped her hands vehemently. The farmer laughed.

"They do tell about ketchin' a weasel asleep in a stone wall," he said, "but 'tis the first time I—or anybody else—

ever see a mink walkin' round in the moonshine to be looked at."

"But I saw him!" said Mrs Graves. "I'm sure I did."

"Seein' him's a sartain sure sign he ain't there!" said the farmer, decidedly. "I'll get the gun and bring down some o' them 'ere bushes, if it'll content ye,—though 'tain't considered just the best way o' prunin' 'em, likely."

"Shoo! shoo!" repeated Mrs Graves, pounding upon the clapboards with her little hands. "There, I guess I've scared him, so he won't come back to-night, any way. But if it's all right, Ahab, why are the coops all so quiet?"

"I s'pose a woman could be answered, sometimes," said Mr Graves, "if so be as she'd ever stand still for two minutes together! But what a man's to do with both sides of a question to once, is more'n I know. First, the coops is noisy —then they's quiet; first, the chickens cries out—then they don't. And nary one suits her! I'm a-goin' to bed. Wouldn't keep awake no longer for all the plaguy minks in creation."

"Well, let's go down and just walk round the house first," said Mrs Graves, pounding on the clapboards. "Shoo! shoo!"

What followed upon that, the two boys did not hear. Hastily lifting their bag of ill-gotten game, they stole away from the cover of the house to that of the nearest bush, and so went on, running like partridges, doubling like hares, till the village itself was left behind, and they were safe in the murky shadows of Vinegar Hill.

"Now we'll just rest a bit," said Tim Wiggins, letting down the bag. "My! I wonder if that old feller's got round the house yet? Tell you what, if she'd had the gun, she'd ha' blowed every one o' them chicken-coops clean away."

"How many have we got?" whispered Sam.

"Don' know,—bag's pretty heavy. Guess we'd just as good sit down here and divide. One's mine for findin' and plannin'; and two's mine for the bag; and three's mine for the throttlin'; and four's mine, to begin. Go ahead."

Sam looked on, scowling, while his companion threw four

chickens in a heap at his feet; but as the facts were not to be denied, thieves' honour bade him submit. He thrust his hand into the bag without a word, pulling out a plump young cock.

"Five's yourn," said Tim, "and six is mine. And seven 's yourn agin, and eight 's mine. And nine 's yourn, and ten 's mine,—and 'leven 's mine. Lucky there ain't nary odd one, or we 'd have to fight for it, sure as guns," said Tim, coolly throwing his lion's share back into the bag. "Was another, too."

"Yes, and you dropped it," said Sam Dodd, fiercely. "You was so scared, when you run, you just flung it away."

"Why didn't you pick it up, then?" said Tim, with a sneer.

"I say, hand out another o' them birds," said Sam, giving Tim a cuff.

"Help yourself!" replied Tim, swinging his bag round with such force, that Sam measured his length on the ground. And before he could pick himself up again, Tim was gone. Worse than that, one of Sam's chickens went with him. Sam turned them over in the moonlight.

"Five was mine,—one ; and seven 's two,—and nine was three,—and *that's* gone ! Eight o' his own, and one o' mine."

With a fierce oath, Sam caught up the two solitary chickens, and flung them from him as far as his strength could throw ; then walked slowly along towards home. The moon was well up now, pouring a flood of soft light in among the bushes, rounding out the shadow of each in darker and sharper lines. The light wrapped up Sam himself, shone in his eyes, made the ground startlingly white and sparkling before his feet. Sam scowled, and muttered between his teeth, and then fairly dodged the fair line ; darting from bush to bush, and keeping now in the thick shade. But it did not seem to make much difference, after all. To be sure, the moon didn't look straight in his eyes ; but whenever he looked out from the bushes, there was her bright face shining down as clear as ever. What was that the lady had said ?

" Think of it, boys, when you are hid away in the bushes."

Sam started on a full run, and never stopped till he was in the very midst of the smoky carouse, which was still going on at his father's house. In the midst of it, taking part in it, steadying his nerves with the bold wickedness of those who were older than himself, both in years and sin.

CHAPTER III.

You would wonder, perhaps, how it was that Sam Dodd went up with the rest to the old church next day, and I don't suppose he could have told himself. Tim Wiggins did not go,—perhaps that was one reason ; for Tim's face and words and manner, whenever Sam met him that day, had been particularly irritating.

" Say, Sammy," he would begin, " had a first-rate broil for breakfast ! How's yourn ? Eat tender, did they ? "

Or, " Sam, how's yer head after that 'ere moonshine ? Made ye look kinder streaked, didn't it ? "

" S'pose yer goin' to tell the old woman up yonder as how you didn't sleep well, and got a headache. Just give her my love, and tell her I's made over all my share o' *t'other* feast to you."

" None o' yer business," Sam would answer, angrily. " Tell ye I ain't a-goin' near her." But when the afternoon came, he did. Something in the strange words attracted him, something in the gentle voice drew him ; but oh, what a " wayside " heart it was, on which the good seed fell ! So *grown up to weeds*, so thronged with evil thoughts and feelings and desires ! Children, pray most of all for those who seem to have no good in them, for they need it most of all. And the prayer of faith has power, even against " the fowls of the air " and their prince.

Everything in Sam's heart was adverse that day. When

he saw the lady in the distance, waiting in the porch, there
came over him a great desire to aim at her with a stone, and
knock her bonnet off, regardless of her head. But Jemmy
Lucas was so close at hand, that Sam thought, on the whole,
it might not be prudent. So he contented himself with
knocking off Jemmy's cap, and then rushing into the porch
with the shrillest whistle that even his well-trained organs
could produce. And when she started, his laugh was the
loudest, his whoop of satisfaction the most overpowering.

Hanging about the old pillars, climbing into the old tree,
pinching Jemmy Lucas, and tickling Peter Limp, and making
faces at little Molly ; so Sam Dodd listened. And yet (you
would hardly believe it) he heard every word that Mrs Kensett said. The golden dishes and gay dresses and sweet
music that graced the King's feast ; the greater splendour, the
unimaginable glories of the heavenly kingdom. Sam lost
not a word. How like music the mere thoughts were !
"Every gate was of one pearl,"—and "the city had no need
of the sun, neither of the moon to shine in it ; for the glory
of God doth lighten it, and the Lamb is the light thereof."
Sam did not understand it all ; the words of the music were
strange words ; and yet the sweet, clear notes somehow
echoed down in his heart.

"Anybody can be a servant of God," so she said ; "and
He bids them tell the truth, and speak no bad words, and to
help other people."

Sam swung himself round and round the pillar, then
straightened himself up, scowling—

"Now that's just what I ain't a-goin' to do," he muttered,
"nor to be, nuther. Who wants to be took care of, I'd like
to know ? Guess when I'm anybody's servant he'll know
it ; and I too."

Again the words fell sweet and soft—

"God loves you, every one. Ask Him to help you."

Sam paused, then as the others knelt down around their
teacher, he spoke an oath between his teeth, and turned
away. The good seed lay scattered, and the fowls of the air
came down and gathered it up.

"Easy talkin'!" said Sam to himself. "Guess if I don't know a trick worth two o' that, I *am* smart. I want somethin' right straight off now, to take the taste o' them kings out o' my mouth." Sam sat down on the grass to think and ponder, while the night fell, and the stars came out in their summer glory. The rest of the little hearers had long ago gone home.

"I owes every one on 'em a turn," said Sam to himself. "Sneakin' round up there, and makin' b'lieve to be better'n they are. *They* settin' up to find the King!" Sam chuckled bitterly. "There's that young 'un now,—guess I'll begin with her."

Sam started to his feet, and went noiselessly threading his way among bushes and houses, till he came to Limp's cottage, which lay far away down at the very bottom of the hill. The owner of course was not at home,—he rarely was at that time of night. You might have found him, perhaps, in the drinking party down at James Dodd's; or, more likely still, in some dark nook of the outside world, deep in consultation with John Crooks. He was off somewhere; and in the one small room which his house contained, Mrs Limp sat, mending his jacket. The smallest and dimmest of tallow candles gleamed faintly through its own smoke like an exhausted fire-fly; the smallest and puniest of babies wailed wearily on the wretched bed. And Mrs Limp sang scraps of lullabies, and plied her needle, and drew sighs a fathom deep. And at the slightest sound the needle redoubled its efforts, as if the temper of the absent Mr Limp was a somewhat doubtful thing, where his mending was concerned. The air of the room was close and foul and hot; heavy with bad tobacco and bad whisky; reeking with the fumes of the supper and the heat of the little stove.

Outside, on the door-step, sat Molly and Peter, talking in the soft twilight; and they too kept watch, ready to scamper away at the least alarm. But one of the crickets in the grass could hardly have moved with lighter feet than Sam Dodd, as he crept up to listen.

"You see, Molly," Peter was saying, "'tain't an over and above sort o' place as we lives in here; and folks ain't

more'n common fond o' me and you,—so guess likely they
wouldn't none on 'em break their hearts with missin' of us.
You ain't no 'count, anyhow."

"But then I don't know whatever the King would do
with me," said poor Molly, wistfully.

"No more don't I," said Peter,—"blessed if I do. But I
tell you what I *did* hear, once, Moll,—some o' them rich
folk's kinder squeamish like, and they don't like to kill off
their old sick horses, and sich; so they has a field a purpose
to turn 'em into, and let's 'em die off nat'ral. My!" said
Peter, reflectingly, "why, there's enough weakly young uns
here in Vinegar Hill to stock a farm!"

Molly was silent a little; the prospect did not look hope-
ful.

"But that don't sound like what the lady said, Peter," she
ventured, doubtfully.

"No more it don't," said Peter, shaking his head. "But
how it's different, Moll, I can't tell ye; so don't ye go for to
ask."

"'God loves you all'—that's how she said," said little
Molly, thinking. "'He wants you every one to be His servants.' But servants has to work, Peter, so I'd have to be
all different, you see."

"Guess likely," replied Peter. "Well, maybe He'd cure
ye up if you once got there."

"Oh, I wish I was there now!" said Molly, with a long
sigh; "I'm so tired, Peter."

"Shouldn't wonder if you was," said Peter, assentingly.
"Well, you might start right off, if you'd a mind ter."

"But I forget!" said Molly, "I forget how."

"What, don't you remember nothin'?" said Peter.

"Only what I said. 'And there's no one too small, or
too weak.' She said that. And oh, I remember now!" said
Molly, with a cry of joy. "She said, 'Ask Him to help you,
ask Him to teach you how.'"

"So she did," said Peter. "And she said for somebody's
sake, too."

"I forget that," said Molly. "But I know she said the

t'other." And putting her hands together pleadingly, little
Molly looked out into the darkness and cried—

"O King! please help me! please teach me! I don't
know how!"

"You shut up!" said Peter, giving her a little shake.
"If you're goin' on like that, I'll be off. What d'ye
s'pose father'd say, if he heard sich a yellin' round his front
door?"

Molly shrank and cowered.

"The King heard, though, Peter," she said, under her
breath, "'cause the lady said He couldn't help it."

"Well, I guess you'd better just hush," said Peter, "or
there be other things as can't be helped, nuther. Father's
comin', this blessed minute; and *he* don't keep no field for
sick folks."

Molly slid down from the door-step into the night, and
Peter disappeared among the bushes; and Sam Dodd set
his teeth in a sort of rage. All sorts of sweet words had
kept coming into his thoughts as he stood there,—thoughts
of the great King, thoughts of His kingdom; loving words
that the lady had said; and right up against them came a
tide of evil, surging, swelling, and at last sweeping all before
it.

"I'll pay *you* off, you little beggar, for talkin' sich stuff," he
muttered, savagely. And always Satan can provide mischief
for willing—as well as for idle—hands to do. Sam went
prowling round the house, and presently came upon poor
Molly's kitten; her white fur making her but too visible in
the twilight. There she sat, watching a rat hole; so absolutely intent upon her duty that she never thought of being
afraid, till Sam's fingers came about her throat with so
fierce a grip, that she could not even mew. I am not going
to tell you all that he did; but when he left the place,
laughing contentedly to himself, the little kitten lay
stretched out by the rat hole, having died at her post.

CHAPTER IV.

THERE is an old story in a very old book of fairy tales (you know they sometimes say queer things), which tells of a battle that raged once upon a time between a bird and a pomegranate. A pomegranate, you must understand, is a very large, handsome, and fragrant fruit, that grows in the East,—in Asia, the very headquarters of fairy tales.

The battle, as I have said, raged fiercely. To secure itself, at length, the pomegranate broke into twenty pieces, scattering the seeds of its life far and wide in all directions; but the bird hopped briskly round, and eat them every one. Or all but one. One single seed rolled secretly away, and hid itself under a broad burdock leaf; and as long as it lay there hid, the bird had not quite conquered, and the pomegranate was not quite dead.

Something like this seemed to have gone on in Sam Dodd's heart. His own evil thoughts and inclinations, the wicked words and wicked persuasions of his companions, had certainly done their best to gather up every good seed which the lady had sown; and yet, hidden away in a corner, one little grain of life still kept its place. It was not in good circumstances for growing, but it was there; and as the afternoon came round, Sam might be once more seen among the little group that gathered round the old church door. But he hung back more than usual, and was a little shy of them all, especially of Molly, who, poor child, looked as if she had cried her eyes half out over her dead kitten.

Still, she did not seem to suspect Sam of any hand in the mischief; there were too many hands about her always ready for just such work. Sam eyed her askance from time to time, as he sat there listening and kicking his feet about; saying very few words of his own, but never losing one that the lady said. Until of a sudden something new caught his eye and his thoughts; and from that moment Sam heard not another word, to notice it, till the talk was almost done.

All around the worn steps of the church, the fresh turf

laid its soft bordering of green ; and the grass had been lately cut, and now the young blades were just shooting up again to repair damages. And as the old keeper of the church grounds was not as keen of sight nor as deft of hand as he had once been, so it happened that there were corners here and there, which the scythe had failed to touch. Tufts of long grass made a lank ring round the tree stems, and others bent down over the church steps ; and little clusters of clover leaves held up their unshorn heads in all sorts of places. They were not at all interesting to Sam Dodd,— indeed, few people would have admired them in their present state,—but as Sam gazed at them idly, with wandering eyes and thoughts which did not go far enough off to lose either word or look from the lady, all at once he saw something else ; and his idle thoughts became, in a moment, the busiest that could be.

At the very foot of the steps a particularly long tuft of grass waved back and forth above the scraper, swaying gently in the breeze ; and deep hid in the shade of its rank leaves, Sam saw a strange glitter of something bright. A gleam that flashed and shone and went out, as he moved his head one way and another to get a better view. It could not be a fire-fly,—the hour was too early, and the air too light. It might be a piece of glass,—but with that strange sort of assuredness which comes to one sometimes, Sam Dodd felt quite certain that it was not. Had anybody else seen it— *would* anybody else see it ? Sam heard no more of the lady's words, and saw nothing, thought of nothing, but that one point of glitter among the grass. How should he get between it and everybody else, without attracting attention ?

Sam swung himself round his pillar, and sat down on the floor of the porch for a minute, and sidled along to the steps ; then slowly and carelessly and by degrees slid down from one step to another, until he sat on the lowest one of all, kicking his bare feet over that very tuft of grass. But he did not venture to give a single look at the bright sparkle that lay twinkling in its depths. Not then. On the contrary, he turned himself quite about, leaning on his elbow, and looking up the steps at the lady; listening now with close attention; giving it as his opinion that nobody need go to the King's feast who was not a mind to. And as he said that, Sam swung his foot a little farther off the step, stretching down until it rested full in the middle of that very tuft of grass where the sparkle lay; and then Sam felt quiet and comfortable. A little impatient, perhaps, as the talk went on; a little angry to see how eagerly the rest of the children listened; for now Sam had turned his heart all the other way, and the sweet words of the story sounded sweet no longer. Scowling, he sat there, eying little Molly, and thinking how glad he was he had killed her kitten; but when at last the others all knelt down around their teacher, Sam's face cleared, and he began to whistle.

He rose up lazily, stretched himself, dropped his cap, stooped to pick it up, and when Sam Dodd snapped his fingers and turned away from the old church door, the bright spot sparkled in the grass no longer.

It was strange though, that as he went rapidly off down the hill, skulking through the bushes, and looking over his shoulder about every other minute, the words of the lady still rang in his ears,—or rather sounded there like some soft whisper: "God loves you all." "He invites you all to the great feast in His kingdom." "We must ask Him to help us, and bring us, for we are weak and He is strong." Sam set his teeth and knit his brows, and did his best to keep the words out of his mind, but they would come. As he mused and walked along, more slowly now, the rest of the children came helter-skelter down the hill.

For you could not expect these children to be quiet and orderly, no matter what they had been hearing, or how they had felt. Like those poor London outcasts who have slept in boxes and corners till they cannot stretch themselves out in a bed, so the Vinegar Hill youngsters would need long training before they could give up their hop, skip, and jump, and walk like ordinary people. Even Molly came along on one foot, and Jemmy Lucas made the air ring with mews, and barks, and crows, and cackles.

"Here you are," shouted Peter Limp, announcing his own approach. "Now then, Sammy, like to know what ye got by bein' so spry?"

"Ain't got nothin'!" said Sam, flushing very red. "None o' yer business, ye little rascal."

"Sam ain't gen'ally over and above, ye know," said Jemmy Lucas. "He's give away all his manners to poor folks."

"And you ain't never had none to give," said Sam Dodd, dealing a cuff at the little boy. "But I say, chaps! who wants more cherries'n he can eat?"

"Deary me!" said Peter Limp, with a slow, drawling voice, "why, ye know, Sam, we ain't none on us fond of 'em! We's been fetched up delicate."

"Guess your trees must ha' started up and blowed quite sudden like, Sam," said Jemmy Lucas.

"There's the biggest lot down to Squire Townsend's you ever did see," said Sam, not noticing either reply. "Biggest cherries too, and so ripe! Why, it's just all they can do to keep theirselves from falling off the tree."

"Oh! and did Squire T. ask us to come?" said Jemmy Lucas, opening his eyes very wide.

"Guess likely he did!" said Sam, with a laugh. "Folks don't do sich things out o' stories, ye little fool. I asked myself."

"But if you're goin' to steal 'em, Sam, the King won't like it," said Molly.

"Maybe not," said Sam Dodd. "That ain't the point in hand. He ain't got nothin' to do with Squire Townsend's things."

"The lady said He looked all the time, and He wouldn't like it," persisted Molly.

"Do you want to get home head first, quicker'n you ever did afore?" said Sam Dodd, turning fiercely upon the child. "'Cause if you do, just keep on, that's all. And I won't make you wait long, nuther. Take yerself off, you little beggar! we wants none o' *your* preachin'!"

"Well, she's a sight better'n you are, Sam Dodd," said

Jemmy Lucas. "And *I* ain't a-going to stand by and see Molly hurt."

"I'll pitch you down first, and save yer feelin's that way," said Sam, furiously. "Be off! Come, Peter!"

But Peter hesitated.

"Blessed if he ain't afeared too!" said Sam Dodd, with a laugh. "Trees ain't so high, Peter; take good care on ye, Peter. Fetch ye safe home to admirin' friends; tuck ye up all slick. Glad *my* daddy ain't so woundy partic'lar as yourn."

"*He* don't care," said Peter, twisting his foot about on the grass; hearing, as he answered Sam, little Molly's under-breath whisper—

"O Peter! the King wouldn't like it!"

"Must be his mammy, then!" said Sam Dodd. "She ain't got used to havin' her dear boy out o' nights! What *will* she ever do, supposin' he should ever grow up? 'Tain't likely, ye know, but still it don't hardly do to think o' how 'twould be if he *should*. Run home, Pety—wouldn't wonder if she wa'n't waitin' tea for ye this blessed minute."

And Sam turned away in the direction of Squire Townsend's, and Peter followed him without another word.

CHAPTER V

IF boys could be made sick with eating countless cherries,—green ones, ripe ones,—stones and all,—then doubtless that unpleasant consequence would have followed the bad night's work of Sam Dodd and Peter Limp in Squire Townsend's orchard. But no, they went about next day as usual, only wearing such a meek look of extra virtue on their faces, as was a sure sign they had been about some extra piece of mischief. But no one at Vinegar Hill was likely to notice that. It was also doubtless that they would have "caught it," as Squire

Townsend said, if only he could have caught them : that
small difficulty was in the way. He knew—and they knew
—that the thing was almost an impossibility. Large, and
stout, and slow, what chance had he of catching the spry
youngsters who went up and down his trees like squirrels,
and over his fence like cats, and pelted him with his own
cherries as he stood gazing from his own house door ? What
use to try to follow *them ?* Why, they would have caught
away the fruit from his very hand, if he had ventured out
into the orchard and succeeded in picking a little in the
darkness.   The Squire could do nothing,—nothing but
groan and scold over his lost cherries and his injured trees.
For the ground was strewn with twigs and tufts of leaves,
wilting in the morning sun as it came up; and the trees were
hung with broken and twisted branches, some split down with
a hard pull, and some with a careless step. Cherries lay scattered about by the handful, bruised and trodden underfoot;
and such traces were all Squire Townsend could find when he .
went out next morning to lose his appetite before breakfast.
Certainly he had never felt less like inviting the Vinegar
Hill boys to come and live with him, than he did that day.

"The young scamps !" he said over and over again, as he
walked through the orchard, for Sam and Peter had not contented themselves with stripping one tree, but had tried as
many as possible. "The little villains ! If I once had 'em
I'd thrash 'em within a half inch of their lives ! and they
haven't left so much as a pocket-handkerchief to spot 'em by !"

No, there was not a sign.   Only One knew who were the
thieves ; only one Eye had seen them, through the thick
branches, amid the darkness of the night ; only one Ear had
heard their wicked words as they picked the cherries, speaking low, lest Squire Townsend might hear.

"Can any hide himself in secret places, that I shall not
see him ? saith the Lord." "There is not a word on my
tongue, but, lo, O Lord, thou knowest it altogether."

Yes, the Lord saw, and the Lord heard,—that same great
King who has said : " Thou shalt not steal," " Thou shalt not
take the name of the Lord thy God in vain." The sin was far

more against Him than against Squire Townsend; and He too was angry : "God is angry with the wicked every day;" but unlike Squire Townsend, He was "ready to forgive." Ready to receive the little outcasts if they would come home to Him, ready to blot out all their sins from His book, where every one was written down, if only they had begged Him earnestly to forgive them, for the Lord Jesus' sake.

"Like as a father pitieth his children, so the Lord pitieth them that fear Him."

Ah, they did not fear Him, these children, not in any way; and they never thought of coming to Him for forgiveness. On the contrary, Sam Dodd got up next morning in particularly good spirits, and began at once to plan new wicked deeds for the next night; for, children, if the devil is once welcomed into a boy's—or a man's—heart, he keeps very busy there, you may be sure.

Sam got his breakfast, and then he found a sunny place on the hill-side, and there stretched himself out on the grass to plan and think and help the devil all he could. The devil proposed things, and Sam consented; the devil caught away the good seed out of Sam's heart, but that was because Sam had not guarded it and watched it, and driven him away. "Resist the devil, and he will flee from you;' but "he that committeth sin"—welcomes it, yields to it— becomes thenceforth "the servant of sin."

Sam stretched himself out in the sunlight, at his ease, feeling quite secure against interruptions; for it was early yet, and the habit of Vinegar Hill was mostly to be up all night, and then sleep all the morning; and after a little satisfied chuckling over last night's work, another thought came over him. Cautiously looking round to make sure that he was alone, Sam put his hand in his pocket and drew forth a small gold pencil; holding it up before his eyes as he lay there, working the slide back and forth with much satisfaction. The large end of the pencil was not gold, but something brighter still; and presently Sam began to twirl it round and round, to see this bright end sparkle, and flash, and dance in the sunbeams; shielding it a little, too, with

F

his other hand, lest perchance the sparkling gleam might glance off too far, and reach some other eye among the bushes. It was wonderfully pretty!—that clear, white glitter, which every now and then seemed to take to itself all the colours of the rainbow; and soon Sam became so absorbed in admiration that he forgot all about everything and everybody else, till suddenly a weak little voice cried out at his elbow—

"O Sam Dodd! what *has* you got?"

"Nothin' for you; and none o' your business, neither!" said Sam, slipping the pencil into his pocket, and dealing the child a cuff as he started up; "take *that*, if you want it. What are *you* after at this time o' day, ye little thief?"

"I ain't a thief," said Molly, dodging his hand; "I ain't after nothin'. And I ain't a-goin' to do nothin' bad, Sam Dodd, never no more."

"Oh! you ain't!" said Sam, with the intensest scorn.

"No," said Molly, "I's afraid; 'cause the King looks right down in among the bushes. What was that you's got, Sam? Let's see it."

"Guess I will!" said Sam, scowling at her. "Sich things ain't good for little beggars' eyes, d'ye see?"

"Well, but *let's* see it," persisted Molly. "Why, it's a'most as bright as the lady's!"

"*Most* as bright!" Sam repeated. "Her'n ain't a tenpenny nail 'longside o' this. Now, Molly Limp, I ain't a-goin' to have all the brats in Vinegar Hill comin' round to look; so if you just tell one on 'em—nor nobody else—as how I've got things as is worth lookin' at, there won't be two inches o' you left standin' not ten minutes after. D'ye understand? No more ain't I a-goin' to have *you* snoopin' round. Take yerself off! Clear out! or I'll let ye try how it feels without waitin'."

Molly vanished, almost before the words were well out, slipping away among the bushes as noiselessly as she had come, but Sam's fun was over. He tucked away the pencil in the deep recesses of his pocket, and moved off muttering and grumbling to himself, and threatening vengeance upon Molly Limp and the whole race of small children to which she belonged. All day he kept rather away from people—out of sight, though watching everything that went on; now curled among the bushes, now stowed away in a leafy tree-top; dodging into the house when he got hungry, and bringing out his slice of bread and meat the back way, to eat it in some unseen corner. "The wicked flee when no man pursueth."

However, the day went quietly by; and when in the afternoon thick clouds came gathering up, and it began to rain, Sam came down from his perch in a more composed state of mind, shook himself clear of the rain-drops, and went into the house to supper.

A rainy day followed; and Sam, who was not too fond of exposing himself, slept away a good many of the dripping hours to recover from past fatigues. He lay there on his little garret bed, dreaming and muttering in his sleep; now hearing the lady's sweet words of counsel, now stealing off with the chickens from the farm, and then again having a hand-to-hand fight with Squire Townsend for the cherries. Then the scene changed once more; and he saw little Molly picking her way along through the mud, holding up her ragged frock to be out of reach of even a spatter, and saying to him as she went along: "I ain't never goin' to do nothin' bad, Sam Dodd, no more." And Sam thought he stooped down to pick up a handful of mud to throw at her, and she slipped away out of sight among the bushes, and he had his handful of mud for his pains.

You may believe that with this sort of work going on in his mind, Sam's sleep was neither very quiet nor very sweet; and as he tossed and threw his arms about in his anger or his fight, behold, the little gold pencil rolled out of his pocket, working its way along through various other things, and slipped softly down upon the floor. But Sam never heard it.

Now James Dodd's house had one characteristic common to many of its class—there was not room enough in it for the work to be done and the things to be stored there; and thus it happened that every corner was in use, and every room served more than one purpose. Especially was this small garret of Sam's in demand; for it was out of sight and out of reach to the comers and goers in the rooms below. Here stood dark-looking chests, carefully locked and corded, and pine boxes nailed up; while on the walls and from the rafters hung all manner of odds and ends. Hats of various dates and patterns, some new, some just worth what in fact what had bought them—a glass of rum. And whips were there to match the hats; and horse blankets were aired there on certain days; and strings of sleigh-bells waved and jingled when the wind rose at night, and came pouring in through the old window frame or a knot-hole in the clapboards. Ropes of onions hung, necklace fashion, round suspicious looking muskets, and tried vainly to give them an air of peace as well as of plenty; while jugs, and kegs, and bottles were scattered and stored in every direction. These were all empty; the full ones James Dodd kept under most careful lock and key. But this particular day, the rain being heavy and business rather slack, James thought some profitable work might be accomplished in his cellar in the way of bottling, and mixing, and racking off, and diluting. Up-stairs he went for an armful of the empty jugs, and was in nowise astonished to find Sam there asleep and dreaming—that was common enough. But something else caught his eye, as instantly as it had Sam's—something which down on the old floor, half under the little bed, glowed, and sparkled, and gleamed out like a live thing. How did it get there? From Sam's pocket? " Most likely," as James Dodd said to himself, with a pretty good appreciation of his son's tastes and habits; and if so, it was no less certain that Sam would show good fight for his prize; and failing to get it back, might give a hint concerning its whereabouts, which would be in the highest degree inconvenient to his father. James Dodd knew all this; and no cat could have been more stealthy than he in his approach to the bed. Never taking his eyes for a moment from Sam's face, the man crept nearer and nearer, reached down his hand with that practised aim which needed not to look,—well used to striking in the dark,—grasped the pencil; and in another second was out of the room, with his hands loaded with the black jugs. And Sam never knew it.

CHAPTER VI.

It was the afternoon of that day when Mrs Kensett—unable to go out herself—sent another message-bearer to invite the children to her house to tea. Sam Dodd had slept well on into the afternoon, and might have prolonged his nap until the evening, had not one of the late sunbeams that came glinting out to dance in the tree-tops, danced straight in through the dusty window of his garret room. Very dusty the window was, and very small, with cracks across it that were out of all proportion large; and the spiders—the only upholsterers that ever entered that room—had hung their drapery about in an extremely fantastic and irregular way. But there's wonderful power in *the real thing*—and the sunbeam made its way through all obstructions, glorified the cobwebs, made the dust look ashamed of itself, shone full into Sam Dodd's face and waked him up: a clear beam of light, despite the cracked window and the dim atmosphere. Just so, children, you can shine *anywhere:* people who are real and true and noble, can always do their work, and do it well.

Poor Sam! that was not what he saw in the sunbeam, though he started up, and leaning on his elbow, peered eagerly out the window.

"Well, I'm blessed if it hain't cleared off!" he said. "High time I cleared out—that bein' the case. Let's see—what's to do? Guess I'll take a turn up yonder and see what's on foot at the church. Wonder now if *she'll* be out? Won't see much o' me, anyhow."

And thus meditating, Sam came down his ladder stairway, and then went with long, swift steps over the rain-bent grass to the top of the church hill, finding the children at their games as usual, but no lady there. As usual, too, Sam joined in the play—teasing, helping, worrying, sneering, making himself generally useful and disagreeable. But when the messenger had come and given her message, and little Molly had made her very incautious speech about the pencil, and Sam had frightened the child nearly out of her wits; then indeed he felt that he had serious work on hand. At once he quitted all sight and sound of the other boys, and went apart by himself to consider what he should do.

"The little fool!" Sam burst forth indignantly, "she ain't got a quarter the sense o' that 'ere dead kitten o' hern! Wouldn't wonder a cent now if she hadn't just done it a purpose—all along o' that! She 's got a proper scare for once—that 's one thing—but how long 's it going to last, ye see? And I durstn't say *too* much to her ;—she 's that sort o' girl, drive her too hard, and she 'll run round t'other way. Then if she went and telled"——

Sam thrust his hands in his pockets, and went wandering round among the dusky bushes in the waning light; scowling and growling enough for ten boys larger than he.

"There ain't no other way as I can see!" he said, at length. "'Twon't never do to have the concern so handy just now. I 'll have to give up carryin' it for a spell. Don't like to, neither—I 've kinder got used to it." And with that, Sam's fingers went lovingly to the little vest pocket where he had kept his ill-gotten treasure. But the pocket was empty. Sam felt of it outside, and felt of it in; and turned the pocket out, and felt all the way down his vest, but no pencil. Then he searched every other pocket of every sort that he had about him, turning out their contents upon a bare, flat stone, and looking eagerly. Plenty of other things came forth into the twilight. Fish-hooks and marbles; snares; stray coins; a pack of cards; a ball; a knot of twine; with various small outfits for games and tricks, with which Sam was wont to turn a dishonest penny now and then. A new pocket-book appeared; a lady's ring; a roll of ribands; but no pencil. Sam thrust them all back again out of sight, and with a savage exclamation of rage and disappointment, he started up and hurried away to the place where Molly had found him in the morning. The rain-drops sparkled yet, in the parting gleams of day, but no other brilliance mingled with theirs; no other jewel flashed up from among the blades of grass. Sam looked and looked—then stood and thought.

"I *did* have it, too, after that," he said. "If she's stole it, 'twa'n't then." And Sam dashed off up the hill to the church, there to spend more vain efforts, and work himself into a greater fever than before. And then it was too dark to even look.

Sam was in a rage. Not daring to ask anybody a single question, not daring even to speak out loud his own chagrin, the boy went muttering to himself words and curses that would have startled any night wind but that which roamed drearily among the bushes on Vinegar Hill. Mrs Limp, patiently mending up the rags which her husband had as yet reserved for his own use, heard a stone come crashing through the one whole pane of glass in her little window. Jemmy Lucas, musing on his broken door-step, was knocked off into the darkness by a swift stick, whizzing by from some unseen hand. But nobody thought much of such things at Vinegar Hill; they were too common. Meek Mrs Limp looked up from her work a moment, glad that the children had gone to bed early, as she marked where the stone fell; its coming so near her own head mattered very little—would have mattered scarce more if it had taken her head off. Jemmy Lucas picked himself up, cried a little, and went in to tell his mother. And she, poor woman, had no better remedy at hand than the one much in use among richer people than she—"to kiss the place and make it well." So Jemmy went to bed comforted; and Peter and little Molly slept right on, unconscious of danger; and Sam Dodd went tearing about like a tempest off the track.

A tempest of God's sending is terrible enough; the wind

that He bringeth out of His treasuries, the lightnings which come and say to Him, "Here we are ;" the marvellous thunder of His voice : yet whatever He prepares is good, and does good. But those fierce human tempests, born of the hot atmosphere of human passion, working their wild way unguided, unchecked—they are wholly and altogether evil ; a fear to everything that is called good.

"I'm bound to be even with somebody, after this !" the boy vowed in his heart, with many a bitter and foul word—and lest perchance he might miss the right person, Sam took up all the mischief he could think of, or that came in his way. Softly he stole in among the horses that were in waiting around his father's door, knotting their tying ropes in untold complications—pulling, and twisting, and looping, till even sober men would have found them a puzzle. One or two he untied altogether, leaving the horses to make their way home at their earliest convenience. Whips were taken from some of the waggons and pitched far into the bushes ; stones were laid on the seats of others ; and at last, when Sam Dodd had carried matters as far as even he thought prudent, he went into the house to sit down and wait for the fun. Sam had smoothed his face charmingly as he crossed the threshold—a more sleepy, careless, stupid-looking boy you need not wish to see ; yet you have seldom seen one, perhaps, more wide-awake ; and even as he entered, Sam found his clue. The men were there at their bad work as usual, some in the chimney-corner, some round the table playing cards ; and with these last sat James Dodd. He looked up as his son entered, a single glance through the dim, smoky light ; but it was enough. A good boy might not have seen—an honest boy would not have understood—the look ; but Sam caught and read it instantly. The covert, searching, inquiring glance—half given, and as quickly taken back—meant just this : his father had the pencil. How he had got it, when, or where ; how he had learned anything about it in the first place ; of all that, Sam could guess nothing. But that Mrs Kensett's little diamond-headed pencil lay even then in the dingy vest-pocket of James Dodd,

Sam knew as well as that it had reposed so lately in his own. For the boy's sharp eyes detected a second glance, given not at him, but at the pocket in question, after which James Dodd went on with his work of cutting and dealing, and never raised his eyes from the cards again.

Sam marched up to the table and sat down, watching the game for a while; then yawned, drank off a glass of the mixed poison, and said he guessed he would go to bed. But once out of the room, with a fierce gesture of his fist towards the closed door, Sam dismissed all appearance of fatigue or of sleep; and climbing to his garret, he sat down on one of the old chests with his head in his hands, to think, study, and plan.

CHAPTER VII.

"THE unfruitful works of darkness," how aptly are they named!—how surely "he that doeth evil hateth the light." "And what shall it profit a man if he shall gain the whole world, and lose his own soul?"

Very fruitless, so far, had been Sam Dodd's first gain of a gold pencil, and fruitless enough were all his musings that night as to how he should get it again. Very black and dark grew his thoughts in consequence. But the evening passed on—something must be done; and Sam resolved that just so soon as the house was quiet and everybody asleep, he would steal into his father's room, find out the chair where his clothes lay, and then softly search out the pencil, in whichever pocket it might lie hid.

"It's a plaguy thing to do!" Sam muttered to himself; "but I don't see as there's nothin' else."

And even as he said it there came floating across his mind—

> "There's room in God's eternal love
> To save thy precious soul."

Sam paused for an instant, holding his breath. But then he started up, swung himself down the stairs, and dashed into the public sitting-room, as if, of all things in the world, he was most afraid of himself.

It was later than he thought. All the men were gone—though how far they had got from the house might be doubted, considering the state in which they left it, and the state in which Sam had left their horses. But the room was quiet and empty. James Dodd stood there alone, and Sam's entrance was clearly an interruption—though to what, Sam could not tell. His father merely faced round upon him, coolly inquiring "how many ghosts he'd seen now?"

"Thought you called," said Sam, gruffly.

"Well, I didn't—and you didn't," said his father, with brief emphasis. And composedly laying off coat and vest, James Dodd proceeded to take others from a closet and equip himself in them. Sam looked on, wondering.

"If anybody comes to the door while I'm out, you're not to let 'em in," said Dodd, as he buttoned his coat. "So just to save you trouble, I'll take the key. Better go back and finish your nap, Sam. Playin' good boy' is hard work." And, with a little mocking nod, he went out, locking the door behind him.

Sam set his teeth as he heard it, standing still in scowling doubt. Then he ran to the back door, and after a glance at its many bolts and bars, all securely drawn and in place, turned off to a side window, and opened that. The next instant he had let himself down, dropping softly on the grass below. Then round the house like a deer; but there was no trace nor sight nor sound of his father. It was so late that even Vinegar Hill had taken to itself a sort of hush, with part of its people asleep, and those who were abroad moving with steps as noiseless as Sam's own. The moon was beginning to silver the dark horizon; the bushes waved slightly in the summer air; the tree-toads cried and answered each other; the night moved on. Again Sam stood still in utter doubt and uncertainty, with not a sight nor a sound to guide him. Then he went a little way down one path, then a little way down another, then stood still once more.

"'Tain't a single spec' of use!" he said, despairingly. "I've just lost my chance." And again, he could not tell why, the sweet words came—

> "There's room in heaven, among the choir,
> And harps and crowns of gold."

That would not do! Sam darted off among the bushes, doubling and turning as if some evil thing were after him. But as he went, I am sure *he* did not know what made him draw a long long breath, that had well-nigh been a sigh.

"I vow, I do s'pose I'm tired!" he said, bringing up under the shadow of the bushes. "Must be that as ails me. And 'tain't no use—I said it warn't, to begin. Just as good go back and get kinder sot up, and then ye see I'll know where I am. *He's* fur enough, by this."

Softly and leisurely now Sam retraced his steps, reached the house, went round to his window—and behold it was shut! So were the other windows, and the doors—every one. Shut and fastened. Sam would have thought little of breaking a pane of glass, had one only been within his reach; but the thick, long window shutters were almost as impenetrable as the doors. Worst of all, as he peered through the big key-hole from which James Dodd had so carefully taken the key, Sam perceived that the key itself hindered his view. And with that, even as he made sure of the fact, his ears caught sound of a brilliant whistle inside the door, which could have come from no throat but that of James Dodd himself.

Children, when the Lord brings His people into times of trial and places of difficulty—and sometimes He does this—He never leaves them there alone. He goes before them, He stands by them, He holds them by the hand. But if ever the devil tempts you, and you follow him, then you will have many a chance to know how Sam Dodd felt that night. Baffled, outwitted, laughed at; his treasure gone, his revenge cut off—Sam felt as if his very wits had forsaken him, and his father had fooled him right through. He did not dare knock, he did not dare give a harder pull at the window shutters; and the open window of his little garret was hopelessly far above his reach. Now the light came gleaming through cracks and keyholes, as James Dodd went whistling round the house—then it shone full and strong from Sam's own window. His father was looking for him!—making sure he was not in. Then suddenly the light was kept back, and from that same little window James Dodd's head and shoulders leaned out into the moonlight. Sam shrank away among the bushes, keeping carefully out of sight, and once off at a safe distance, he threw himself down on the ground and cried for rage. He had lost so much, and he had gained nothing!

Meanwhile, stealthy steps came up from another quarter, and Sam was roused at last by a pretty smart application of somebody's foot.

"What's here?" said the voice of Jem Crook. "'Tain't nobody fainted 'long o' hevin' too many feelin's, I don't think."

"Leave a feller be, can't ye?" growled Sam.

"Ha! ha!" laughed Jem Crook, "what's to pay now? Looking for small change in the grass, Sammy? Hain't been no overturn o' one o' yer father's rich customers? I say, Sammy, let's go shares."

Sam swore at him, but deigned no other reply.

"What ye lyin' there for, like a smashed toad?" said Jem Crook, contemptuously.

"'Tain't none o' *your* business, if I take a likin' to sleepin' out doors, is it?" said Sam, raising himself on one elbow. "It's so confounded hot inside o' all them winder shutters!"

"Old Dodd inside?" said Jem.

Sam nodded.

"Well I wouldn't wonder if he did make it sort o' warm, by spells," said Jem Crook. "Quite a lively notion o' stirrin' round, he has. Hows'ever, *I* ain't got time to attend to him. Time *I* was gettin' breakfast."

"Breakfast!" drawled Sam. "Didn't the poor boy get no supper?"

"Ah!" said Jem Crook. "Won't go into partic'lars, fear o' makin' yer mouth water. But I finds I gets breakfast easiest overnight, Sam Dodd. Ye see, new milk's partial to my constitution,—and 'tain't nigh so handy to get it after the cows has been druv home, as it is afore. Barnyard's farther off."

"And folks is nearer," said Sam.

Jem Crook nodded.

"Well, that ain't a bad idea, on the whole," said Sam, getting up. "I'm as dry as a brook bed myself. Which way, Jem?"

I'm a-going to the parson's this time," said Jem. "Find it agrees with me to change cows pretty often."

"But the parson ain't got but one," said Sam, hesitating.

"No more he ain't," said Jem, carelessly. "Hope it's a good one. Come on!"

And Sam did "come on," though with a queer little feeling of compunction.

The parson was nothing to him. Sam had never come within range of even one of his kind words, and had stolen his apples with immense satisfaction. But somehow now, the parson and Mrs Kensett and the words of that hymn had all got mixed up together in Sam's mind, and he could not separate them, do what he would. Still some grains of good lay hid in his heart, struggling to grow: still the fowls of the air kept close watch to gather them up. Ah, had Sam but watched against them!

"If it's a good cow," said Jem Crook, as they walked along, "then ye see there'll be enough left from my breakfast to pay Widow Camp for the six cents she'll owe me about that time."

Sam made no answer. His thoughts were busy again with the King's feast, and the kind lady who had told him of it, and the feast she had promised them herself at her own house. Jem Crook glanced at him once or twice, but for a while said nothing. Then he burst forth—

"I say, Sammy, what an uncommon, wonderful, A 1 woman that 'ere is, up to the church arternoons! I vow

I'm so fond of her I don't hardly know what to do. Time seems long till arternoon comes. Days *is* kinder long now, ye know," Jem added, with a deep sigh.

"Goin' there to-night?" said Sam, abruptly.

"Goin' where?"

"Down to her house to tea."

"Ha! ha! ha!" said Jem Crook. "Why, *'tis* to-night, ain't it?—leastways s'posin' this was to-day—which it ain't. To think o' my forgettin' an invite out to tea!"

"Well, are you *goin'?*" said Sam, impatiently.

"Don't see as I can, noways," said Jem. "My best company manners ain't come yet, Sam—express must ha' broke down, likely. And there ain't none ready made about town. Not as I knows on. And besides," added Jem, dropping his voice to a confidential whisper, "I never *does* care so much about goin' out to tea when I has new milk for breakfast. Kinder satisfies me like, for all day."

And Jem swung himself over the bars into the little meadow where the parson's cow was feeding, and said no more.

CHAPTER VIII.

IT was the day of the great tea-drinking at Mrs Kensett's, and now afternoon had come, and the little ragged guests were on their way, eager and shy and happy, to a wonderful degree. Sam Dodd was not with them, you may remember, nor Tim Wiggins, nor Jem Crook; but Sam watched them every step of the way. Yet they never saw him. Under cover of fences and hedgerows and bushes, he followed on; though for just what use and purpose Sam could hardly have told himself. Yet he followed, and when they were once inside the house, he took post outside the garden, watching till the back door should open, and the children come forth that way. For Sam's quick eyes very soon spied

out the table in the arbour; and there is little doubt he
would have made nearer acquaintance with it, had not the
gardener been on duty; watching quietly as he raked the
walks, while the pleasant-faced woman brought out the
things for tea. The sight, the smell, of these delicacies, did
not tend to sweeten Sam's temper. He might have been in
the house there too, ready for his share, had he chosen ; and
instead of that, he was away off, hanging about, and afraid
to be seen.

"Well, I don't want 'em, I tell ye!" said Sam, in his
silent rage. "O' course I *could*, if I was a mind ter. But
what's cakes, I'd like to know?" And with that, Sam
Dodd drew in a long long whiff of fragrance, trying to get
just as much as possible of the aforesaid cakes.

"Strawberries! blessed if there ain't!" he began again.
"And sich bread and butter—why, it's just white and yeller!
And biscuits—and little pies ! If I don't make them young
beggars laugh t'other corner o' their mouths afore bedtime !"

And there Sam grew silent in spite of himself; for just
then the pleasant-faced woman brought out a large loaf-cake,
frosted all over, and even (it did certainly look so) sprinkled
upon its white top with coloured sugar-plums. The sight
fairly took his breath away. Oh, to spring in there, across
the hedge, break all the dishes, knock down the gardener,
frighten the woman out of her wits, and bear off the cake in
triumph to Vinegar Hill ! But highly as he esteemed his
own prowess, Sam felt that to attempt all these various ex-
ploits at once, would be a little too much, even for him.
Some one of them might fail, and that would spoil all the
rest. Gentler thoughts, too, came for a moment into the
boy's mind ; how kind it was of the lady to do all this,
almost proving true what she had said about the King.

"For in course," Sam remarked to himself, "it wouldn't
be not nigh so much for Him to do, once He'd made up His
mind to it, 'cause He's richer'n she, and has got lots o' fellers
to do things. My ! what a cake ! Wonder if t'other thing
was true, now ? And there ain't the least speck o' doubt
but there's goodies inside," added Sam, with his trains of

thought slightly mixed up. He stood silent again, peeping through the hedge from behind an old apple-tree; and then of a sudden, the talk began inside the garden.

"Well, she do take a sight o' trouble!" said the old gardener, leaning on his rake handle.

"Why, no, she don't," said the woman with the pleasant face, trying hard to make room for a refractory plate of biscuits. "Maybe she would, if she wasn't Mrs Kensett. But it's only pleasure to *her*."

"I see, just so," said the old gardener, nodding his head. "There'll be consid'rable pleasure scatterin' round when supper-time comes, I'm thinkin'."

"She would have the best of everything for 'em," said the woman, coaxing her plates into good behaviour. "If they never did afore, in all their born days, they should now, she said."

"What's the use, Mrs Fritz?" said the old gardener, speaking out at last the problem on which his mind had worked fruitlessly for some time. "What's the good of it all, when all's done, anyhow? And what'll the young scamps know of the differ?"

"Why, the use is to let 'em know somebody has a care for 'em," said Mrs Fritz. "Supposin' the Lord had said that about us, where'd we be then?"

But at that the old gardener shook his head hopelessly.

"Supposin' *He'd* never made ready better things than we'd been used to?" Mrs Fritz went on. "Supposin' *we'd* never had a speck of icing to *our* cake? Don't you see, Mr Pink? 'We love Him because He first loved us.' And Mrs Kensett she says to me; 'Freely ye have received, freely give.' 'I should feel ashamed,' she says, 'to take the best and give the poorest.'"

"Well, there's no denying that to be like the Master," said Mr Pink, nodding his head again in assent. "And I do s'pose we've got to believe He loves they youngsters, if they *be's* a bit trying now and then in cherry time."

"Loves 'em!" echoed Mrs Fritz. "Why, man, He *died* for 'em, every one. What's cakes and sugar-plums now?

I declare—now and then—times when I get thinkin' of it," said the good woman, her eyes shining with kindness, as she arranged and rearranged her dishes, "thinkin' of it, and lookin' at them "——

"Well," said Mr Pink, who had waited anxiously for the end of the sentence, " then you feel as though you 'd like to give 'em a good washin' and whippin' ?—reg'late 'em, like ? I do."

"I don't," said Mrs Fritz. "I forget all about the dirt and the rags and the wickedness, and I can't seem to see a thing, but a whole parcel of children the King wants up yonder in His kingdom. And all I can think of is, how ever I can push 'em along and shove 'em in—and they just look lovely !" And with that Mrs Fritz wiped her eyes on her apron, and went off in haste to the house after another dish.

Softly Mr Pink resumed his work, the light touch of his rake on the gravel walk sounding in sweet, quiet peace with all the world. And Sam stood and listened. Then of a sudden, the old gardener began to sing—

> "The Lord into His garden comes,
> The spices yield their rich perfume,
> The lilies grow and thrive :
> Refreshing showers of grace divine
> From Jesus flow to every vine,
> And make the dead revive."

The thoughts, the images, were all new to Sam Dodd ; he did not understand them ; and yet something in the wild sweetness of words and tune made him listen, straining his ear to catch the whole. He listened as the old man muttered and hummed through two or three half-forgotten verses, then burst forth again in full song—

> "The worst of sinners here may find
> A Saviour pitiful and kind
> Who will them all relieve.
> None are too late if they repent ;
> Out of one sinner legions went—
> Jesus did him receive.

G

> "Come, brethren, you that love the Lord,
>   Who taste the sweetness of His word,
>   In Jesus' ways go on :
>   Our troubles and our trials here
>   Will only make us richer there
>   When we arrive at home."

And with that, Mrs Fritz, who had come softly back with the sugar-bowl, herself took up the strain :—

> " There we shall reign and shout and sing,
>   And make the upper arches ring,
>   When all the saints get home.
>   Come on, come on, my brethren dear,
>   Soon we shall meet together there,
>   For Jesus bids us come."

"Don't you see, Mr Pink ?" she said, as she set down her bowl. "And there ain't a young savage of 'em all but what 's bidden, as much as you or I." She went off. Sam heard her brisk steps upon the gravel, and the slow scratching of Mr Pink's rake—and he thought and wondered. "Bidden to come," there it was again. And what was the old gardener singing now ?

> " Oh, how I love Jesus !
>   Oh, how I love Jesus !
>   Oh, how I love Jesus !
>   Because He first loved me."

Strong and clear the chorus rang out, but this time the old gardener's memory seemed to have quite lost the hymn that should have gone with it. He muttered and murmured to himself as before, humming over four lines of something ; but Sam could not make out a word. Then again came the chorus, full on the summer air—

> " Oh, how I love Jesus !
>   Oh, how I love Jesus ! "

And still Sam listened. And for a while you would have thought some little grain of good was going to take root and grow—finding a softer spot than usual in the wayside soil. Perhaps, who knows ? But quick, suddenly, Sam set his

foot on it, and then, almost without a call, came a host of wicked, bitter thoughts, and cleared the ground. "It was trodden underfoot, and the fowls of the air came and devoured it."

How did this happen, do you ask? Well, the Bible says such things happen when any one "heareth the word, and *understandeth* it not:" and to understand God's word, you must begin to keep it. I had directions once for knitting some piece of work. They were written down, and I read them over, but I could make nothing of them. This part seemed confused, and that unnecessary. At last, in despair, I took my needles and knit the first stitch, then the second, then the third; till one row was done, and another and another—and then the beautiful pattern began to show itself. The directions were all right, but they puzzled me unless I just took them *stitch by stitch*. And it is often so with the Lord's commands. Do the first one you can think of; and then the very next, and then the very next. And then it will be true of you with the rest—

"A good understanding have all they that keep His commandments."

But poor Sam Dodd!—this was just what he did not do. For a minute he was almost persuaded, for a minute he did think of rushing into the house, telling the lady all about her pencil, and begging her to help him seek the King. And then he put that thought right down under his foot, and opened his heart to all the wicked thoughts that would come. He took them all in, every one as it came; and again the good seed was gone in a moment. He did not dare stand there any longer; for now the house door opened, and there came forth a small tumult of small voices, and Sam knew whose they were well enough. And it would never do to be so near the hedge on one side, with Jemmy Lucas and Peter Limp close to it on the other. Very different eyes theirs, from the fading sight of the old gardener or the busy glance of Mrs Fritz. Sam drew off and off till he was out of hearing as well as out of sight, and then he stretched himself out on the grass in his old fashion, to plan and to think. And the sunbeams crept higher and higher, and the birds began their evening song; cow-bells came tinkling home from the woods, and smoke curled up from out the village chimneys; and a wild, mixed scent of roses and strawberries and ferns and pinks and clover filled the air.   And still Sam lay and thought, and still, in spite of himself, more fragrant than the roses, more glowing than the sunbeams, the whole eventide seemed full of the old gardener's song—

> "Oh, how I love Jesus!
> Oh, how I love Jesus!
> Oh, how I love Jesus!
> Because He first loved me."

CHAPTER IX.

THE tea was long over, the children long gone, and now Mrs Kensett lay resting on her little white couch by the open window.   The lamp was put down low so as not to interfere with the lingering twilight; and there could just be seen the little lady's white dress, and her motionless repose, and a brow as calm and clear as the evening sky itself.   She lay there quite still, looking out.

And on a sudden, Sam Dodd stood at the window, appearing nobody could tell how or whence, dropped there in a moment like some dark shadow.

"Why, Sam!" said Mrs Kensett, after her first breath of surprise, "can that be you?"

"Guess likely 'tain't no one else!" was Sam's civil reply.

"But then why didn't you come to tea?" said Mrs Kensett, sitting up.

"Couldn't!" said Sam.

"Couldn't—or wouldn't?" said the lady, with her pleasant voice.

"Suit yerself," answered Sam, as briefly as before.

"Well, come in now, and you shall have some tea still,"

said the lady. "I should like another cup myself, and we'll have it together."

"Can't do that nuther," said Sam. "Don't care about comin' in." And from the increased distance Sam put between himself and the window, it was pretty plain that he *did* care about staying out.

"Well, Sam, what then?" said Mrs Kensett, leaning back among her cushions, whereupon Sam Dodd ventured a step nearer.

"Come to tell ye about that 'ere jigum what you lost up to the church," he said, abruptly.

"Oh! my pencil," said the lady. "What of it, Sam? Have you found it?"

"Just wish I could!" said Sam, earnestly. "Fact is, 'tain't so easy to find things, if you don't know where they be. But in course I couldn't miss hearin' what's said, and there's folks as swears it's been sparklin' round Vinegar Hill."

"And what then, Sam?" said the lady, not seeming much surprised. "What if it has?"

"Why then," said Sam, coming a step or two nearer yet in his eagerness, "anybody as comes after it, don't ye see, might get a word as would help him spot the right feller."

"The one who found it, do you mean?" asked Mrs Kensett.

"No, no!" said Sam, hurriedly; "what's the odds who found it? I mean him as has *got* it!"

"But if you know who it is," said Mrs Kensett, "there is no need of my sending. You might ask the man yourself Sam, and then bring the pencil to me."

"*Don't* know," said Sam. "Didn't say as I knowed nothin' at all about it. And I ain't a-goin' to ask him if I did. And 'twouldn't be no sort o' use. Them sort o' folks and things don't part company for askin'. You just send down and nab 'em both together. I'll trip him up."

But Mrs Kensett did not seem attracted by this fascinating offer. She lay quite still on her sofa, and for a minute or two said nothing. And before any words came, Sam heard a low, deep-drawn sigh. Then she spoke.

"I shall not send, Sam! I should like to have the pencil again, I have used it so long ; and I will pay its full value to any one who will bring it back."

" Why don't ye send and get it, then ?" said Sam, his face darkening.

"There might be some mistake," she said, " or something might come of it for which I should be very sorry. I offer the reward—I shall do nothing more. But now, Sam, I do want your help in another much greater matter ; about another much greater loss."

"What yer lost now ?" said Sam, alive on the instant. " 'Tain't yer watch ?"

"Oh no," said Mrs Kensett ; "it is nothing of mine. It is something of yours."

"Somethin' o' mine !" Sam repeated, very considerably astonished, and falling back a step or two, with eyes that glowed and glittered in no kindly way. "Somethin' o' mine ! Guess likely *that's* a big mistake, anyhow. Ain't never been nothin' o' *mine* lost, nowheres ! "

"It is not lost yet," said Mrs Kensett, "but it is in very great danger. If you give precious things to bad people to keep, Sam, what happens then ?"

" Why, they keeps 'em ! " said Sam, emphatically, think-ing of the pencil. "Leastways, if they don't hand 'em over to nobody else. Any fool could ha' telled ye. But that ain't me—not exactly ! Like to see myself a-doin' of it ! "

"Well," said Mrs Kensett, raising herself up from the cushions again, and laying one hand on the window-sill, "if you give Tim Wiggins and Jem Crook your soul to keep, Sam, *they'll* hand it over to the devil. And when he gets it he'll keep it."

"They'll hand it over to the devil !" Sam repeated, in the extremity of his astonishment. "Well, if you don't go a little ahead for tellin' stories ! Like to know where they'd find it, fust ?"

" Why, they find it," said Mrs Kensett, "just as other things are found—when you are careless. Bad words open one lock, and bad thoughts pry off another ; and bad actions lift the lid of the chest right up ; and whoever can persuade you to speak the one or do the other, has gone just so far towards stealing your soul. And when you listen to them, and do what they say, it is just like giving them your soul to keep. And then, as I said, *they'll* hand it over to the devil."

"Well, of all queer folks I ever *did* see!" Sam broke forth again. "How d'ye know I've got one, to begin?"

"You might better have none," said Mrs Kensett, "than to give it into such hands. Why, your soul isn't but half your own, now! Afraid to do what Tim Wiggins will laugh at, afraid *not* to do what Jem Crook demands—why, Sam, you might far better be my little pencil, lost in the grass, without a soul, than to be a boy able to think and feel and know, and yet give yourself into such keeping."

Sam Dodd was absolutely too much dumbfounded to speak a word. He stood there, trying hard to collect his wits, and found them quite beyond call for a minute or two.

"Who telled ye nothin' about Vinegar Hill folks?" he said at last, sulkily breaking the silence. "Like to hear what *you* know about 'em, or me nuther."

"I know," said Mrs Kensett ; "I have seen ; I can tell."

"It's that 'ere little sneak of a Molly Limp!" said Sam, working himself up into a passion. "I'll settle *her* business!"

"It's not Molly at all," said Mrs Kensett ; "it's not anybody, Sam, but yourself."

"'*Twas* her, too!" said Sam, furiously. "I ain't said the first thing."

"Neither has Molly," said Mrs Kensett. "But never mind that, now. Sam, the Lord Jesus came down from heaven and died to save that precious soul of yours, and will you let it be lost, after all?"

"No!" said Sam. "Tell ye I ain't give it away to nobody!"

"Ah, but you must!" said Mrs Kensett. "You must give it to the Lord Jesus to keep, or it will surely be lost. No one else is strong enough to guard it from the snares of wicked men ; no one else has power to deliver it from the wiles of the devil. Jesus is able to keep all that we commit to Him, Sam ; but every soul *not* given to Him will be lost."

"Look a-here !" said Sam ; "I vow I ain't a-goin' to stand this no longer ! You just stop a worryin' your head round me and Tim Wiggins and the devil and the rest o' folks, will ye !" And Sam darted away into the darkness, and was seen by the lady no more that night. She did not know that he crept back to the window, softly, softly, as soon as the blinds were closed. She did not know that he stood there to watch her while she read, to listen while she prayed, to hear those strange words of entreaty for all the little stray waifs of Vinegar Hill—most of all for him—for "poor Sam !"— for that precious soul of his which was in such danger. Sam frowned, and shook his head, and bent close to the blinds that he might not lose a word.

"Save him, O God !" she cried, "by Thy mighty power, for the sake of our dear Lord Jesus !"

And Sam saw two or three bright tear-drops fall upon the little table by which she knelt. He stood there, looking and listening, perfectly absorbed.

Suddenly a shrill, peculiar whistle sounded, as if from near the foot of the garden, and in a second Sam had darted away. Gliding noiselessly off by the fence, and into the shadow of the next trees—forward, and across and back— till he was well away from the house. Then he stopped, and from his new position sent up an answering whistle, wild and shrill as the first. A whip-poor-will's cry answered that, and was at once responded to by Sam. Then came the shrill bark of a little puppy, and the mew of a cat—and then Jem Crook flung his arms about Sam, and drew him down upon the grass in a sharp round of roll-and-tumble.

"Where you been ?" said Jem Crook, when this was over, and the two stood up again, breathless and panting. "What made ye stay so late to tea, Sam ? Rest all home long ago. Guess she couldn't part with ye, eh ?"

"Ain't been to tea—nowheres," said Sam, gruffly. "Been mindin' my own business—just you mind yourn."

"Come all the way up here, and didn't get no tea!" said Jem Crook. "Tain't no great wonder as he's so sweet. What did the rest have, Sam? Let's hear."

"Tell ye I wasn't there!" said Sam.

"She's been a-pourin' salt water all over him, sure as eggs!" said Jem Crook, "till he's lost his appetite. Oh dear! There's some now on his coat collar, this blessed minute."

"Don't ye hear?" roared Sam, flinging Jem off. "I say I ain't been there!"

"Well now," said Jem, "yer know, Sammy, as how she allers *did* take to yer partic'lar. Why, it's only this very mornin' as I met her myself, trottin' off alone to Vinegar Hill, to invite yer, special. And she says, 'You'll be sure and tell him, Jem?' So o' course I promised."

"And o' course you didn't," said Sam.

"O' course," said Jem Crook, with a slow drawl. "Hadn't time, ye see—and disremembered—and all sorts o' things."

"And hadn't seen her—to begin with," said Sam, "so don't make much odds. Let ye off this time."

"Well, I does 'fection that 'ere woman, uncommon!" said Jem Crook. "Don't know as I ever *did* like anybody quite so much. Sammy, let's go find some duck eggs lyin' round somewheres." And the two small dark shadows crept away.

<hr/>

CHAPTER X.

"Fond of duck eggs, ain't yer, Sammy?" said Jem Crook, affectionately, as they walked along.

"Not over and above," answered Sam, with no touch of responsive tenderness.

"Well, now, ain't *that* a disapp'int!" said Jem, "when I was a hopin' as yer might sort o' relish 'em.

"Better not venture yer precious time hopin' round me," said Sam, thinking of the two bright drops he had seen fall on Mrs Kensett's little table.

"Dear ! dear !" said Jem Crook, "what 's a feller to do ? Ye know yer 's been rather weakly like, Sammy, this spell 'long back, and yer friends is anxious."

" Generally is—till they gets knocked down," growled Sam.

" Fact is," said Jem, linking his arm in Sam's and taking no notice whatever of the rebuff, " they *does* think, Sammy, as how yer plays ball altogether too reg'lar. Kinder wastes away yer strength, ye know. And them steps *is* damp, up to the church. Why, *I* 've give up goin'."

" Don't tell nobody, and they won't find it out," was Sam's complimentary rejoinder. " You might stay away from most any place, Jem Crook."

" Ah, but I ain't some folks !" said Jem, hugging Sam's arm very tight. "' Where 's Sam Dodd ?' bawls one. ' Confound him !' says another, and we waited and waited, and then a chap sung out like a rocket : ' Sam Dodd 's hired out down to the village to do chores !' And we was that cut up, yer could ha' floored the hull on us with a tail feather o' Squire Townsend's big gobbler !"

" Shouldn't wonder," said Sam, with a sneer. " And you ain't none on yer worth the trouble. Try yer hand on another, Jem Crook, you made that up so spry."

" Ha ! ha !" laughed Jem under his breath. " Don't yer make no noise, Sammy, now don't ! Ducks is awful skeery."

" What 's the use o' goin' round the world after 'em for ?" said Sam, suddenly perceiving that Jem had turned back in the darkness, and was now approaching Mrs Kensett's house again. " Ain't a livin' duck *here*."

" They lives to the back o' the house," answered Jem, creeping along under the shadow of the hedge. Sam stopped short.

" I say !"—he broke forth—" I ain't a-goin' to touch none o' *hern*, you know."

" Yer don't think as I'd expect it of ye, Sammy ?" said Jem Crook in an aggrieved voice, and standing still in his turn—" when she allers *did* make as much muss over yer as a hen with one chicken, and 's just been a-coddlin' ye, and cryin' over ye, and that. Guess *I* know beans—and radishers—

and punkins." And Jem turned away, and began creeping along under the hedge again, without another word.

Close at his heels went Sam, thinking every step of the way of the lady's words, and every step of the way making those words good. Had she not said he was afraid not to do whatever Jem Crook required ? So he crept along hanging back in mind, but going forward in body, till at last Jem's jeering tone and words did their work, and Sam Dodd threw off his strange and new and inconvenient feelings. By the time they reached the edge of the little brook where stood the duck-houses, Sam was quite ready to do his part. But Jem took care not to push matters too far. With great show of consideration he despatched Sam to one of the neighbouring duck-houses, while he himself undertook that which belonged to the premises where Mrs Kensett lodged. Only when the sport was over, then Jem took his revenge.

"I vow," he said, standing up to survey the pile of duck eggs, "I've put 'em all together ! Which is hern, Sammy ? Got any ear marks to tell 'em by ? What 'll ye do ? 'cause ye *might* get one o' hern, by mistake. Tell ye what—I can keep 'em all. Anythin' to save yer feelin's."

"Like to see ye doin' it ! " said Sam, fiercely. "You just touch one o' them eggs more 'n belongs to yer, and there 'll be a smash-up o' the whole concern."

"Ha ! ha ! ha !" Jem Crook chuckled to himself, as he pocketed his share, to have it at once in safe keeping. And Sam pocketed his, and said to himself that he would bring them back again, and didn't do it.

With new eagerness now, he set himself to find out the hiding-place of the little pencil. Not that he might carry it back to Mrs Kensett—if she wanted it, she might get it, Sam declared to himself ; and if she didn't, it was not his fault.

"Why, I never did make such an offer to nobody," he said, feeling very virtuous and very cross, at once. Had she not hindered the revenge which he had planned so nicely ? But Sam did not mean to lose the pencil, if he did the revenge. Day and night he waited and watched ; sometimes inside the house, sometimes hid behind a shutter and peering through the window ; sometimes dogging his father's steps along the lanes and the by-ways which James Dodd frequented. In vain : no sparkling pencil-head ever glimmered in the man's hand, or gleamed out from his vest pocket, or twinkled between his fingers : and Sam grew more and more savage as the days went on. A fear to all the small boys of Vinegar Hill, a terror to Molly Limp, Sam by and by came to hate the very sight of Mrs Kensett, and resolved to stay away from the old church door altogether. Close and strong grew the tightening bonds between him and Jem Crook and Tim Wiggins in those days ; skilfully and surely did they on their part search for every grain of good seed that had fallen on Sam's heart ; until he was, as they said to each other, "all himself again"—his old, hard, wicked self ; given up to weeds of the worst kind.

"That he which soweth, should sow in hope." Verily, it is a hard thing to do that sometimes ! Yet still Mrs Kensett's heart yearned over the boy, and still she scattered the good seed whenever she had a chance ; giving Sam, each time she saw him, some word or look, or bit of sweet counsel, which would somehow, by the blessing of the Lord, lodge in the boy's heart, and hide there for a while, unseen. If only Sam had watched against the fowls of the air !

One evening, a few days after the children had brought home their Bibles, a knot of the little waifs sat huddled together among the bushes on Vinegar Hill. This particular spot was a favourite gathering-place for the smaller children, being off the general track of the men of the hamlet, as well as at a distance from the special play-ground of the larger boys. Here then—it was a warm night in July—the children sat, having played till it was too dark to play any longer : and hither came Sam Dodd, softly creeping up behind the bushes, to hear their talk. Sam was suspicious of everybody, in these days.

"Well, I *does* keep it safe, too ! and I will," Jemmy Lucas was saying.

"Where does he hide it, Jemmy ?" said another, "in yer

boots ?" which raised a great laugh at the expense of little
Jemmy, whose bare feet were as familiar with the winter
snows as with the summer dust.

"No, I don't," he answered. "And I ain't a-goin' to tell
ye—that's more."

"Hide it where old Dodd keeps his things," said a third
boy. "Guess that's a safe place."

"'Taint't not nigh so safe as he thinks," said a fourth.
"Tim Wiggins knows all about it. And some o' these days
old Dodd'll miss somethin' nother—shouldn't wonder."

"Why, did Tim tell you 'bout it ?" inquired Neddy Flint.
"How d'ye know ?"

"Heard him sayin' it over and over to himself," said the
boy. "Guess he thought, maybe, as he might forget. I
was a-comin' by there one night, and down came Tim, slidin'
down of a rope as he'd fastened somehow out o' Sam's winder.
And he'd been a-lookin' through some place ; and says he—
'Next red stair to top begin to count, and count two ; and
there's a spring in the corner.'"

"Does Sam know ?" inquired Jemmy Lucas.

"Guess he don't !" said Neddy. "*He* ain't up to snuff !"

Sam waited no more words—did not even tarry to knock
down Neddy Flint—but sped away home as noiselessly and
swiftly as ever he could. Well he knew the staircase, with
its red stairs here and there, put in at some time of repairs
—well he knew how the adventurous Tim, swinging by a rope
from Sam's own little window, might have got footing on
another window-ledge which commanded the whole stairway. And the half moon cut in the window shutter, gave
space enough for so practised an eye as Tim's. Sam hurried
home, and found a full room and his father presiding, just
as usual. And for a while Sam lingered there, joining in
whatever was going on, then crept away—up to his own room
first, then softly out on the stairs once more—then counting
down—repeating to himself : "Next red stair to top begin
to count, and count two."

Upon the stair below these two, Sam paused, and turning
round began to feel, and examine, and search for the spring,

with such intense eagerness that he forgot everything else, till suddenly a violent blow came upon the side of his head; and Sam Dodd staggered against the banisters, and then fell heavily down the stairs.

CHAPTER XI.

It was towards the middle of the next day, when Mrs Fritz, hurrying home from some one of her many errands about the village, suddenly fell in with Jemmy Lucas and Molly Limp, walking hand in hand, and looking very much troubled.

"Well, children," quoth Mrs Fritz, kindly, "what's the matter now? Who's lost a cap, or torn an apron?"

"Oh, 'tain't that!" said Molly, while Jemmy Lucas answered, "We was just a-comin' for you."

"No, it was for *her*," said Molly.

"Well, so it was," said Jemmy Lucas, "that's what I meant. Is she to home, ma'am?"

"My mistress? Mrs Kensett? Why, yes, she's home," said Mrs Fritz. "Who wants her?"

"Oh, Sam Dodd—dreadful!" said the children. "He's breaked his collar, and's all cut up besides."

"You see, ma'am," Jemmy Lucas went on more coherently, while Molly broke down in a great sob—"you see, ma'am, he's went down the stairs head first."

"Went down the stairs!" repeated Mrs Fritz.

"Yes, ma'am. Some does say as old Dodd pushed him down. And they's got him on to the bed, and there ain't a livin' soul there to know if he's dead or 'live."

"Why, bless your heart!" cried Mrs Fritz, in dismay, "don't *you* know? Run and find out, this very minute."

"Oh, he wasn't dead," said Jemmy Lucas. "But old Dodd's took hisself off, and the other boys they's allers got somethin' on hand."

"And hasn't the doctor seen him?" cried Mrs Fritz, once more.

"Why, yes, ma'am," said Jemmy Lucas. "Old Dodd sent *him*, and he's come and set the bones. But he couldn't stop."

"Well, you run home, like good children," said Mrs Fritz, "and take the best care you can, till I or somebody comes."

"We's afraid o' Sam," said little Molly, shrinking.

"Never mind, he can't hurt you now," said the woman. "Run home and do all you can for the poor fellow, and pray the Lord to keep him quiet. The Lord can do anything."

Mrs Fritz hurried off again in her own direction, and the two little children once more took hold of hands, and ran all the way back to Vinegar Hill.

"Poor feller!" Molly repeated, pity fairly getting the better of fear. "And the Lord *can* do anythin,' Jemmy."

"Well, Sam couldn't do much to ye now," said Jemmy, "anyhow."

"I'se so 'fraid of his swearin' at me!" said Molly, with a shiver. "And that makes the King angry. And I then feels as if He was angry with me just for hearin' it. But we'll beg Him to keep Sam quiet."

They ran along out of the village and past the church, and down among the bushes, deep in consultation as to how they would take care of Sam, and what various things they would do for his comfort; when suddenly Jemmy Lucas stopped short.

"Game's up, Molly!" he said. "There's Jem Crook's head out o' Sam's winder. Nice takin' care *he*'ll do!"

Molly stopped too, much disappointed.

"But maybe he ain't a-goin' to stay, Jemmy," she said.

"Maybe not," answered Jemmy Lucas, "but there ain't much 'maybe' about your and my stayin', Molly Limp. Howsever, we'll go as fur's we can."

The house door stood wide open, no hinderance there; and so did the other door at the foot of Sam's stairway; but as the children set foot on the first step, the face of Tim Wiggins looked down upon them from the top.

"Hullo, babies!" he said, "what's to pay now? Run home to yer mammies; we don't keep no infant school in these parts."

"We 're comin' to take care o' Sam Dodd," said Jemmy Lucas. "The lady telled us to."

"Oh, she did!" said Tim Wiggins. "Well, you just skurry off back again, and tell her Sam's *took* care of—first-rate."

"But we wants to come up," said Molly.

"Does yer?" said Tim, with a sneer. "Couldn't let ye up, nohow. Stairs is too steep. Feared ye'd find out how it feels to fall down 'em." And Tim seated himself on the top stair, with a look and air that were unmistakably threatening.

"We'll sit down and just wait till she comes," whispered Molly to her companion. "She won't be very long."

"No, yer don't!" growled Tim, not catching the words, but taking full effect of the action. "I say, clear out o' that! I 'm goin' to 'speriment flingin' boots and shoes and sich like down the stairs, and some one on ye might take a notion to get hit."

It was an argument not to be answered. Little Molly and Jemmy Lucas gave way, perforce, before it. They went off, consoling themselves with the promise of keeping close watch for the lady, or for her deputy, Mrs Fritz, whichever might come.

So the day wore on, and Sam knew perfectly well who kept close watch over him, and made as though he knew it not. Anger and pain and mortification racked him almost beyond bearing, but not a word could Jem Crook or Tim Wiggins get; not a look even would he give them, except when they were looking another way. Sam felt that he hated them both heartily, if for no other reason, yet because they were strong and lithe as ever, and he lay there helpless. The hours wore on very wearily. Sometimes the boys left him quite alone, and Sam could hear them roaming over the house, or at least so much of it as was not locked up. Sometimes they went down and played beneath his window, their ringing shouts of laughter and frolic making the pain ten times worse, and the weariness almost unbearable. It was hot and close in that little garret-room, and Sam's watchers at length forsook it altogether, and delighted themselves in the cool shade below.

"If he wants somethin', he can just holler," said Tim Wiggins, stretching himself out for a nap. "Keep an eye, Jem, don't let none o' that 'ere small fry get in. Sam's a'most spiled now."

Jem Crook opened one eye and shut the other, alternately, for about ten minutes, but then he too went to sleep; and Sam might have wanted something a good while before his weak voice could have roused them up. At first he was glad they were gone; in his feverish, restless state, Sam found the strange quiet of the house rather pleasant. But soon he wearied of that, and grew more restless than ever. Better the mocking faces and tormenting laughs of Tim Wiggins and Jem Crook than his own thoughts, with that silent array of chests and jugs and horse blankets and guns. What was it the lady had said? "He sees you, boys, wherever you are," and Sam did not like the remembrance. He covered his head up in the clothes, and then bits of hymns that the lady had repeated, and of those Mr Pink had sung, seemed to ring in his ears. Sam threw down the coverlid with an oath, and there stood the lady herself before him; gentle, pure, and loving, as she always looked.

In his surprise, Sam was very near repeating his former expression, or something still worse; but instead of that, he only spoke out his thoughts pretty plainly.

"How'd you get here?" he said. "How come they to let ye up?"

"If you mean the two boys I saw asleep on the grass," said Mrs Kensett, "I did not ask them. And I should have come, Sam, just the same if they had been awake. I wanted to see you. How do you do?"

"Confounded!" was Sam's unqualified answer.

"Poor boy!" said Mrs Kensett, laying her hand on the hot forehead, "it is very hard to lie still and bear pain. I

know, for I have tried it myself. See, Sam, I have brought
some cool fresh water to bathe your head."

Sam scowled. But he was too weak to resist, and it took
but a touch or two of the cool wet linen to smooth away all
the wrinkles. His brow unbent, and a heavy sigh of relief
escaped his lips. Then the eyelids fell more gently, and
for the first time that day the weary boy went quietly to
sleep.

Neither sound nor stir disturbed him. Jem Crook, who
had waked up just in time to see Mrs Kensett's white dress
disappear through the doorway, crept noiselessly up the
stairs once or twice, to note the progress of things ; but
liked appearances far too little to venture in. James Dodd
was not yet come home ; and the sunbeams silently quitted
the little garret, and began to climb the roof.

For a while Sam slept on ; then pain was too much for
weariness, and roused him up. His wandering eyes looked
full into those of his kind nurse.

" Well, whatever *did* yer come for ?" he broke forth, with
something of his old manner.

" To take care of you," said Mrs Kensett.

" He won't let ye, when he comes back," said Sam.

" Oh yes, maybe he will, if you mean your father," said
Mrs Kensett.

" They makes an awful noise down-stairs nights," said
Sam.   " You 'll be just scared to death."

" No, I think not," said Mrs Kensett, with a smile.   " But
you must not talk, Sam. I am going down-stairs to get
your tea, and then you must go to sleep again."

Alas ! Sam's words proved true. Going down to the
kitchen, Mrs Kensett met there the master of the house ;
and was at once informed, with great distinctness, that her
services would be neither wished for nor permitted. James
Dodd " didn't like strangers in his house, and Sam would
get more care than he deserved, without troubling the village
folks."

With a sorrowful heart Mrs Kensett mounted the stairs
once more, carrying up Sam's cup of tea, and served him

with it tenderly and carefully. Then she set down the cup and came and knelt by his bedside.

"Sam," she said, " you were right, your father will not let me stay. But God will stay with you, and no one can hinder Him. Sam, will you think of Him? Will you trust yourself to Him? Will you try to be His child? This is what the Lord Jesus says : 'If ye shall ask anything in My name, I will do it.' 'If ye love Me, keep My command. ments.'"

She prayed for him there, with all her heart in her voice and words ; then bade him good-night, and came away And as she passed round the first clump of bushes, Jem Crook and Tim Wiggins came stealing round the other side, and darted into the house, and up the stairs.

"When any one heareth the word of the kingdom, and understandeth it not, then cometh the wicked one, and catcheth away that which was sown in his heart. This is he which received seed by the wayside."

GOLDEN THORNS.

GOLDEN THORNS.

———◆———

CHAPTER I.

"And some fell among thorns; and the thorns sprung up and
choked them."

DID you ever see a sower sowing his seed? Then you know
that he does not seek out the good spots, and the smooth
places of the field, but tries to cover the whole alike, not
knowing which shall prosper, "whether this or that." Only
as the best ground gives (to human eyes) the fairest chance
for the seed to grow, where indeed is no chance at all, but
only the blessing of God; so does the sower scatter his
grain more thickly on the thinner soil and in the barren
corners, that if one seed fails another may spring up and
bear fruit.

In Palestine, by the shores of the Sea of Galilee—there
where the Lord Jesus spoke His wonderful parable of the
sower—there are, as I once told you, no fences. One field
passes on into another, and the highway runs right through
and the rocks start up here and there, and the thorn-bushes
strive for possession. The seed falls and lodges in all sorts
of places, and meets with all sorts of fate. And it is just so
with that field which we call the world. No dividing lines
(there should be none); the seed sown broadcast, then
caught away, withered, choked, and springing up unto everlasting life.

As Mrs Kensett went forth to sow, that Sunday afternoon, scattering the truth wherever she could find a place, it came to pass that one little seed fell among thorns. Yet I suppose if you and I had looked for the thorns, through all that field, we should never have expected to find them there. *There,* in that smoothest spot of all, where the ground had been ploughed and harrowed for full forty years. Where the stones had been picked up, and the weeds rooted out, until it was a very fair looking piece of ground indeed. Whence then came the thorns? Ah! the heart is deceitful —who can know it? The thorns were not grown then, only the sprouting seeds lay in the soil; and the moment the one good little seed tried to grow, up sprang the thorns and choked it.

If Sam Dodd went home that first Sunday with a good thought in his heart, so had Farmer Graves one in his.

"I declare," he said to himself, as he plodded along, looking back now and then after Mrs Kensett—"I declare, if she bean't a-goin' to that crow's nest in spite of me! Women do beat the world!" Which *sounded* as if they beat the men—though that was not at all the farmer's intention. Something of the same idea, however, perhaps occurred to himself; for he went on more guardedly.

"They're just near about as heady as my white Bess. Why, she'll go the hull day long, and be fresh at the end o't, if you'll only let her go t'other way! And that's the way *she's* goin', sure enough," said Mr Graves, turning round once more. "Like to know what she'll do when she gets there. 'How many church members'—that's what she said. And 'the blessing.' Does seem now," said Mr Graves, thrusting his hands in his pockets and striding on once more, "does seem as though trowsers could manage them bushes better'n petticoats. Guess I'll *consult* 'Lizy Ann."

With which claim and surrender of masculine superiority, Mr Graves turned aside from the high road, and dived down a shady woodland path till he reached his home. It was one of those where "an early candle" gleamed already from the windows. Not of the parlour, however—that lay dim and solitary in Sunday state seclusion. But in the bright kitchen, the neat busy figure of Mrs Graves flitted to and fro, as she made ready the substantial "supper," which was wont to follow the two Sunday services and the Sunday lunch.

Out-doors there was just light enough to show you how comfortable everything was. Wood-house and well, chicken roost, barn, garden and orchard, had all their place, were all in order. Sleek cows were in the yard, plump horses in the stable ; countless chickens and turkeys were tucked away in feather beds below stairs, and a whole array of older poultry occupied the roosts. From the garden came the odour of ripe strawberries, and June roses and honeysuckles flung their sweetness abroad on the evening air. Beyond the dell, over many a rich rolling acre, stretched the farm; its various crops showing good cultivation, skill, and progress.

"Ain't a *much* better bit o' land than that nowheres," said Farmer Graves, as he stood still to look. "First-rater crops you *couldn't* find. And ain't she just a woman, though," he added, as a savoury waft of supper came through open windows, and brought him face about to the house. "Does seem as if we'd kinder ought to do something for them as ain't not nigh so comfortable. But Vinegar Hill!—why, you'd want to turn in saleraters by the pound."

"Yes, and instead of standing out there talking about saleratus, you'd better come in and attend to things you *do* understand," said the bright voice of Mrs Graves, floating pleasantly out into the darkness. "Saleratus, indeed ! Indeed, yes, even *my* biscuits'll want it, if you'll give 'em chance enough. What's up in the stars now, Mr Graves ?"

"Well, that I couldn't say," answered the farmer, slowly, as he marched into the kitchen. "Biscuits is sweet as a rose yet, 'Lizy."

"I should hope so, yet," said Mrs Graves. "What were you speechifying about there, if it wasn't the stars ?"

"Well," said Mr Graves again, proceeding to take off his Sunday coat and fold it up—"well, 'Lizy, I was talkin' round some, as to them folks in houses where the biscuits *ain't* sweet."

"Ah," said Mrs Graves, "I'll warrant you. There's enough such houses in the world. Just look at that," and the little woman tumbled out a panful of white, smoking puff balls, that were nearly as light as the young princess who had lost her gravity. Mr Graves hurried on his every-day coat, and sat down without waiting another minute; and for a little while made no further remark, even about the biscuits, having, in fact, so much to say to them.

"Ham ain't bad, neither," said Mrs Graves, as she watched him.

"Couldn't be no better," said the farmer. "And the coffee's just extra. That 'ere dun cow does yield the wonderfullest cream."

"If there were half a dozen children to eat it," said Mrs Graves, trying to laugh off a deep-drawn sigh.

"Yes," said the farmer, abstractedly. "Wonder now what them Vinegar Hill young ones has for supper? 'Tain't cream, I'll take my affidavy."

"Vinegar Hill?" said Mrs Graves, in astonishment. "Can anybody guess what put that in your head? Haven't been there, have you?"

"Not I," said the farmer. "But I seed some one as was goin', 'Lizy; so I s'pose that put it in my head. That 'sponsible little lady as stops to Miss Smith's—well, *she* met me as I come along home."

"She wasn't going to Vinegar Hill, I take it," said Mrs Graves.

"Well, she just was," said the farmer, "headed for Vinegar Hill, and all steam on, the minute I telled her the way."

"I want to know," said Mrs Graves. "'Twasn't clever of you, Ahab, to let her go, I must say."

"Maybe you'll go a leetle step farther, and just say how I could help it," said the farmer. "No, no, guess you wouldn't like it if I took up the business o' crossin' feminine notions."

"Guess *you* wouldn't," said his wife. "What under the sun did she want at Vinegar Hill? Why, she's a lady, every inch."

"Just so," said the farmer. "She didn't want much under the sun, ye see, bein' as the luminary was already down, but she wanted to go and fetch up them children and folks gen'ally. Talked like a book, she did, about how many church members it would take to make that 'ere hole dry and comfortable."

"Ahab,—do tell !" said Mrs Graves. "How ever did she count to do it ?"

"Why, I can't tell ye nothin'," said Farmer Graves. "There she stood a-talkin' to me 'bout workin' faithful, with the blessin'; and what was I to say ?"

His wife glanced at him, with a strange quiver of face for an instant, but she made no reply.

"O' course," Mr Graves went on, "I always do count to do my work faithful; you don't never see a corner o' *my* wheat field grown up to blackberries. There ain't ten foot o' the farm nowheres as hain't been ploughed and harrowed and had the weeds killed off."

"Except Vinegar Hill," said Mrs Graves, musingly.

"That ain't on my farm, I'm thankful to say," said the farmer.

"No, but I was thinking," said his wife. "I do suppose, Ahab, *that's* what Mr Cross meant, when he preached that sermon—don't you know ? 'The field is the world.' And Vinegar Hill's a patch of weeds in one corner."

"You may swear to the weeds," said Farmer Graves, with some asperity. "But I kint cultivate a field o' *that* size, nohow. Have to grow up to grass, for all me."

"What was she going to do ?" asked Mrs Graves.

"Don' know, no more'n my old horse," said the farmer. "Kinder made me feel bad, too, to see her setting off alone so."

"If those children had some of this milk now," said Mrs Graves, filling her husband's bowl. "Why, Ahab, it does seem as if we might pull up a few of the weeds."

"Transplant 'em to the penitentiary," suggested the farmer.

"No indeed," said the little woman. "Put 'em in the garden and make flowers of 'em."

"Wouldn't wonder now one bit if that's what she was after," said Farmer Graves. "Does take you, 'Lizy, to make out most things."

"Well, come to think of it," said Mrs Graves; "it *is* a shame to let such a place be. Right next to the church, too."

"Fact," said the farmer. "But, bless you, 'Lizy! I ain't got time to see to it. And you couldn't walk so fur, and I wouldn't let you, that's more."

"Why, you've got ever so much more time than I have," said his wife, laughing. "What with the house, and the garden, and the chickens, and the bread, and the dishes, and the mending, and making."

"Smart little woman," said Farmer Graves, nodding his head. "But you don't begin to know what it is to have a hull farm on your shoulders. Tell you what, though, 'Lizy, we might both on us go, some afternoon. Take a play spell, like."

"What'll we do when we get there?" asked his brisk little wife.

"I can't tell ye," confessed Mr Graves.

"Because I'd like to find out, beforehand," said Mrs Graves. "What was *she* going to do?"

"Now, there's an idea," said the farmer. "I can't tell ye that at this present, but it's likely I kin find out. And then some day when things is all done up, and there ain't more chores than common, we'll go. I do believe I'd feel the better for havin' somethin' done. What's this she said now? 'How many church members would it take, if they worked faithfully, with God's blessing?' Them's the very words."

"Take to do what?" said Mrs Graves.

"Why, to sweeten it—that's Vinegar Hill. I'd been callin' it a sour spot. Give us some more sugar, 'Lizy; seems as though the taste had got into this cup o' tea."

Mrs Graves put in the sugar, and then mused in silence.

CHAPTER II.

"Go to Vinegar Hill this afternoon, Ahab?" said Mrs Graves, as she dished up her neat and substantial breakfast, Monday morning.

"Guess it's safe to say I've got other weedin' on hand as is more important," answered the farmer. "You see, 'Lizy, potatoes has got to be took in time, or you can't do nothin' with 'em. Ain't no hurry, is there?"

"Why there's always a hurry about weeds, isn't there?" said Mrs Graves.

"Fact!" said the farmer. "But some kin wait better than others."

"Well, how can you tell which to pull first?" said Mrs Graves, stirring her coffee.

"Why, it's just which crop is most worth," said the farmer, "or sometimes which weeds 'll run up to seed the quickest. And for all I kin see, potatoes 'll pay better'n anything *this* year."

Mrs Graves sighed a little, and stirred her coffee, and looked at the great pitcher of milk, upon which even her husband made small impression.

"What sort of a crop's started up there, among *those* weeds?" she said, musingly.

"Vinegar Hill?" inquired the farmer.

Mrs Graves nodded.

"Love ye! I kin't tell," said her husband, all astonishment. "Now you've just gone and got your head sot upon gettin' hold o' them young scamps," he added, deprecatingly.

"Thought of 'em the whole night long," said Mrs Graves, with another nod of assent.

"'Cept when you was a-huntin' minks," said the farmer, with a sly look. "She thought she see a brown mink airin' himself in the moonlight! How's the chickens this mornin'?"

"Oh, I don't know—I'm not thinking of chickens now," said Mrs Graves. "I was wondering how long it'll take *those* weeds to go to seed."

"Bless ye! they're seedin' down and startin' up the hull time!" said Farmer Graves. "Nothin' there *but* weeds, little woman."

"But if the weeds were cleared off, and the ground planted?"

"Don't she talk like a book, now?" said the farmer, admiringly. "Well, I'm real sorry now, 'Lizy—that's a fact; but I *kin't* leave those potatoes, nohow you kin fix it. They'll spile, just as sure as the world, if I don't attend to 'em."

"Well, so might t'other place," said Mrs Graves, persistently.

"Kin't," said the farmer. "Bad's it kin be, now."

"I don't believe that, any way," said his wife.

"Don't know nothin' 'tall about it—that's the reason," said Mr Graves. "Tell ye it *couldn't* be no worse. Chance is, it'll be better."

"Guess I'll believe that too — when *your* weeds stop a-growing," said Mrs Graves.

"Well—I ain't no match for a woman at talkin'," said Mr Graves, getting up from the table. "Never was—and don't never expect to be. But I tell you what it is, 'Lizy, if we get on right smart with that 'ere potato field to-day, mebbe I'll tackle up and drive ye over to Vinegar Hill to-morrow." And Mr Graves marched out of the house as if he was glad to get away.

"Better go and look after them chickens soon as ye kin, 'Lizy," he said, putting his head back inside the door. "Case that 'ere brown mink might ha' skeered 'em, you know."

Now if Mr Graves had said nothing about the chickens, the chance is that his wife would have gone out as soon as she could, to satisfy herself concerning the said brown mink; but as it was, she sat still, and presently fell back into a muse again, eyeing her great pitcher of milk. Too far off was Vinegar Hill for her to walk there, even had she been sure her husband would let her go alone—and yet there was the milk, and there were all those children. How still the house seemed! and even the cackling and crowing and gobbling and quacking and cooing which went on outside—mingled as it all was with faint lows and grunts and squeals from a a greater distance, seemed but to deepen the stillness. She could hear the rustle of the wind through the tree-tops, and the dancing glee of the little brook ; but within doors neither voice nor footfall broke the silence. Mrs Graves sighed once more—that pitcher of milk was so big and so full; then broke down and cried a little ; then dried her eyes and looked round the lonely room. But with that, business habits took up their old rule, and she began to bustle about much as usual. Clearing away dishes, and filling the tin curd-form with its sour-sweet complement, and preparing for dinner, and making ready to wash. And in the midst of it all, with a panful of scraps and scrapings, Mrs Graves sallied forth to feed her chickens. Of course the fattening ones must be first served ; and singing lightly to herself, her spirits all come back again at the first touch of thrift and work ; Mrs Graves marched gaily round the house to where the coops had been set for safe keeping ; but at the very first corner, wet with the dew, draggled and smeared and stiff, lay the young cock the boys had dropped in their hurried flight from the coops. The coops themselves did, indeed, stand where she had left them the night before, but with loosened slats now, and pushed aside from their trim order ; and instead of the bright eyes and hungry bills of her favourites thrust out between the bars, there were dismal-looking tufts of feathers caught and sticking and scattered about, and for the rest but silence. Mrs Graves set her pan right down in the grass where she was, and stood still in dismay.

"I said so !" she cried to herself. "I just *knew* that brown mink was around ! Only Ahab's *such* a sleepy-head, after dark."

But stooping to examine the dead chicken, the bright little woman began, after all, to doubt whether the brown mink had really added this to his long list of crimes. For the chicken's neck was unmistakably wrung, and the slats of the distant coops were unmistakably pulled out and flung aside. Mrs Graves left the chicken in the dew, and crouching down in front of the coops, considered the matter in profound silence.

"It's just some of those misguided children!" she said at last, pitifully. "It never was the mink, and it couldn't be any other living soul that I can think of. Wonder what Ahab 'll think *now* of weeding that field ? Guess 'twould pay, at this rate. A round dozen of prime chickens, so fat they could'nt but just see to eat more ! But my ! my !—if I tell him he'll *never* go there, nor let me neither !"

Mrs Graves sat thinking, her head on her hand—then suddenly rose up and replaced the slats in their proper positions, nodding her head sagely the while. Then caught up her pan and carried it off to the barn-yard, and on her way back picked up the dead chicken and carried that into the house. But then she stood thinking, thinking, all the morning work unheeded, as if it would do itself.

"No!" she said at last; "I never did do him a false turn, and I guess I ain't a-going to begin now. Things'll have to take their chance."

She ran hastily out to the coops, pulled out the slats and threw them on the grass, and then ran back to her work in earnest ; flying about, to make up for lost time, with the spirit of half a dozen, at least.

.

CHAPTER III.

"TELL *you*, little woman," said Farmer Graves, as he sat down to dinner that day, "there's no reasonable doubt but what potatoes does make a man hungry."

"Taken one way," said Mrs Graves, smiling at her husband's plate.

" Well, yes," said the farmer, "it's accordin' as you take 'em—like most things. But what on airth, 'Lizzy !—been and killed your store chicks afore they was ready ?"

"Not I," said Mrs Graves, with some emphasis. "And there's but one there, Ahab."

"Thought ye'd try 'em first to see?" inquired the farmer. But his wife shook her head.

"Didn't think anything of the sort."

"Then she's a-tryin' to get round me, sure as guns," said the farmer, helping himself to more potatoes. "Coaxin' me up with fried chicken and notions jest to do what she'd a mindter hev done. But I kin't do it, 'Lizy—telled ye I couldn't—and I kin't. Not if you was to line the road with chickens."

"Pretty small danger of my doing that at present," said Mrs Graves, again with some quickness. "Make the most of this one, for it's all you'll see for some time."

"He's a first-rater," said Mr Graves, plying the bones with great skill and spirit. "Don't know as ever I eat a more tenderer fowl. But tell ye, 'Lizy! the hull lot on 'em ain't worth—not two rows o' them pink eyes."

"I won't say they are—now," said Mrs Graves. "What can't you do, Ahab?"

"Can't go foolin' round the country *after* somethin' to do," said the farmer, energetically.

"Oh, but you half promised you'd take me to Vinegar Hill to-morrow," said his wife.

"Promised? not I!" said the farmer. "Guess you dreamt it, 'Lizy, your head was so full."

"No, no—*half* promised," answered Mrs Graves. "You said 'maybe,' and I'm sure that's half a promise."

"Oh, well, t'other half hasn't come to fetch it," said the farmer, putting his knife and fork upon double duty. "There's the potatoes, and the corn; and by that time there'll be hayin', and then'll come harvestin'; and the fall ploughin's got to be looked after sharp—and 'tain't no fool of a job to gather in the apples. No use goin' into that crow's nest, ye know, if I don't *do* somethin', and I ain't got a speck o' time."

His wife sat and watched him, long after her own meal was finished, but she did not push her point, nor say another

I

word just then about Vinegar Hill. She watched him, and supplied his plate with the daintiest bits from every dish, but gave no further hint of what she wanted to do nor of what other people had done. And Mr Graves finished his dinner with great satisfaction, and hurried away to the field once more, with no more thought of Vinegar Hill to trouble him than if it had been in another continent.

It was towards the end of the afternoon, and Mrs Graves —work all cleared away and working-dress off—sat alone in her neat front room. The muslin curtains might have been a wreath of last year's snow for whiteness ; not a shred nor a speck were on the carpet ; and table, door-knobs, candlesticks, and andirons made the room dazzling with the long late sunbeams. Lithe sprays of sweet-brier waved before the windows, the bees hummed in and out, and Mrs Graves stitched ceaselessly on her husband's Sunday collar.

"Now if Ahab would drive me over there," she thought, "and we could find a nice child—it don't seem right to take him from his own home, neither—but then he might be an orphan, and not have any." And the needle flew in and out faster than ever to the tune of kind thoughts. Then came a sharp little rap at the outer kitchen door. And not laying down her stitching nor laying off her thimble, Mrs Graves stepped quickly into the kitchen and threw the door wide open. She was a pleasant picture to look at, the smart little farmer's wife, in her light print gown and brisk black shoes and spotless stockings. Cheery, happy, useful ; if a wish lay hidden in her blue eyes, they seemed to sparkle none the less, and few people found it out.

Before her now stood a boy of some thirteen or fourteen years of life experience and hard knocks; by dint of which, as it seemed, he had daily grown rougher, stronger, and harder : in no sweet rippling brook had he been tossed and cradled. Half-grown, half-formed, *not* half-washed; his clothes with no suit in them, either to him or each other ; his face sharp and vacant by turns. Just now it was hopelessly vacant; only the stealthy eyes roamed hither and thither without a moment's rest.

Many of these characteristics Mrs Graves remembered afterwards, but at the time she gave them no thought. Her mind had been so full of her new project all day, that the boy suggested but one idea; and instead of the usual inquiry in such cases, Mrs Graves promptly demanded "where he came from?"

"I come from the road, 'long by the fence," the boy answered, clearing his face yet more of any expression.

"I guess you did!" said the farmer's wife. "Where beyond that? Where do you live, child?"

"Don't reckon as *you'd* know where it bees," said the boy. "Pretty folks gen'ly don't; they takes the t'other road. Don't live much nowheres."

"Pretty folks are quite as apt to know things as ugly ones," said Mrs Graves. "Where do you live a little?"

"Wal," said the boy, with a sort of slow drawl, "there's Pinetop, and Lonesome, and the rest. I visits a good deal down to Vinegar Hill."

"I thought so!" said Mrs Graves, triumphantly. "What sort of a place is Vinegar Hill? That's just what I want to know."

"Vinegar Hill?" said the boy, glancing up at her for an instant, and only that; "guess yer'd better ask folks what lives there reg'lar: *they* kin tell ye. 'Bout a large place, it is, of the size. And it's pretty full stocked with folks and things—spe'shly things—arter the winter supplies comes in."

"What's your name?" inquired Mrs Graves, with extreme briskness.

The boy glanced at her again, quick and sharp as a needle; then vacantly as before. "Folks calls me Tim, when they wants me."

"Well, what did you want of me this afternoon?" said Mrs Graves, studying the boy much as if he had been a fossil of some rare and extinct species. For all answer to which, Tim held out a tin pail, heaped with the red wild strawberries of the woods.

"Thought yer might take a notion to 'em," he added.

"Oh, I do!" said Mrs Graves, all eagerness to see more of a real, live specimen from Vinegar Hill. "We've got plenty in the garden, but I love the taste of these. Come in, Tim, and I'll get a dish."

Tim peered into the bright kitchen with an air of some doubt; but the room was empty—he ventured in. Empty, that is, of people, for otherwise that kitchen seemed pretty full. Fresh loaves of cake were cooling on the table, and loaves of bread, both white and brown, helped fill the air with a rich scent of peace and plenty. The sun flickered in bright and warm through the screen of lilac-bushes; the cups and tins and brasses all gleamed and laughed as joyously as their statelier neighbours in the parlour. But Tim Wiggins walked up to the table—scoured as white as hands could make it—and set down his pail with a scowl. It was so good to look at—so hard to get—all this comfort and good cheer!

Mrs Graves saw the scowl, and straightway imagining that Tim was longing for a piece of cake, and not even pausing to turn out the berries, she fetched a knife from the pantry and cut him a slice large enough and sweet enough to clear the brow of most boys; but which Tim took and eat without much change of appearance.

"And so you live on Vinegar Hill?" she said, measuring out the berries into a great bowl.

"Didn't say so," replied Tim. "Got any chickens down this way to sell? I knows a man as wants forty dozen."

"I hope he'll get them," said Mrs Graves, "but all mine are disposed of."

A queer little sound, coming from she could hardly tell where, made the farmer's wife pause suddenly and look up from her purse and the dimes she was counting out for Tim Wiggins. And in a minute she felt perfectly sure of two things—it was Tim who had laughed in that extraordinary way, and it was Tim who had emptied her coops—she felt both things to the very tips of her fingers. But to think of those forlorn children wanting her chickens enough to come and take them, went to her heart as well. She sighed, missed her count, and had to begin all over again. Tim Wiggins grew impatient.

"Be quick, can't ye?" he said, roughly, and with a glance out of the window. "Didn't yer never buy nothin' afore? Here—gives us the cash," and snatching the coins from her hand, Tim caught up his pail, and vanished from the house in a style that fairly made Mrs Graves draw her breath. She went to the door—but there was no sign left of Tim Wiggins: road and meadow and hill were in very summer stillness and rest, and looked as if there could be nothing worse than sunshine in all the world. The sun lay fair and full upon the broad country, touching up grass and corn and trees and fences with his shifting gold; and far down the road, giving strength and emphasis to the long shadow of Farmer Graves. The shadow danced up and down with strange vagaries, but the farmer tramped sturdily along, and before him a long string of cows—black and white and red and dappled and dun—wound slowly down the sunlit hill into the valley.

"And that child saw him!" cried Mrs Graves, "and didn't dare to wait!"

CHAPTER IV.

Mrs Graves turned from the window and began to bustle about getting tea. The kettle was soon on, and the table set; and then she went back and forth, cutting smoked beef, and cheese, and cake, then hulling a part of her late purchase; and finally—after a minute's look at them, she rolled up her sleeves, and plunged into some mystery of flour and eggs. Then with her quick bakery all done, and keeping hot in the oven, Mrs Graves glanced round the kitchen to see that everything was right, and started off for the barn and the milking field. But at the last house threshold she paused— asking herself for well-nigh the twentieth time, "Well, what *did* the boy come here for?"

It was hard, even for her, to give a pleasant answer to this; and her thoughts went on—

"Maybe he wanted to find out if I had any more fat chickens,—maybe he wanted to see if I'd got anything else. Maybe he's round now!"

And with that the little woman's foot made a decided pause,—it would never do to go off to the barn and leave the supper unprotected!

"He's welcome enough to my share of it, poor thing!" she said to herself; "but Ahab's got to have his. And 'twouldn't help matters *much* to have Vinegar Hill get *his* supper. Ahab'd spare some other things 'fore he would a berry shortcake. Wish that young one had some! I'd like to feed him up, for once, and try and comfort the badness out of him. There—now I'll go set my pans."

"Old Brindle's doin' wonderful, 'Lizy," said Farmer Graves, as he came in. "Have to get another milk-pail, at this rate."

"And another hand to milk?" said his wife, as she poured the foaming treasure into her bright pans.

"Another hand to milk?—not I!" said the farmer. "Many hands don't make light work in my field, nor barn neither—nor barn-yard. Zach Green's as many hands as *I* want."

"Why, you're always afraid you won't get things done in time," said Mrs Graves; and she carried the pails out into the kitchen, and began to wash them vigorously. The farmer followed her, and stood looking on.

"Always *do* get 'em, though," he said.

"But you might have an easier time of it."

"Times is easy enough," said Farmer Graves. "And they'd only be harder. 'Tain't every man you kin git as 'll bring his dinner and board to home; and I tell ye, 'Lizy, I won't have you slavin' yourself to death for half a dozen lazy fellers—not if you want it ever so bad."

"I don't want half a dozen," said Mrs Graves. "And it's a pity if I couldn't take care of one boy and not hurt myself. Now, Ahab, make haste, supper's just ready."

"Smells mighty good—whatever it is ; " said Mr Graves, as his wife stooped down and opened the oven door.

"It won't—after it gets as black as my shoe," said Mrs Graves ; "so be quick."

"Quick as you like," said the farmer, hurrying out again. "I 'll just head off that 'ere brown mink, afore it gets dark."

Mrs Graves laughed to herself a little, but then she sighed and looked grave.

"Poor things, poor things !" she said. "And it 'll just set him dead against them."

She ran about, filling the tea-pot, and setting the last things on the table ; chief among which was the strawberry shortcake, fresh from the oven, and now smothered in yellow cream. The farmer came stamping in, even in greater haste than he had gone out.

"Why, 'Lizy !" he said. "Why, 'Lizy !"

"Yes, yes," said Mrs Graves, pushing him gently into a chair,—"we 'll talk about it by and by. But meanwhile the shortcake's getting cold !"

"A berry shortcake, too !" said Farmer Graves, subsiding —"first of the season, and sure to be first-rate. But what on airth, 'Lizy !"

"What 's the matter ?" said his wife. "Ain't it large enough ?"

"Why, that 's another thing, now," said Mr Graves, sur- veying the dish more carefully. "Expected company, did ye ? and they never come."

"Didn't expect anybody but you," said his wife. "And you 're pretty sure to come at supper-time."

"Fact !" said the farmer. "But I ain't—not *quite* so sure to eat enough for a whole tea-party. Must have been thinkin' o' folks, anyway."

"Well, I was that," said Mrs Graves, with an air of candid confession. "Only it wasn't exactly what you'd call 'folks,' maybe."

"Vinegar Hill, I 'll be sworn," said the farmer.

Mrs Graves nodded.

"'Tain't out of her head yet !" said Mr Graves, despairingly. "And first thing I know, I'll find myself swoopin' round down there, some fine afternoon, when I'd ought to be home and to work. Hain't sent 'em your chickens, have ye, 'Lizy, to begin with?"

"No," said Mrs Graves, coolly, "somebody came and took them."

The farmer dropped his knife and fork, and gazed at her.

"You don't!" he said. "Took the chickens! what! and didn't pay for 'em?"

"Paid me a fright last night," said Mrs Graves, "and a surprise this morning."

"'Twan't the mink then, after all," said Mr Graves, with a gleam of satisfaction. "'Lizy! it was some o' them Vinegar Hill scamps!—ain't a soul else in the village would do a neighbour such a turn. One o' the very young rascals you're aching to get here and fetch up by hand. And he's fattenin' on your store-chicks this blessed minute!"

Mrs Graves laughed at that, clapping her hands softly, and with her face full of dancing light; but then she suddenly dropped her head down on the table, and sobbed out a whole heartful of other feelings. Mr Graves looked on helplessly,—then helped himself in a bewildered way to another piece of shortcake.

"Never did know what to do with women," he said, shaking his head; "don't s'pose if I'd been one I'd have known what to do with myself, 'Lizy!"

"Well?" said his wife, looking up and drying her eyes.

"You ought to be mad—hoppin'," said the farmer, in a puzzled tone. "Just what I telled ye, child; ain't such another crows' nest in the country."

"But oh, Ahab," said his wife, "they *must* have been in need, or they'd never have come so far to get my chickens."

The farmer gave a most uncompromising grunt.

"Don't foller, nohow," he said. "Ain't a thing in the world they need so bad as a first-class whippin'; but they don't come to get *that*—and wouldn't stop for it, likely, if they was here."

But to that Mrs Graves had nothing to say, with certain recollections of her afternoon's visitor coming up.

"Shouldn't wonder, now, if 'twarn't one o' them very boys you're hankering after," Mr Graves began again, glancing across the table at his wife.

"Well, what if it was?"

"Cryin' over him, warn't ye, in imagination?" said the farmer. "Wishin' you had some more fat chickens you could let him have cheap?"

"Come, Ahab, hush!" said Mrs Graves, rousing up. "I ain't quite a fool, I guess. But you said yourself, it didn't seem right to have everything and give nothing. And I can't help crying sometimes, when I think of all those children gone to loss. Suppose one of 'em was ours."

"Suppose a load of hay!" said Farmer Graves, energetically. "Suppose the moon was a cheese, what sized chunks could ye cut? 'Tain't no use supposin', 'Lizy. One of 'em *ain't* ours—and ain't a-goin' to be."

"Not till you change your mind," said his wife, softly.

"Well, no," said the farmer. "Give us another bowl o' tea, 'Lizy; this one tastes as salt as the ocean!"

"But we'll go over there, and see what we can do for them?" said Mrs Graves, as she emptied the cup and refilled it.

"See just as well here," said the farmer. "Can't do nothin' for such folks. I know as well as if I'd seen 'em every one. There was a pair of 'em coastin' round the farm this forenoon—and I'd a sight rather see two weasels. A scarecrow's a picture to 'em."

"I suppose it was one of them that came here with the berries, then," said Mrs Graves.

"Like enough!" said her husband. "Look out for anythin' you've got lying round loose, if *they've* beat a track to the back door. I'll go and shut up the rest o' the fowls, the first thing. Such chaps ain't noways particular, and 'll take up with the tough, easy, if they can't get the tender. One o' *them* boys to help me milk?—nice mess o' milk *he'd* fetch in!"

"But we'd teach him and improve him, you know," said Mrs Graves, following her husband out; "and if he did take a little at first, Ahab, he'd soon get over that; and we have plenty."

"There went a woman!" said Mr Graves, "and 'tain't hardly worth my while to foller! Let's see your chicken coops, 'Lizy; best look at 'em to-night, for there's no tellin' where *they*'ll be in the mornin'! How in the name o' silence he got all them cocks out without makin' more noise, passes my wits."

Mr Graves went into a close examination of the matter, and his wife stood silently by, biding her time.

CHAPTER V.

IT seemed, after that, as if the Vinegar Hill children were almost as curious about Mrs Graves as she was about them; or else perhaps the slice of cake given to Tim Wiggins had caused the excitement. Certain it was, that she soon began to know a good many of the wild youngsters by sight, and even by name: not always the right name, it must be confessed. But on one pretext or another, they came to the farm very often,—much oftener than Mr Graves thought at all desirable.

"All comes o' carin' about folks that ain't worth it," he said. "Once let them young scamps find out you've got sweet cake and sweet looks and sweet words standin' ready for 'em, and they'll come round you like flies in a honey-pot."

"But it don't hurt me as much as it does the honey," remonstrated Mrs Graves. "It amuses me."

"Risky kind of amusement, to my thinkin'," said the farmer. "'Muses you to feed them with sugar, and 'muses them to see where you keep it. You give them cake—and they count your cheeses. By and by it'll come *my* turn to be amused with hearin' the spoons is gone."

"Now, Ahab," said his wife, laughing, "you be quiet! I've got a little sense."

The farmer gave a dissatisfied grunt.

"Look out you don't lose it, 'Lizy," he said. "Boys has a wonderful way o' pickin' your pocket!" and off he went to his work.

Hardly was he well out of sight, when one of the very boys in question made his appearance—so suddenly, indeed, that one might well suppose that he had been lying in wait for the farmer's departure. But for a wonder he bore no excuse in his hands,—neither berries nor flowers, nor the wild greens of the meadow. Silently the boy slipped in, and stood watching Mrs Graves as she washed her churn.

"Well!" said the little woman, looking at him kindly, "what do you want? did you come to help me churn? You're too late this time."

"Why, that's the very thing!" cried the boy, who was no other than our old acquaintance, Jem Crook. "O' *course* I couldn't help bein' late, when I had to do up mammy's churnin' fust."

"Oh—your mother churns too, does she?" said Mrs Graves.

"Often as she can get cream enough," answered Jem, gravely.

"What does she do with the butter?" asked Mrs Graves. "Does she make more than you want?"

"More 'n we eat," said Jem. "Poor folks has to take their bread 's they can get it, and let the butter go. 'Tain't fun bein' poor."

"And you'd like to churn and eat the butter too, then?" said Mrs Graves.

"Ah!" said Jem Crook, smacking his lips. "Fact is, I *did* hear as some un 'nother was arter a boy o' my size down this way."

"What can you do?" asked Mrs Graves, looking at the wild, acute, not unhandsome face, whereon fun and skill and

lawlessness gleamed out through dust and tan.   "I think
might like to have you for my boy;—what can you do?"

"Turn my hand to most things," answered Jem, decidedly.
"Fetch ye woodchucks for dinner, and a brile o' young
squir'ls for breakfast.   And as for supper—why, there ain't
a berry grows 'thout my knowin' of it."

"Then you can do something besides mischief?" said Mrs
Graves.

"Oh, we's give up mischief now, and goes to Sabba'-school
reg'lar," said the unblushing Jem.

"Who is 'we'?" said the farmer's wife.

"Chaps down our way—down to Sour Lonesome and Grab."

"Sour Lonesome and Grab?" repeated Mrs Graves—"why,
I never heard of such places."

Jem chuckled.

"Guess likely there's jest a few things you *ain't* heerd on,"
he said, with a dash of his usual impudence.

"Aren't you a Vinegar Hill boy?" said Mrs Graves.

"Some folks calls it so," said Jem, "but 'tain't hardly fair,
it's a real sweet spot."

"Well, where do you go to Sunday-school?" said Mrs
Graves.   "Not here in the village?   I never saw you
coming into church with the rest."

"Oh, *we* never gets no farther'n the steps, replied Jem.
"Teacher's fond o' air,—and some o' the boys is restless."

"Yes, I think that is probable," said the farmer's wife,
surveying the young Arab before her, whose eyes, hands,
feet, and muscles generally were not still an instant.   "Why,
then, you must be one of the strange lady's class?"   Jem
nodded.

"Strangest woman *I* ever comed across," he said, briefly.

"Well, what does she teach you?" said Mrs Graves,
growing interested.   "What does she say to you?"

"Lots!" said Jem.   "Heaps!   Queer as a ghost story,
and 'bout as likely.   Fust she sits up and talks, and then
she kneels down and talks."

"Kneels down?" Mrs Graves repeated.   Again Jem
nodded.

"Seems to like ter," he said. "Seems as though she felt more comf'tabler. Talks better'n ever."

The farmer's wife stood thinking—the words struck home with a minute's sharp pain.

"Well," she said, rousing herself with a sigh, "I must send you away now,—I have something to do."

"Ain't got nothin' for *me* to do, likely?" said Jem. "Wants a job this mornin', the worst kind."

"Oh, then I must find you one," said the warm-hearted little woman. "Let me see.—There's Mr Grave's lunch !— could you carry it to him for sixpence?"

"Run all the way!"

"Well, I don't want you to run," said Mrs Graves; "if you walk briskly it will do. Sit down, child, and I'll get it ready. By the way, what's your name?"

"Used to called me 'Crooked Jemmy,' when I was little," answered the boy, dropping into a chair.

"'Crooked Jemmy!'" repeated Mrs Graves, standing still to look at him once more. "Why, you're straight enough, now."

"Looks so—don't I?" said Jem, with a queer laugh.

Mrs Graves made no answer to that—the laugh chilled her a bit; and she went silently about the business of preparing her tin pail. Jem Crook looked on in equal silence and some wondering admiration. First went in two substantial pieces of cake, then a slice of cheese, then a generous quarter of pie, then another slice of cheese; then an immense sandwich.

"Quite clear 'tain't his dinner?" quoth Jem Crook, at this stage of the proceedings.

"Very clear!" said Mrs Graves, laughing, as she stowed away a cold potato or two. Her cheerfulness came back at once. Perhaps the poor boy was hungry, and that gave his laugh such a strange sound. "Don't you want some lunch yourself, Jemmy?"

"Wouldn't object," answered the boy, glancing at her. "Run the faster."

So Jem Crook was served with another lunch, the mate

to that prepared for the farmer, and disposed of it in a style that would have made even that mighty trencher-man open his eyes. Then he started up.

"Give us the pail!" he said, abruptly. "Time's up." And with a dash which reminded Mrs Graves rather startlingly of the movements of Tim Wiggins, Jem made for the door.

"You know the turning to the wheat field?" Mrs Graves called after him. Jem swung the pail round his head as it had been a lantern and he a station-man, and started off on a full run.

"Know it?" he shouted back—"guess I *does* know some things, and no mistake!"

Mrs Graves stood watching him, doubtfully.

"Poor boy! poor children!" she said. "Now if he should get Ahab's lunch all mixed up! He does hate cheese and gingerbread *that* way!"

However, Jem was already out of sight, and it was as useless to pursue the subject as the boy; so Mrs Graves went back to her work.

One thought went with her—followed her about—came in *apropos* to everything and nothing—it was that new thought of Mrs Kensett. Jem Crook's uncouth words had drawn the picture as well as far more delicate English could have done, and Mrs Graves could not forget them.

"Seems to like ter!" he had said. "Seems as though she felt more comf'tabler. Talks better 'n ever!"

What sort of a strange life must she lead, who felt more at home in heaven than on earth? Mrs Graves mused, and went on with her work, and passed the whole morning as in a dream; her hand now and then drawn hastily across her eyes, her eyes many times going off out of the window, in a silent gaze which yet saw nothing of all that there appeared.

CHAPTER VI.

THE sunbeams had struck noonday with their noiseless bells, and the shadows had echoed it, before the long figure of Farmer Graves was seen advancing from the wheat field. Mrs Graves watched him through the window and dished up her dinner at the same time.

"He's late!—never guessed I had pot-pie," she said to herself, as she heaped the platter with her savory compound; piling up white puffs of dough that were as light as her biscuit. "I don't suppose he ever dreamed of such a thing. But he's in a hurry now,—wonder if he smells it already!"

The little woman laughed brightly to herself, giving more attention to the dinner now, and less to the window; and she had just gone into the pantry for bread, when she heard the farmer's voice and step in the kitchen.

"'Lizy!" he said, "'Lizy! Days when you're goin' to be too busy to look after me, I'd like the compliment o' notice aforehand, so's I kin look after myself."

Mrs Graves put down her loaf on the pantry shelf, and stood aghast. Had he had a sun-stroke? was the wheat-field too much for his brain? She caught up her bread again and hurried out.

"Ahab!" she cried, "you're sick!"

"Sick?" said the farmer, "no, I ain't; but I'd ought to be."

"You'd better go right to bed," said his anxious wife.

"Bed!" echoed the farmer; "guess I won't go far, in no direction, till I get somethin' to eat. How long d'ye s'pose a man kin live without eatin', 'Lizy?"

"Dinner's been ready ever since twelve o'clock," said Mrs Graves, in an aggrieved voice. "It's you who are late, Ahab."

"Late, am I?" said the farmer, "didn't know as you took no 'count o' time, down here. Thought you'd got mornin's and afternoons and next week all mixed up together. I'd a good notion not to come at all. When a man's forgot to home, he'd as good stay away."

"If anybody 'll tell me what you 're talking about, I shall be thankful," said his wife, folding her hands and looking at him. "*I* think you 're crazy."

"Don't know why I shouldn't be," said Farmer Graves, seating himself at the table and grimly surveying the empty plates. "All day cradlin' wheat, and not a speck o' lunch. Ain't been too busy to get dinner too, hev' ye ? "

"Lunch !" cried Mrs Graves, a light breaking over her. "I sent your lunch hours ago ! "

"Sent it—how 'd ye send it ? " said the farmer. "Shut the pail up and set it rollin' down hill ? It didn't roll *my* way, that 's all I know."

But at that Mrs Graves, finding her clue, and immensely relieved thereby, clapped her hands, and almost danced about the kitchen.

"You poor Ahab !" she said. "No wonder you 're cross. But see there—it 's all straight now, ain't it ? " and she placed her smoking dish before the disturbed farmer, hastily flanking it with an array of snowy potatoes and crimson beets and the greenest of green peas, with crisp lettuce and flaky bread, that might, altogether, have tempted a **far less** hungry man than the farmer.

Mr Graves made at first no reply to this appeal in words ; and it was not till deeds had carried him well on through his dinner that he began to think words might be desirable. Somewhat soothed and mollified by that time, he laid down his knife and fork, and leaning back in his chair, looked across the table at his wife, who on her part had been only playing with her dinner.

" *Was* I cross, 'Lizy ? " he said.

" Very ! "

" Well, a man who 'd be cross with a woman as kin get up a dinner like that," said Mr Graves, " has got a bear somewheres, for his distant relation ! "

Mrs Graves laughed a little at this rather masculine way of stating the debt and credit of a household, but other comment she made none.

" Thought the bear 'd got here instead o' me—now, didn't

ye?" said the farmer. "But come, 'Lizy—why on airth *didn't* ye send me that plaguy tin pail?"

"I told you I did send it," said Mrs Graves.

"What became of it, then?" said the farmer.

"Oh, well—you may as well know first as last," said his wife. "There was a boy here, Ahab, wanting a job, and I gave him sixpence, and your lunch."

"To eat?" said Mr Graves.

"No—nonsense!" said his wife. "To carry to you."

"And he kind o' made a mistake o' purpose, and went t'other way," said Mr Graves, nodding his head. "I see! Who was it, 'Lizy?"

"Well," said Mrs Graves, playing with her piece of bread, "it was one of those boys that want looking after."

"*He*'ll be looked after—if I ever catch him," said the farmer. "What—you don't mean one o' them young choke-cherries from Vinegar Hill?"

Mrs Graves gave an unwilling assent.

The farmer laughed till the tears came.

"That's just the best joke!" he said. "Why, 'Lizy, 'tain't hardly worth while takin' 'em into the house, when we kin hev' 'em so for nothin'! First they steal your chickens, and then they steal my lunch. Why, they couldn't do much more for us if we had 'em altogether!"

"That's just what I say!" said his wife, rousing up. "I say it's a crying shame to let those children go on so—just running to ruin as fast as their feet will carry them. It's like Farmer Dawson's patch of Canada thistles—seeding the whole country. I say it's a shame! And if we could pull up only one of 'em, there 'd be a thousand less seeds scattered next year."

"Love us! how she runs on!" said the farmer. "2.40 time, and nothing less! But I tell ye, 'Lizy, it's the prickliest kind o' work to pull up them 'ere thistles. Mow 'em down; that's the only way."

"And don't they start right up again, after you 've mowed them down?" said Mrs Graves.

"Well, what if they does?" said Mr Graves.

K

"Then I call it poor farming," said Mrs Graves, "doing work that won't stay done."

"Guess likely the work as you took in hand this mornin' 'll stay done," said the farmer. "'Tain't likely *he*'ll start up again for a spell. If ever I catch him, there'll be a little added to it. He'll get such a thrashin' that he'll think he didn't know what the word meant, afore."

"You'd better take some more pot-pie, Ahab," said his wife, with her merry laugh. "Do, for pity's sake, eat dinner enough to make you forget your lunch!"

"Ain't so easy to forget as you'd think," said Mr Graves acting, however, upon her prudent suggestion. "Cradlin' wheat since daylight, without so much as a quirlcake!"

"Well, think of those children, who *never* have any," said his wife, returning to the charge. "I don't see how you can sit there and eat your dinner in peace. Why, they'd never come after chickens and lunch, if they weren't half starved."

"Crazy—ravin' crazy—that's what *you* are," said the farmer. "Like to know why I shouldn't eat my dinner? *'Tis* mine, I s'pose, so long's I've got it."

"Well, Ahab," said his wife, "you know you did promise to drive me over there; and then we could find out what the children want, and stop their taking it in this dreadful way."

The farmer gave a sort of a grunt.

"'Fraid they want some things they ain't very like to get," he said. "And so'll you—if I don't cradle my wheat. 'Lizy—guess I'll take my own lunch along this afternoon. Might be somebody else come along as 'ud want it."

Mrs Graves shook her head at him, but she packed up the lunch as desired, and Mr Graves took it with a grumble.

"Needn't ha' kept the pail," he said. "S'pose he didn't want to eat *that*. Mebbe he thought 'twould come handy for a school pail—when he goes somewheres to learn the ten commandments."

The farmer shouldered his cradle and walked away, and his wife looked after him, smiling; but in her heart she felt that Vinegar Hill so far had been a failure.

CHAPTER VII.

SHE thought it was a failure, and in a sense that was true, but in another sense not. The sunbeams which never fall on the fruit, do yet help to mellow the air, and could the many powerless wishes be struck out of this world's atmosphere, the world would be far colder than it is. "In that it was in thine heart," said the Lord to David, "thou didst well that it was in thine heart." And from David's time down, I doubt if one true-hearted wish or purpose has ever quite fallen to the ground. Yes, it may fall indeed, as a seed does, hiding itself away, lost for a time, then to spring up and bear fruit.

But it was with a rather sad heart that Mrs Graves watched her husband away from the door that bright afternoon, and then turned back to the kitchen to clear away the remains of the feast.

"Yes, it would be nothing short of a feast to them," she said to herself, as plate after plate received the contents of the half-emptied dishes, ready to set by in the cellar. "And there's about enough here for half a dozen, now; Ahab always will have so much on the table. I wonder if *she'll* be at 'Society' to-day?"

And quickening her steps at the thought, Mrs Graves flew hither and thither like a very sprite, and had the dishes washed, and the kitchen in order, and herself dressed and back in the kitchen again before some people would have waked up fairly to what there was to do. In undoubted visiting trim this time she came, with snowy dress, and black mantilla, and a ruffly white sun-bonnet to crown all. Half smiling at herself, half vexed, the farmer's wife then went nimbly about from window to door, front door and side door and lower door; perfectly conscious that she was more anxious than usual to fasten up the house securely, and all inclined, if she could, to lay the blame of that upon the farmer himself.

"It's enough to make one nervous, the way he talks," she

said ; as having drawn the last window bolt, she stepped
out of the great back door, and locked that too, dropping
the key in her pocket. "Wish I could go round by the
wheat-field, but it's just the other way." And with a parting glance at all the weak points in her citadel, Mrs Graves
set forth in earnest for the house where "Society" met that
afternoon.

There was the usual gathering. Life-worn faces and toil-
worn hands ; earnest eyes and sober mouths, and foreheads
that had kept a certain high, calm quiet through all Time's
furrowing work. The minister's wife and the schoolmaster's
sister, and the sheriff's daughter, were all there ; with others
who had no special name, unless one derived from the broad
acres which their husbands tilled.

Among them all sat Mrs Kensett. It was her first
appearance at "Society," health, or some other reason having
always hindered her hitherto. And from the moment Mrs
Graves set eyes on her, she herself had neither eyes nor ears
for anybody else. Beginning at first in true "Society"
fashion, with only stolen glances across the top of her needlework, the farmer's wife was very near forgetting her work
altogether, before the meeting was far advanced. For Mrs
Kensett was a great study to her, a wonderful problem : this
little frail woman, so quiet looking, so retiring and unob-
trusive, so plain in her dress, and yet (if Jem Crook spoke
true) so familiar already in the courts which are not of earth.
Mrs Graves never forgot her for a single moment, and waited
with the most intense anxiety to hear her talk.

But Mrs Kensett seemed in no hurry to take the lead.
She kept steadily at her "seam," as the Scotch people say, a
very model for "Society" workers, putting in her word now
and then, looking up brightly when others spoke, but giving
not the least token of any intention to deliver a lecture on
Vinegar Hill, or the state of the world generally.

"She don't mean to teach us !" thought Mrs Graves,
despairingly. "And she'll never know how much I want
to learn !"

Click, click went the needles as before.

"There!" said a motherly-looking woman, capacious in heart as in dimensions, and holding up to view a small pattern of blue check, "there's one shirt done, anyway. Wonder who'll wear it, now? I never can finish off one o' these mites o' things, but I wish I could wrap up a blessin' in it. Poor little freezin' souls!"

"Why so you can," said Mrs Kensett, looking up with her bright smile. "That's the very thing to do. I don't believe those old times of the early church are so far past as people think; when the shadow of Peter and the handkerchief of Paul wrought such wonders."

"But those were miracles, Mrs Kensett," said the minister's wife.

"Yes," said the little lady, "they were visible ones. And the miracles now-a-days are unseen. I think that is much of the difference."

"Well, how in the world am I to put a blessin' in this?" said Mrs Peasely, again displaying the small shirt. "'Twon't stick."

"Stitch it in," said Mrs Kensett, with a smile. "Take every stitch, and fit every seam with a thought of prayer in your heart for the unknown little wearer. Money might slip out, and a book might get lost, but a prayer never!"

Mrs Graves dropped her work and looked, drinking in every word, watching the sudden roses that bloomed in the pale cheeks as if they had been veritable flowers from the other world.

"Do tell!" ejaculated the amased Mrs Peasely, once more holding up the blue shirt, and gazing into its folds as if to see where a blessing could possibly hide. "Now don't that just beat all?"

"But you don't think prayers get answered in *that* way, do you?" said the schoolmaster's daughter, while the minister's wife sat with uplifted brows, plying her needle at the "double quick."

"In every way!" said Mrs Kensett. "There is no possible way in which prayer has not been—may not be answered. No one word, no single thought of earnest, honest prayer ever fell to the ground unanswered."

" Stitch a blessing in !" repeated Mrs Peasely, once more. " Well, I never !"

There was a little silence after that ; people had nothing to say, or had too much, which was as bad, and it was Mrs Kensett at last who spoke.

" I am glad this subject has come up," she said, " for it touches something about which I wanted to take counsel with you all to-day. I am but a stranger, you know, and not so well acquainted with people and things here as the rest of you. What is the best way to get hold of those children on Vinegar Hill ?"

" Get hold on 'em ?" said a saturnine looking woman, after another pause of astonishment had marked the effect of Mrs Kensett's words. " Get hold on 'em ! You may be glad and thankful, too, if they don't get hold on you !"

" Yes, and that proves the need there is that we should begin first to get hold of them," said the lady, with a pleasant smile.

" Can't get ahead of Vinegar Hill," said the other speaker. " Why, 'twas only last week they cleared my clothes-line clean out !"

" And my duck-house," said another.

" And half his potato patch went last night," said a third. " Tell you what, he *was* real mad, for once."

" Yes, I know, but how shall we make them better ?" said Mrs Kensett.

" You think prayer won't do in this case," said the school-master's daughter.

Mrs Kensett flushed a little, but she answered steadily—

" Prayer can do all, where no work is possible, and only there. God is ready to do for us all that we cannot do—all that we *can*, He leaves in our hands."

" Well, I am glad Vinegar Hill isn't in my hands," said the girl, pertly. " Father says it 's quite impossible to reform such folks."

" What do you think, Mrs Peasely ?" said Mrs Kensett, turning to her.

"My dear," said the puzzled Mrs Peasely, "I don't know. When I hear you talk, I seem to think—and then again I *don't* know. One way's adoptin' some of 'em, right out. I wouldn't mind tryin' my hand a bit, if I hadn't got ten o' my own. And there *are* days, when it don't seem as if I could stand two or three additional. Ask Mrs Coon there, she knows. Why, she's picked up full six orphans out o' the mud, and washed 'em, and turned 'em out Christians."

"Ain't turned 'em out yet," said little Mrs Coon, trying to laugh off her confusion, at being thus brought into notice. "But that is all I can think of for Vinegar Hill. If we could take some of 'em right out, lift 'em up like, it might make a beginnin'."

"And who'd take care of us—with our houses full of thieves?" inquired she of the saturnine countenance.

"Well, you know we ain't just secure, now, by all accounts," said Mrs Coon, "and I guess maybe *that's* where Mrs Kensett thinks prayer would come in."

"Yours wasn't all first-class, to begin with," said Mrs Peasely.

"Mrs Coon has great skill," said the clergyman's wife, mingling her dignified words in the conversation. "I always wondered at her success. Why, one of those boys"——

"All six of 'em," interrupted Mrs Peasely.

"One of those boys," the lady began again, "was bad enough for Vinegar Hill. Mrs Coon has wonderful skill."

"I s'pose I had a knack at gettin' fond of 'em," said Mrs Coon, "but there ain't no skill about it. Give 'em a sight of Jesus, that's all. I guess most of 'em ain't worse'n that thief, afore he was on one cross, and saw the other. And it kind o' takes wonderful with 'em all, to think o' somebody's carin' for 'em."

Little Mrs Coon paused, and shrunk back again into her timid silence, and the rest sewed on without a word. Only upon Mrs Kensett's face there shone the light of a hidden smile of gladness.

When the silence was broken again, it was by a summons to tea.

CHAPTER VIII.

MRS GRAVES carried home no report of the meeting. She
kept her own counsel, and for a number of days did not even
mention Vinegar Hill. It was the farmer himself who next
broached the subject, coming home one night in not the best
of humours.

"I vow to patience," he said, "I'd like it if folks could
let folks be!"

"Who's been abusing you now, Ahab?" said his wife
with a laugh. "You've come back all standing, so far as I
can see."

"You don't see fur," said the farmer, "and likely 'tain't
fair to expect it of a woman, but then why kin't they let be
the ones as *kin* see?"

"Oh, it was a woman, was it?" said Mrs Graves.

"Yes, 'twas a woman," said the farmer, with a sort of
groan. "That's all the trouble. I'd settle a man, quick
enough. But what kin ye do with white muslin and sich?"

Mrs Graves laughed, beginning to have her own thoughts
as to what had happened.

"White muslin isn't much," she said, mockingly.

"That's accordin' to how you find it," said the farmer.
"Does look kind o' innocent in a bale, I'll allow; but float-
in' off in the air, ye see, is different."

"Did you meet a bale of white muslin floating off in the
air?" inquired Mrs Graves, with great solemnity. "Why
didn't you fetch it home? I want some new dresses."

"Now, 'Lizy, ye needn't to laugh," said the farmer. "No,
I guess 'twarn't a hull bale, though it looked a' most like it,
flickerin' here and there as the wind blew. And I didn't
fetch it home, 'cause I'd seen enough of it on the road.
Now, what d'ye think o' that?"

"I think you met the stranger lady," said Mrs Graves.
"She's the only one in the village that wears white every
day."

"Well, I just did," said the farmer. "And you wouldn't

believe, 'Lizy, but she asked me—up and down—to adopt some o' them Vinegar Hill scamps. 'Settin' an example to the neighbourhood,' she called it. Act'ally did. So says I, 'If I set 'em an example by takin' leave o' my wits, they'll some on 'em be slow to foller, likely.'"

"And what did she say to that?" inquired his wife, who was listening with more eagerness than she cared to show.

"She gave me a queer kind o' look first," said the farmer, "just as if she thought I knew so much better'n that, 'twarn't hardly worth while to tell me. And then she turned all sober like, and says she, 'Mr Graves, you never did anything that would more surely prove you a wise man, than to try to help those children.'"

"'Maybe 'twould,' says I, 'but I don't seem to see it.' Then another thought got hold of her, and says she, 'Wouldn't your wife like it? Would she mind the trouble?'"

"O Ahab, what did you say?" cried the little woman, clasping her hands. "Did you tell her I'd longed for it?"

"Well, no, I didn't," said the farmer, slowly. "She'd enough to say, 'thout my helpin' her on. I did tell her you was the lovin'est little soul in all the State, and a heap too good for anythin' that ever come out o' Vinegar Hill. And *would* ye think, 'Lizy, she said, 'So much the better, that's just what they want.'"

"Oh, she knows!" cried Mrs Graves again, with a look of delight. "Well, Ahab?"

"Well, 'Lizy," said the farmer, "what was the good o' my talkin' any more after that? I just come away."

"And was that all?" asked his wife. "Didn't she say any more?"

"Said enough, *I* thought," said the farmer. "No, 'twarn't quite all, 'Lizy—if ye must hear about it," he added, with some unwillingness. "She said a queer thing just as she was goin' away. I'd been tellin' her as how I couldn't afford it—hadn't got time, and that; and she turns right round upon me, and says she, 'Mr Graves, why do you put all your money out at the lowest interest ? *That* is not like a wise man.'"

"So, says I, firin' up a little, I don't! Somebody's telled you wrong. Always get the most for it I kin."

"'Ah, no!' says she, with her voice changing into a musical box, 'you told me so yourself! Mr Graves, "He that giveth to the poor, lendeth to the Lord, and that which he hath given, will He pay him again." And when the Lord pays, He gives higher interest than you can even begin to count.' And with that she come away, and I too."

"Feeling like a wise man?" inquired his wife, trying playfully to keep down and hide the various feelings that yet made her voice shake a little.

"No, I didn't," said the farmer; "I felt just like a fool, 'Lizy, if that's what you mean. Just the way with a woman's talk, always! Goes jiggerin' round, tumblin' all your ideas head over heels, knockin' 'em down faster'n you kin set 'em up."

"I wish some of 'em would stay knocked down!" said his wife, with a half laugh, though her eyes were wet. But she ran off to get the tea-pot, and said nothing more.

It was the afternoon of the next day, midway between the noon and the evening, that Mrs Graves was coming home from the field, whither she had been to carry her husband's second lunch. It was an expedition she was very fond of, on fine days, and when she was not specially busy; while the farmer on his part declared that the sight of her was better than twenty whetstones to his scythe, or an extra team to his plough. And the little woman took the greatest possible satisfaction in his work, which was always well and thoroughly done; and entered into the merits of some new machine, or the question of weeds, or the state of the crops, almost as intelligently as if she had been a farmer herself. That had been the way always. But of late, a new thread of feeling had come in, winding itself in and through and about all the rest; and there were times when the farmer's wife felt all this thrift and prosperity as a sort of burden, instead of a joy; times when the very richness and beauty

of the crops oppressed her. How little of that overflowing plenty they two could use, how small a part of its value would supply all their other wants! Were they putting out all their money at bad interest? for little as Mrs Graves knew of the matter, she felt, deep down in her heart, that the only sure investment was that of which Mrs Kensett had spoken. *That* interest would come to them, living or dead; but the other? some far-away cousin of the farmer's would have it all. She could not have put her thoughts in so many words, perhaps, but they swept over her none the less, as she stood looking across the fields that warm, sunshiny afternoon. One crop after another met her eyes, the green furrowed potatoes, and the waving maize, and the whitening buckwheat, with other fields all sunburnt and ready for the sickle, and others where the rough stubble showed—

"Three months of sunshine, bound in sheaves."

The reapers were bending to their work, the cows lowed softly from the distant hills, the air was one full low-toned chorus of twitter and hum and rustle and murmur, that was indescribably sweet. Mrs Graves listened and looked, leaning her arms on the long, weather-tinted rails at the bar place, then turned away with a sigh; and through her mind came floating long-forgotten words, heard she could not tell when:—"Thou shalt remember the Lord thy God, for it is He that giveth thee power to get wealth." How fully and sweetly they chimed in with the universal song!

Mrs Graves pushed her thoughts aside with another deepdrawn breath, and went swiftly down the road towards home. And as she went, turning quick round a sudden corner, she found herself within ten feet of Jem Crook, who, on his part, was taking a full-length siesta by the roadside.

Jem felt himself caught for once in his life. But his sharp, practised wits did not forsake him. Up he started, and, cap in hand, marched straight up to the farmer's wife, making her the profoundest of bows as he came on.

"Ain't I in luck, now!" he said. "Been down to the

place after yer, and was just resting here after my disappint, ma'am, and here yer be!"

"Been to the house after me!" repeated Mrs Graves, with no pleased sensation. "Did you want some more lunch?"

Jem's eyes twinkled in spite of him.

"Why, that's just it!" he cried. "I was a wantin' to see yer to tell yer how it was."

"I guess I know, without any of your telling," said Mrs Graves.

"You'd never guess!" said Jem Crook, lengthening his face about one half; "why, the chap as come and took it from me was a reg'lar seven-footer, a tramp he was, too, and o' course I couldn't do a thing. Did fight long's I durst, and then the feller keeled me over, and when I come to he was gone."

The boy's cool effrontery was inimitable. Mrs Graves laughed, and could not help it.

"Now, listen, Jem Crook," she said. "You know that there isn't one word of that true, and *I* know that it's no use for boys to come telling such stories to me. You poor, forlorn child! did nobody ever teach you better? What would Mrs Kensett say to your doing such things?"

But with that, Jem took to his heels and ran.

———

CHAPTER IX.

So passed on the last days of summer, and white frosts began to deck the fields by night, and red and yellow leaves flapped gayly in the brisk autumn wind. Butternuts sprinkled the grass with their olive green, and chestnuts slipped silently from their prickly homes, and hid away in the dry leaves beneath. But neither chestnuts nor butternuts lay long. First in the field were the squirrels, who, as they worked "for dear life," and never lost a minute, and never made the mistake of lugging home an empty nut, naturally had the most complete success. They could reach, too, all those extreme clusters and topmost twigs where even Vinegar Hill feared to climb. But if "Eclipse was first," it was by no means true that the rest were "nowhere." Farmer Graves declared, on the contrary, that they were everywhere; his largest nuts, his favourite trees, his most secret spots of woodland, discovered—rifled—carried off—past help. The farmer strove in vain for even his fair share.

"You needn't to fret over them young vagabonds *this* winter, 'Lizy," he said, one night, as he brought in the milk pails. "If the chickens gives out, and they gets tired o' ducks, they can do for a spell on biled chestnuts."

"Well, they don't know any better," said Mrs Graves, excusingly; "or at least not so much better as they might."

"No—not so much better as they might," said the farmer; "that's it exactly. If they was rolled round a little in some o' them 'ere chestnut burrs they're so fond of, they'd know considerable better, I expect. I vow, I think Vinegar Hill could turn out a boy for every tree on the place!"

"Never mind," said his wife, soothingly; "I mean never mind the chestnuts. I wish we could mind the boys, I'm sure."

"I'll mind 'em!—when I get a chance," said the farmer.

"But, Ahab," said Mrs Graves, "if everybody that could would take one of those boys, then *they* would help improve the others."

The farmer gave a grunt of extreme scorn and disapproval, and applied himself to his supper.

"Everybody that kin, may," he said. "I ain't one o' the kind. How're ye goin' to do it, to start with? Ask an eel to come and live with ye and do chores—maybe he'll come."

"But Ahab," said his wife again, "if you won't do that, and if you won't let me go there—why not let some of 'em come here once or twice a week? I could teach them some things, I know."

"Love ye!" said the farmer, "ain't they here every livin' day, as it is? If there's a foot on the hull farm where they *don't* go, I'd like to know it and go there myself. 'Once or twice a week,' she says!"—and again the disturbed farmer found words too small for his feelings.

"Well, we've got enough still," said his wife. "And so we should if we had one of the boys here in the house."

"That's as you think," said the farmer. "But I ain't quite rich enough yet to hev my pocket picked every day. Even 'once or twice a week' would be more than's agreeable."

"But you know what Mrs Kensett said," persisted his wife.

"She's another woman," said Mr Graves, turning the question out upon that broad, unfenced waste of stones and thistles.

"If I had one of those children here," said Mrs Graves, "just at first it wouldn't be all pleasant, I dare say, but after a while it would make the house so cheerful you wouldn't know it."

"Think likely," said the farmer. "Question is what 'ud become of me? S'pose *I*'d be so cheerful, I wouldn't know myself."

"Now, Ahab, say you'll let me try!" urged his wife.

"No, I won't," said Mr Graves; "and that's just where it is. I don't never object, 'Lizy, to *your* chuckin' money out o' the window, whenever you take a notion; and you know I don't; but I ain't agoin' to have other folks doin' it, and 'tain't no sort o' use wheedlin' me round. I won't,—and there's an end."

"Well, will you drive me over there to-morrow afternoon and let me see the place?" said Mrs Graves. "Come, Ahab —please do! And then I'll promise to be quiet for a whole month to come."

"'That 'ud be somethin' worth payin' for!" said the farmer with a sort of resigned desperation. "That'll be to the first day o' winter, mind. Yes! I'll drive ye—as you drive me— all over creation!"

With which unpromising promise Mrs Graves was so much delighted, that she was very near executing an impromptu and highly original dance on the kitchen floor, before the eyes of the astonished farmer.

But the next day *was* a day of promise; with that wonderful hush in which autumn enwraps the world, and the golden glory of the sunlight, and a faint, faint haze, in which even the leafless trees looked glowing and tender. Mr Graves went to the field with a groan for his (to be) lost afternoon, and his wife sang over her work from the time he went till he came again. She cooked him the nicest of dinners, and made him the daintiest of puddings; but Mr Graves seasoned it all with a sauce of his own compounding, which somewhat impaired the effect.

Mrs Graves, however, was too much elated to mind trifles; and she chattered away all dinner-time, in a fashion that even turned some of the farmer's groans into a laugh. And a far more disturbed man than he might have relented, a while later, when the little woman came out in bright crimson dress and ribbons of a deeper shade, and danced up to her place in the waggon, one could hardly tell how.

"If you ain't on wires this day," said Farmer Graves, mounting to his own seat, "then *I* ain't learned in machinery. What ye going to do, 'Lizy, now we're off?"

"Why, we're going to Vinegar Hill!" said the little woman.

"I ain't likely to forget that," said Mr Graves—"no more'n that I *ain't* goin' to plough. But what d'ye expect to do?"

"Well, I'm going to see the place, first," said Mrs Graves; "you're going to drive me all round it, slowly, so that I can see. And then I'm going to look at every child I meet, and study 'em all I can, and find out all about 'em I can."

"Here's an afternoon's work!" said Mr Graves. "What good'll all that do ye? Kin't come round me that way."

"I'm not trying to come round you any more, Ahab," said his wife, a touch of sadness coming into her voice. "I want to see and study," she went on, slowly. "I want to think if maybe there's some little thing I can do, without taking any of your time or money—or doing anything you wouldn't like."

And at that Farmer Graves touched up his horse to a good rattling speed.

"'Tain't *my* money," he said, huskily. "It's every dollar of it yourn—just as much, and more. What's the use o' talkin' like that?"

But his wife sat looking off at the hazy hill-sides—"with a smile on her lips, and a tear in her eye"—and answered never a word.

"Do what you like with it," he said. And Mrs Graves knew that he meant it—and didn't mean it,—and accepted both conditions with a little stir of both love and sorrow in her heart, as a woman must.

"One sinner destroyeth much good," was certainly true of Vinegar Hill, so far as atmosphere was concerned. Long before they were fairly at the edge of the hamlet, the sweet autumn air lost its sweetness, and came freighted with the smell of burnt leather, or burning straw, or the fumes of bad cooking, or of tobacco ; or else heavy with a sort of chaos of scents, made up one was glad not to know how. The grassy roadside, which had been so fresh and clean, was trodden now, and strewn with rags and shreds and broken glass and bones. Half-starved dogs prowled sulkily about, or rushed in hot haste after the waggon ; looking as if they could, upon occasion, enact the part of wolves with good success. And by the road, and on the fences, and under the bushes everywhere, were half-clad dirty children of all ages—tangled, hungry, and foul. They rolled on the grass, they cheered on the dogs, they threw stones at the waggon, or shouted and jeered as it went by.

"O Ahab!" his wife cried, "what a place!"

"Ay, ain't it!" said the farmer. "And this ain't only the outside. I shan't drive in, 'Lizy. Might be too much for ary one on us. And I guess you kin see enough, most anywheres round here."

"Oh, *do* look at the children!" cried Mrs Graves again, clasping her hands. "I never saw anything like it in all my life!"

"O' course not—just as I telled ye," said the farmer.

"And the Lord wants to borrow money and time and labour for these children," said Mrs Graves, in a tone as if she were half-dreaming. "That's what she said, Ahab; it sounds so strange!"

But to that the farmer made no reply. He had checked his horse at the main entrance to the hamlet, and before them lay a labyrinth of huts and stunted bushes; the one half hiding the other; and the one seemingly as full as the other of child-life. Such child-life as Vinegar Hill could show.

"Ahab," said his wife, suddenly, "would you be afraid to have me come as far as this—if I'd promise not to go a step further?"

"Shan't do it!" said the farmer. "Ain't there nothin' else pretty as ye kin find to look at?"

"I don't want to look," said his wife, sighing. "I want to teach these children something—how to wash their faces and mend their frocks, if I couldn't anything else. I don't know much, myself."

"Not quite everything, yet," said Mr Graves, with superior wisdom. "And this ain't just the best place for ye to learn. 'Tain't a place for a man to go—let alone a woman. Nobody hadn't ought to—without it's folks like themselves—and they'd ought to stay away."

"Ahab!" cried his wife, "I saw a bit of a white frock off yonder in the bushes!"

"Maybe they've been and stolen yourn—since we come out," said the farmer.

"See here, little boy," said the irrepressible Mrs Graves, beckoning to one of the children—"who is that I saw in the white dress?"

"Her that used to be a stranger in the village," said the child, approaching the waggon. "Molly Limp's sick, and she comes reg'lar. Real good she is, and tells lots o' stories."

"What's the matter with Molly Limp?" inquired Mrs Graves.

"She ain't much—that's all I knows on," says the boy. "And days she's wus, and says she's goin' 'way off"—and the child waved his unwashed hand up towards the fair blue sky, all shining with the sunset.

"*Where's* she going?" said Farmer Graves, somewhat awed and startled.

"I don' know," the boy answered. "Some place where the lady telled her of. And I say I wouldn't mind goin' myself, if I was her. Looks kind o' grand—when there's stars and clouds."

There came floating softly by, as he spoke, bright drifts of coloured light—they seemed hardly more substantial; and the west flamed up with crimson, and the blue between shone fairer than ever, with dashes of opal and bands of green. Grand?—Oh how grand even the visible heavens seemed, with their flush, and tremour, and glow, over that dark spot of earth! Mrs Graves glanced hastily up, and then her head sank, and she began searching in her pockets for she could not well see what. The farmer caught the look, and it chafed him.

"You're a large boy—o' your size!" he said, surveying the small soiled specimen before him. "How does she know she is a-goin' to get there?"

"How d'ye know yer ain't?" responded he of Vinegar Hill with a grin, and Mr Graves had nothing to say. If Molly Limp's certainty were even but equal to his uncertainty, as it struck home at that moment, why even then the poor child among the bushes was far richer than the owner of all his fair fields. And Neddy Flint, reclining by the roadside, knew that his shot had told.

"When you get through, 'Lizy," said Mr Graves, with some impatience, "we'll go. Don't know as *you've* got nothin' to do at home—but I *hev.*"

And Mrs Graves hurriedly let fall upon Neddy Flint a small avalanche of cake, and spoke not a word more until they reached home.

CHAPTER X.

THE winter set in early. A few more bright days, a mere touch of Indian summer, and then the wind, and the clouds, and the snow, seemed to take possession. Early and late the farmer and his men pressed on the out-door work, and early and late wrought the farmer's wife at her in-door occupations. Pumpkin pies, and hulled corn, and baked apples, took the place of summer dainties, and were just as welcome to the owner of all this abundance ; the big wheel spun merrily round, throwing off its blue yarn for stockings, and its clouded mitten yarn, and its finer white thread for the use of Mrs Graves herself. With all her wonted skill, and thrift, and industry, she kept everything under way ; and the house and farm had never looked more smiling and prosperous. Was the mistress of the house as smiling as ever? Farmer Graves sometimes asked himself the question, and could not tell. He would have been in no doubt had he seen her when she was alone. For often then, there was a shadow of thought upon her face, and her eyes gave wistful glances through the shut windows ; and the loaded tables, and filled store-rooms and heaped up bins, sometimes called forth a sigh that was very deep and real. Loaded waggons or sleds went weekly to the village market-place ; and cattle were driven away for sale, and prancing horses left the barn-yard with new owners ; and on them all, Mrs Graves seemed to see written—"Low interest." "A bad investment." Who would be the better of all this money that was daily coming in ?—not even themselves, for they had enough before. And the snow lay deep on the smooth fields, and the wind roared and raved round the well-built farm-house, trying in vain to get in. But at Vinegar Hill?—Mrs Graves shivered sometimes as the thought came over her, and the farmer would pile on more wood, and say—

"Why, 'Lizy, you're cold!" and she would answer "No," and make her knitting-needles fly till they were a mere twinkle in the firelight. She kept her word well, and never even mentioned Vinegar Hill till that month was over. Nor indeed after that, having little heart to do it any more. If she had had her will, half the turkeys on the place would have gone to the children among the bushes; but they went to market instead; and the others came, one by one, upon the farm-house table, cooked just as the farmer liked them, and bearing no token of the sighs with which they had been basted. Mrs Kensett had gone back to town for the severe weather, and the farmer's wife thought and thought of Molly Limp, sick, alone, perhaps even already taking her flight "'way off!" beyond snow and storm and winter. Or, if on earth still, were that child's bare, weary feet walking in paths of love and knowledge, where her own busy and happy steps had never entered? Once or twice she did try for another expedition to Vinegar Hill, pleading the sick child's need; but the farmer had no mind to cross lances again with any of those young Arabs. He was always "threshing," or "chopping," or "hauling wood;" apples or potatoes or pork or wheat were always in the way; and the sturdy farm teams went merrily on through the snow to mill and to market and to the forest, but never even tried to break the road to Vinegar Hill. The white drifts lay there unstirred, and the farmer's wife looked wistfully across them, and wondered what might be going on beyond. Then she grew restless and superstitious; eyeing the money her husband brought home as if it were already rusted, and shaking out her closet stores every week or two, with a sudden fear of moths.

"Do *you* have much bother with 'em?" she inquired of little Mrs Coon one day at "Society." And the shy doer of kind deeds answered with a laugh that moths never could find anything to eat in *her* house.

"'Tain't full o' waste things, you know," she said, in explanation. "He's well enough off, too, and there's enough comes into the house—but I tell him I never can keep a thing ten minutes if I ain't wearin' it. And not always then! That's the best way *I* know to air your goods," said Mrs Coon, with one of her sudden blushes. "Put 'em on poor folks, and it'll get done to purpose."

Doubtless that was the best way!—if one only could! as Mrs Graves thought to herself. What had come over her husband lately? he was not used to be so close-handed. Had his views changed? or was it hers? It seemed sometimes as if he thought she was in league with all Vinegar Hill against his purse. Yes, he had changed. "The thorns sprang up with it"—there was a deep truth in that, which his wife did not know.

Neddy Flint had made the most of his load of cake, not only in the way of eating, but also of talking. And by degrees, the story—drifting about in the hamlet, and magnified now by the addition of a ham and two loaves of bread —came to the ears of Peter Limp's father. Things had gone ill with the man of late, his thirst for drink increasing as his funds ran low. Everything available had passed into the hands of James Dodd, until little remained in the house but wife and children; and now as they were not saleable, Limp thought to turn them to account in another way. Neddy Flint's story had started a new idea.

And so it was, that towards the end of a stinging January day, Mrs Graves saw a strange little procession approaching the house—if procession that might be called which consisted only of two. A tall, thin boy, in trousers much too short, and jacket to match, with the veriest wreck of old boots on his feet. Slowly toiling on, for the snow was deep and dry as sand, he dragged behind him a rough sledge, on which was a basket and a little bundle of rags and face. So it seemed to Mrs Graves as she looked out. In another second she was at the door.

"What in the world have you got there?" she cried out. "Is that a child?"

"Guess likely," said the boy, pausing to take breath, "seein' it's Moll."

"But you'll kill her, dragging her about in this weather," cried the farmer's wife again, as she looked at the little face, which was almost as white as the snow-drifts.

"And father'd kill her if she didn't come," answered Peter; "so it's take yer choice, and not pay nothin' extry."

Mrs Graves darted down to the side of the sled, and, picking up the little bundle, bore it back into the house.

"Are you frozen to death, child?" she said.

"I's cold," said Molly, through her blue lips. Then rousing herself—

"O Peter, we mustn't stop! We must hurry; mother'll be so cold!"

"Where is your mother?" said Mrs Graves, who had the child in her lap, and was trying to disentangle her from a mass of patches and patchwork that made Molly look as if she were packed in a rag-bag. "Is she out, too?"

"*She's* home," said Peter, "and that's her petticoat. She put it round Moll, unbeknown to father, when we started."

"And oh, she'll want it so bad!" cried little Molly, trying to work her way down to the floor.

"She won't care," said Mrs Graves, with a sudden assumption of motherly knowledge, "sit still, child. What did your father try to freeze you to death for?"

"He'd drinked up all there was in the house," said Peter, "and o' course he can't never stand *that*. And then Molly and me was started off to find somethin' some place else."

"Do you mean he sent you out to beg?" said Mrs Graves.

"Guess he warn't partic'lar as to how we got it," answered Peter, with a laugh. "But there ain't much lyin' round now, without it's snow."

Mrs Graves was quite beyond words. She set Molly down in the chair, and brought out bread and bowls, and warmed some milk, making the children eat a good hearty meal, watching them pitifully the while, and quite at her wit's end what to do.

"And if I were to dress Molly all up warm," she said, "would your father take the things away?"

"Swaller 'em afore you could count three," said Peter, expressively. "Why, he'd drink up that 'ere petticoat, if he could once get a hold on it."

"We's got to take it in careful," said Molly, with an anxious look.

"Goin' to hev more snow, 'Lizy," rang out a cheerful voice

at the door, and in came Farmer Graves, stamping his feet to clear them from a share of the white drift, and bearing two foaming pails of milk. The thin, half-clad children looked at the pails, and at him, with a wistful admiration that again took from the farmer's wife all power of speech. She stood by Molly, choking down her tears as best she might. The farmer's brow clouded a little.

"Didn't know as ye had company," he said, "or I wouldn't hev come in so unceremonious. Be they goin' to stay to supper?"

And Mrs Graves, with her quick woman's instinct, answered—

"No, I've given them some bread and milk." Then, self-control giving way a little—

"O Ahab!" she cried, softly, following him into the pantry, "mayn't I keep the little one all night?"

"S'pose she gets sick afore morning?" said Mr Graves, handling the heavy pails as if they had been toys. "What then?"

"Then I'll take care of her," said Mrs Graves, boldly.

"Think likely you would," said the farmer, dryly, "and afore the next night you'd have the extra pleasure o' takin' care o' the hull family. Never know where you'll stop, if you begin feedin' crows."

"But, Ahab"—urged his wife.

"You just run back into the kitchen, and see they don't put *that* in their pockets," said Mr Graves, "and I'll come t'ye."

So Mrs Graves went back, and held out Molly's poor little feet to the fire, and bade Peter come nearer and warm himself well, thinking busily how she could do.

"Ahab," she said, as her husband came from the pantry, not waiting for him to speak, "they'll freeze to go home so, at least the little one will; it's growing colder and colder. And their father drinks up everything they get, and how in the world shall I manage?"

Vexed as he was, the farmer could not help chuckling, privately, at the neat way in which his wife had drawn him in.

"Bless ye, 'Lizy," he said, "they're used to it! Didn't freeze comin', did ye?" he added, bending down by Molly; "and t'ain't no farther back." But, getting a good look at the child's face, Farmer Graves straightened himself up again hastily, his own face very grave indeed.

"What d'ye ask me for?" he said, with a vexed sort of protest in his voice. "How kin I tell? Drinks it all up, does he? I wouldn't wonder. Kin't ye give 'em a little for him to drink up, and a good deal to hide for 'emselves?"

Mrs Graves clapped her hands, in a sort of struggle of tears and laughter.

"You're just the best Ahab that ever was!" she cried. "Now if I can only manage to do it"——

"*That's* easy," said Peter Limp, bringing his experience to bear. "We'll take somethin' in hand, yer see, and then lose t'other things by the way, and find 'em agin, when father's off to old Dodd's."

"*He's* used to the business!" the farmer muttered, his face clouding over once more. "Come, 'Lizy, hurry up! 'Tain't exactly the time o' day to count your fingers. Time they was right off."

In haste, with dim eyes, Mrs Graves ran hither and thither, giving the children bread and meat to take in hand, and yet more, both of food and clothes, to be "lost" by the way.

"The moths won't ever get *this!*" she thought, joyfully, as she wrapped a warm cloak round Molly, bidding her be sure and keep it out of her father's sight. Then lifting the child in her arms, she carried her out to the little sled, and packed her on it in the best way she could. And the farmer followed helplessly, and looked on. When his wife once took things into her own hands, he was no match for her.

The weather had changed for the worse. Dull gray clouds hid all the sky, and the wind blew fitfully across the drifts, bringing flurries of dry snow. Labouring on through the gathering night went the little sled; a mere speck at first upon the white, and then beyond ken altogether. But even then, the farmer's wife still stood looking.

"I've done all I can!" she said to herself. And then Mrs Kensett's words came back to her, bringing a sense of comfort; and with a strange, new eagerness she ran away to her room, to lay off the burden of all that she could not do upon the Lord.

And the night settled down upon the bright farmhouse, and upon the wild, rough bushes on Vinegar Hill.

"Well got along with, 'Lizy," said Farmer Graves, as he stirred his cup of smoking tea. "If I'd been a half hour late to-night, you'd hev had 'em on your hands, and no mistake. It's snowin' now right down, and so dark you kin't tell which is sky and which ain't. And if there's anybody in town makes better short-cakes than these be," added Mr Graves, helping himself liberally, "I'd like to know it."

"*He that received seed among the thorns is he that heareth the word; and the cares of this world, and the deceitfulness of riches, choke the word, and he becometh unfruitful.*"

PLANTS WITHOUT ROOT.

PLANTS WITHOUT ROOT.

———◇———

CHAPTER I.

"Some fell upon stony places, where they had not much earth: and forthwith they sprung up, because they had no deepness of earth: and when the sun was up, they were scorched; and because they had no root they withered away."

You cannot make anything grow, you cannot make anything stand long, upon the mere surface of things. The house must have a foundation, the plant must have a root, or neither the one nor the other will ever be worth much. For a little while, in the quietness of good weather, they may seem to endure—while indeed as yet there *is* nothing to endure; but the storm and the heat will do their work sweepingly when they come. Therefore make sure that all your hope is built upon Christ, the only Rock foundation—make sure that you are "rooted and grounded" in Him. For—

"If my house is built upon the Rock,
I know it shall stand for ever!"

Well, the children had received their Bibles; carrying them off in great triumph, as the first real possession many of them had ever had: and Jemmy Lucas had already contrived a hiding-place for his, and Peter Limp and little Molly sat together on the old door-stone.

"And you'll read to me every day, Peter?" the little one was saying. "And we'll set right out, and wait for nobody."

"Don't see no use in waitin', that's a fact," said Peter. "We was to set out, she said."

"And then we was to keep on," said Molly.

"In course," Peter assented. "Guess I won't want to turn back, for one. 'Tain't so dreadful pleasant here. Where's we to begin, Molly?"

"Oh, with beggin' the King to help us," said Molly.

"That's good work for you," said Peter; "yer's got so little to do. 'Cause I's got to look out for us both."

"Yes, and it's good you're goin' too," said Molly; "you's so big, and I's so little."

"Good I's goin' too!" echoed Peter. "'Spose I warn't? —guess likely you wouldn't try settin' out alone?"

"Oh yes, I would," said Molly, seriously. "I's got to. The King sent word, Peter."

"Who'd help ye over the bad spots?" said Peter, looking at her.

"Oh, He'd have to do it all Hisself then, you know," said Molly, gazing up into the evening sky, as if the difficulty did not trouble her much.

"Yer'd look well at that," said Peter—"botherin' the King with your slow steps. Like t'see ye!"

The child looked at him wistfully, but had no answer ready.

"You pay attention, Moll," said Peter, encouragingly, "and I'll get ye along. 'Cause you and me's got to be reg'lar and diff'rent."

"I'd like it," said Molly. "How, Peter?"

"Guess 't'll be most every how," said Peter, with a knowing shake of the head. "We's got to toe the mark, sharp!"

"I's glad," said Molly again. "Oh, I's so tired o' hearin' 'em swear!"

"'Tain't none o' yer business what they does," said Peter. "Guess likely yer own concerns 'll give ye consid'rable to do. And we's got to be hush about it, too, Moll, or it 'll be too many for us. There's father now—what d'ye s'pose he'd say?"

"I's going to tell him, though," said Molly. "The King's asked him too."

"Yer ain't a-goin' to do never sich a thing," said Peter, sternly. "Why he'd shut both on us up quicker'n yer could wink. Get t' the kingdom fast, that way, yer would!"

"But the King could get us out," said Molly. "He can do everything, Peter."

"Don' know about that," said Peter, with another shake of the head. "He might could and He mightn't would. 'Taint safe to count. We'll set out, Molly, me and you, and creep along so nobody won't think nothin' at all."

"But they'll see if you does different," said Molly. "And I don't want to creep, Peter—I wants to hurry."

"Hurry along then!" said Peter, something sharply. "It's a fust-rate chance—father's comin'." And the two children disappeared into the twilight, just as Walter Limp's staggering form came in sight.

"Hist!—Molly!" said Peter, from one bush.

"I's here, Peter," whispered little Molly, from another.

"We'll start all fair in the morning," whispered Peter in turn. "I's got to go now and meet the fellers."

And Peter started off, and Molly crept slowly into the house, and sat down and watched her father from the farthest corner she could find.

Walter Limp was in one of his worst moods that night. He sat himself down by the table, and made that and the room and the very house itself ring with his wild stormy outbreaks. Mrs Limp listened trembling, as was her wont on such occasions; her needle flying in and out with frightened, nervous haste; and Molly looked on, shuddering, from her corner. This was no time to tell anything!—nor even to move, if she could help it; and Molly shut her eyes and thought, and tried not to hear, and could not help it. But oh, joyful remembrance! next day she was to set out for the King's house! and no such sights and sounds would ever trouble her there. No more tired shoulders, no more aching head; and as thought after thought swept through the child's mind, with visions of white robes and golden streets, little Molly's head drooped quite down upon the old board floor, and in dreams she was already in the kingdom.

Later in the night, when her father had stormed himself quiet, Molly roused up to find herself laid on her little heap of straw in the next room, and her mother softly loosening the few fastenings of her frock. The pinched, care-worn face that bent over her ; the baby's faint wailing from the next room ; the smoking, guttering tallow candle—poor little Molly !—it seemed a harsh awaking. She shut her eyes again with a heavy sigh, and——

"Oh, I wish we *was* there !" broke from her lips.

"What 's it, Molly ? what 's it, dear ?" whispered Mrs Limp under her breath. "Don't make no noise !—what you want, love ?"

"It 's so fur to the King's house !" sighed Molly, and again the weary child dropped off to sleep, and her wondering mother stood and watched her.

It was one of Walter Limp's peculiarities—not too uncommon a one, alas—that he never chose to be at home, except just when he was least of all fit to be there. The moment he got past that point in his drunken fit when his mere presence was a curse and a terror, that moment he went off to regain the lost ground as speedily as possible. So when Molly crept from her little bed next morning, the house was very still. Mrs Limp sat hushing the baby, and a small dish of porridge stood waiting on the hearth.

"There ain't no bread, dear," said Mrs Limp, trotting the baby up and down. "He 's eat it all, Molly. And there warn't but a crumb, anyway."

But this morning Molly did not care. She sat down on the floor, and began taking spoonfuls of porridge, thinking the while of her bright dreams and the dingy waking reality.

"Mother, where 's Peter ?" she said at last.

"Took his breakfast and went," said Mrs Limp.

"When 's he comin' back ?"

"Why, I don't know, no more 'n the dead," said Mrs Limp

"Don't *they* know nothin'?" said Molly.

"Dear heart!" said poor Mrs Limp, "how's I to tell that neither? I ain't quite dead myself yet." And Mrs Limp wiped her face and trotted the baby, with an air that said she wouldn't be very sorry to have that, quite, come.

"We'd know if we followed on, she telled us," said Molly, musing. "And we was to set out, and keep on, and bime-by we'd be there. Mother, how fur *is* it, you s'pose?"

"Fur?" said Mrs Limp, "to Peter?"

"To the King's house," said Molly.

"The King's house?" repeated the astonished Mrs Limp. "When I know where it is, I'll tell ye."

"It's a great ways—I knows that," said Molly, still half to herself. "But we's got to go. Oh, there's Peter!—now we's off!"

And Molly left her unfinished cup of porridge, and ran out of the house at a rate so much quicker than common, that Mrs Limp looked after her with a weak feeling of fear that the care of a crazy child was about to be added to her other troubles. But nothing mattered very much now.

"You's so late, Peter!" Molly was saying, catching hold of Peter's jacket by its depending fringe.

"Late!" quoth Peter, "guess likely as I was up time enough to see *you* in bed."

"I's up now, though," said Molly.

"Well, and yer ain't much to see, if yer is," said Peter, surveying his little sister, whose face, however, looked bright and almost beautiful that morning.

"But we's got to set out to-day, Peter," said the child. "Where's the books?"

"Safe enough," said Peter. "Just you wait a bit till the boys is off, Molly—I'll fetch 'em."

And Molly sat down upon the door-step in the morning sun, and waited; and even as those golden beams came on, so higher and higher rose upon her little weary life the promise—

"Unto you that fear My name, shall the Sun of Righteousness arise, with healing in His wings."

M

CHAPTER II.

"The place where he read," as the Bible says, was the fifth of Matthew. Mrs Kensett had put a mark there, among other places ; and there Peter opened the book and began to read ; now very loud, as he had learned in his brief schooling ; and then dropping his voice to a whisper, afraid to be overheard.

"What 's multitudes ?" said Molly, stopping him at almost the first word.

"All the folks there was, guess likely," said Peter. "But don't ye ask too many questions, Moll, 'cause there 's lots o' hard words here I don't know myself ; so we 'll just skip 'em by, I guess, till we comes to them we *does* know."

"But don't really skip 'em," said Molly. "Read 'em all out, Peter, they sounds good."

So Peter read out the long list of blessings—not one of which rested on a single head in all Vinegar Hill. The "pure in heart," the "peacemakers," the "merciful"—where were they to be found in that community of foul deeds and words, of cruelty and fighting ?

"Guess likely this here ain't meant for us," said Peter, with a sudden pause—some feeling of contrast reaching him even through the hard words. "Yer see, Moll, part's for some, and part's for t'others."

"She didn't say so," said Molly. "And we 's got to learn 'em all. Read on, Peter."

Peter read on : "'Ye are the light of the world'"—but who knew what that meant at Vinegar Hill ?

"'Whosoever therefore shall break one of these least commandments, and shall teach men so, he shall be called the least in the kingdom of heaven.'"

"There !" cried Molly, "that 's just what she said. 'The least little thing'—don't you remember, Peter ? We wasn't to do the least little thing the King didn't like."

"Swearin' and sich," said Peter.

"Oh, she said, '*that* was a great big thing !'" said Molly.

"Easiest done o' anythin' *I* know," said Peter. "Why it slips out o' a feller's mouth afore he knows it's there. Tain't not nigh so hard as liftin' chickens."

"Well, you's got to do it no more, anyway," said Molly.

"That's a fact," said Peter. "Here it is, Moll, sure as guns : I say unto you, 'Swear not at all.' Ain't this here just the queerest book for trippin' a feller up ?"

"Oh, I wish I could read it too!" said Molly, peering over at the mysterious black marks.

"Why, I'll read to ye," said Peter. "Saves yer the trouble, Moll."

"But you read to yourself all the time," said Molly, watching him, as Peter's eye, caught and fascinated by the strange things, went wandering over the page.

"It do beat all!" he burst forth. "This here book's enough to make a feller jump ! Just you open yer ears, Moll, for once." And Peter read—

"'Ye have heard that it hath been said, Thou shalt love thy neighbour, and hate thine enemy : but I say unto you, Love your enemies, bless them that curse you, do good to them that hate you, and pray for them that despitefully use you and persecute you.'"

"Then I's got to pray for Sam Dodd," was little Molly's comment, after a wondering pause. "O Peter ! ain't it good words !"

"Don' know yet," said Peter, "some on 'em 's too dreadful hard for my likin'.'

"What's next ?" said Molly.

"Sounds like some sort o' givin' a reason for it, like." said Peter ; "but it don't make it come no handier to do."

"'That ye may be the children of your Father which is in heaven ; for He maketh His sun to rise on the evil and on the good, and sendeth rain on the just and on the unjust.' Now what d' yer think o' that ?"

But Molly did not answer. Rough as the voice was and untaught the accent, the words fell like music, and Peter's stumbling speech and imperfect reading could not hide the wonderful love of God, which sounded 'hrough every one

"The children of your Father which is in heaven." Molly shut her eyes and sat wrapt in invisible sunshine, hearing angels sing.

"That's a'most the end o' this here part," said Peter Limp, with a perplexed glance and shake of the head at his little sister. "I don't just make out the rest. 'Be ye therefore perfect, even as your Father which is in heaven is perfect.'"

"What's perfect, Peter?" said Molly, without opening her eyes.

"Oh, I didn't know but yer was gone off to sleep," said Peter. "Why, perfect's got nothin' bad into it, yer see. If it's an apple it ain't specked, and if it's pertaters they ain't false-hearted, and biles all right, jest as them did out o' old Peasely's lot."

"But this ain't things, Peter," said Molly.

"Sounds like folks," said Peter, studying the verse and reading it aloud once more, to help his understanding.

"How'd people be, if *they* was perfect?" said Molly, shutting her eyes again, but this time to think.

"Whew!" said Peter, going back to his definition— "they'd be *some*, wouldn't they! 'thout specks, and bilin' all right—guess I can't even begin to think."

"But we've got to be," said Molly. "That's what it says, Peter. 'The children of your Father'—that's the Great King. O Peter, ain't it good!"

"Fust-rate," said Peter, "if a feller knowed how to come at it."

"*She* telled us to ask," said little Molly, thoughtfully. "And I's done it, too. Read some more, Peter."

"Guess, I'd better try another place," said Peter, "and see if it's easier."

So Peter turned on, passing one mark and another which Mrs Kensett had put in, until he came to almost the last in the book.

"Now this here's a good way off, yer see, Moll," he said; "so guess likely it'll turn out different. 'My little children, these things write I unto you, that ye sin not.'"

"Don't sound to be much odds, neither," said Peter, rubbing his head in a puzzle. "One says, 'Be perfect,' and t'other says, 'Sin not.' They's as like as two peas."

"Well, she said that too," said Molly, studying the difficult question. "She said the King didn't like nothin' bad."

"That's the very plague o' the hull thing," said Peter. "You and I, Moll, we feels mighty good now, yer see, sittin' here readin'"—and Peter stopped, and began considering the words again.

"What's next?" said Molly.

A well-directed handful of soft mud, coming full in Peter's face at that moment, somewhat interfered with the answer to this question; and it was only because Molly snatched the book away, that the mud did not fall and cover that too.

"Ha! ha!—he! he!" came the voices of Tim Wiggins and Jem Crook from among the bushes. "Why, he's gettin' sich a scholard, he don't hardly take time to wash his face, mornin's!"

"Dear! dear! don't he look kind o' pale and interestin' now?"

"Guess he won't need no sweet'nin' to his cakes *this* mornin'," said Jem Crook.

"Now don't ye stir him up to come out for a walk," said Tim Wiggins, "'cause yer know he's read till he can't hardly see."

"My little children, these things write I unto you that ye sin not;"—how easy, how hard!

Peter Limp started up with a terrible oath, and clearing his eyes in part, with a desperate hand he dashed the book out of Molly's lap, and started off on the full run after his tormentors; while they on their part were not slow to lead off at a tearing pace. They were all out of sight in a moment, and only a distant shout now and then told of the course the chase was taking. And Molly sat alone on the doorstep. She had gathered up the precious book, carefully smoothing down the tumbled leaves with unsteady fingers, and holding it far away that no tears might drop on it, and now sat pale and trembling, a frightened shudder running over her whenever she remembered Peter's oath.

"Oh, the King will be so angry!" cried Molly, wringing her little hands. She slid down off the stone, and laid her face on it in utter despair.

CHAPTER III.

As for Peter, the other boys had led him a wild chase before he even drew breath or began to recollect himself, back and forth among the bushes, far over the hill and into the meadow, where at last Tim Wiggins and Jem Crook threw themselves down upon the grass in a boisterous fit of merriment.

"He does look so woundy cur'ous!" said Tim.

"Help yer wash yer face, when I gets through laughin', Peter," said Jem.

For all answer to which, Peter began to fire a swift volley of stones, sticks, clods, and rubbish at his tormentors. At first this only redoubled their shouts; but as the missiles came thicker and faster, Tim Wiggins's face grew threatening.

"Look a here!" he said, sitting up;—"does yer want that 'ere mug o' yourn stuck in the pond and held there? 'Cause if yer does, I'm yer man."

"Just as good be done right off, too," said Jem Crook, rousing up in his turn, "Saves washin'."

Peter Limp stayed his hand at these suggestions; but when he tried to speak, the mud—already drying upon his face—cracked and curled into a dozen wrinkles, making matters even worse than before. The two boys rolled over upon the grass in the ecstasy of their enjoyment.

"Why, Squire Townsend's best porker ain't a bit more strikin' to look at!" cried Tim Wiggins.

"I say, Pete, lend us yer face for a crop o' oats," said Jem Crook.

"Wouldn't need no ploughin'," said Tim Wiggins.

Peter fell upon them, and pinched, and kicked, and cuffed, and bit; and the two mastered his hands and feet, and rubbed his face back and forth upon the turf, until there was some danger of getting rid of the mud at the cost of the skin.

"*Now*, he looks like folks!" said Jem Crook. "How *does* yer do, Peter? Been out o' soundins so long, I'd kinder got melancholy, and didn't know as 'twas you."

"What was yer about up there, at yer books?" said Tim Wiggins, with a scowl.

"Readin'," said Peter, sulkily.

"Nice work for mornin', ain't it?" said Tim. "If I catch ye at it agin"——

"Why, I wouldn't wonder if 'twarn't the very one the white lady giv' him," said Jem, "and he's goin' to play good-boy, for a change! 'Tis kind o' slow down there to Limp's—when he ain't home. Lively, then, ain't it, Peter? Flogs yer round consid'able, don't he?"

"'Taint none o' yer business what he does, nor what I does, nor what nobody does," said Peter, comprehensively. "I was a readin' to Moll; and I'll do it, too, if I'm a mindter."

"Why so he shall! in course!" said Jem Crook. "Does yer allers read so early, Pete? I say, I'm a comin' round some mornin' to hear."

"Help yer pernounce," said Tim Wiggins.

"Tell ye what the words means," said Jem Crook.

"Guess likely yer will—when ye finds out yerself," said Peter, scornfully.

"Come, stop yer chaff," said Tim Wiggins; "let's go get some apples. I'm as thirsty as a bucket. There's a hull lot of 'em down to Peasely's."

"Fust-raters, too," said Jem Crook. "Come on, Peter," —and Peter did not dare say no. Indeed, at first he hardly thought of saying no, the force of old habit was so strong.

It was as natural to Peter Limp to go on such expeditions as it was to go to bed. But as he went along, the words that Molly and he had been reading began to sound strangely in his ears. "Love your enemies," they said, and he was planning with all his might how to do these two boys an ill turn—how to pay them off for what they had done to him. "Sin not"—it said that too; and here he was on the way to Farmer Peasely's to steal his apples. Peter felt but half himself as he tramped along over the dewy grass, and the worst of all was that he did not see how to get away. Suddenly a bright thought came into his head.

"Wants to go slower, does yer?" he said, with a scornful glance at his two companions. "Sort o' weakly, ain't yer? Jem Crook's beat out, and Tim Wiggins is thirsty!"

A smart shower of cuffs and pinches was the answer to this sally, in the midst of which Peter Limp started off on the full run towards the orchard, and the other boys followed. Indeed in the eagerness of self-assertion they soon passed him, and Peter quietly fell behind a little more and a little more—then dodged behind a rock—then made for the woods; and once under cover, he set off straight for home.

His little sister had lifted her head from the door-stone by this time, and now sat there all quiet and alone, with a very sad, wistful face indeed. Her small ragged apron was stretched protectingly over the Bible, and Molly stroked the much-loved book with tender fingers now and then, as if to soften down the affront which had been offered to its teachings.

"I's back agin, Moll," said Peter, trying to put a good face on the matter, and to hide the mortification he really felt. "Takes most a hull day to get quit o' them fellers, when once yer begins."

"O Peter," said Little Molly, "we was a settin' out!"

"So we be's," said Peter, shirking the obvious point of her words. "Come on, Moll, hand it over. We's read a heap now, but I don't mind givin' ye another turn."

"You throwed it down, Peter!" said Molly, still guarding her book.

"Well--and yer picked it up," said Peter, holding out his hand. "A feller can't help doin' everythin' under the sun."

"But does you know what you's said?" asked Molly, dropping her voice to a sort of frightened whisper.

"Bother!" said Peter, impatiently, "how long's *you* been so partic'lar? If yer ain't a-goin' to read, *I'm* goin' off."

"Here's the place," said Molly, giving up the book with a sigh. "I's kept my finger in. Begin again, Peter."

Peter would quite as lief have tried his fortunes at another place, but he took the open book and began where Molly bade him.

"'My little children, these things write I unto you, that ye sin not.'"

"Now you *sees* that's spoke right to us, Peter," said Molly.

"Do sound like it," said Peter.

"And she said the King knowed everythin'," said Molly, "so that's how it comed to say we was children. Guess that's just all for me and you, Peter."

"Why there's more young uns 'n you," said Peter.

"But the King knowed how we'd be settin' out," said Molly, gazing straight up into the blue sky, "and so He put that down. Read it over, Peter."

Peter read it over, and then went on to the words which came next in course.

"'And if any man sin, we have an advocate with the Father, Jesus Christ the righteous.'"

"What's that, Peter?" said Molly, bringing her eyes back and her head down.

"Don't just seem as though I could tell yer," said Peter, looking puzzled; "we's got to miss that, Moll, it's too hard."

"No, we mustn't," said Molly, eagerly; "take part first, Peter."

"Part's easy enough," said Peter, considering the passage. "It's about them folks as will cut up, arter all. 'If any man sin'—yer see some on 'em does, Moll."

" *We* can't," said Molly, decidedly. " What's next, Peter ? What's 'advocate ? ' "

"Oh, I can tell yer *that*," said Peter. "Squire Townsend's son—*he's* advocate."

" *This* ain't him," said Molly.

"Guess likely no," said Peter ; " this here's another."

"What does him do ?" said Molly, with her face in a hard knot of puzzled wrinkles.

" Well," said Peter, with a competent air, " he gets folks off as is kind o' hard up. Yer see, Moll, fust the sheriff he nabs 'em ; and then them that's had things took, *they* comes and swears to 'em, and wants the judge to send folks to jail without waitin' a minute."

"And then they has to go ?" said Molly.

"Straight off," said Peter, " leastways they would, if young Townsend did'nt speak for 'em. But he comes and talks and talks, and then the judge lets 'm go off home agin. I heard him once, when old Dodd was up for stealin' Peasely's sheep."

"Who gets him to talk ?" said Molly, who was plainly working out some problem in her mind.

" Oh, they sends him word," said Peter. " Guess likely Sam went that time."

" That's what she told us, Peter," said Molly, slowly, as if she were trying to recollect : " it must have been the advocate. ' Tell Jesus when you's wicked,' she said ; ' and tell Him when you's frightened, and tell Him when you feels bad ; and beg Him to help.' ' If any man sin '—What's it say, Peter ?" And Peter read—

" ' If any man sin, we have an advocate with the Father, Jesus Christ the righteous.' "

CHAPTER IV.

IT was early, early the next morning, when Jem Crook and Tim Wiggins—true to their evil word—crept softly up to Peter Limp's house. Stationing themselves each side of the door-way, they kept their watch, as the dawn brightened and the stars grew dim, waiting for Peter himself to come out.

"Wait, Peter—I's ready," they heard Molly say; and then appeared Peter on the door-stone, closely followed by his little sister. But Molly shrank back at first sight of the enemy, and instinctively hid the book in her apron. Peter's arms were seized at once.

"Now for the apples!" whispered Tim Wiggins.

"Sorry ter interrupt yer studies, Peter," said Jem Crook, " but them farm chaps does get afoot so early!"

"Hurry up!" said Tim Wiggins; and between the two, Peter went scudding over the ground much faster than he liked in *that* direction.

"I don't want no apples," he said, striving to free himself. "Ain't had my breakfast yet. Let go, I say!"

"Why, in course he ain't," said Jem Crook, taking a firmer grip. "The poor boy's had no breakfast—and wont get none afore tea-time, and the only thing as he *can* get is apples."

"Tell ye I don't want none!" said Peter, with another effort. "If I ain't left more breakfast home 'n *you* 've seen this mornin', it's a pity."

"Guess 'twont spile," said Tim Wiggins.

"Set it by, Peter, and we'll come help yer eat it to-morrer," said Jem Crook; and again Peter was hurried on as before.

Presently the orchard came in sight, all dewy and glowing with the morning freshness; and wherever the sunshine reached the trees, they seemed to be nothing but sparkles. The boys relaxed their hold of Peter now, for fences and trees are best met single-handed; but they never slackened their watch; and he presently found that he could not make the least move in any side direction, without being at once surrounded and headed off. And Peter felt miserable enough. What would Molly say, what would the lady think, if they could see him now? Where were all his grand beginnings and resolutions?

"Well, so I *is* beginning," he repeated over and over to himself; and then, even as he said it, came the words, "That ye sin not—that ye sin not." How they rang in his ears! Now when a boy knows what to do, and is ashamed or afraid to do it, it follows, as a matter of course, that he is a dead failure for the time being. He is no sort of a boy for any purpose whatsoever. A bag of sand is about as interesting, and much more respectable.

So it was with Peter Limp—the two other boys had him in their power completely. They made him climb for them, enforcing their orders with threats which Peter (being afraid to obey his conscience) did not dare to brave. They made him clamber out on particular branches, after particular apples; and when at last the heap on the grass was large enough, they made him sit down by them and devour the roughest and hardest specimens that they could pick out.

Things were precisely in this stage, when Farmer Peasely's great waggon appeared, coming slowly over the brow of the hill. This brought matters to a crisis. Jem Crook and Tim Wiggins had already filled their own pockets to the utmost, and having besides eaten as many apples as even they could stand, they were now lolling about on the green floor of the orchard, much at their ease. But the moment the waggon appeared, they started up; and once more seizing Peter, they hurriedly crammed his pockets, and the breast of his jacket, and even his old boots, with apples; and then pulling out a tattered handkerchief, Jem Crook filled that too, and hung it round Peter's neck. Then they ran—how they did run! out of sight in a minute; while Peter, by no means inclined to have the sole benefit of Farmer Peasely's heavy ox whip, stumbled after them as best he might. Well for him that there were woods near by!—well that he knew every by-path and corner and dodging-place. Farmer

Peasely had no chance, and knew it, and gave up the pursuit. But as Peter went chuckling along, more leisurely now, and even (with the force of old habit) thinking that after all it wasn't a bad morning's work, he had but reached the bushy confines of Vinegar Hill when his tormentors were upon him again, and again Peter Limp was nothing in their hands. They shook him out as if he had been but a sack of apples himself—handkerchief, boots, jacket, pockets; and having before this emptied their own, Peter's ill-gotten load disappeared in short order.

"*Ain't* he a rump, now, to wear hisself out for other folks?" said Jem Crook, patting Peter affectionately on the back—"why there ain't hardly nobody as *I*'d run so for. Sun's hot, ain't it, Peter? Didn't hardly want yer jacket, did yer, Peter? Hope there's somethin' to drink at home —kinder makes a feller thirsty to fetch apples," added Jem, setting his teeth into one of the largest of Peter's load.

"Guess likely yer didn't s'pose I was a fetching 'em for *you*," said Peter Limp, getting his breath a little, and making a grab at the apple.

"No, we didn't s'pose it—we *knowed* it," said Tim Wiggins, with a sneer.

"Hand 'em over!" said Peter, manfully.

"Hand 'em over!" Jem Crook repeated in a mocking tone, as he took three or four apples from his pocket and began to set them in motion in the air, with true juggler's skill. "Catch 'em, Peter! have 'em on yer head or yer nose?"—but Peter, trying first one application, and then the other, drew off a little.

"*I* don't want 'em nowheres nor nohow," he said, with well-dissembled scorn; "why I know where there's more apples 'n ever you two fellers set eyes on. And them ain't but pig-squeals to 'em! Pity if *I* can't find apples!"

And Peter turned away with great disgust. But once fairly away from his companions, and out of hearing of their jeers, his foot slackened and his head dropped. Then *this* was the morning's work, after all! *this* was what he got in exchange for his new principles; this was the reward of being afraid to own them. Peter dropped down under one of the bushes, and thought no pleasant thoughts. Tired, out of breadth, angry, ashamed—he had done all the climbing, and the hardest of the running; he had toiled and panted along under a load which had all past into the hands of Tim Wiggins and Jem Crook. Never before had they put so much upon him, never before had he been so unable to take his own part. Other times without number he had robbed orchards in just such company, and had laughed and whistled and sung with the gayest; but this morning? —ah, he had gone all the way to the ringing of those words: "My little children, these things write I unto you, that ye sin not."

Peter Limp's head sank lower, and two or three strange, hot tears came welling up from some new, unheard-of spring. "Wonder what Moll *would* say!" he muttered to himself— "wonder what she's doing, anyway!" And with that Peter rose up and went to see.

Little Molly was in her old place on the door-stone—perhaps the quietest she could find at that time of day; rocking herself slightly from side to side, and gazing wistfully up at the blue sky. Peter crept up and sat down by her, more ashamed than he had ever been in his life. But he tried to hide it.

"Sky's so interestin'—guess likely yer won't care about readin' none, to-day, Moll," he said.

"I's thinkin' about the advocate," said Molly, bringing her eyes down. "And I's been waitin' for you, Peter."

"Wouldn't wonder if yer had," was Peter's reply.

"Where's you been?" said Molly, suspiciously,

"I's been—round, consid'rable," said Peter, with some hesitation. "There, Moll, there's an apple for yer." For Peter had managed to secrete two in his cap.

Molly took the big apple, and turned it round, and looked at it—but the child's instinct was learning to know good and evil.

"Where'd you get it?" she said at last.

"Why—I jest picked it up," said Peter, hesitating again,

and beginning to eat his own. "It come off a tree fust, in course."

Molly looked at the apple again, turning it slowly round as before.

"Peter," she whispered, "did you took it?"

Peter hung his head a little at that, and was not ready with an answer.

"They does crowd a feller up so," he said at last.

Molly looked at him, and looked at her apple—and then, before Peter could stop her, she flung it with all her little strength away. The apple rolled and bounded and hurried down the slope, and landing in the very midst of a conclave of pigs, was there instantly devoured without scruple. Molly drew a long breath.

"I's glad!" she said.

"Well, I do guess likely yer're about the meanest girl afoot!" said Peter, in high displeasure. "What's the use o' that now? what d'ye mean? Say?"

Molly looked up at him with her wistful eyes even brighter than usual.

"We's set out, Peter." And that was all she said.

———

CHAPTER V.

When Saturday night came, Peter Limp and his little sister were in deep consultation, curled up on the open hillside with only a screen of bushes between them and the hamlet, the sunset lingering in the west, the shadows coming on; the air just stirred with the parting song and the farewell hum of many a bird and many an insect.

"Yer see, Molly," Peter was saying, "I does get most beat out. Yer'd think now, as they'd let a feller alone as lets *them* alone—and 'stead o' that, they's arter me the hull blessed time, and there ain't a speck o' chance to do nothin'!"

"We's got to find some other place for readin'," said Molly.

"Ain't a place," said Peter, despondingly.

"But we's got to find it, Peter," urged his little sister, nothing daunted. "O Peter, the words is so good!"

"Guess likely that's true," said Peter. "All about the crowns, Molly, and the big city."

"And the advocate," said Molly; "I telled Him all about what you's did, Peter."

"Yer needn't to mind me," said Peter, somewhat hastily. "Guess likely I can talk the loudest, if it comes to that. And them words is jest a poser—they's too hard for me, that's a fact. Now, young Townsend *he* gets paid."

"What does they give him?" asked Molly.

"All sorts o' things," answered Peter. "Old Dodd, he outs with a hull heap o' shiners. And Sam, he tugs along a bag o' apples, or a string o' fish, or a lot o' eggs—anythin' old Dodd happens to have on hand."

Little Molly sat silent, gazing up at the bright-eyed evening star which looked down at her so wonderfully. Oh, what was up there!

"Does you think we's got to pay Him, too, Peter?" she said. "T'other advocate?"

"Why, we ain't got nothin', to begin," said Peter. "And yer couldn't chuck it up there, Moll"—and Peter eyed the star in his turn.

"How's we to do then?" said Molly.

"Can't tell yer," said Peter. "Maybe He'd look arter you for nothin', 'cause yer's so small."

Molly sighed a little, rocking herself from side to side in her old fashion.

"I's asked Him, Peter," she said, "and the lady said He'd hear. But I's got nothin'."

"No more yer haven't," said Peter. "Wouldn't wonder now if the book didn't tell—if we could find the place. We's got to read more, Moll, and it passes me to know where we'll do it."

"We might go sit on the church steps," said Molly.

"Won't do," said Peter, "if we didn't go when the folks was in, and *that* wouldn't. Tell yer what, Moll, we might go and sit just close under the winders, after everybody 'd done comin', and then whip off afore they 'd got through. The rest o' the fellers gives the church a wide berth, them times."

And Sunday morning dawned upon this new project.

It is safe to say that very few of the people who climbed the church hill that morning, thought much of the little bushy slope which—as Farmer Graves said—had "slid off from its back door." They knew, indeed, that the bushes were there, and that life, dark and unlovely, lay hid within that shadow; but that they themselves had anything to do therewith, any duty arising therefrom, any privilege concealed therein, was a very rare thought indeed. As yet, "they all slumbered and slept." And if they had been told that morning that a part of the congregation would be from Vinegar Hill, not a mother of them all but would have taken firmer hold of the little hands that nestled in hers, not a man but would have fastened a button or two extra; and even the minister himself would probably have remembered with pleasure that he had left his pocket-book at home. Yet the case was even so. Close hid in the tangle of the very nearest bushes to the church, crouched Peter Limp and his little sister, waiting.

"They 's all goin' in, Peter!" said Molly, longingly.

"Never do you mind," was Peter's answer—"let 'em go, the sooner the quicker. Then we 'll creep up, Moll, and do heaps o' readin'."

"What 'll *they* do, Peter?" said Molly.

"Can't tell yer—that 's a fact," said Peter. "Only they talks and sings consid'rable. Yer can hear if yer 's a minuter, after we gets fixed. There—guess that 's the last feller— he 's long enough arter all the rest."

And as he spoke, there rose and swelled upon the still air the first song of the congregation—sweet, grave, earnest. It thrilled the two poor little hearts that were thirsting off in the distance.

N

"O Peter, you *thinks* we'll hear?" said Molly, anxiously, as she hurried along.

"Sartin sure!" said Peter. "Why, that 'ere minister—he don't never let down a peg arter he once gets up. And the winders is histed."

And just under one of the windows, crouching close to the wall, the two children took their place, unseen, unheard, for there were no window-seat members of that small congregation. The music paused for a moment as they came up, but almost before Molly had time to look disappointed, it rose again upon the stillness—

> "Great Advocate, almighty Friend,
> On Thee our humble hopes depend;
> Our cause can never, never fail,
> For Jesus pleads, and must prevail."

The words rang out with the clear, full music of faith as well as utterance, and the little waifs listened, breathless.

"O Peter!" sighed Molly, as the last note died away, "that's him!"

"Hist!" said Peter, "they's a talkin'."

"No, they's readin'," said Molly, straining her ears. "O Peter, *what's* it?"

The spoken words were harder to catch, and the children stood even on tiptoe in their eagerness.

"Let's we go round by the door," said Molly.

"Guess likely you won't catch me at that," said Peter. "We'll just sit still, and read ourselves, Moll."

"I's goin'," said Molly, creeping swiftly along under shelter of the wall.

"Well, if yer wants to be took up, yer can just go," said Peter, following at a safe distance. "They's got the door open, in course."

Molly's courage failed her a little at that, and she ventured no nearer the door than the extreme end of the old porch. There she perched herself, while Peter curled down by her in one of his favourite positions. They could hear much better now.

"'Ho, every one that thirsteth,'" so the words rang—
"'come ye to the waters, and he that hath no money, come
ye, buy and eat.'"

Even Peter roused up at that, drawing a little nearer the
door, and nodding his head to Molly as if he thought they
had come to about the right place. But Molly gave him
little heed. With the eagerest intentness she listened to
every word, waiting for some more that she could understand. They came presently.

"'Seek ye the Lord while He may be found, call ye upon
Him while He is near. Let the wicked forsake his way, and
the unrighteous man his thoughts; and let him return unto
the Lord, and He will have mercy on him; and to our God,
for He will abundantly pardon.'"

The congregation inside listened with quiet attention to
the words they had heard so often; some of them with a
glad thrill of joy that they *had* sought the Lord and found
Him: within the church the call and the offer came like a
wonted shower upon a favoured land. But without, where
those little handfuls of desert sand lay heaped—who can
tell how the drops fell there? Molly listened, with her face
pale with excitement, and then broke into one of her low fits
of sobbing—hushed, kept in, but that shook her little frame
from head to foot. And even Peter laid off his wariness,
and fairly drew himself along to the very edge of the door,
that he might have a good look at the place from which
such wonderful words came.

"You may just bet he's a readin' our book, Moll!" he
said, drawing himself cautiously back again. "And all we's
got to do is to find the right place. I say, Moll!—shut up!
Folks'll hear."

"O Peter!" said little Molly, raising her tear-wet face,
"I's so glad! O Peter, it's so good. I's nothin' to pay,
and He don't want it!"

"How d'ye know?" said Peter, whose mind was not up
to such quick conclusions.

"He said so," Molly answered, undoubtingly. "'He that
hath no money'—that's us, Peter."

"Guess *that's* so, anyway," said Peter.

"And we's to come right now," said Molly, "while He's near ; and oh, Peter, I's so glad !"

"Yer don't s'pose it means near these here steps, young 'un ?" said Peter.

"It says so," Molly answered again—"'cause *we's* here. And we's to call, and He'll be found." And Molly crept down upon her knees, and folded her hands and looked up into the blue sky with all her heart in her eyes.

"If yer don't quit, Moll, I'll take yer right straight off," said Peter, in some dismay. "Get on yer feet, now—so's we can run at a minute. There ! they're all in a stir, I tell yer."

The two children scuttled away off the steps, and crouched in their old place beneath the window, held fast by the music which came pouring forth again, as the people stood up to sing. But Peter would not wait a minute more after that.

CHAPTER VI.

It was uphill work. Do their best, Molly and Peter could not find even a corner reading-place where they were not disturbed. At home, the baby cried, or their father stormed, or poor Mrs Limp was ready with a whole host of demands upon their time and attention. There wasn't a minute's quiet *there*. And out doors—sometimes there was and sometimes not. If the two had managed to dodge all the sharp eyes of the hamlet ; if there was some general marauding expedition of more than usual interest on foot—then Peter and little Molly could creep away unmolested, and, hiding under the bushes like two rabbits, read and talk over the wonderful words of the Book of life. Now and then Jemmy Lucas joined them ; for neither his strength nor inclination led him much with the other boys. He was no match for their stormy play or ruthless fights.

"I's most beat, Molly," said Peter one day, when they had been dodging and doubling and running, till they were out of breath. "'Twon't never pay, *this* won't."

"But we's got to go on, Peter," said little Molly, for the hundredth time: the only answer, in fact, which her small store of logic could supply.

"Don't know about that," said Peter. "We's got to if we can."

"We's telled the King, and He's telled us," said Molly.

"What d'yer tell Him?" said Peter, a little crossly. "He don't want none o' yer talk."

"I's telled Him everything," said Molly. "And He hasn't stopped sayin' 'Come,' not a minute."

"Much you know about it," said Peter. "Yer see, Moll, the thing's here. 'Tain't only the chaps—it's father. Now how's a feller to walk straight, I'd like to know, when somebody's allers a makin' him walk crooked? 'Tain't no longer ago 'n last night, after you was a-bed, that I just had to go find him a chicken for his breakfast."

"But you didn't, Peter!" cried Molly.

"Tell yer I *had* ter," said Peter. "Why, I just lives in fears o' my life, the hull time."

"And did you tell the King all about it?" said Molly, very much distressed.

"No, I didn't," said Peter. "If He knowed it, 'twarn't no use, and—I warn't a-goin' to be the one, anyway."

"But you's got to have Him forgive you, Peter," urged Molly.

"Got to's easy said—that's all I know," was Peter's reply. "I ain't got time to do so much talkin' as yer has, Moll. We's set out, yer see, but we goes on a bit different."

"But the King'd help you, Peter," said Molly. "Why, He helps me right off."

"Guess likely yer wants it pretty bad," said Peter, surveying the little thin, pale creature beside him. "Now I's got to help myself. That's the rub."

Molly listened, unsatisfied; yet with no reserve force of words to answer.

"Peter," she said, suddenly, "I's a-goin' to tell father all the lady says."

"Just see yer don't!" said Peter, turning sharply upon her. "What would that be for?"

"We'd oughter," said Molly. "I feels so."

"Guess *I* don't feel so, nor nothin' like it!" said Peter. "And if you does, yer more of a fool 'n I thought yer. Tell father!"

"Maybe he'd go to," said Molly, wistfully.

"Maybe he would!" said Peter, with great scorn. "Now you Moll, if yer says one word o' all this to a livin' soul, I won't never read to you no more. So there."

"Will you tell him then, Peter?" urged Molly.

"Guess likely I will—when I wants to get killed," said Peter.

"You's might tell him, and run away very fast," suggested Molly.

But this idea was so intensely amusing to Peter, that he rolled over and over upon the grass for sheer delight.

"No, no, Moll," he said, recovering himself, and sitting up once more, "we'll keep on, all quiet and reg'lar, and let him find it out for himself same as we did."

"We's didn't," said Molly. "The lady telled us."

"Didn't we went up there fust?" inquired Peter, in a great state of virtuous indignation. "How'd the lady ha' found us if we *hadn't?* And didn't I take yer days and days to hear the musics?"

"I wish 'twas time to go again," said little Molly. "Where's you goin' to read, Peter?"

"Most anywheres," said Peter, opening his book with a competent air. "Guess likely over here at the end's a good place, and easy found."

And beginning to read at the very first verse that caught his eye, Peter burst into the midst of the description of "that great city, the Holy Jerusalem," and read it out to his awe-struck little listener. For hard as the names were, and strange the image, there was now and then a gleam of brilliant glory from among those unknown words, which not even

Peter's stumbling speech could quite conceal. The twelve
gates, with their stately enumeration ; the mysterious size
of the city ; the costly garnishing of its foundations, seemed
to fill the very air with magnificence, until the children
almost held their breath. For little as they knew of "jas-
per," and "chalcedony," and "sardius," in particular, yet
with the general name of "precious stones," Peter Limp
was unhappily but too well acquainted. And the golden
street and the light, clear as crystal, needed but little
explanation.

"Tell yer what, Moll," Peter said at last, breaking off ;
"this here's the King's house, and no mistake."

"Where we's goin' to ?" said Molly, in a half breath.

"If so be "—said Peter, doubtfully. "Don't seem easy to
see how we's to get there, Moll—but if we should, yer know,
then that's it."

"We was to set out, and to keep on," said Molly, rehears-
ing her short lesson. "And to beg the King to help. Read
on, Peter."

And Peter read on.

"'And the city had no need of the sun, neither of the
moon, to shine in it : for the glory of God did lighten it,
and the Lamb is the light thereof. And the nations of them
which are saved shall walk in the light of it. And the gates
of it shall not be shut at all by day : for there shall be no
night there.

"' And there shall in no wise enter into it anything that
defileth, neither whatsoever worketh abomination, or maketh
a lie : but they which are written in the Lamb's book of
life.' "

The strange glory and power again shining all through
the hard words, fell upon the two children and held them
spell-bound.

"Don't sound much like us, that don't," said Peter, after
a pause.

"But we's goin' to," said Molly, eagerly. "And we's
got to, Peter ! We ain't got to do nothin' bad, never again."

"Easy talkin' !" said Peter, with a sort of a groan.

"S'pose we *was* there, Moll?—what d' yer reckon the King 'd say? You just go down to the village, and step on somebody's clean floor, and see what yer 'll get. And gold streets! —whew!"

"But the King says, 'Come,'" urged Molly. "And they don't."

"There's somethin' in that," said Peter. "Have with yer, Moll!—we 'll try it a spell longer."

"*I* ain't a-goin' to give up—not, never," said Molly. She dropped down on her knees, hiding her face in the tangle of wild grass that spread all around. But Peter heard no word.

"What's this ye 're doin' here?" said a rough voice. "What's the reason ye aint off makin' a livin' like other men's brats?" And Walter Limp, suddenly appearing from behind the bushes, dealt no light blows right and left upon the children.

"I say, what's this ye 're doin'?" he demanded again, with an oath that made Molly shrink even more than his blows.

"We wasn't doin' nothin'," said Peter, doggedly. "Who's to know where the livin' is?"

"Oh yes, we was doin' somethin'," said Molly, mastering her tears and her fears together. "We 's been a readin'."

"Readin'!" growled Walter Limp. "Let's see yer book." Peter picked it up from under the bush where it lay, not daring to refuse, and handed it to his father. Walter Limp's face grew blacker than ever.

"Robbin' the church, hey?" he said. "I 'd recommend to ye to steal somethin' else next time. And if I catch ye again amusin' yerselves with my property 'stead of bringin' it to me, I 'll kill ye both—d' ye hear?"

And having knocked Peter down, and given Molly a parting cuff which made it hard for her to hear anything, Walter Limp walked away, book in hand.

For awhile the two children lay there on the grass sobbing, and made no attempt to pick themselves up, or give themselves aid and comfort in any way. How dark the world was, after that shining city with the golden streets!

"What's it you read, Peter?" Molly said at last, in her little weak voice.

"Don't make no odds what I read," said Peter, gruffly "'Tain't for us, Moll—I telled ye so."

"But the King knows," said Molly, raising herself up a little with effort. "O Peter, I think I'd die right off if it ain't ! The King *must* know, Peter."

"Yer'll have a chance to die, afore yer think, maybe," said Peter, in the same tone. "He's got one book now, and when he catches us with t'other, guess likely he'll finish the job, and be done with it."

"Peter," said little Molly, earnestly, "you mustn't say lies !"

"Guess I'll say what I'm mindter to *him*," said Peter.

"But the King heard too," said Molly.

Peter moved a little restlessly at that, but made no other reply for a while; and Molly lay looking at him.

"We's got to do's we can !" he said at last. "And what that'll be, it'll take more'n me to tell yer. T'other book's got to keep hid—that's one thing."

"And we's go up to the preachin'," said Molly.

"Ain't no preachin', not for days and days," said Peter.

Molly turned her eyes away, and began softly repeating to herself, "There's no night there, and they don't want the sun, and the street's all gold, and the gates ain't never shut."

She hid her face down in the grass again, and lay very still.

CHAPTER VII.

WHAT was to be done now ? In vain the two children pondered, and planned, and consulted, talking to each other in whispers, at all sorts of stolen minutes through the next morning, and still nothing could be decided. Only one thing was clear, it would never do to bring Molly's Bible within reach of the ruthless hands that had confiscated

Peter's ; and therefore for the present the book must lie safe in its hiding-place, and the two children must do without their reading.

"Telled ye so, Molly !" said Peter, with the gloomy satisfaction of one who has prophesied a misfortune that has come to pass. "Telled ye he'd blow it all to splinters. How's we to get on now, I'd like to know ?"

"But it's good we's read so much, Peter," said Molly, with a girl's superior hopefulness. "And we 'members some. And we'll go on as fast as we can."

"Guess likely we will, till we gets tripped up a little oftener," said Peter, savagely. "Much you remembers !"

"I's goin' on," said Molly, simply. "And I does 'member a deal, Peter. I knows ' My little children,' and about the advocate, and ' there shall be no night there.'"

"Pity there warn't none here," said Peter. "It's twice as hard to tend to the nights as 'tis the days. The fellers is allers busiest then, and it's a sight harder gettin' off."

"And then father's home," said Molly. "That's the worst. Peter, if we goes on fast, how long'll it be 'fore we gets all away ?"

"Guess if yer asks me how long it'll be if we goes on *slow,* I can tell yer better," said Peter, despondingly. "We won't never get there at all, Moll, and that's the way it's like to be. Hedgin' of yer in and shuttin' of yer out, and what's a feller to do ?"

"You's might tell the King," said Molly.

But Peter shook his head at that, as something not in his line ; and presently wandered off in search of better counsel or amusement or adventure, or whatever he might chance to find. And so passed on the morning.

"I say now—what's up ?" inquired Tim Wiggins, as he came swaggering along through the bushes, and suddenly found himself in an unusually large assembly of his compeers. It was the afternoon of the day following that on which Peter Limp had lost his Bible ; and Peter himself stood in the centre of the ring, looking somewhat red and altogether disturbed.

"What's the game?" said Tim Wiggins again, sliding himself in among the rest. "Anybody come into a fortin' without the sense to keep it dark?"

"Why, that's just where it is!" cried Jem Crook; "and yer's hit it exactly—only kinder on t'other side. There's Peter's *lost* all the fortin' he ever expected to get!"

"I ain't, neither," muttered Peter Limp, angrily.

"Like to know what he had to lose—and I'd go look for it," said Tim Wiggins.

"Too late for yer," said Jem Crook. "Have to wait till next time, Timpty. *This* here one's swallered!"

There was a roar of laughter at that, in which Tim joined, without in the least knowing why.

"Blessed if I know what yer all up to," he said then.

"Ask Sam Dodd," said one of the boys.

"Why, his daddy's drinked his book up—that's all," said Sam, thus appealed to. "And if it only'd disagree with him as well as it does with Peter, it 'ud be for the good o' the country."

The boys shrieked and laughed and shouted and danced round Peter, whose face certainly did not improve during the process.

"Drinked it up, Timpty—think o' that!" said Jem Crook. "His handsome book as he was so fond of, and took reg'larly, mornin's, 'stead o' his breakfast. And his daddy gets hold on it, and likes the taste on it so well, he swallers it all to once, 'stead o' makin' it last, as Peter did. And now there ain't a speck on it left for nary one."

An indescribable hubbub followed this speech of Jem Crook's; and anger and sorrow and shame struggled and fought in Peter's heart, till he was very near bursting into tears and helping on the excitement that way.

"Serves him jest right, for tryin' to make b'lieve better 'n other folks," said Tim Wiggins, with a scowl. "If old Limp had swallered him along with the book, it wouldn't ha' hurt *me* none."

Another storm of shouts and jeers burst forth at this, and Sam Dodd inquired—

"What's that you said about settin' up to be good, Tim?"

"He," said Tim, "Peter, settin' up to be better'n the rest of us. Guess 'tain't in him to be exactly what yer'd call good. Not first-chop."

"If I see him at it again!" said Sam Dodd. "I say, boys, guess we'll let him off this time, 'cause he's lost his book and feels kind o' watery; but he hadn't better try it over."

"No! no!" shouted the chorus, closing round Peter Limp. "We'll make *him* swaller it next time, hull."

"Ain't one on ye never had a book o' yer own," said Peter Limp, rousing up a little; "so in course it don't suit that nobody else should."

"Where'd he get it, anyhow?" said one of the boys.

"The white lady giv' it to him, to help him play pretty," said Jem Crook. "And it's had the most astonishin' effect in a short time. Why, he's giv' up to like apples, and kind o' lost his taste for chickens, and don't care about roastin' ears without Farmer Graves counts 'em out hisself. Sam had a touch o' the complaint, but Peter's took it powerful."

"Needs watchin'," said Tim Wiggins.

"And doses o' the very thing he don't like," said Jem Crook. "That's my notion o' physic."

"Watchin' did heaps for Sam," said Tim Wiggins. "Come on, Peter, I'll watch yer for to-day."

"And we'll go where the physic's handy," said Jem Crook.

"Guess likely I ain't a-goin' nowheres with nary one on yer, *this* day," said Peter Limp.

"Peter ain't much of a hand at guessin'," said Tim Wiggins, "and never was. Hurry up, boys!—fetch him along. I say, I can't wait here all day."

"I ain't a-goin', I say," repeated Peter.

"Shows yer don't know what's good for yer," said Sam Dodd. "There's a chance now for yer to walk on yer feet; but yer *may* have to go on yer head."

"That's the game!" shouted the boys, "on his head! on his head!"

"Peter," whispered a little voice near him, hid away in the bush against which Peter was leaning. "I'd let 'em try. You're pretty big, and they's easy tired. 'Twon't hurt ye much, Peter, a little way."

Peter knew the voice of Jemmy Lucas.

"Where's they goin'?" he whispered, in return.

"Widow Canty's," said Jemmy Lucas, "to steal her young pigs. She's sick a-bed. I wouldn't, Peter! They're splendids!"

But Peter stood irresolute. He didn't want to go—*that* was very certain; but it was also sure that if he must go, he would rather go on his feet, despite Jemmy's comforting assurance that the other way wouldn't hurt him much. Certainly it didn't *sound* pleasant.

"They're goin' to run off some o' Graves's sheep arter that," whispered Jemmy.

"Molly'd pray to the King for help," he suggested, presently.

But that was a lesson Peter Limp had not learned. And even as you may see a little half-rooted plant blow hither and thither in the wind, holding fast to nothing, even so stood Peter, kicking his foot into the dusty turf, and hanging his head, the very picture of irresolution.

The other boys meanwhile were holding a deep consultation, but never slackening their watch of Peter, so that he seemed to feel their hands on him all the time. What was he to do? how was he to help himself? True, as Jemmy had said, Molly would have prayed for help to One stronger than she; but in these times of trouble Peter's thoughts went all the other way. He liked setting out to seek the King when nobody hindered him—the idea of travelling to the kingdom was very pleasant then—but if he must go through thick and thin for it, Peter began to think it would hardly pay.

You see, children, he was not what the Bible calls "rooted and grounded in love." There was a little shoot of good in his life, a little leafage of better things; but it came from no deep-struck root; his heart had not yet laid fast hold of the Lord Jesus as his one only King and Saviour. "He that believeth in Him shall not be confounded;" but no one can go many steps towards heaven in any other trust. And so poor Peter Limp, not having chosen the Lord wholly, could not be brave and strong against the taunts and threats of the boys of Vinegar Hill. He wished himself anywhere else, and Jemmy Lucas too; for his words just brought up to Peter the face of little Molly; and Peter knew what *she* would say, well enough. Weak as she was, Molly would have braved the whole ring of boys, sooner than yield to them one inch, Peter knew. And why? Ah, the mere thought of the Great King and His goodness was so precious to Molly, that I think she would have given up her life first, sooner than turn back from seeking Him.

"Now then, for roasters!" said Tim Wiggins, breaking up the consultation. "I's got to look arter Peter, so all yer other fellers has got to look out for yerselves. Come ahead, Peter—you and me, we've got to lead off."

"And he just went!" said Jemmy Lucas, describing the scene afterwards to Molly. "They just led, and he just follered. And if they tells him to swaller one o' them little pigs right down hull, he'll do it!"

CHAPTER VIII.

Little Molly Limp had been long wrapped in tired sleep and resting dreams, before Peter came back; and then he slunk away to his own corner heap of straw, without a word to anybody. Nor could Molly get any information from him next day. To all her anxious inquiries Peter turned a deaf ear; or at most made such answer as, "Who telled yer I'd gone nowheres, Moll? Well, yer can ask him *where* I went, too, if he's so knowin'."

And Molly at last gave up the subject, and tried to engage Peter upon the somewhat difficult task of remembering

Bible verses. It was hard work for Peter. Molly thought it very fascinating to sit on the door-step in the sun, saying over and over to herself the scattered words and sentences that she could call to mind. But Peter's memory was not so good, or he cared less to tax it ; and so it came to be the way that Molly talked and Peter listened—listened most of all, it must be owned, for any token of unseen foes.

The Bible money lasted Walter Limp till just the next day, and after that he was more savage than ever ; always suspecting that there was hid treasure in the house, always on the watch to find it. Then he would drive the children out of the house, declaring they should not enter it again without their hands full of something. And the days began to grow **very short**, and the evenings were dark and chill.

Those were hard times. Poor Mrs Limp trotted her puny baby after the old-fashion ; and Molly coughed, and grew thinner than ever, creeping out to sit in the sun when it shone, and looking up into the far-off blue above her head, and saying to herself first one and then another of the beloved Bible words that she could remember.

As for Peter, he was restless—tired of worrying and being worried ; tired of trying to hide his better thoughts and intentions, which yet he would neither confess nor forsake.

"Moll!" he whispered to his little sister one evening, " does yer want to go somewheres ?"

"Where's it, Peter?" said Molly ; "I guess I's too tired."

"Be yer too tired for preachin' ?" inquired Peter, in the smallest voice that could be heard at all. Molly gave a little jump.

"I thought that 'ud wake yer up—but now just yer sit still," said Peter, putting his hand on her arm. "If yer stirs a finger, Moll, or one on yer toes, even, afore the time comes, we won't none on us go, nowheres."

" You 's *said* preachin', Peter," said Molly, under her breath, and subsiding into an absolutely motionless state.

"Well, 'tain't preachin'—it 's prayin'," whispered Peter,

" down to Sam Coon's. We's just tumble in, Moll, like usual, till father's safe, and then for it!"

The children slipped quietly away to their sleeping places, long before Walter Limp came home; but such wakeful eyes as peeped at him from across the straw and from under the rags, were not often seen just there at that hour. Then they had to dodge Mrs Limp, too, who would certainly have been roused to ask where Molly was going; and it was not until much later than they wished, that the two stood free and safe in the dark star-light out of doors.

Hurrying along, then, fearful of being late, afraid of being stopped, as silent, as noiseless, as timid (for the time) as any wild creature of the woods, Peter and little Molly scudded, rather than ran, over the bushy hill which people called their home. But neither fear nor danger ceased there; for Sam Dodd and Tim Wiggins were seldom in at that time in the evening, and were more likely than not to be on the high-road or hiding about the village. So still the two scudded along in silent haste and dread; seeking the cover of every fence and tree, lest even in that moonless night the keen eyes of their tormentors might find them out. But once fairly in the village, Peter carefully avoided all bye-ways, and kept at the front of the houses; for, as he told Molly in a whisper, "the chickens was all at the back."

" That's Coon's," he added presently, pointing to one of the houses in the street, rather larger than most of the rest, and with two or three open and lighted windows. "They's at it a'ready! Now keep yer eyes wide, Moll, and yer'll see sights."

Mrs Mason, in her book of wonderful missionary pic-tures,* gives one that is of special loveliness to me. I must give it in her own words. She had gone on a trip into the Mopaga country of Karens, along a winding mountain road.

" We went plodding on, and even after reaching the nar-row opening in the sky by clinging to the roots, rocks, and whatever could help us, still no house appeared, nor the

---

* " Great Expectations Realised."

slightest vestige of any village; but, following our guide,
we wound along on the side of the hill, down, down, down,
and were about to step off into a gorge as black as night,
when a dozen hands were raised, and a whole flood of mountain music burst up the ravine, and held us spell-bound!

"It was the little congregation of Wechaduc, yet far
distant, at prayer and singing—

'Rock of ages, cleft for me,'

in their own native tongue."

Different from this—yes, its very converse—was the wonder that greeted the eyes and ears of Peter Limp and little
Molly; and yet as truly a wonder, and one that held them
as breathless. For as they came softly up to the lighted
window of Mrs Coon's house, and caught sight of the people
within, those same people rose suddenly to their feet, and a
sweet, wild tune, and words that were sweeter still, came
filling the evening air with tenderness.

> "Hark, my soul, it is the Lord;
> 'Tis thy Saviour, hear His word;
> Jesus speaks, and speaks to thee:
> 'Say, poor sinner, lov'st thou me?
>
> "'I deliver'd thee when bound,
> And when bleeding, healed thy wound:
> Sought thee wandering, set thee right,
> Turn'd thy darkness into light.
>
> "'Can a woman's tender care
> Cease toward the child she bare?
> Yes, she may forgetful be,
> Yet will I remember thee.
>
> "'Mine is an unchanging love,
> Higher than the heights above:
> Deeper than the depths beneath,
> Free and faithful, strong as death.
>
> "'Thou shalt see My glory soon,
> When the work of grace is done;
> Partner of My throne shalt be;
> Say, poor sinner, lov'st thou Me?'"

O

Rapt, entranced, as the children were, they said not a word to each other, nor moved a muscle till the hymn was done. And then a prayer followed so immediately, that there was no chance to talk. Getting closer and closer to the window, with the softest and lightest motions, Peter and Molly stood at last where they could see as well as hear ; where they could watch the faces of the people who were saying and singing such wonderful things. Prayer followed prayer, and hymn followed hymn ; and then there was reading ; and then there was speaking—and still the two young listeners stood still in the darkness, nor ever lost a word. If Molly once or twice cried " Oh !" it was breathed out too softly to reach any ears but Peter's ; and if Peter, on his part, made occasional notes of admiration, they were but silent nods to himself or nudges to Molly.

"We's got to 'member all the easy words," Molly whispered to Peter once ; and after that bent all her attention to catch and hold those little fleeting parts of speech that went by so very easily. And if it had not been dark, and there had been anybody to see, Molly's face would have been found all knit and wrinkled with the difficulty.

But not so Peter's. *He* had no idea of turning play into work at that rate ; and besides, as he muttered to himself—

" Guess likely I couldn't do it, nohow. Not if I *was* to try *ever* so. This sort o' folks don't talk easy."

Perhaps it was well for little Molly that her brother was less absorbed than herself. In the midst of the last hymn, Molly felt herself seized by the shoulder, and Peter's hand was upon her lips.

"Don't yer breathe," he said in her ear, drawing the startled child down from the neighbourhood of the window to a little dark corner below the steps, and holding her there so that she couldn't move an inch. There they hid, until the people began to come out from the meeting, and then, to Molly's amazement, Peter suddenly drew her right in among the little crowd, and they walked behind Mrs Peasely, and before somebody else, for ever so far.

One by one the villagers dropped off from the line, leaving

the street here, and leaving it there, for some quiet, peace-ful-looking home; and when at last the two little waifs stood alone in the starlight, they were far enough from Mrs Coon's, and quite near the turning to Vinegar Hill.

"Peter!" Molly ventured then, under her breath.

"What yer want?" growled Peter.

"O Peter!" said Molly, reassured by his louder tones, "doesn't you wish we's lived here?"

"Guess likely 'tain't much good wishin'," said Peter, in the same sulky tone. "I say, Moll, I's tired out!"

"I's tired, too," said little Molly, with a long sigh. "But oh, we's heard such good things, Peter! And we'll come, every time."

"Guess yer will!" said Peter, savagely. "Not if I knows it. I ain't a-goin' to dodge round this way no longer, Moll —I's goin' to give right straight in. There was them fellers huntin' us high and low."

"To-night?" said Molly, her voice sinking again to a frightened whisper.

"Yes!" said Peter. "That was what I pulled yer down for. They'd ha' found us in two seconds more."

"Well!" said Molly. "But we's can't help it, Peter. We's got to go on."

"I ain't," said Peter. "Tell yer I'm sick of it. What with father huntin' me out, and them huntin' me in, 'tain't a pig's life."

"O Peter," said little Molly, "we's heard such things. 'Poor sinner,' Peter—that's me and you. And when He said, 'Does you love me, poor sinner,' I said yes, Peter— oh, I said yes!"

Peter looked down at his little companion with a strange thrill running through him, but he just pushed Molly into their wretched home, and shut the door without a word.

CHAPTER IX.

WHETHER Molly's words had their effect—whether having
been so successful after all, made him bolder; certain it is,
that Peter Limp contrived to find out most of the church
meetings that were held, and to get some share of the words
spoken thereat. Sometimes he went alone, sometimes he took
Molly; first giving the other boys his company all day, to
allay their suspicions. And either he had grown skilful,
or else they were especially busy, for a good many days and
nights passed by without particular disturbance. But Peter
was not happy. He couldn't go back to his old ways of
doing and talking with any sort of comfort, for he had had
a taste of better things; and he got not half the good of his
new ways, because he was for ever afraid they would be found
out. And I can tell you, children, once for all, whoever
would *really* be the Lord's servant, must be one openly.
What would you think of a soldier who should refuse to
wear uniform and march in ranks, for fear the enemy would
get a shot at him? Poor Peter, it was pretty much what he
was trying to do. He had made great talk at first abou,
helping Molly, but as it turned out, it was Molly who helped
him. And so, sometimes catching the glad trust of her little
heart; sometimes urged on by her words, or drawn on by
her example, Peter—liked Herod—"did many things." Also
he contrived to *not* do a good many. Sometimes he kept
out of his father's sight, so that he could not be ordered to
go and steal something "to keep the house a-goin';" or if
that plan failed, Peter would spend all his energies to beg
or find something that might serve his turn. Mrs Graves
was not the first farmer's wife who had been laid under
contribution; nor was the snow-clad visit to her house
the last one, by many, that the two children paid to the
kindly villagers and farm folk. For the people were very
kind, even to children from Vinegar Hill; and Walter Limp
began to think that begging might prove as good a trade as

stealing, at least taking the risk into account. But begging, in such a small neighbourhood, could not last.

"We's goin' round to Skillet's to-morrer," Peter said to his little sister one night, as they sat whispering over their day's work and their plans. "That'll be a long pull for yer, Moll—most down to Graves's they lives."

Molly shivered a little, in anticipation, but made no reply.

"Has ter, ye see," said Peter, with a glance at her. "Least-ways if yer wouldn't sooner mouse it into the parson's corn-crib."

"Oh no!" said Molly, earnestly. "We's go, Peter; beggin' *is* honest, ain't it, Peter?"

"Guess likely 'tis—sorter," said Peter Limp, with some hesitation. "Make the most on it, Moll, while yer can Next week we's got ter live by our fingers."

"*We* ain't," said Molly, decidedly.

"Tell yer we's *got* ter," said Peter, in rough tones. "This here and King's is the last livin' places left. 'Taint no sort o' use goin' to some—and we's been to t'others."

"We's go again," said Molly.

"Blessed if *I* do," said Peter. "Tell yer, Moll, they's tired o' us, like—and seein' all, yer can't hardly blame 'em."

"We's pray what to do, then," said little Molly.

"*That's* no good," said Peter, decidedly, "'cause we knows now. I'll tell yer, like a book. We'll worry on a bit, and then we'll take up old tricks again, and *not* worry."

"Peter, I ain't never a-goin' to do tricks, no more!" said Molly, with a whole covenant in her little white face.

"Then yer won't do nothin'," said Peter. "Father'll kill yer, sure as guns."

Molly rocked herself softly from side to side—somehow the idea did not seem to terrify her much.

"Would it be *all* done then, Peter?" she asked. "I wouldn't ache no more, nor nothin'?"

"Guess likely there'd be a good deal done," said Peter, once more giving her a side glance; "and you among the rest. Reg'larly done for, you'd be. Now, Moll, just shut up—does yer hear? If we can't help it, we can't—and 'tain't noways agin us, as I see."

"But we's *got* to mind the King, Peter," said little Molly, with a gleam of joy lighting up her face. "And oh! I's so glad!"

"*I* ain't got to do nothin' as can't be done," said Peter, with a dissatisfied grunt. "Telled yer so all along. However, Moll, we'll hold on a spell yet; and we'll be off to Skillet's in the mornin', fust thing."

"Peter," whispered Molly, under her breath, "lets we read just a little!"

"What, now?" said Peter.

Molly nodded.

"'Spose father comes in?" said Peter.

"He won't," said Molly. "I'll ask the King not to let him."

"Well, if you can get him kep' out," said Peter, with a look half of scorn, and half of a certain awed wonder which often came over his face at Molly's speeches.

Molly gave a little joyful exclamation, and hurried away to fetch the much-loved book from its hiding-place. Curling down then by the twinkling chip firelight, which they had kindled behind the stove, Molly sat with eyes and ears intent upon Peter, and Peter opened the book cautiously.

"*Did* yer ask Him?" he whispered to Molly.

Molly nodded.

"Read on, Peter," she said; "anywheres."

Sitting uneasily, glancing over his shoulder, Peter read "anywheres."

"'Be ye therefore followers of God, as dear children.'"

"What's dear children, Peter?" whispered Molly.

"Why, young 'uns as their folks is proud of, I guess," said Peter, hesitating a little. "Children as loves 'em, Moll, and gets loved back."

A shadow fell on Molly's eager face, plain to see even in that dim light. She looked round at poor listless Mrs Limp, about her old trade of patching and piecing, the baby asleep for once; then gave a timid glance towards the dark

window, and with a little shiver and a little sigh came back
to Peter and the book again.

"Guess likely we's ter foller like as we *was* sich, yer see,"
said Peter, in answer to her puzzled look.

"But we's all different, Peter," said Molly, sadly. "What's
it mean, Peter?"

Peter looked puzzled in his turn.

"Here's the next thing," he said, reading on as if to get
through the difficulty that way—

"'And walk in love, as Christ also hath loved us, and
hath given Himself for us.'"

"Then if He's giv' Himself for us, He wants us, Peter!"
said Molly, rousing up with her eyes like two fire-flies.

"Does sound so, sure enough," said Peter ; "but if *that's*
it, Moll, it's too queer for me."

"And if He wants us, and gets us," said Molly, pursuing
her own train of thought, "*then* we's His dear children—
don't you see, Peter? And we's to feel so, too."

"Them may as can," answered Peter, with a little grunt
of extreme doubt and difficulty. "How's yer goin' ter feel,
I'd jest like to know?"

"Happy," said Molly. "And glad. He's giv' Himself for
us 'cause He's wanted us—only think, Peter!"

"Too hard for me," said Peter, with a shake of his head.
"Guess I'll try a bit further on. Queer!" said Peter again,
as he fluttered over the leaves and began in a new place—
"seems as if it was everywhere, in all sorts o' places. I's
turned away on, Molly, and here's the fust livin' thing I
comes upon—

"'We love Him, because He first loved us.'"

A heavy, lumbering step on the threshold startled both
the children from their musings. Molly turned white with
fear.

"There—telled ye 'twarnt no sort o'. use askin'," said
Peter, reproachfully. "Father's come, this blessed
minute."

But even as he spoke, Walter Limp stumbled and fell,
measuring his full length upon the floor ; and long before

the besotted man could rise to his feet again, Molly and her book were both in safe hiding, and Molly was giving thanks that the King *had* heard.

Not hear ?—

" Ask, and ye shall receive."

" The Lord is nigh unto all that call upon Him, to all that call upon Him in truth. He will fulfil the desire of them that fear Him ; He also will hear their cry, and will save them."

Peter Limp, on his part, also disappeared out of the little room ; but instead of going to bed, he went out for a walk.

It was clear starlight, but only that as yet, and so Peter thought to himself that there was no need of his meeting any of the boys unless he was a mind to. For indeed they were a great trial to Peter just now ; and instead of bravely fighting the difficulties they threw in his way, Peter shirked them as far as he could.

So wandering noiselessly round among the bushes, considering with himself what he should do when begging was quite played out, Peter went step by step towards the village, and began to peer in at one window and another to see what the folks were about. Windows were shut too tight now, in the cold weather, for him to hear anything ; but the bright lights and fires and faces were a good picture in many a house. Knitting-needles and books and apples and nuts came in to play their part ; and Peter almost forgot he was cold, standing in the snow to watch.

He had stood long in front of one particular window, where there was most to see, when of a sudden a huge snowball whizzed by his head, and went crashing through the panes of glass. In quick succession came a volley of smaller balls against his own head, and Peter drew back in haste. It was time, too ; for the house door flew open, and not only the head of the family, but *every* head of the family, was thrust forth into the darkness. Stumbling back to be out of reach, Peter came full against Tim Wiggins.

" Ain't they just the stoopidest ? " said that worthy under his breath. " Hold up, Peter ! Now then—here she goes!"—and another well-directed ball of ice and snow landed full in the doorway, making great confusion among the heads there assembled.

"Boys!" shouted the owner of the house, shielding himself carefully this time behind the door.

"Look alive there!" said Tim, in the same undertone, despatching his ball this time against the door itself.

"I'll have you all sent to prison!" screamed the excited schoolmaster, for he it was. "And have you thrashed first, till you won't care where you go!"

"Steady's the word!" responded Tim; and another clink of broken glass told of further execution in the sitting-room. At the same minute the wild cry of a nighthawk sounded through the air, and Tim dropped his next snowball, and seized hold of Peter.

"Game's up," he said, "and we's the winners. Now for it!"—and away the two ran, till village lights were far behind, and only the stars looked down.

CHAPTER X.

"WHAT yer up ter now?" was Peter Limp's gruff question when they had reached the shelter of the bushes. "Smashin' things up gen'ally, for nothin', don't *gen'ally* pay."

For an answer, Tim Wiggins sounded forth the wild, melancholy cry of the nighthawk again, and then, with a sharp "quack, quack, quack!" of reply, Jem Crook and Sam Dodd came upon the scene, each bearing a large bag.

"Grabbed 'em all, Tim!" said Jem Crook, dropping his bag in the snow. "And if they ain't heavy, I just wish I mayn't eat 'em—that's all."

"How many?" said Tim, handling the bag.

"Nine quacks and seven gobbles—all told," said Sam Dodd.

"And three cock-a-doodles," added Jem Crook, "and the

folks is scared out o' what little sense they's ever had.
'Twan't much.   They'll never miss it, likely."

"What does yer think *now*, Peter Limp?" said Tim,
"'bout smashin', and sich?   Peter's taken cur'ous, boys—
got a sort o' inquirin' mind come to him—wants to know
what we's at."

"Shouldn't wonder if more 'n one couldn't play that game,"
said Sam Dodd.   "Say, Peter! what was *you* at?—moonin'
round them 'ere winders like a chickaninny?"

"Why, it's like 'twas he cracked 'em!" said Jem Crook,
with a slow drawl.   "Come to think, I *did* hear as how that
'ere schoolin' feller's winders was all cracked up and down
—fourteen ways for Monday.   *Must* ha' been Peter!"

"I'll swear I see him do it," said Tim Wiggins.   "I was
a-comin' by all peaceable like, with just a pound o' soap for
my mother, and tuppence taffy for the young 'uns, and I
heered the biggest kind of a smash-up—and there he
were."

"How'd he do it, Tim?   Tell us the story, Tim!" said
Jem Crook and Sam Dodd in concert.

"Oh, he ups with a ball this fashion," said Tim Wiggins,
forming a well-packed missive of snow, "and he lets fly—
so"—and Tim's ball knocked Peter's cap off in the coolest
manner imaginable.   The other boys took the hint following
his lead; and as Peter on his side was not slow to reply,
the game was lively for a few seconds.

"Hold on!" said Tim Wiggins then, "stop yer nonsense!
This ain't business.   And it ain't play-time.   Shoulder yer
bag, Jem—come along, Peter.   There's lots more to do."

"Guess likely there is," said Peter, dusting the snow off
his cap; "but yer see I ain't got time for it.   Fact is, I've
got to get an early start, come mornin', and so I's bound for
a wink or two to-night."

"Where're ye goin' in the mornin'?" said Sam Dodd,
gruffly.

"Skillet's," Peter answered, with brief unwillingness.

"Why, ain't that a'most too much!" cried Jem Crook,
embracing Peter with affectionate earnestness.   "And we

was jest agoin' there ter night! saves yer all trouble and everything, and yer gets company thrown in."

"Tell ye I don't want none," said Peter, swinging himself clear, "I ain't agoin' nowheres with none on ye *this* night. I'm agoin' straight home."

Peter walked off in state, astonished at his own liberty, half expecting every moment to be seized from behind, and with all sorts of contrary thoughts confusing his heart. How easily the other boys had filled their great poultry bags!—how cleverly they would sell some to far-off villagers; what grand roasts and stews they would have of the others! And what miserable scraps of pieces he would bring home from Skillet's next day, if, indeed, he was so happy as to get anything at all—and how little even of such spoil would fall to the share of Molly and him! Peter drew a long sigh, and thrust his hands deep down into his pockets, where indeed there was room for anything that might come.

"*Don't* pay," he said to himself. "I telled Moll so, and so it is. What *she* finds in it now"—— And with that, sweet, scattered words of reading and song and prayer came floating through Peter's mind as if in answer. But Peter sighed again, and shook his head.

"Why he feels so lonesome, there's no tellin'!" said the voice of Jem Crook at his ear, while that worthy's hand was slipped deftly through his bent arm. *I* knowed how 'twould be. I telled 'em so. And I jest give up the fun, and come off to give *him* a little quiet turn in the air. Moon's comin' up shiny, ain't it, Peter?"

"Take yerself off!" was Peter's gracious return.

"And—my!—*ain't* the snow kinder white?" pursued Jem Crook, turning Peter round, and walking him off away from Vinegar Hill. "Glad o' yer company, Peter—case o' ghosts, yer know."

"Tell yer I'm goin' home!" said Peter, not much enlivened by this last suggestion.

"We'll go round this way, takin' a turn or two first," said Jem Crook. "Fact is, Peter, yer daddy's in a state to-night.

He was a kickin' out the winders when I come by—swearin' for yer, like mad."

"Where yer goin' then ?" said Peter, his desire to go home cooling off on a sudden.

"Don't yer make no noise, Peter, and I'll tell yer," said Jem Crook in a whisper. "I allers *was* fond on yer, Peter. Fact is, I don't like these goin's on myself—but how's we ter keep out on 'em ?"

"You and me might, together," said Peter, taking sudden courage. "They couldn't do much with two."

"'Tain't not nigh so bad as one—that's so," said Jem Crook, reflectively. "But the white woman's been gone a spell, hain't she ?"

"*She's* gone," said Peter. "But then Moll and me, we reads and talks, and hears tell too, by spells."

"Down by the winders and sich ?" said Jem Crook, with a sharp glance.

Peter nodded.

"Now I'll tell yer what," said Jem Crook, slapping his companion on the back, "suits me, that does, to a splinter ! S'pose there's somethin' goin' on to-night, Peter ?"

"Past time," said Peter, "they's early folks, mostly."

"Oh, it's past time, is it ?" said Jem Crook. "It *is* late. And yer starts early in the mornin', Peter. I *did* want ter creep round and see what them other boys is up to—they's gone ter Skillet's, I *guess*," said Jem, hesitating. "But if yer'd mind "——

"Guess likely *I* shan't mind," said Peter, chuckling. "Like ter head 'em off—the worst kind !"

"Come on, then," cried Jem Crook, with sudden spirit, and away they went at a sharp pace, getting further from Vinegar Hill every minute.

It was rather a long way to the Skillet's farm—a sort of out-lying nest of barns and crops and cultivation, with a good cheery house for a centre. All dark now, in the midst of the thick white snow ; with everything that could sleep gone to repose long ago. The boys went silently along, seeking the shadow of fences and bushes ; though, indeed, *shadow*, strictly speaking, there hardly was. Suddenly, Jem Crook sent forth the wildest, wierdest cry of a screech-owl, that ever that respectable bird could hope to imitate.

"I say now!" said Peter Limp, rather more than pleasantly startled, "what yer about, Jem? we ain't to hev no signaling, yer know."

"O' course not!" said Jem Crook, "jest wants to find out where they is, Peter. If they's hereabouts, one on 'em 'll howl."

And sure enough, the howl of a seeming dog, second in character only to the screech-owl's music, next moment rose on the air.

"That's them!" said Jem Crook. "Now if I don't answer, yer see, they'll think as it *were* an owl. This way, Peter—they's a runnin' sheep, jest as sure as nothin'."

Creeping round behind the barn now, and so on to the barnyard fence, the two could just make out in the dim light two other dark figures like their own. Huddled together before them, frightened, and crowding into the corner of the yard, was the flock of pretty, white-wooled creatures, of which Farmer Skillet was justly proud.

"Will yer let 'em?" whispered Peter, in great excitement —it was a new sensation to come on such a scene as a detective.

"Let 'em get to work," answered Jem, in the same tone. "When they's run the things off, Pete, you and me, we can fetch 'em back, and make old Skillet shell out."

"But they'll keep 'em!" said Peter.

"Not if we takes 'em away," said Jem Crook, contemptuously. "Feared o' the sheep, Peter?—or maybe it's the chickens. *Did* hear a rooster just now."

"Ain't afeared o' nothin'," said Peter, stoutly.

"Jest yer stand still a minute then," said Jem Crook, "and watch this here gate, while I goes round to look at t'other. If I fasten that a bit, they can't get out noways but here."

Jem stole away, and Peter watched and waited. What were they all about? Some of the sheep came scurrying along near where he stood, frightened, and not knowing which way to flee in the darkness. Then Peter heard a rush —and then he was almost sure he heard the further gate open and shut. All was still again—and Peter stood on one foot, and then on the other, and felt his patience grow as cold as his fingers.

"Guess likely now he hain't got a thing to tie it with!" said Peter to himself, "and here's the very thing in my pocket!—twine as would a'most hold old Skillet fast himself. Guess I'll slip round and back—'tain't best to be here always. *Did* think I heerd a noise off towards the house."

Peter slipped round stealthily, but the gate was wide open.

"Jem!" he whispered, "Jem Crook!"—but no Jem Crook answered. Peter listened.

Not a sound but the soft breathing and bleating of the sheep, still too much alarmed to leave their corner. Not a shadow broke the dim, even line of the wall, not a step crunched the snow.

Peter Limp was not quick of thought, but it did not take him long to spell this out. With an exclamation which savoured much more of his old life than his new, he flung to the heavy gate, and turning sharply away, came in sharp contact with a heavy stick, which laid him flat upon the snow.

CHAPTER XI.

STUNNED, bewildered, helpless, Peter **Limp** lay for a minute under a shower of blows, nor even tried to raise himself. But then he struggled to his feet, facing some tall figure in the starlight.

"Curse yer!" he said, savagely, "what's yer arter now?"

"What are *you* after?" said young Skillet, taking Peter by

the collar and giving him a shake. "How many of our sheep have you set a running? hey?"

"Run along arter 'em and mebbe yer 'll find out!" said Peter Limp, striving to free himself. "*I* ain't a-teched nothin'—'thout it 's this here plaguy gate."

"What were you doing to the gate?" said young Skillet, with another shake.

"I say!—let me be, will yer?" growled Peter. "Guess likely I 's a right to shut anybody's gate—if I 's a mind ter."

"And *I* say, what were you doing here?" repeated the young man.

"Come ter ask arter yer health," said Peter, doggedly. "*I* ain't teched yer sheep; and if yer 's so anxious about 'em guess likely yer jest wastin' time over me."

Something in this suggestion seemed to strike Mr Skillet, for latching the gate with a kick, he collared Peter more firmly and dragged him along towards the house. Here, into some out-house, or out-standing closet, or shed—he could not quite tell which—Peter was thrust, and securely locked in; while the young farmer, calling together his hands, set off with lantern and dog to see after his flock of sheep.

Peter stood still—or rather lay still—in the dark, huddled together in a heap on the floor, just as he had been tossed in unceremoniously by young Skillet. Then by degrees he raised himself up, and began to feel round the place he was in. It seemed half full of empty barrels and lumber, and Peter went hitting his head against sharp corners, and tearing his fingers with outstretched nails, till he was quite tired of *that* amusement. There was no window—nothing more than a few pigeon-holes high up towards the roof, and no door but the one by which he had come in. Peter sat down again and studied the situation. He had scarcely felt the cold thus far, in his eager excitement, but now cooling down a little in mind, Peter began to perceive how sharp the night was, and how keen-edged the wind that came in upon him through every knot-hole and crack.

"Friz ter death all night, and beat ter death in the mornin'," said Peter to himself, reviewing the situation, and

with that he jumped to his feet once more, and began a yet
more careful examination of his prison. Some of the floor
boards seemed partially loose, but the weight of lumber on
them was too great for Peter's single strength, or would take
too much time and make too much noise in the removing.
Then he tried the boards of the siding. Nailed fast, of
course, all of these were, but Peter at last found one which,
rusty or broken nails, held but slightly. A vigorous push at
this, then a very pinching clamber through the opening, and
Peter Limp stood free and unwatched in the starlight—unwatched, except by the all-seeing One to whom the night
shineth as the day ; whose eyes run to and fro through the
whole earth, to search out those who serve Him, and those
who disobey. And some thought of Him crossed Peter
Limp's mind at this minute, as he looked hastily up towards
the sky, with a strange recollection of the reading of that
very night—

"Be ye therefore followers of God, as dear children."

"'Tain't no sort o' use for me," said Peter, with a kind of
long-drawn sigh. "Molly—she's different. And I can't
hold out no longer ! Jest see now what's come o' it *this*
time," he went on, working himself up. "If I'd ha' been
with 'em all reg'lar, o' *course* they wouldn't ha' gone off like
that. Wish I knowed how ter square up with that ere
Skillet afore I go !"—and Peter looked about him and began
to consider.

He was near the house, but every window and door was
fast shut, and there was no sign or hope of booty in that
direction. Peter walked slowly along towards the barns
again, keeping a wary look-out on all sides, but pretty well
assured that young Skillet and his men were far distant in hot
pursuit after the sheep. The night was wearing away now,
and the old moon came softly up in the eastern sky, flinging
pale shadows and a pale light upon the snow.

"He sees what you do—He hears what you say"—so rang
Mrs Kensett's words of long ago, in the ears of Peter Limp ;
and with them came the words of later reading and talks
with little Molly—

"My little children, these things write I unto you, that ye sin not."

Peter hesitated and drew another long breath—then shook himself free of thoughts and hurried on.

"There's no livin' so," he said to himself; "and I's got ter pick up somewheres. *I* can't go a-beggin' and waitin' like Moll. Now in course it'll never do ter come up here in the mornin'—so I'd as good take all I wants to-night."

And with a certain hardiness of determination Peter Limp went stealthily about in his old fashion, seeking for spoil. In that cold weather most available things were stored away, quite beyond the reach of the frost or of him; but, having once set his mind to evil, Peter was not so easily balked. In the very dim light of the barn and stable, he went feeling round; pulling a bag from one corner and a basket from another; then finding his way to the corn-crib, it was but a few minutes work to fill both bag and basket. Sooth to say, Mr Skillet had thought himself so far from Vinegar Hill, that he had grown careless of bolts and bars. Stumbling over a bridle, Peter took that too; and finally, as the last step in the process of "squaring up," he set the stable door wide open, and coolly untying the halters of two or three horses that stood there, left them to finish the matter their own way.

Then Peter made off. The moon had risen higher and higher, and more than one shrill cock-crow told that the small hours of the night were slipping fast away; and far off in the distance, Peter saw one or two faint moving specks of light, which could only have belonged to young Skillet and his men, returning from their fruitless chase after the sheep. Peter quickened his steps—got clear of the farm and all its belongings, dodged, and turned, and went backwards, and zigzag, to confuse his track in the snow; and at last struck the high road, and from it turned gladly into the dirty, well-marked track which led to Vinegar Hill.

Gladly, did I say?—nay, there was very little sign of gladness in Peter Limp's heart that morning. "Telled her it wouldn't pay!" he kept repeating to himself; but for all

P

that, when he had dropped the heavy sack and basket into some dark hiding-place, Peter found that after all, the weight had been on his heart and not on his shoulders. He would not venture an encounter with his father at that hour of possible returning consciousness ; and curling himself down between his bag and basket, Peter slept an uneasy, troubled sleep, until the morning sun had risen bright and clear over all the frozen world. Jem Crook stood by his side.

"So *that's* what yer up to ?" said Jem, with a kick at the basket. "Don't care about mutton, 'cause yer prefers corn ! Yer did it well, Peter—didn't think it was in yer. I vow I thought yer meant it !"

"*Did* mean it," said Peter, rousing himself sulkily.

"And don't," said Jem Crook.

"Pretty work *yer* made of it," said Peter, carrying the war into the enemy's country. "Leavin' a feller there all night."

"Couldn't get t' yer—that's all," said Jem Crook, with a sly twinkle in his eyes. "Hain't slept more 'n ten winks, jest for thinkin' of it. How *did* yer get home, Peter ? and how *did* yer leave young Skillet ?"

"Ain't seen nor heerd o' young Skillet," said Peter, gruffly, and yer'd best not ask arter him *too* close, Jem Crook. Get out o' the way !—I'm agoin' in."

"Goin' ter read ?" inquired Jem Crook, in his most affectionate manner. "Won't yer give me no inwite, Peter ? —I'd like ter hear yer, fust rate."

"Tell yer no !" said Peter again, in no gentle tones. "*I* ain't got time for sich stuff; jest foolin' yer I was, last night, Jem. Hist."

They were in full sight of the house door now, and at this moment it opened, and little Molly came out on the door-step.

The thin, pinched little face and figure smote Peter to the heart, and he faltered and fell back a step.

"Peter ! Peter !" she called—"where's you, Peter."

"I's here," said Peter, advancing with bag and basket, while Jem Crook stopped and looked on grinning. "What's the row, Moll ?"

'O Peter," said the little girl, "is you ready? We's got to be right off, Peter. Father said so afore he went."

"Catch me goin' up to Skillet's this day," said Peter, "and yer 'll catch most anythin' yer a mind ter. See here, Moll—that 'll last more 'n one day, I reckon."

"Where's you been, Peter? where'd you get it?" said Molly.

"Kind o' trade it was," said Peter, lifting his sack inside the door. "One o' them 'ere farmers thought as how I'd done somethin' for him, and wanted ter pay, yer see, Moll; so I fetched home this."

Half-anxious, half-satisfied, the child looked up in his face —then back again for Jem Crook; but Jem had disappeared, and Molly drew a breath of relief, and came in and shut the door.

"I's so glad," she said. "And we 'll read all day!"

"Now jest yer shut up about readin'," said Peter, turning to her roughly. "I's got somethin' else ter do, Moll. 'Twon't pay, that wont."

And Peter rattled down his corn in a heap in the corner, tossed the bag upon the little chip fire, and rushed out of the house to lose his thoughts in the snow.

———

"*He that received the seed into stony places, the same is he that heareth the word, and anon with joy receiveth it; yet hath he not root in himself, but dureth for a while; for when tribulation or persecution ariseth because of the word, by and by he is offended.*"

AN HUNDREDFOLD.

AN HUNDREDFOLD.

CHAPTER I.

"But other fell into good ground, and brought forth fruit, some an hundredfold, some sixtyfold, some thirtyfold."

"An hundredfold!"—it sounds like a great deal. But one day when I was at the "Grace Mission," I thought that even an hundredfold did but faintly express the wonderful harvest; for there, above the long "roll of honour," was a little roll of glory : so bright, so glorious, that it seemed to shine through all the room. From every point my eyes went back to that.

The room was full of children—children gathered from the very blackness of city darkness; and a band of earnest teachers led them onward to the light. Weary sometimes, and sometimes sick—fighting in the van of the children against sin and death and hell : "in labours more abundant, in perils oft."

On the wall were written the names of the roll of honour; names of children who for long months had never missed a lesson, nor ever came with one imperfectly learned. A long, long list it was. But above these were three names that stood all alone, "having escaped." "Asleep in Jesus," was their record—the shorter roll of glory :—

" George Davis."
" Rosie Bender."
" Em. Petherbridge."

That was all.

Was it only "an hundredfold" the teachers had already
reaped? It seemed to me, as I looked, that no words could
measure it. Three endless lives, caught from the death-tide
that surged all around, and gone to be with Jesus for ever!

Look through the tall windows of the mission-room and
see the dingy house walls, the untidy fluttering rags, the
foul look of everything that presses close around you.
Then think of three—were there *but* three—who have
"washed their robes, and made them white in the blood of
the Lamb." When we see the great multitude, which no
man can number, stand before the throne, *then* we shall
know the harvest there is in one rescued soul.

"What a sweet lady, Peter!" said little Molly Limp, as
the two threaded their way home among the low, brushy
covering of Vinegar Hill, one night after their Sunday
lesson.

"Ain't she, though!" said Peter, admiringly. "But I
tell yer what, Moll, yer'd better not go tellin' 'em at home
all she said."

"Why not?" said Molly, stopping to cough.

"Father'd think you was a-callin' *him* names, pretty
strong, guess likely," said Peter.

"But I wouldn't be," said Molly.

"*That* ain't no sort o' consequence," said Peter. "Wouldn't
he come out!—'bout swearin' and sich!"

"But he'd ought to know, if it makes the King angry,"
said the child, earnestly. "Don't you see, Peter?"

"O' course I sees," said Peter; "but I wouldn't be too
set upon makin' *him* angry—not if I was you, Moll."

"But if I doesn't tell him, maybe he'll make the King so
terrible angry that the King'll kill him, Peter. You might
help," said Molly, suggestively.

"Sartain," said Peter, "and get kicked out o' doors too.
I might do that, yer know."

"Well," said Molly, "that wouldn't hurt you as much as
it would father to get killed."

But with that Peter broke into a tumult of shouts and
somersets.

"Guess I'll risk him!" he said; and away he went, rolling and wheeling among the bushes, and Molly followed slowly on by herself.

"God is our King," the child repeated, as she trotted down the hill: "God is our king."

The idea was so new, so wonderful, that Molly's thoughts could get no further; and when she opened the house door, and crept in, the sound of a loud oath from her father's lips struck her with a shuddering sense of fear. Did God hear that? did the Great King of heaven really know how His glorious name was spoken in this poor little house on earth? Molly stole off to the furthest corner of the room where her mother sat, and crouched down out of sight; making no noise and giving no sign, except a painful start now and then, as some fiercer word than usual reached her ears. Walter Limp and one or two of his neighbours were telling over old deeds, or plotting new ones, and even poor passive Mrs Limp shivered a little once or twice, and clutched her pale baby with a firmer hold, as she listened. That was the ordinary way of this poor little household, whenever the man who should have been its light and protector came home. Only now, a new sort of fear had found place in Molly's heart, and instead of wondering what her father would do to her, she sat marvelling what perhaps God would do to her father.

Nothing happened that night, to anybody, more than common. Peter stayed out, as usual, till long after other people were asleep; and Molly dreamed and tossed, and the baby fretted, and poor Mrs Limp sighed; and Walter Limp and his companions sunk away from their games and their talk into heavy, brutish sleep. That was what the sunbeams saw, when they came glinting in with their pure brightness next day. They were used to the sight.

Little Molly, too well accustomed to the state of things to notice anything, so long as all was quiet, roused up from her tumbled bed-heap in the corner with the first gleaming light. Hastily fastening her scanty frock, she stole out of the door, unwashed, uncombed, unsmoothed in any way,

and planted herself on the doorstone to catch the sunbeams.
How fair they looked ! how sweet was the morning hush !—
for even Vinegar Hill was pretty quiet at that time; and one
or two little birds really ventured to sing in the rough
bushes. Molly saw and felt it all, drawing one long sigh
after another.

"If we knowed how," she said to herself; repeating over
then the charmed words, "God is our King."

Suddenly Molly looked down at her hands. Children,
you can't think how black they were ! And from the hands
to the frock Molly's eyes went with a certain new, wondering sense of disapproval. Nothing looked like the Great
King's child. Nothing *felt* like it—for when Molly put her
hands up to her head, the rough hair stood out in every
possible direction. Molly sat right down on the old step
and began to study the matter. Then suddenly hearing a
stir behind her in the house, she jumped up again, and crept
silently away among the bushes towards the further side of
the hamlet.

Coming there within sight of a little lean-to shanty,
backed up against the side of the hill, and with two barrels
set one on the other for a chimney, Molly gave a whistle
shrill enough and cautious enough for the worst boy on
Vinegar Hill, and then waited. Presently a little shutter
window in the hut was thrown open, and out jumped
Jemmy Lucas, in a state of hair and hands that matched
Molly's, and a shirt and trousers that went well with her
frock.

"Hi !" was Jemmy's expressive greeting, as he came sliding and hopping and flinging towards her with a perfectly
indescribable motion. "What's up, Molly ?"

"I's got things to talk," said the child. "And Peter ain't
home."

"*He* ain't worth lookin' arter," said Jemmy Lucas; "sure
as a bad cent to turn up somewheres."

"Oh, I ain't lookin' for him," said Molly. "I's lookin'
for you. See here, Jemmy "—and Molly held up her little
black hands.

"Berry thorns?" suggested Jemmy.

"No, 'taint thorns," said Molly, coughing—"they's so dirty!"

"Well—I guess they is," said Jemmy Lucas, after a moment's consideration of the subject. "Does look like it, Molly, come to think. But they ain't a speck worse'n mine." And Jemmy stretched forth two paws that might have gone with anything.

"And I's all rough, too," said Molly, putting one hand to her head again. "And torn up."

Jemmy nodded.

"Bushes can't do yer no harm, Molly," he said—"no-wheres."

"Jemmy," said Molly, drawing nearer and speaking in a doubtful whisper, "does you s'pose the King likes it?"

"The King!" echoed Jemmy Lucas in extreme astonishment. "Oh, yer means Him as *she* telled about?"

"Yes," said Molly. "If we was agoin', Jemmy—settin' out, you know?"

Jemmy pondered.

"It's easy took off, Molly, anyhow," he said. "Leastways I don' know as it's 'xactly *easy*, but I guess it'll *come* off."

"S'posen we was to try?" said Molly. "And they was to look like hers, Jemmy? all white and pretty."

Jemmy gave a low whistle.

"Don't see how that could be, noways in the world," he said. "But they'd be whiter'n they is."

And with one impulse the two trotted off yet further down the slope, to where a noisy, sonsy little brook ran for its life to get away from Vinegar Hill. Such scrubbing, then! Such rubbing of faces and rubbing of hands! And at first with such small effect!

"It'ud save trouble to jest skin 'em, *I* know," said Jemmy Lucas, looking ruefully down at his hands, whereon the dirt seemed only to grow more conspicuous under the washing. "Molly, you's as streaked as a garter snake!"

"But we's tried," said Molly, accepting this compliment as a token of progress. "And we'll do it agin, Jemmy."

"Get the streaks on to-day, and get 'em off to-morrow," said Jemmy. "My! don't my face jest feel queer! What's you at now, Molly?"—for Molly's new-washed fingers were slowly and with much difficulty threading the mazes of her tangled hair.

"I's slickin' it a little," said Molly, knitting her brows very hard at some pull of unusual sharpness and strength. "Now we looks more like the King's children—doesn't we, Jemmy?"

"They looks pretty queer, if we does," said Jemmy Lucas. "Is you goin' to set right out, sure enough, Molly?"

"Oh yes, I's goin'," said Molly. "And so's Peter. And we's goin' to help each other along."

"Well, so's I, too," said Jemmy Lucas. "Only I hasn't got the first notion how—and 'taint jest the best place to get a start. Ain't a soul here ter give a feller a shove off inter where he'd float."

"*She* said, Jemmy," said Molly Limp, speaking quite low and confidentially, "that we was just to do every little thing that comed up, and to ask the King to help. What's the next thing, Jemmy?"

CHAPTER IL.

DID any of you children ever try to do each little thing you could think of, to please the Great King of heaven and earth? Did you ever begin, fancying there was nothing you could do, except perhaps just one little trifle; and then find that as fast as one was done, another stood ready? So that you could always find something to do for God? some little way in which to please Him? Well, it was just so with Molly Limp. When she had washed her face and hands, she thought of smoothing her hair; and when that was done, she remembered that she must ask the King's help. So down there in the bushes the two children knelt, as they had seen the lady do; and then they tried to remember and say some of the words that she had spoken. And then they parted and went off to their poor homes, with a new, strange, sweet feeling of something better to be had than all those homes could furnish.

"What's yer up ter now, Moll?" was Peter Limp's morning salutation, coming suddenly upon his little sister as she trudged along. "What's yer got in them 'ere rags?—Let's see."

"I's got nothin', Peter," said little Molly, letting fall her tattered apron which she had wrapped round her hands to keep them clean.

"Where yer been then?" demanded Peter. "Out all night and nothin' ter show?"

"I ain't been out all night," said Molly. "Jemmy 'n I's been talkin', Peter. We was tryin' to keep what the lady said."

"Oh! yer's settin' up fer great folks, guess likely," said Peter, with some scorn. "Wont do, Moll—wouldn't grow here if yer did stick it in the ground. I've been a thinkin' it over, and that's what I says. And so the other fellers says."

"They ain't good," said Molly.

"Well, I jest 'spicion they ain't," said Peter. "And no more ain't us. What's that ter do?"

"I'm agoin', Peter," said little Molly, with a resolute face. "I'd like it so much! And I's never goin' to steal nor nothin', no more."

Peter gave a little whistle.

"Guess likely yer ain't goin' ter get whopped, nuther," he said. "If yer goin' ter set up like that, Moll, look out, or yer'll catch it."

Molly coughed, shivering a little, but the look on her face did not change.

"I's determined," she said. "And so's Jemmy. Come, Peter!"

For all answer Peter Limp thrust his hands in his pockets, and walked on, deep in meditation.

"Sounds fine," he said at last—"sounds mortal fine, Moll, this here follerin' the King, and sich. Thing is, how 'll it feel?"

"It feels good," said Molly, decisively.

"I means t'other part on it," said Peter. "Sticks ain't pleasant round yer head, and father's old boots ain't no softer'n when they was new. If they ever was new," Peter added after a moment's reflection.

"But, oh, Peter, just think of the King's house," said little Molly, with her sharp cough. "And we wouldn't be sick no more!"

"Do sound sort o' wonderful," said Peter. "If we could jest slip along easy, now, 'thout no one's knowin'. Tell yer what, Moll, don't yer be in sich a tearin' hurry, and we 'll see. Jest yer wait a bit, till I sorter look round, yer know, and then likely we 's both off like a 'motive."

And with this promise little Molly was fain to be content.

"We ain't set out yet," she explained to Jemmy Lucas, "we 's a gettin' all ready, and I 's got to wait for Peter."

"Glad I needn't ter," said Jemmy Lucas. "Peter drives the likeliest pair o' snails in all Vinegar Hill. Wouldn't wonder if he wasn't tacklin' of 'em up now. I telled mother this mornin' what I was up ter, Moll."

"Oh!" cried Molly, "Peter said I shouldn't tell father. What 'd her say, Jemmy?"

"She was took all up," said Jemmy Lucas. "Yer see, Molly, mother's heerd o' lots o' things, afore she ever see Vinegar Hill, and this here's one on 'em. So she giv' a great long sigh, that 'd a'most took yer off yer feet, and turned all red and white in a minute. And says she, 'Jemmy!'—as surprised as could be."

"And she liked it?" said Molly, anxiously.

"Don't know about that," said Jemmy Lucas. "She wouldn't say a thing—and I asked her about forty questions, I guess, right straight ahead."

"What was they all?" said Molly.

"Every livin' thing I could think of," said Jemmy Lucas.

"How fur 'twas, and who was goin', and what they done when they got there."

"At the King's house?" said Molly.

Jemmy Lucas nodded.

"And she didn't tell?" said Molly.

"Never a word," answered Jemmy Lucas. "Only once, and then she fetched another sigh a mile long, and says she, 'Jemmy, shut up! I can't tell yer but just one thing—the road's straight. And ef yer walks crooked, yer'll never get there,' says she. I couldn't make her say another word, Molly."

The two children sat and pondered this strange answer, puzzling their wits to know what it might mean.

"What's the odds, anyhow, between 'em?" said Jemmy Lucas, holding his head with both hands as if to catch and stay the shy ideas. "Yer walks straight, and yer walks crooked—what's the odds, Molly?"

"You walks straight when you's in a hurry to get there," said Molly, thinking hard.

"That's so," said Jemmy Lucas. "Only I don't walk— I runs. What next, Molly."

"And when you's afraid they'll see, you runs crooked," said Molly again, bringing her Vinegar Hill experience to bear upon the question.

"Fact!" said Jemmy Lucas, more emphatically than before, "yer's jest hit it. When folks wants ter get there, and ain't afraid ter be seen, they walks straight. But I say —Molly!"—and the boy stopped short with a more puzzled look than ever. Molly looked and waited.

"How's it about liftin' chickens?" Jemmy began again, under his breath. "A feller don't care to be seen then, Molly. And it's the same with runnin' sheep and takin' in washin's."

"Then they's crooked," said Molly, decidedly.

Jemmy's face lengthened.

"Supposin' they is," he said; "then how's folks goin' ter live straight?"

But Molly left that question as too hard for her.

"Look, Jemmy," she said, getting up off the grass, "I's

goin' to walk straight all the way home, too. I ain't agoin' to creep round through the bushes no more."

"Come ahead!" said Jemmy Lucas, jumping up in his turn—"we'll see how it feels in a jiffy. But I say! Molly, you ain't in a hurry to get *there*"—and the little boy stopped short, and pointed expressively up the hill towards the tumble-down home of Walter Limp. Molly stopped for a minute too, but then walked straight on.

"It's practisin'," she said—"we's makin' believe, Jemmy" —and Molly's face settled into a look of grave determination that would have suited the reality.

Yes, and reality it was. "Making believe," they called it ; and yet as the two children followed their straight line up the hill, surmounting patiently every hindrance of stick or stone, taking the rough spots and the hard spots and the dusty spots even as they came, they were in truth gathering purpose of heart and habit of foot for far more serious encounters.

Midway up the hill Jemmy Lucas paused again.

"S'posin' we meets some o' the boys, and they stops us?" he said. "Jest to teaze, yer know?"

"But we can't stop, Jemmy," said little Molly, hurrying on faster than before.

"And you ain't afeard?" said Jemmy Lucas, quickening his pace to match hers.

"If we was afeard, we'd go by the bushes," said Molly, with a little shake in her voice that gave a strange air of plaintiveness to the brave words.

"And if we'd took somethin', we'd go there sure," said Jemmy Lucas. "When yer wants to get there's quick as yer can, Molly," he went on, summing up, "and when you's ain't afeard folks'll see yer, and ain't ashamed ter have 'em see yer—guess that's the time to walk straight."

"Here, you young rabbits!" called out a rough harsh voice. "What yer doin' there, spilin' the grass? Get off and stay in the bushes where yer belong. If I catch yer out here again, sunnin' yerselves!"—and a handful of weeds came full upon Molly's head.

"Leave her be!" said Jemmy Lucas, facing round. "I say, Sam Dodd, you jest let Molly alone."

"I'll make a football o' *you* and kick yer down hill, if yer don't shut up," said Sam, fiercely. "Get out o' my way there!—I'm comin' up myself."

"Take ary side you's a mindter—we ain't partic'lar where yer goes," answered Jemmy Lucas, mockingly, but keeping fast hold of Molly's hand the while, and hurrying her on as straight as he could.

"Yer ain't—ain't yer?" replied Sam. "Guess I'll take my own way then, as I gen'rally does. Here goes—heads I win—tails you lose "—and Sam Dodd, preparing himself with a run, took a flying leap over the two children; first knocking them down with the end of a long stick as he came, to make the work easier.

As soon as she could get breath again, Molly picked herself up and started off up the hill as before; and Jemmy Lucas, though rubbing himself rather ruefully as he went, followed on without a word. At the top of the hill the children stopped and looked round, but especially down at the unmarked way by which they had come. No Sam Dodd in sight now; no harsher sound upon the summer air than the chirp of a lonely grasshopper near their feet, and the notes of some bird far up above their heads. Molly looked up and listened.

"How does you like it, Molly?" said Jemmy Lucas, doubtfully.

"We's walked straight all up the hill," said Molly, "and now we's here. I likes it—it feels grand!"

——

CHAPTER III.

Do you know how a seed begins to grow? First it sends out a little, little bit of a root into the dark earth where nothing can be seen; and then it sends out a weak, small leaf or

Q

two up into the sunlight. And the root grows strong in the dark, and the shoot grows strong in the sunshine; and each spreads and enlarges and increases every day. The mightiest oak begins its life so, as well as the poorest little weed that we tread under our feet.

Vinegar Hill was a hard place for anything to grow—shade and blight and mildew were likely enough to attack anything good that started there; and little Molly's new life found very few gleams of fostering sunshine. But the unseen work is always the most important—it is not the plant's beautiful stem, nor its wealth of leaves, nor its crown of flowers, that will help it to withstand the frost and the drought, but only its depth and strength of root. So, though Molly's show of good things was but like a weak, sickly, nondescript little leaf at first; yet unseen, unknown, her faith had laid strong hold of the King's message, and that root was growing and strengthening every day. "He invites you all to come"—the words became her daily life. Steadily, surely, the little plant struggled on; cheered now and then by the warmth of Mrs Kensett's words, revived by the shower of blessing which fell around the old church, or perhaps chilled and broken down by Peter's unsteadiness and final return to his old ways. Yet still on!—sure sign of life, still growing: until slowly the little plant had lifted its head above even the shadows of Vinegar Hill, and no earthly hindrance could shut out the light.

Meantime, hunger and cold were no strangers in Walter Limp's cottage. Limp's own drinking habits began seriously to interfere with the thieving trade at which he was an adept; and Peter, steel his conscience as he might, was still shy of bringing home unlawful booty for Molly to see. He never liked to meet her eyes at such times—they always seemed to say over to him the words—

"We's set out, Peter!"

It was a hard winter too, cold and snowy; and poor Mrs Limp grew more and more dreary, and Molly's little pinched face looked bluer and thinner every day.

"You's so hungry, Molly!" Mrs Limp would say—not

with tears—that fountain was long ago dried up, but with a weary, anxious look. . And Molly would answer, half to herself as it were, the wonderful words she had long ago learnt almost by heart.

"The King made a marriage; and He sent people to call the folks; and some of 'em wouldn't go. But we 's goin'—Oh, ain't it good! And bimeby we 's sure to be there!" Molly would end, her voice failing a little as she rubbed the patient, hungry tears away from her eyes.

"If yer goin' to be there, yer 'd better be about it," said Walter Limp, rousing up out of his stupid sleep. "Clear out, I say—yer won't get nowheres sittin' here. Get out o' this! —and don't yer dare to come back 'thout both hands chuck full o' sunthin'. Off with yer!"—and trembling and faint Molly fled away.

Nothing but snow outside—where should she go?

"Peter!" she called timidly—but Peter was off on a high carnival of skating. Molly stood still a minute—then thinking she heard a step in the house, darted off as fast as she could to find Jemmy Lucas. James Lucas himself was just staggering from the house as she came near, but Molly dodged him, and running round the back way crept under shelter. Such shelter as it was!—with holes in the roof and cracks in the siding, through which last night's snow had sifted softly in, and now lay in white heaps upon the floor. Jemmy Lucas, with an apple in his mouth and a broom in his hand, was just beginning to spread the heaps upon the floor, sand-like, as a preparation for sweeping the same. A handful of ashes in the old stove, an empty cracked plate upon the table, seemed to say that, in the matter of supplies, the families of James Lucas and Walter Limp were about equal.

"Warn't much to begin, Moll," said Jemmy Lucas, catching her sharp first look at the plate, and taking the apple from his mouth. "Hain't you had nothin'?"

Molly shook her head.

"That 's 'zactly what my father gen'ally leaves," said Jemmy. "So we 's got that and no more. 'Cept my apple

—and the only way that comes to be here was 'cause it
rolled away where he couldn't find it. And mother she
knew, and didn't tell. 'Tain't so large as it 'ud ha' been if
it had growed longer, but it's a hull one, for all. And a
half's a half."

And Jemmy Lucas, making desperate efforts to break the
little green knurly thing in two, at last succeeded, and pre-
sented one half to Molly with an air that might have suited
a dish of pommes farcies.

"You's got to take it," said Jemmy, as Molly put her
hands behind her—'cause it'll be a long job if I has ter
keep runnin' round yer arter yer hands. And if we each has
half, that's a hull one for breakfast—don't yer see?"

But at last the hungry child's fortitude gave way. Molly
dropped on the floor and burst into tears.

Mrs Lucas drew one of her "mile-long" sighs, and, stooping down by Molly, took the child on her lap, and began
chafing her hands and feet.

"The Lord help us!" she said; "what are we all a-
comin' to, 'long o' these men! Take a bite o' apple, dear—
Jemmy 'd sooner you would 'n not."

"I 's jest chuck the hull thing inter the ashes, if yer
don't," said Jemmy, rashly.

To this terrible threat Molly was forced to yield, and the
two halves of apple disappeared slowly and with much lingering enjoyment;—knots and hard places and seeds and core,
all included.

"Apples does make a man o' one, don't they?" said
Jemmy Lucas, giving himself a rousing shake. "Now,
Molly, what's afoot?"

"I 's got to go and find things," said little Molly, plaintively. "Father said so."

"Where 's yer goin' ter find 'em?" inquired Jemmy
Lucas.

"I 's got to look," said Molly, sighing. "And the Lord
He 'll help. You 's said so?" she added wistfully, looking
up at Mrs Lucas.

"No, I didn't," said the woman, hastily; and she rose from

her seat and put Molly down. "Don't see no signs of it, for my part."

But Molly repeated gladly—

"He 'll help—He 's the Great King. And bimeby we 's be there! Come, Jemmy."

And hand in hand the two children went forth to see how the help should come; Mrs Lucas kindly taking the broom, to finish the snow-sanding of her floor herself.

The air was stinging—and at first the children set off to run. But that made Molly cough, so that she had to stop and take breath, while Jemmy Lucas blew on his fingers and danced his feet. They went on more leisurely then, once in a while turning their backs to the wind and running gently so for a little, and then again facing it bravely. But if the little hard apple had really had any good effect—and I suppose it must, since everything does something—the work done was so slight, and so soon passed away, that neither of the children could remember that they had had any breakfast at all. Jemmy's mouth, as he blew and blew upon his fingers, began to work and twitch with more than cold; and two or three little tears slid down Molly's cold cheeks so fast that they hadn't time to freeze as they went.

"What 's we to do, Jemmy?" Molly stammered out.

"Don' know yet," said Jemmy Lucas, looking appealingly all round him at the snow. "I jest wish breakfast grew on bushes—I know that."

"But it would freeze hard," said Molly, with a wistful look at a bare, whistling clump of twigs by the road-side.

"Who 'd care?" said Jemmy Lucas. "Pity if we couldn't break it up, if 'twas all friz. Jest think, Molly, if there was a hull pot o' hot coffee a-hangin' friz up to this here bush!"

"It wouldn't be all coffee," said Molly, her face brightening at the very thought. "There 'd be bread on one branch."

"And gingerbread!" said Jemmy Lucas. "I wouldn't care about no apples, 'cause I 'se had one a'ready, yer see."

"You 's only had half," said Molly.

"Well, you had t'other—and that was jest as good," said Jemmy Lucas. "O Molly!—jest look at the cows!"

The roadway here lay through the rich, well-tilled farm of Squire Peasely, with small show now indeed on the white fields; but well the farmer knew what wealth of grain and fertility lay warmly hid under that snow blanket. By the very side of the road were the farmer's capacious barns, with plenty thrusting her cheery face from every crack and crevice. The cows stood gathered in the barnyard under warm sheds, the fowls came lazily forth to pick up the scattered grain at the barn door.

"Molly!—jest listen once!" said Jemmy Lucas, applying his ear to the slatted gate. Molly laid hers there too.

A sweet soft sound came distinctly from under one of the sheds—a sort of double sound, with a quiet, regular beat, beat.

"They's milkin'—sure as guns!" said Jemmy Lucas. "Don't I wish I had the cleanin' o' the pails!" The boy's eyes gleamed with interest and eagerness, but Molly only answered by a little sob.

"Does you think the King really knows we's set out, Jemmy?" she faltered.

"O' course he does," Jemmy said confidently. "But yer see He's got so many to look arter, Molly—mebbe we's got to wait our turn."

"We's was to set out—and then we's was to keep on—and bimeby we'd be there," Molly said dreamily, and leaning yet more upon the gate. Cold and hunger were again fast getting the upper hand.

"Don't yer, now, Molly!" cried Jemmy Lucas. "We'll run right on, and we'll be all warm and comfortable in jest a few minutes. And we's got ter go," he added hurriedly, as the sound of the milking ceased. "They's got through, I guess, and like as not they'd be mad ef we was here when they comed out."

And even as he spoke, a bright, warm-faced, round-cheeked man, well muffled up in jacket and mittens and comforter and fur cap, appeared from under the shed, and came towards them, pail in hand.

CHAPTER IV.

"WHAT's here? what's here?" said the young man, with a tone that tried to be rough and couldn't. "What's wanting now? Rather late in the day for chickens, ain't it?"

"Please, sir, we was a listenin' you milk," said Jemmy Lucas.

"Listening me milk!" the young man repeated. "If that don't beat the Dutch! What sort of a dodge d'ye call that, hey?"

"Please we was," Molly repeated, rousing up a little at sight of the stranger. "It sounded so good!"

"Yer see, we took breakfast sort o' early," explained Jemmy Lucas.

"Reckon ye did," said the man, shortly. "Supposin' you freeze solid to my gate—what then? Run on, run on! if you want to keep the life in ye."

"But yer see, she can't run a great deal," said Jemmy Lucas, "and the wind ain't quite so much here."

"Ain't it?" said the young farmer. "Must be pretty consid'rable elsewhere, I should think. What ails her that she can't run?"

Molly lifted her white, tear-marked face for an answer, but the man asked for no more.

"Good patience!" he ejaculated—"she'll die on my hands. What'd you fetch her out such a day for, you young scamp?"

"Old Limp sent her," said Jemmy Lucas, "and I come to help. And breakfast was so long ago."

"What was breakfast, anyhow?" said the young farmer.

"Oh, we had an apple," said Jemmy Lucas, simply. "Leastways, Molly had half, and so did I."

The young farmer set down his pail, and leaning over the gate, lifted Molly across as if she had been a feather. Then with the child still held fast under one arm, he took up his pail again and strode across the barnyard, bidding Jemmy Lucas follow.

"Do s'pose I'm showin' 'em the way," he muttered to himself; "but it's got to be done, all the same."

He flung open the great barn door, and, putting Molly down in a soft heap of fragrant hay, began rummaging about in quest of something.

"Was it you that run off a dozen o' my sheep a spell ago?" he inquired of Jemmy Lucas.

"No, sir," said Jemmy, thrusting hands and feet into the warm hay.

"And you don't know the taste o' my apples, I s'pose, neither?" said the man.

A few months ago Jemmy would have returned an unblushing "No," but now he only coloured and hung down his head.

"'Twarn't one of 'em you had for breakfast?"

"Oh no, sir!—not nigh so good!" Jemmy said, eagerly, remembering the next moment in utter dismay what he had said. But the young farmer only laughed.

"Who learned ye to tell the truth?" he said, coming back from his search with an old battered tin cup, which he dipped in the pail and held to Molly's lips without another word. But he was not prepared for the starving eagerness with which she drank. Never taking her lips from the cup, the child's eyes came once and again to his face with a wistful, grateful gladness that was something to see.

The young farmer dashed his rough mitten across his own eyes with some energy.

"Hang it!" he said—"and I should ha' been off to mill long ago if that 'ere calf hadn't been so plaguey long about his breakfast. And Dolly won't let a soul touch her but me. There now," he said, soothingly, as Molly drained the last drops; "that'll do to begin—let him have some next, —'cause you had part of the apple, you know."

Back and forth went the cup, from one child to the other, till the pail—which had held but a moderate supply—was empty.

"Was that all you had?" inquired Jemmy Lucas, with some compunction, peering in.

"I reckon not," laughed the young farmer, his spirits rising as the milk disappeared; "this here was only Dolly's strippings. 'Twas about the richest we had, I guess—but anyhow it's gone to the poorest place. So that squares it up. Now, youngsters, if you can run, you've got to, for I'm in the worst kind of a hurry. You ain't quite the same chaps you were a spell ago?"

"Guess not!" said Jemmy Lucas, throwing a deft somer-set into the middle of the heap of hay. "We's all thawed out and filled up. Come ahead, Molly."

"And next time you want somethin' o' mine," said the young farmer, "you come and ask for it like a man—d'ye hear? Don't go to helpin' yourselves."

"Catch me!" said Jemmy Lucas, giving three leaps out into the snow. Molly turned and held out her hand, all thawed now and warm, and her shy eyes were full of loving gratitude, but she said not a word. The young farmer gave the hand a good grip, marvelling the while at its cleanness, and then stood at the gate by his empty pail, watching the children till they were out of sight.

"Milked, and churned, and brought the butter!" he said, with a laugh, as he turned off to the house. "Fair yield, too. Wonder what mother'll say!"

"Jemmy," said little Molly, as they trudged along through the snow, "I guess he's one of the King's folks!"

"You s'pose the King telled him what to do?" said Jemmy Lucas, curiously.

"He must," said Molly. "How'd he know we was hungry?"

"'Twouldn't ha' took an extra spry man to find that out," said Jemmy Lucas. "Howsoever, he might ha' knowed and not ha' done it. Next door to breakfast on bushes, warn't it, Molly?"

"We's never had nothin' so good in all our lives," said Molly.

"Not half—nor a quarter," said Jemmy Lucas. "Now ef we could jest pick up somethin' as would stop your father's mouth, Molly, we might go home and read verses."

Where was it to come from? Untrodden snow on all
the fields, and along the road deep cut white channels
wherein the children's feet toiled painfully. The cows in
the barnyards, the chickens grouped under the sheds, the
houses tight shut up around their glowing fire-centres.
Only abroad and adrift were the two little children. The
sunbeams struggled faintly through a gray vail, the day
was growing colder.

"Jemmy," Molly said in her pitiful voice, "don't you
guess we'll find somethin' pretty soon? I's asked the
King—and He won't forget, Jemmy?"

"It 'ud be easy enough ef we could jest help ourselves,"
said Jemmy Lucas, thrusting his hands deeper down in
his pockets as if to put them out of the way of temptation.
"That's how I used. Look, Molly—see that 'ere pigeon
a-sittin' up on the barn? Why, he wouldn't be nowhere,
in a minute, ef I was jest to send arter him. Leastways
he'd be here," Jemmy added, softly, and clapping his empty
pockets.

"But you mustn't!" said Molly.

"Ain't a-goin' to," said Jemmy. "I'd be afeard o' bein'
seen, and, so it 'ud be crooked."

"And if you walks crooked, you won't never get there,"
repeated Molly, looking wearily round. Oh, how hard it
seemed to get there, walking straight!

"That's what she said," assented Jemmy. "All the
same, the way them hens cackles is fit to drive a feller
mad! Let's run, Molly."

So from walking to running still through those deep
sleigh tracks, till the dangerous barnyard was passed, and
Molly was forced to stop for breath.

"I can't run no further, Jemmy," she said. "Let's say
words."

"Well, say on," answered Jemmy Lucas.

"'My little children'"—Molly began slowly. "Ain't it
pretty, Jemmy?"

"What's next?" said Jemmy Lucas.

"Ye—must—sin not," said Molly, supplying forgotten parts.

"That fits," said Jemmy Lucas. "'Tain't jest the easiest road, Molly. 'Bout as nice as steppin' along top o' this here soft snow, 'stead o' down in the ruts. Fust thing yer know, yer's in up t'yer eyes. What'd yer s'pose now ever made the King give such queer d'rections?"

"He don't like it," said Molly.

"Helpin' yerself?" Jemmy suggested.

Molly nodded.

"'Twon't pay then, in course," said the little boy. "Molly you's all beat out. And there ain't a livin' thought o' nothin' in sight. I guess we'd as good go home, and take it as it comes. 'Twon't be more'n common, likely."

"O Jemmy, I's afeerd!" said little Molly. "And Peter ain't much there to help now, and when I's knocked down I gets all dizzy like."

Jemmy Lucas gave a sort of groan.

"Jest wish some great big feller'd knock *him* down to some purpose," he said.

"But you mustn't say such things; and you mustn't wish 'em, either," said a kind, comfortable voice. The children stopped and looked round.

A little box sleigh, painted blue, and drawn by an old gray horse, had come silently up while they talked, and having no bells to warn them, had come near enough for the driver to hear Jemmy's last words.

An oldish woman, common looking but for the uncommon kindness in her face, held the reins loosely in her blue-striped mittens, and eyed the two children with grave eyes.

"You mustn't say such things, little boy," she repeated. "It's wrong."

"Is it?" said Jemmy Lucas—"seems as if everythin' was. Well, I guess you can't make it out right for old Limp to go knockin' Molly down, ef he does have the luck to be her father."

"Knock her down? Oh, that is dreadful!" said the woman, changing colour.

"He does it, though," said Jemmy Lucas. "That's why

she's out now. And my father would, only I'm too spry for him."

"Do you mean that she's out in all this snow to keep him from knocking her down?" said the woman, gazing at Molly.

"She's out lookin' for somethin'—for fear," explained the boy. "He's drunk up everythin', and wants more."

"Oh, I see," said the woman. "She's going to the store."

"No, she ain't, neither," said Jemmy Lucas. "What's the good of a store 'thout the tin? And we can't take things no more, so it's puzzlin'."

"Oh, you've given up that, have you?" said the woman, smiling.

"The King don't like it," said Molly, speaking for the first time, "so we's different."

"Poor little pilgrims!" said the woman, twinkling her eyelashes, "are you following the Great King?"

"Oh yes, we's set out," said Molly, joyously. "But it's so fur!" she added, sighing.

"Maybe not, maybe not," said the woman, gently. "The Lord Jesus takes some little tired ones by a short road, dear. Just gathers them up in His arms and bears them away. And I wouldn't wonder a bit if He did you. Keep on, dear, and don't be down-hearted. And now, see!—here's just what you want, hid away down under my buffalo."

She stooped down, rummaging about, and presently pulled out a little tin can and a loaf of bread.

"I was takin' 'em somewhere's else," she said, "but I've no doubt the King meant 'em for you. The bread'll freeze solid, I do suppose, but it'll thaw again—that's one thing. And now do you take some soup yourself, the minute you get home—d'ye hear? And fetch me my pail some day, down to the furthest end o' the village—Mrs Bingham's. And just trust and follow on, and you'll be there afore you think."

CHAPTER V.

"I DECLARE!" said Jemmy Lucas, as the little blue sleigh drove off, "it do pay ter go round with you, Molly Limp! Why, I never had so much happen, not in all my born days."

"Think o' the King's tellin' her to put the things in for us!" said Molly.

"And her not knowin' it at fust," said Jemmy Lucas. "Yer see, Molly, we didn't know ourselves we was a comin' this way, so in course she couldn't. But the King He knowed all about it. Wonder how He telled her we was the ones!"

"He telled her soft," said Molly, the old dreamy look coming over her face. "I's heard Him, Jemmy, often."

"What's He tell you?" said Jemmy Lucas, curiously.

"He says 'Bimeby,'" said Molly; "and He says 'My little children'—and 'the Advocate.'"

"'Him's the one as takes 'em up and carries 'em,'" said Jemmy Lucas.

"And gets 'em all forgived," said Molly, "when they's done crooked, Jemmy."

Jemmy looked at her and nodded, as if he took the full force of the words.

"We's best to hurry home now, Molly," he said, noticing then the pale wan face of his little companion. "You's so tired!"

"Yes, I's tired," said Molly, patiently turning round and beginning to trudge back towards Vinegar Hill.

"Wish I could carry yer, Molly, every single step o' the way, I do," said little Jemmy, seizing both pail and loaf as his share of the burden. "But 'tain't no use standin' here no longer, 'cause she's out o' sight, and it's time we was home."

"What time's it, Jemmy?" Molly asked.

"Well, by my watch," said Jemmy Lucas, screwing up his eyes, and trying to locate the sun as exactly as possible behind that gray veil—"'tain't quite so easy ter pull it out in this sort o' weather, but by my watch, Molly, I should say—it was—goin' on—arternoon!"

Which definite announcement had at least the effect of quickening Molly's steps with some indefinite fear.

"Yer can't hold on like that," said Jemmy Lucas, "so wot's the use? I say, Molly, don't yer wish we jest had a pair o' wings apiece? It's mortal cold down in this here snow."

"Where's you get 'em?" said little Molly, wonderingly.

"Don't jest know," said Jemmy Lucas, pondering. "Yes, I does too!—Molly, I's goin' ter fetch 'em out o' this here tin pail—straight!"

Molly stopped short and looked.

"I say," pursued Jemmy Lucas, "she didn't tell us ter wait till we got home for it. Then we's jest take it now while we can get it, and it'll be every bit as good as a cutter ter fetch yer home. Open yer mouth, Molly, and hold fast all I give yer!"

And Jemmy Lucas in great haste pulled off the cover of the little tin pail, and gave Molly a cautious sip of its contents.

"Tiptop, ain't it?" he said, smacking his lips for sympathy. "What's it like, Molly?"

"Jest you's try," said Molly, the light coming into her eyes. "You's got to get home too, Jemmy."

"Fact!" Jemmy responded, and dealing out another cautious sip to himself. "Why, it's a'most like solid meat. Must ha' been hull pounds and pounds biled up in this, Molly. Somethin' like a dozen, I guess. Have another? Ef we drops down, and don't never get back, the old man won't get none o' it—so."

There was great practical wisdom in this remark, and a few more mouthfuls of the strong broth were distributed with great comfort to all parties. The children began to feel like somebody else.

"Jest wish I could let yer have some bread 'long with it," said Jemmy Lucas, handling the loaf. "But if we was ter break it, Molly, like as not old Limp 'ud say so. And I ain't got no knife ter speak of."

But with that the boy took from his pocket a large clasp knife, bright and new.

"Don't it cut?" inquired Molly, innocently.

"Cut!" cried Jemmy Lucas. "Why, I's most doubtful ter have it in my pocket, fear it'll cut all shut up. 'Tain't that. But yer see, Molly," he added, dropping his voice to a confidential whisper, "the knife ain't 'xactly straight, so that's the trouble."

"You's tooked it?" asked Molly, in the same low tone.

Jemmy Lucas nodded.

"I finds I don't never enjoy usin' it, fear o' bein' seen," he went on—"so it's a clear case o' crooked. And I's goin' to put it back where it come from, the fust chance."

Molly smiled approvingly, and the little pail being once more tight shut up, the weary little pilgrims, refreshed and strengthened for the time, took up again the line of march for Vinegar Hill.

"D'ye s'pose now, Molly, the King telled her how ter make it so strong?" said Jemmy Lucas, his wondering thoughts going back to the broth.

"He must," said Molly, undoubtingly. "He knowed which way we was comin', Jemmy, and how tired we'd be, and all about it. And so He just telled her to have it ready."

"Beats me how it's managed," said Jemmy Lucas. "T'other lady, up ter the old meetin'-house, must ha' spoke true, Molly. 'Bout His seein' everythin', yer know. Tell yer what, it don't feel nice when yer's got old Graves's knife in yer pocket!"

"But you's goin' to take it back," said Molly.

"Fust chance," Jemmy repeated. "Yer see, Molly, it won't never do ter put it down, 'thout I's sure there ain't none o' t'other chaps hangin' round ter pick it up. And they's allers down there, I do think. So I has ter wait. But I ain't usin' of it."

"And the King's lookin' on the whole way," said Molly. "See, Jemmy—as we puts our foots down in the snow, He knows. And sometimes the Lord Jesus takes 'em right up.'

"Wonder why He don't you, then," said Jemmy Lucas.

"Maybe He's busy now," said little Molly, simply. "But He's lookin', Jemmy. And He's pleadin' too—and so it's all forgived. And it can't fail, 'cause He does it."

Molly walked on silently after that, her little fingers pressed tight together under the old ragged shawl, and Jemmy Lucas was quiet too, studying his little companion's words and looks with unspoken awe and admiration as they went towards Vinegar Hill. The winter twilight was already beginning to veil the sorrows and tone down the hardships of that "sour spot," and Jemmy Lucas brought pail and loaf and Molly all safe to the door of Walter Limp's hut, long before that worthy thought of quitting his boon companions at James Dodd's.

"Now you's got to come in, Jemmy, and take half," said little Molly, giving the boy's ragged sleeve a gentle pull.

"Guess I will!" said Jemmy Lucas, freeing himself from that slight obstruction. "And when I does, I guess yer'll know it, and I too. Make the most of it yer can, for gracious! I ain't a-goin' ter take not a drop nor a crumb. Come ter think, though, I'll take the pail," the boy added, stepping inside the door. "'Twont never answer ter let old Limp get hold o' that. I'll hide it, straight off, Molly; and then some day you and me'll go carry it back."

No sooner said than done. The broth was quickly turned into an old jug, and Jemmy Lucas scampered off with the pail, skilfully dodging every boy and man that came in his way, and draining the while every last drop that could be drained into his own mouth.

Molly watched him from the door till he vanished in the gathering darkness, and then went back into the little hut with a happy smile upon her lips.

"Molly, can't you's get some chips, dear?" said poor Mrs Limp, who, having put broth and bread carefully away, was now trotting the baby again. "It's cruel cold—and when he comes, there'll be our two heads off."

With silent patience little Molly went forth again into the night, groping round with bare hands among the snow-covered chips at the door, till she had filled her old basket.

Then she came in and lit a very small fire in the little rickety stove, and sat down, and held out her hands towards the cold iron.

"Where'd you find so much, Molly?" said Mrs Limp. Molly told.

"Did you's take some, mother?" she inquired.

"I durstn't, Molly," said poor Mrs Limp, sighing. "He'd be certain to ask. I durstn't to touch it."

Molly rubbed her hands slowly, holding them still out towards the stove, and for a while was silent.

"Think o' the King's askin' us all, mother!" she said. "Ain't it wonderful?"

"Love the child!" ejaculated Mrs Limp. "Whatever are you's talkin' about, dear?"

"It's all ready, too," Molly went on, scarce seeming to hear her. "And we's all asked. And I's goin'?"

"Listen her once!" said Mrs Limp, under her breath, and eyeing Molly as if she were a sort of weird thing, quite beyond ordinary comprehension. "Where's you goin', love?"

"I's goin' to the King's house," said Molly, curling and twisting her hands in a dreamy sort of fashion over the old stove. "And Jemmy's goin'. And we's got to walk straight and different. We's set out, mother,—and we's to keep on; and bimeby we's be there. Why, she said maybe afore I'd think!" said the child, a gleam of joy coming like a stray sunbeam across her wasted face. "And we won't be sick never no more; won't ache nor nothin'. And they's got plenty, plenty!—Oh I wish we was there!"

"Molly, you's tired, dear," said poor Mrs Limp, soothingly. "And it ain't quite so cold in bed. And maybe you'll sleep right on till mornin'."

"Will there be bread for breakfast?" said little Molly.

"We'll see," answered Mrs Limp, evasively. "Who knows?"

Molly got up slowly, and crept away to her so-called bed, rolling herself up there in the tattered covers as best she could. And before the tired eyes had time to close, Mrs

R

Limp came to the bed, with the baby tucked under one arm, and in her hand a small cracked mug.

"It's got to be, if he kills me for it," she said. "And it wouldn't matter much. Drink it, Molly—fast as you can, dear, and don't tell."

And with the comfort of these few more spoonfuls of the broth, little Molly was soon asleep.

It may interest those who are curious about things, to know that Walter Limp swallowed every drop of the broth that was left, that very night, as soon as he came home. And with the first light of the morning he took the loaf of bread, and went forth and sold it for another dram.

CHAPTER VI.

LITTLE Molly Limp woke up when the late winter morning had fairly set in, feeling very stiff and sore. Sleep among those old rags was not such a warm, balmy thing as to banish all remembrance of the pinching hours of the day, and Molly huddled herself up in a new position, and tried in vain to forget her back-ache and her tired little feet. Then she unrolled herself and crept out into the next room.

"He's just took it all, Molly," said Mrs Limp, as Molly's eyes went round the room, looking for both the bread and her father. "But he's took himself off with it—that's somethin'."

Yes, it was something; and with that cold comfort Molly sat down in a corner of the hearth, and the breakfast hour passed by with empty hands.

"It smelt so good!" said little Molly, refreshing herself with the remembrance. "And it was a whole big loaf, wasn't it, mother; nobody hadn't even cut a piece off."

"'Twas big to look at; 'twouldn't ha' been so very big to eat," said poor Mrs Limp, trotting her baby. "You and me could ha' stood it, easy."

Molly glanced hungrily up, but she said nothing. Then came the blessed sunshine streaming in, through gray clouds and dusty window; and little Molly's thoughts were caught and held and carried away.

"They don't never want the sun up there!" she said. "They hasn't no need of it—only think, mother!—'cause the King's face shines so. And they don't cry any more, and they never says they's sick; and the sorrow and sighing has all runned away."

"It's all run this way, then, I guess," said Mrs Limp. "What's you talkin' about, Molly? Seems sometimes lately as though you was sort o' silly. Ain't sick more'n common, is you, dear?"

"I aches a good deal," said Molly, with her patient face. "Just think, mother, I won't ache at all bimeby!"

"I'll be glad, for one," said Mrs Limp, humouring the child, as she thought.

"Only we's got to walk straight," said Molly. "And sometimes, when they's very tired, you know, He takes 'em up and carries 'em. Oh, I's so glad! And He'll help—He'll help," the child repeated to herself.

"This here's a pretty sort of a go, I do s'pose!" said Peter Limp, bursting into the house at this minute, followed by two or three more. "I say, Moll, where's the rest o' yer pickin's? We's all sharp for breakfast."

"I's got nothin', Peter," said little Molly.

"No, I reckon not," said Peter, roughly. "Yer's so mighty fond o' yer daddy, guess likely yer give him the hull on it."

"He tooked it," said Molly. "All the soup last night, and the bread this mornin'."

"Soup, too, of all things!" said Jem Crook. "Why it's better'n better. Guess I'd as good marry Molly out o' hand and set up ter housekeep. Sich a market woman!"

"And bein' too good ter eat none of it herself," said Tim Wiggius, "o' course there's the more left."

"I say, Moll!" Peter went on, "where'd yer find it? Ain't no use sittin' there as if butter wouldn't melt in yer mouth. I telled yer t'other thing wouldn't pay—had ter come the old dodge, didn't yer ? "

" I didn't took a bit of it, Peter," said little Molly, looking up with her wistful eyes. " I ain't agoin' to do nothing bad, never no more. You knows I 's set out, Peter."

The colour flushed into Peter's face, spite of all he could do, and he stood silent for a minute. Jem Crook burst into a loud laugh.

" Ain't she jest the rarest little fox as walks ! " he said. " Come on, boys—might ha' knowed she 'd ha' had it all eat up by this time."

And away went the troop, whirling out as they had whirled in, only that Peter had an uneasy pain somewhere in his breast which he could not quite lay off upon the cold weather ; and Molly and Mrs Limp and the baby sat thinking. If that baby laid up knowledge at all in proportion to its ceaseless examination of things in general, with those sadly precocious eyes, its store must have been immense.

" Molly ! " said Mrs Limp at last, in a whisper, " they 's all gone now, dear—and he won't be back afore night—and we 's got somethin' ! " said Mrs Limp, with almost a smile.

Molly looked up in wonder.

" It come yesterday," said Mrs Limp, enjoying her secret. " And I was put to where to hide it, fear o' his gettin' it. And it 's round in under the stove, Molly, where the ashes goes ; we 's had so little fire, 'tain't full."

Sure enough, in among the ashes, under the oven so long unused, lay a neat little package, or rather two ; so well wrapped up that the ashes had done no harm, though indeed both mother and child were far too hungry to mind trifles. And what a breakfast ! For in one package there were actually ham sandwiches !—slice after slice of white bread neatly folded together, with savoury ham between, and cold potatoes sliced up for garnishing. And the other package was a little paper bag of parched corn.

" I ain't even looked at 'em," said Mrs Limp, watching Molly ; " I just hid 'em away as hard as I could. There was a boy as fetched 'em—'for Molly Limp,' he said. But who sent 'em, he never telled."

"It must have been the King!" said little Molly, beginning to eat her sandwich with eager hunger and deliberate enjoyment that somewhat disputed the ground, "'cause nobody else wouldn't have knowed, mother."

"'Twarn't no king," said Mrs Limp; "'twere a small boy."

"But the King sent him," said Molly. "We's eat part, and keep part; and I's give Jemmy Lucas some o' the corn."

"There's a plenty for to-morrer too," said Mrs Limp, who was eating her share with even more than Molly's eagerness. "And he wont never know a mite about it. He ain't apt to kiss nobody when he comes home," said Mrs Limp with severe pleasantry, "and if he did, he couldn't smell nothin' more'n what he allers fetches along.'

The meal was finished, to-morrow's portion safe hid away in the ashes, and poor Mrs Limp, drowsy under the unusual refreshment, leaned her head against the old chimney and went fast asleep. Molly, too, dozed, curled up on the floor with Jemmy's corn in her pocket, and only the baby's wide-open eyes kept watch and ward over the little hut. Only they, that anybody could see. But not all the stars in their courses—not all the many kingdoms and concerns of this lower world—not all the wise and good and distinguished people that were on the earth—could make the Great King of heaven and earth forget, even for one moment, the poor, shattered old hut on Vinegar Hill, where dwelt one little child who had set out to seek and to follow Him.

By and by, in came Jemmy Lucas. He crept round softly by Molly and roused her with a touch.

"Molly!" he said, "no need ter wake *her* up, yer know; but ain't you's sleeped most enough?"

"Oh, I's all awake," said little Molly, straightening herself up. "Look here, Jemmy—just you's feel down in my pocket!"

Down went Jemmy's hand, finding its way with the deftness of long practice among rags and misleading holes, and up it came again, with a full grasp of parched corn.

"Molly! you's a brick!" said Jemmy Lucas, gathering up and conveying to his mouth a few stray kernels that had dropped by the way. "Hold yer apron; mind that 'ere hole, Molly! Corn's fustrate!"

"You's got to eat it all!" said Molly, with a face of delight. "I's got a little for me in t'other pocket. Slip it in somewheres, quick, Jemmy, 'fore nobody's sees it."

"Her?" inquired Jemmy Lucas, nodding towards the sleeping Mrs Limp.

"Oh, I's telled her," said Molly, "but Peter might come, or the boys. They's been once, now."

"They's all safe," said Jemmy Lucas, "off a longways, Molly. I seen 'em go, and then I come straight here. Astonishin' corn, ain't it?"

Jemmy slipped the corn into his own pocket as he spoke, taking therefrom grain by grain with immense satisfaction, and listening wonderingly to Molly's story of how it came.

"And does yer think the King sent it, sure enough?" he asked.

"Nobody else knowed," said Molly.

"Fact!" said Jemmy Lucas. "Parched corn don't grow on none o' our bushes, that's certain. Jest do wish I knowed how He tells folks, though. I say, Molly, you reckon the Book tells? S'posin' we read some, and find out."

"Peter's book's tooked away," said Molly, jumping up with glad eagerness; "but I's got mine. Wait till I fetch it, Jemmy. We keeps it hid away in the well," she added, sinking her voice to a whisper; "'cause you knows father don't never go near there."

So off to the old well Molly went, to find her treasure lying hid there among the moss and ice, wrapped in fold after fold of an old torn quilt, and then laid in a little old box, and then shoved in between the stones. Molly came back and sat down by Jemmy Lucas, and carefully took off the wrappings, and gave him the book with her old direction—

"Read anywheres."

The book opened easily at one of Mrs Kensett's marks, and Jemmy began at the top of the page, and read straight down.

.   .   .   .

"A man's life consisteth not in the abundance of the things which he possesseth."

CHAPTER VII.

"Queer, ain't it now?" said Jemmy Lucas, stopping short, and looking at Molly. "Things turns round in this here book till yer hardly know where they is. Rich folks allers seems ter live so easy like,—and we jest rubs and goes, yer know, Molly."

"What's next, Jemmy?" Molly answered; her usual resource in all Bible difficulties.

"It's a story 'bout a rich man—a terrible rich man," said Jemmy Lucas, glancing over the passage. "Had more'n he knowed what t' do with. Jest listen, once."

And Jemmy spelled out slowly the parable of the rich man whose ground "brought forth plentifully." Molly sat and pondered.

"Fust he had everythin', and then he didn't have nothin'," said Jemmy Lucas. "Beats me, Molly!"

"But you see, Jemmy, it warn't really so much to begin," said Molly.

"Why, it was lots!—hull lots!" cried Jemmy Lucas. "Fairly bothered him where ter put it."

"Then I guess he didn't love the King," said Molly; "and so it all seemed to turn to nothin'."

"That's so," said Jemmy Lucas, reading the words once more. "O' course, the King's more'n the hull village, barns and all. D' ye s'pose it means that, now?"

Molly nodded, her face lighting up.

"We's follerin'," she said, with a sudden feeling of untold

wealth. "And bimeby we's be there—in the King's house, Jemmy. Only think!"

Jemmy Lucas shook his head, as if the subject was still too much for him, and read on.

"'Therefore I say unto you, Take no thought for your life, what ye shall eat; neither for the body, what ye shall put on.'"

Jemmy Lucas looked down at his well-patched trousers; where, indeed, the patches had so nearly replaced the original stuff, that it was hard to tell which was which, and then glanced at Molly's wan, pinched face. Then he broke into a laugh.

"I can't make the fust thing out of it," he said. "Folks don't take much care o' things out this way, Molly; and I should say it were a heap better ef they did."

"Read on, Jemmy," said little Molly.

"'Consider the ravens: for they neither sow nor reap; which neither have storehouse nor barn; and God feedeth them.'"

"What's ravens?" inquired Molly.

"They's jest birds," said Jemmy Lucas. "So, in course, they don't have no barns; but does He feed 'em, I wonder? Thought they jest picked up a livin'. I say, Molly, let's we get up 'fore light some mornin' and watch."

"You s'pose He throws it 'way down out o' the sky?" said Molly.

"Must," said Jemmy Lucas, "'thout He gives the trees a shake ter send the seeds off. And no livin' bird 'ud wait for that."

"Maybe He puts the seeds there a' purpose, all ready," said Molly.

"Guess you've hit it now!" said Jemmy Lucas, though something loth to give up his own brilliant idea of the feeding. "He puts it all ready when He has time, and then when they's ready they picks it fer theirselves."

Jemmy read on again, slowly, through words and meanings not always quite clear, and yet where something of the beauty and something of the intent shone through with a

power which no ignorance could withstand. "'The way-
faring man, though a fool, shall not err therein.'" Molly
Limp sat drinking in the words. Jemmy Lucas, on his part,
was hardly less absorbed.

"'If, then, God so clothe the grass which is to-day in the
field, and to-morrow is cast into the oven, how much more
you, O ye of little faith?'"

"'And seek ye not what ye shall eat, or what ye shall
drink, neither be ye of doubtful mind. For all these things
do the nations of the world seek after; and your Father
knoweth that ye have need of these things.'"

"There! there!" said Molly, leaning forward in her
eagerness, and laying both hands upon the book. "I said
He knowed! O Jemmy! does you hear?"

"Guess I does," said Jemmy Lucas, going the words over
again to himself; "it is jest tiptop. Does you reckon He
allers knows, Molly? 'Cause 'tain't every day as things
comes."

"It's most every day," said Molly; "somethin' or 'nother.
And if we's sure He knows, Jemmy, then we's can wait—
oh, ever so long!"

"I does s'pose that's safe—seein' who it is," said Jemmy
Lucas, still pondering. "'Your Father knoweth that ye
have need of such things.' Yer see 'tain't none o' our fathers
'bout here, Molly. They knows, too, and they doesn't act
up to it. But in course the King's different. 'Don't yer be
doubtful,' it says; so it must be sure to come. Well, I's
been doubtful lots o' times, Molly; and so's mother."

"But we's ain't goin' to be, no more," said Molly, joyously. "Read on, Jemmy."

Jemmy Lucas read on slowly, dwelling on every word.

"'But rather seek ye the kingdom of God; and all these
things shall be added unto you. Fear not, little flock; for
it is your Father's good pleasure to give you the kingdom.'"

How rich the music of the words!—how wonderful the
promise!—how weak, how poor, how needy, these little ones
to whom the promise came; filling their craving hearts with
more than their hearts could bear! The boy's voice trembled:

his lips were all in a quiver as he read; and Molly hid her face and sobbed, but so softly that she lost not a word.

"He likes it!" she cried at last. "It's good to him too!"

"Goes right down here—I knows that," faltered Jemmy Lucas, taking hold of his throat with both hands, as if the trouble were there.

"And we's to seek it, and He'll give it," said Molly. "What's seek, Jemmy?"

"Lookin' might and main, and follerin' on it up," said Jemmy Lucas. "That's the great thing."

"What comes next?" said Molly.

Jemmy Lucas read on through the next two verses, pausing long at the last.

"What's treasure?" inquired Molly again.

"Best thing yer got," said Jemmy Lucas, promptly.

"And we's got to have ours 'way up there," said Molly, leaning back her head to catch a glint of sunshine through the old roof.

"In course," said Jemmy Lucas. "Yer see, Molly, reckon we'd be jest put to it ter keep it down here. Can't hide away much in the well; and yer daddy'd find it, likely, some day, besides."

"But the King keeps it now," said Molly, contentedly.

"Like ter see it once, jest," said Jemmy Lucas. "Fact is, Molly, I can't hardly s'picion what the kingdom mought be like."

"It's the best we's got," said Molly, with her quiet little face all bright with the far-off reflection. "And nobody can't get it—and bimeby we's be there."

"Foller it up, that's the thing," said Jemmy Lucas, referring to his book. "Jest think, Molly, there can't no thief so much as come nigh it!"

Of all the wonderful words to the little waifs of Vinegar Hill, this was surely one!

The children shut up their book, and hid it away once more,—it was time now, and Mrs Lucas and the baby both woke up; and Jemmy Lucas ran away to his own poor home, first making an appointment with Molly to take home Mrs Bingham's tin pail the very next day.

Walter Limp came home in an unusually bad humour that night. Unusually early too, and with more power of speech and of locomotion than common. Either the loaf of bread had brought less than he expected, or he had drunk it up too soon, for he went roaming and storming round the house in a fashion that made his wife and children flee to the darkest corners they could find. Peter, indeed, having stayed long enough to find out that there was no prospect of supper, took himself off entirely; but poor Molly and Mrs Limp had no such resource. With a curious sort of instinct, the man perceived that—somehow or other—these two forlorn ones were a trifle less forlorn than ordinary; they had more strength to get out of his way, more composure under his blows and curses. That such a thing as ham-sandwiches could be or could have been in the house, did not indeed enter Walter Limp's head; but that some atoms of comfort had come and gone, he felt sure. Just sober enough to guess that, just tipsy enough to find it hard to follow out his conclusions, Walter Limp stormed and raved that night like a wild beast rather than a man. Mrs Limp, much heartened up by the good food and rest she had had that day, set herself determinately to keep the small supply that still remained, for herself and Molly. Ah, when did ever a drunkard's wife succeed in doing that!

"Yer 've got a stock in hand somewheres," he said, fiercely. "I knows it jest, as good as if I'd seen it. Hand it over, I say!—or it 'll be the worse for yer both!"

"We 's got nothin'," Mrs Limp repeated, trotting the baby in a far corner.

Molly, on her part, heard this denial with a stirred heart. "When you 're afraid to be seen, that 's crooked;" and surely Mrs Limp was desperately afraid of being found out. Did the King mean they should tell what He had sent them? did He mean they should hide it? What was "straight," in such a thicket?

Molly searched her memory for any Bible words on the

matter, but could find none; only the verse Jemmy had read that afternoon kept coming up like an answer.

"Fear not, little flock." Did that mean they were to tell, and then not be afraid?—not afraid for their supplies?—not afraid for themselves? It did seem more straight to answer "Yes" than "No," to Walter Limp's repeated demands. Yet her mother kept saying no. Molly, in her own dark corner, pondered this question till she was tired, sure only of one thing, that every "No" from the other corner made her shrink and wish it unspoken.

"I'll fetch yer to terms," said Walter Limp, at last. "I'll take every mortal thing out o' this here old pen, and see how yer'll like that. May as well begin with the stove —come you here and bear a hand. Put the brat down on the floor, I say, and come!"

"But we'll all freeze up!" said his wife, piteously. "We's most froze now."

"Folks as eats all day long don't friz easy," said Walter Limp, wrenching down a joint of the old pipe.

"But it ain't cleaned out, Walter," said poor Mrs Limp, putting her baby on the floor, and coming timidly up.

"Clean it out, then!" said Walter Limp, with a terrible oath. "Full o' ashes, is it?—didn't know as yer kept sich roarin' fires. That's the way my money goes."

"It ain't full," said poor Mrs Limp, kneeling down, and beginning to fumble with the stove doors. Her husband watched her. Suddenly another oath burst from his lips, and in a moment she fell senseless beneath his hand. Some unwary touch or motion had betrayed her secret; and in the very moment of slipping out the two little packets into the old bent tin that served for an ash-bucket, Walter Limp saw and seized them, gave one glance at the contents, and rushed storming from the house.

Little Molly laid down the baby then (she had crept round to take it up), and came and rubbed her mother's face and hands, and did all she could to bring her to. It was not the first time she had ever done such a thing,—not the first time she had seen her mother senseless, with the red drops starting from some sharp cut on face or head; but now Molly had for help the King's name in her heart. Yet somehow, as the child remembered the sweetness of that Name which is above every name, it shook her as not pain nor fear could often do, and hot tears fell fast with the cold water which she was sprinkling on her mother's face.

"He knows!" thought Molly, "He knows!" And it seemed almost as if her heart would spend itself in one long sob.

CHAPTER VIII.

VINEGAR HILL was not easily disturbed. A woman knocked down, more or less,—an extra child sick,—what did it signify? So though poor Mrs Limp went about next day with her head bound up, and though Molly's eyes and cheeks were bright with fever, nobody paid much heed, or felt uneasy about it. If Limp had killed his wife outright, the other women of Vinegar Hill would only have said—

"She's quiet, anyhow, if nobody else ain't;" and the men would have expressed their opinion that such indulgence in the matter of a wife was "risky." But unless the affair had got abroad, so as to entail prison consequences—which might not have been, at Vinegar Hill—nobody would have been even much excited.

Walter Limp did not come home again that night, which was, at least, a small bit of miserable comfort. Molly sobbed herself to sleep on the floor, and Mrs Limp sat by her, holding the baby, in a stupid passiveness of both body and mind. What was the use of trying to put one's self to bed in rags? The head might ache a little less for the time, or the heart forget its dull pain; but it was only the worse to wake up to them both as a new thing. And so the poor woman sat motionless through the rest of the long, dark hours, stunned and dizzy yet with her fall, and scarce heeding the dawn

when it crept in ; nor the cocks—that would crow, even at
Vinegar Hill ; nor the clear sunbeams that would look down
there, if only to see what they could do. Little Molly slept
on, her heavy, fevered sleep ; and the morning was far on
before the weary child sat up on the floor, and began to look
about her.

"There ain't nothin'—if that's what you's alookin' for,"
said Mrs Limp, stolidly.

Molly dropped her face in her hands, but made no answer.
She sat still a long time.

"Molly, you's worse this mornin'," said Mrs Limp, with
just the faintest little stir at her heart. "You's real bad,
dear."

"I's thinkin'," said Molly. "I's tryin' to 'member what
the King said. We's not to be doubtful, 'cause _He_ knows,"
the child went on, resting her hot cheek against her hand.
"He knows we wants 'em. And we's not to fear, and we's
just to foller. Oh ! it's so good, mother."

"I's glad anythin's good, love," said poor Mrs Limp.

"Jemmy 'n me's goin'," said Molly again, without lifting
her eyes. "And the King's telled everybody. And some
of 'em won't come."

Molly's head drooped down lower, and her thoughts wandered, and her words were unconnected ; and Mrs Limp, at
last, put the baby on the floor, and carried Molly off to the
best bed she could make out of her wretched materials. Not
that day, nor the next, did the child go with Jemmy Lucas
to carry home the tin pail. More than one week passed by
before Molly was able to sit up. And how did she live all
that time ? Well, it was hard to say. Jemmy Lucas
brought the freshest cold water for Molly's thirst, with
every apple or semblance of a dainty of any sort that came
into his hands. Mrs Limp sold her old petticoat, secretly,
for bread ; and other women of the hamlet did what they
could. From the baskets of odds and ends which some of
them begged at the village, many a half-cup of broth, many
a half-picked bone, found its way to Molly Limp. Secretly,
of course ; these women had, most of them, domestic tyrants

or terrors at home, as well as a host of clamorous children ; but their hearts opened easily to the need which, for the time, was even greater than their own. Very weary feet ran over to Limp's—"jest to see how the child was," at the end of the day ; very tired hands brought pails of water, or held the baby for a little, to relieve Mrs Limp ; and hard, care-seamed faces softened, and were even beautified, as they watched over the sick child. Molly was a wonder to them all, those days. Her chance words were so strange, her stray smiles so happy. Vinegar Hill had seen nothing like it in all its life before. To some it was all a riddle ; to others, who, as Jemmy Lucas said, had known things long ago, before they ever came to that sour region, it was all like the touching of an old, long-broken string—a thrill of inexpressible discord, that went through them like a pain. Jemmy's own mother was one of these—keen to catch every word the sick child said, quick to understand them, turning away from them with bitter stricture of heart. Especially was this the case when Jemmy Lucas himself was there to answer. The faintest word Molly spoke, he could hear it ; and if it was but a word—all scattered and disconnected—Jemmy Lucas knew just where and whence it came. And as Molly tossed, and muttered, and cried out, in her fever-dreams, Jemmy Lucas caught up the words and put them together, or in the setting where each belonged, proclaiming them then to the amazed listeners, as something quite too good and precious to be kept to himself.

"It's the Lord Jesus she means now," he would say ; " the Advocate, yer know ; Him as gets us forgived when we's been doin' crooked."

"There!—yes, Molly, the King knowed. And so *that's* how the chicken bone come," he said ; looking round at his mother with a glad smile. "But He's got the best keeping of it—she's thinkin' o' that now. And—O Molly ! yer needn't ter be in sich a takin' ter get there, and me here ! " And Jemmy fairly broke down and cried, while poor Mrs Lucas threw her apron over her face and ran home as fast as she could.

However, the Lord's time was not yet ; and the little life struggled back again to its ordinary place among the winds and frosts of this lower earth. Looking frailer and fainter than before, and yet bright with a certain shining which made all Vinegar Hill say—

"Whatever's come to Molly Limp!"

While some added sagely, that "next time old Limp scared that 'ere child ter death, she'd go for good." But it was not the fright and sorrow of one particular night that had laid such hold of Molly, save as a finishing touch to the long days of exposure and want which had gone before. And now, as the child's need showed less extremely, and the poor neighbours fell back, perforce, to the supply of their own more pressing wants, life in Walter Limp's little hut began to wear its most pinched and eager face. Peter would have brought home a good deal, after the old fashion, but Molly was sure to ask—

"Did you's tooked it, Peter?" and Peter did not like to meet the question. He kept himself in good case, and kept himself away. Walter Limp, on his part, drank up everything he could lay hands on, in-doors or out ; and poor Mrs Limp left the baby with Molly, and toiled down to the village and back, bringing scanty supplies of cold buckwheat cakes, and well cleaned ham bones, and frozen potatoes, with such other dainties of like nature as "the bairns wadna' eat!" The bairns of the village, that is. But Molly never complained, and left all the chafing and fretting to her mother. Did not the King know? Was not "her best" in His safe keeping?

"Then we's can wait," thought Molly.

Yet sometimes, even so, the days seemed long ; and in the brilliant winter light and air the blue sky looked higher than ever, and further away from Vinegar Hill. Molly sat and gazed at it sometimes, till almost her soul took wing for very longing.

But oh! how fast the good seed grew in those long, wintry days! how fast the child was learning! Learning to rest her weariness upon the Lord ; learning the lesson of absolute trust in Jesus; learning to tell Him all,—the words she had no chance to speak to her father, the words spoken to Peter that did no good, the words of which her mother was in such sore need, yet could not understand. All these— the hopes, and fears, and wishes, not put in words to the child's own mind, not very defined even to herself, went up to heaven, just as they were, and the Lord knew. He could read the "look up" of Molly's eyes; He could weigh the burden of every long-drawn breath. Not for nothing did the child hide in her heart those words,—

"Your Father knoweth."

So passed by the last winter days, and spring came. Fitfully, as if playing hide-and-seek, having her white trimmed with green, and her green with white; and wearing now buds of promise, and now gems of ice.

"Why, yer's getting on *ever* so much!" said Jemmy Lucas one day, as he ran up and surprised Molly in her old seat on the door step, to which she had ventured for the first time. Molly smiled, but made no reply.

"Yer cheeks is pinkerin' over," Jemmy Lucas went on; "and *now* we's got to carry home the pail."

"Has we?" said Molly, wistfully.

"In course," said Jemmy Lucas. "I's been jest waitin' for yer, and I's feered o' my life every day somebody else'll find it. And yer knows ef they *did*, Molly!"—and Jemmy finished with a long whistle.

"So it ought to be took home," said Molly.

"Sooner the quicker," answered Jemmy Lucas. "When'll yer go?"

"Where's it, Jemmy?" Molly said, unconsciously seeking a reprieve. "Does you think you knows?"

"Guess I's been there a matter o' four times a'ready, ter make sure," answered Jemmy Lucas. "'Tain't more'n twice as far's old Peasely's—or maybe three times. Go this arternoon, Molly? Walk's splendid."

"Yes, I's go," said little Molly, plaintively. "Jemmy, does you's foller all the time?"

"Straight ahead," said Jemmy Lucas. "Fur's I can see."

s

"Ain't it good !" said Molly. "Does you's know, Jemmy, Peter read some this mornin'? I asked him, and he did. 'Twan't much, 'cause he went off right short—in a hurry, like. What's 'faithful,' Jemmy?"

"Why, it's standin' ter what yer's said," answered Jemmy Lucas. "'Tain't breaking yer word, nor nothin'."

Molly smiled—leaning her head back to gaze up into the blue sky.

"We's to be 'faithful,'" she said. "That's what it telled, Jemmy. 'Be you's faithful,' if you's dies."

CHAPTER IX.

The village Sewing Society met that afternoon at Mrs Bingham's, far out of the village as it was. But the day was fine, the roads still smoothly frozen up, and the needle-workers mustered in force. And so it fell out, that when Jemmy Lucas and Molly Limp knocked timidly at Mrs Bingham's door, that good woman fetched them right into the midst of the conclave, having, as she said afterwards, "a purpose." The sewing had been put by, and the workers had read together their parting chapter, and now were just standing up to sing a hymn.

If you could have seen them look, when Mrs Bingham came in, pushing before her the two Vinegar Hill waifs, like morsels of humanity wrapped up in rags to bind body and soul together; so curiously bound, and tied, and pinioned—and after all—fluttering ! The utterly white face of the one child, the small red hands of the other, all chapped and bleeding with the cold; the strange, unmatched foot gear, evidently collected, one shoe at a time, from ash heaps and road sides, and showing every possible variety of rent and tear. No stockings, no comforters, and as near as could be, no anything else ! The village mothers gazed in extreme dismay ; for do you know, the ragged child that we work for at Sewing Society, is not the *real* ragged child of the streets, else would our needles move much faster, and our tongues in quite another direction. The child *we* work for is going to be so *very* comfortable, that it's hardly possible she can suffer much now. She is going to look so nice in her new cape and apron, that it's hardly worth while to inquire whether she has a frock; or if we are making the frock too, can it be that she has nothing to eat!

There is nothing like seeing the real thing; and all Society work would be much improved if a live model were brought in now and then, as into an artist's studio. You all know how these objects look in the street; but fetch one into a room full of warmth and comfort; put it in a framework of ease and plenty and prettiness,—clean floors, soft carpets, fireshine, and the remains of your lunch,—and *then* see!

There was not a woman in Mrs Bingham's little room whose heart did not give a sudden bound of pain, and settle down into a restless, steady aching, as the two waifs came in. Mrs Bingham put the sick child in a rocking chair by the fire, motioned Jemmy Lucas to a little bench at her side, and then going back to her own place in the astonished circle, she led off the hymn with heart enough for a whole choir:

> " How sweet the name of Jesus sounds
>   In a believer's ear!
> It soothes his sorrows, heals his wounds,
>   And drives away his fear.
>
> " It makes the wounded spirit whole,
>   And calms the troubled breast;
> 'Tis manna to the hungry soul,
>   And to the weary, rest.
>
> " Dear Name! the rock on which I build,
>   My shield and hiding-place;
> My never-failing treasury, fill'd
>   With boundless stores of grace:
>
> " By thee my prayers acceptance gain,
>   Although with sin defiled;

Satan accuses me in vain,
And I am own'd a child.

"Jesus, my Shepherd, Saviour, Friend,
My Prophet, Priest, and King,
My Lord, my Life, my Way, my End,
Accept the praise I bring.

"Weak is the effort of my heart,
And cold my warmest thought;
But when I see Thee as Thou art,
I'll praise Thee as I ought.

"Till then, I would Thy praise proclaim
With every fleeting breath;
And may the music of Thy name
Refresh my soul in death."

If the picture needed any last touches, it had them now. The light, and joy, and privilege, in which all the singers lived, in which they had been brought up; the rest, and peace, and blessing, that wreathed—for them—both this life and that which was to come; they saw it all, with those pinched, weird faces gazing at them out of the darkness. More than one voice failed in the singing, and the last words of the hymn died away in sobs.

To the surprise of everybody, Molly Limp was the first to speak. She had sunk back in her chair in such utter, faint exhaustion, that Mrs Bingham watching her, doubted if she was able to notice anything. But Molly had caught the very first words of the hymn; and as it went on she straightened herself up in the chair, holding fast to the arm, and so turned herself slowly round, to face the singers. And after that she never moved. A faint colour flitted back and forth over her white cheeks, and her eyes opened wide and full; but she gave no other sign, and so sat till the singing was done. Then, fixing upon the last thing she had wanted to have explained, Molly spoke—

"What's it mean about the music?"

This brought everybody round her at once. One came up to answer, and the others to hear and look on.

"What music, dear?" said Mrs Bingham, kneeling down

by the chair, and taking the child's numb hands in her own.

"The music 'of Thy name,'" said Molly.

"Oh, that?" said Mrs Bingham. "Why, if you loved the Lord Jesus, dear, you would know that the mere sound of His name is very sweet, because He loves us, and because we love Him."

"I knows," said the child, quietly. "But I means—what's it—when's it"——and Molly stopped, looking puzzled.

"She means 'bout the 'freshin'," said Jemmy Lucas.

"'And may the music of Thy name
      Refresh my soul in death;'

"Is that it?" asked Mrs Bingham.

Molly nodded. Those standing round just glanced at each other, but hardly a breath was heard.

"Why, my child," said Mrs Bingham, tenderly, "when people are dying, sometimes they feel very weary, and in pain; but then, if they love Jesus, His name sounds in their hearts like sweet music and gives them rest. Just as you almost forgot how tired you were as soon as we began to sing."

Molly smiled.

"I knows," she said again, leaning her head back.

"Dear heart!" cried Mrs Peasely, at this point; "if you don't give that poor little soul somethin' right off, Mrs Bingham, she'll melt down afore your very eyes."

"Yer see, she didn't get nothin' for breakfast," explained Jemmy Lucas; "'cause old Limp, he took it."

Nothing for breakfast! and of course nothing for dinner, and the sun already dipping towards the west. Such a commotion as followed that announcement! If Mrs Bingham had not kept sharp track of her common sense, Molly would have had to eat enough to kill a well child in no time. And as it was, it was well that Jemmy sat close at hand, with a capacity for much and pockets for more. Molly was served carefully with what was best for her by her kind hostess, and the child presently revived a little, and tried to get up.

"We's in a hurry," she said; "we's fetched the pail, and it's so fur back? We's go now, Jemmy."

Mrs Bingham studied the child's face for a minute, kindly keeping her down in the rocking-chair.

"Jemmy,—if that is your name," she said, "I think she'd better stay here to-night, and get rested. Then you can come over again in the morning."

Jemmy's eyes opened wide; but Molly stirred uneasily under the detaining hand.

"I's got to go, please," she said, wistfully. "I ain't rested in the mornin'—never."

"Poor little dear!" said Mrs Peasely, wiping her eyes.

"'Tain't so easy, ma'am, when yer's next t' nothin' under yer, and less 'n that atop," said Jemmy Lucas, deprecatingly, as if the ladies might think it was Molly's fault.

"How in the world did she get here, all the way from Vinegar Hill?" said Mrs Graves, whose close pressed lips had spoken no word hitherto.

"Oh, we druv it," said Jemmy Lucas; "'way we allers does."

"Druv it?" repeated half the women present.

"Yes 'm," said Jemmy Lucas; "that is, we footed it as tight's we could. Only Molly, she had ter stop,—and *then* the wind were powerful cold. Counts more 'n when you're drivin'."

The women whispered together, and consulted. Jemmy Lucas sat staring at the fire—what a thing such a blaze was; and Molly, after her one faint remonstrance, quite subsided, and spoke no more. Her heavy eyes saw but dimly the figures clustered round her. She heard their voices as in a dream; and when one and all declared she must be taken to bed at once, and that to go out in the cold again that day would most certainly kill her, little Molly submitted without a word.

"Molly, is yer goin' ter stay?" whispered Jemmy Lucas, in deep wonder.

"I'se so tired, Jemmy," said the child, closing her eyes. "But we's set out," she added, dreamily; "and I's follerin', and bimeby we's be there. How longs bimeby, Jemmy?"

Two or three kind ones, bending over Molly, drew back rather hastily at this,—Mrs Graves to hide her thrill of pain, Mrs Peasely to wipe her eyes, and Mrs Bingham to come round in front of the child, and softly lift her up.

"I don't think it's very long now, dear," she said, tenderly; "but the Lord knows."

The smile that flitted across Molly's face was utterly sweet and peaceful.

"He knows," she repeated, "He knows; and we's to wait."

Her head drooped upon Mrs Bingham's shoulder, and she fell fast asleep; and so the good woman carried her into the little bedroom next the parlour, and took off from Molly the rags, and patches, and signs of Vinegar Hill, which she was not to wear any more at all.

"She's a sick child," said Mrs Peasely, coming back to the fire, where Jemmy Lucas still sat; "and it's *my* belief"—but Mrs Graves touched her arm, and she stopped short.

"Who are you, little boy?" said Mrs Peasely, then. "Be you her brother?"

"I's Jemmy Lucas,—and she's Molly Limp," the boy answered. "We's together, mostly."

"Where did she learn?" said Mrs Graves, in her quick, impulsive way. "She said she knew this, and she said she knew that,—how did she learn?"

"'Bout the King, and sich?" said Jemmy Lucas.

"Yes."

"White lady, up ter the old meetin'-house," said Jemmy Lucas, lucidly. "And now her's gone, we reads."

The two women looked at each other, and Mrs Graves said—

"Some of Mrs Kensett's work."

And Mrs Peasely nodded her head a good many times.

Jemmy Lucas carried the news back to Vinegar Hill; but except that poor Mrs Limp felt a dull sort of satisfaction that the child was beyond her father's reach, and that she herself, and the baby, slept under an extra allowance of rags, the thing made little odds.

CHAPTER X.

THAT is a blessed word in the history of the old Israelites, which tells how the Lord went before them every day to choose out their camping ground for the night's rest. He—who knew all the way, its dangers, and difficulties, and needs—He chose. And so for every one of the true Israel, God is doing still the same. "What shall we do?" "Where shall we go?"—so we say restlessly, in some hard corner of circumstances, some rough passage of daily toil. Hide then in your heart these words—"God knoweth." Words often spoken in tones of hopelessness and unbelief; but do you take them silently in faith. "Commit thy way unto the Lord; trust also in Him, and He shall bring it to pass."

It was the first time Molly Limp had ever slept in what you and I would call a bed; and something so strange and new would have almost hindered her sleep altogether, had she not been completely worn out and spent. She could not even notice all the comforting processes she went through in Mrs Bingham's kind hands, nor the clean little nightgown in which she was wrapped, nor the wonderful pillow on which her weary little head was laid. In a sort of stupor, that was partly fever and partly fatigue, Molly went passively through it all, and never unclosed her eyes again until morning.

Good Mrs Bingham sat by her all the night, watching the cheeks that were now too deep coloured, and the breath that was so quick, and yet so fluttering. But when Molly at last awoke, it was to see the gentle face of Mrs Graves; who had run over, as soon as her husband's early breakfast was disposed of, to see Molly, and let Mrs Bingham rest. Molly looked round in supreme wonder, from the white sheets to the gay carpet, and the looking-glass, catching the sunbeams, and one or two simple little pictures on the wall. A smell of breakfast, too, came sifting through cracks and doorways from the kitchen, and altogether Molly felt very much bewildered.

"Now then—who's ready for breakfast?" said Mrs Bingham, coming briskly in. "Why, Molly, you've had the grandest sleep that ever was."

"Is I waked up?" Molly asked, doubtfully.

"Just try and see," said Mrs Bingham, smiling. "Don't you want to get up and sit in my lap, and have some breakfast?"

"I'll take her," said Mrs Graves, eagerly. "I can wrap her in my shawl."

"Ah, I guess we can do better than that," said Mrs Bingham, with something like a sigh. She went to a small press in the room, and took thence a little calico double-gown, old and faded and soft. She brought it tenderly, as if the very touch were precious.

"They won't mind up there," she said, half to herself, "I guess they'll be glad." And she wrapped Molly carefully in the double-gown, but then turned aside and let Mrs Graves carry her out.

Molly made no remark while all this went on; and when they were out in the warm little breakfast-room, she watched the fire and the breakfast, and the kind faces near her, but still said not a word. The child was in a state of utter passive exhaustion. She did not want to speak; she did not want to stir; but neither did she want to eat. Sitting there dreamily in Mrs Graves' lap, Molly wondered what it all meant. At home, with little or nothing to eat, she was always hungry; and now here, with hot gruel and toast and all sorts of nice things, Molly did not want to touch one. At home, too, she used to huddle over the old stove, as if even its cold covers were a comfort; and now she rather wanted to get away from Mrs Bingham's great fire, and wished Mrs Graves would not sit so near. She wondered if that was the way in rich folks' houses always, or if summer had come. Then her mother and the baby were warm too. And what did Mrs Bingham mean by "they won't mind up there?" Who was "up there?" Up there was the King's house,—hadn't she seen its blue walls many a time, all shining in the sunlight, and its thousand lamps at night? But then it was quite sure now that she would have to be carried, feeling as she felt this morning, Molly Limp could never get there in any other way; with so many aches and pains, with such tired feet. Yes, it must be that the Lord Jesus would carry her.

"'Cause He knows," little Molly murmured to herself, turning her head wearily on her friend's breast. "And bimeby we's be there." Her eyes closed again in heavy sleep.

Mrs Bingham cleared away the breakfast, and went off to take some rest, and Mrs Graves sat still before the fire, with Molly on her lap. Well she remembered the little face that had appeared to her earlier in the winter, peeping out from the strange muffling on the sled; and well and truly could she read what the winter had been since that, in the child's sharper features and wasted limbs. Hunger, misery, starvation even, so near their own over-full barns and larder? Mrs Graves smothered a great cry that came up from the very depths of her heart, but to sit still there any longer and think, was impossible. She laid little Molly down on the old chintz couch by the side of the fire, and herself walked restlessly up and down the room. What should she do? what could she do?

It was quite a relief to hear a knock at the door, and to have Jemmy Lucas come in; all frozen with the cold, and out of breath with running to keep himself warm.

"I's come for her," he said. "I couldn't get here afore. Ain't started off by herself, is she?"

"Oh no," said Mrs Graves. "Come in softly, and you shall see her. Molly's asleep."

"Sleepin'!—deep down in the mornin'." Jemmy gave a short whistle under his breath, and followed Mrs Graves into the room. But there he was unmistakably taken aback.

" Whatever's yer done to her!" he said. "That ain't Molly."

" Come nearer and see," said Mrs Graves.

" 'Tain't her hair, anyway," said Jemmy Lucas, advancing cautiously. "Well, she do look like it now."

" Like what?" said Mrs Graves.

" Molly and me, we's follerin' the King, yer know," said Jemmy Lucas, simply, "and so we was allers atryin' ter wash up, like. But it don't stay, down our way," he added, feeling his own face, as if the streaks had been ridges. " Why, yer 'most has ter wash the water."

" You and Molly are following the King," Mrs Graves repeated, with a sharp twinge at her heart.

" Oh yes, we's follerin'," said Jemmy Lucas. "And Molly, she's allers wishin' we was there. That's why she keeps sayin' bimeby so often."

Mrs Graves remembered the child's whispered lullaby, as she sank to sleep. She stood watching the little pale sleeper, and answered not a word. But now little Molly stirred and woke, roused, perhaps, by the familiar tones of Jemmy Lucas; and Mrs Graves took her seat at the other side of the fireplace, and left the two children to their talk. But she noticed that Molly took little part in it, giving her answers by a smile, or in the fewest words possible; and now that the fever flush had passed away again, the child was almost as white as the pillow on which she lay.

" O Molly," said Jemmy Lucas, "isn't you 'most ready?"

" I's too tired, Jemmy," little Molly made answer.

" But yer never staid abed's long's that down home," urged Jemmy Lucas.

" I's tireder now," said Molly.

" Hasn't you had no breakfast, Molly?" Jemmy inquired in an anxious whisper.

" I guess I has—I don't 'member, Jemmy," said Molly, wearily.

" Then yer's had it, in course," said Jemmy Lucas, decidedly. " Yer'd 'member if yer hadn't. I does. Look, Molly,"—and the boy drew his tattered jacket round him, with an air that said he knew of no hindrance to its compressing him to the size of a pipestem.

Molly stroked his face with her hand.

"Jemmy, Jemmy," she said. Then after a little pause, "We's wait, you's 'member."

"'Cause the King knows," said Jemmy Lucas. "Why, Molly, I does really s'pose I has that over a matter o' twenty times—days when my jacket's too big, yer know."

Molly smiled, stroking his face softly.

"Yer see, daddy smelt it out—I'd a lot o' things they gave me here," said Jemmy Lucas, dropping his voice. "And o' course when that's the case, yer'd as good turn a rat in at once. So mother'n me we jest smelt the pocket," the boy added with a gleam of fun. "Good's fur's it went, Molly, but 'tain't quite the stuff to go round the world on."

Whether some word of this caught Mrs Bingham's ear as she came in, or whether she merely made up her own premises, certain it is that Jemmy Lucas was shortly served with as good a meal as ever a boy had. And it is no less sure that he did as good justice to it as ever a boy did,—which is saying something. But they could not tempt Molly. She took the spoonfuls of broth or gruel that were given her, but with a weary air that told plainly they had no relish ; and then her head went down on the pillow again, as if absolute, unbroken rest were the only thing she craved. Mrs Graves had gone home to her own dinner. Mrs Bingham in the next room sat down to hers, and Jemmy Lucas, with his jacket a much better fit, sat on a little bench and gazed at Molly.

"Yer's fell on a real streak o' luck, Molly," he said. "Don't wonder yer doesn't want to come home. Breakfast in the mornin', dinner at noon,—and sich a fire ! Why, it's most the King's house, ain't it ?"

"I aches yet," said little Molly, applying an infallible test to the region that held such wonders. She moved wearily, looking up at the smooth white ceiling. "It doesn't shine through a bit," she said.

"It's shinin' outside though, like sixty," said Jemmy Lucas.

"Do it look blue?" Molly asked.

"Blue as the world," Jemmy answered.

Molly sighed,—clearly even holes in the roof have their bright side!

CHAPTER XI.

"This is one of the cases to be cured beforehand," said the old village doctor, as he stood gazing at the little patient for whom he had been summoned. "Look here,"—and he stripped back the sleeve of the faded double-gown, and showed the bone that lay there where should have been a round, plump arm. "How d'ye expect to make up such arrears as that? You can't do it!—you've lost your chance." And the old doctor marched off leaving his words like an arrow in the heart of his two hearers.

Oh, chances lost that can never be regained! Oh, arrears that can never be made up! Mrs Graves and Mrs Bingham stood still where the doctor had left them, each bearing the sharp pain for herself in silence.

Molly, in her slumberous state of half unconsciousness, in which she sometimes passed much of her time, paid little heed to either words or looks, that went on around her. Rest, in a warm room, on a soft couch, was so utterly good and new to her; and the child's exhaustion was so extreme, that mind and body sunk down together into a perfect hush. So she would lie for hours, almost without stirring. She could not sit up, she could not eat, except as they persuaded her to take a spoonful at a time. The broth that had been so delicious, was only a weariness now to Molly Limp; and the beautiful white bread, once so longed for, was taken, and held, and laid down again, untasted. It went to Mrs Bingham's heart to see the child's patient attempts to eat, when they urged her; and yet more, the

patient bearing of the long fits of restless weariness and
pain, which took their turn with those of sleep. The quiet
little face could always call up an answering smile, though
Molly's words were very few. It was all so strange to her
—the faces and the voices, and the words—not one thing
like anything she had ever heard or seen before in all her
little life. She was not pining for home—that could hardly
be expected; and she was not wondering and wishing for her
mother,—how could poor Mrs Limp bring the pale baby all
that distance through the snow without her breakfast, even
if she had dared absent herself for so long a time as would
be needful? And what could she do if she came? Molly
had more care and attention in one hour now, than her
wildest dreams of possibility could have crowded into a
whole year. So the child reasoned it out to herself, in her
unformed, untutored way, and lay still, full of thoughts
and shy of the very kindness which surrounded her. For
you know she was but a little waif, after all, and never
could be anything else till she drifted safe and saved upon
the eternal shore. The village people had lost their chance
with Molly Limp, and she had passed into the Lord's own
hands, with nothing between her heart and Him. *There*
Molly really rested; there was the deep secret of her patience;
and often when the lookers-on saw her lips move, and
thought her dreaming, the child was hushing herself with
one of her old lullabies.

"Bimeby we's be there. He knows."

Jemmy Lucas was a great comfort; and it came to be the
way that Jemmy Lucas was at Mrs Bingham's much of the
time; getting also much heartened up by unwonted dinners
and suppers, and much smoothed to outward appearance by
kindly touches of brush and soap, and needles and thread,
from the hands of Mrs Bingham. Then Molly brightened
up when he came in, and would lie by the hour and hear
him talk in her own vernacular. She was rarely in bed,
these days, but, wrapped in her little double-gown, lay white
and still upon the couch in the sitting-room, where was more
light and air and fireshine. Long sunbeams walked slowly

through the room, and Molly watched them; and little
birds twittered and hopped on the twigs outside the window, giving wonderful pleasure—for spring had come in
earnest.

"I's got a supprise for yer, Molly," said Jemmy Lucas
one day as he came in, his jacket wrapped round him very
tight, but not seeming too big for him, after all. "What
does yer guess now I's got?" and Jemmy gave the breast
of his jacket a sounding thump.

"You's got—your pussy," suggested Molly, with a faint
smile.

"Well, you's out for once," said Jemmy Lucas. "My!
wouldn't she jest have squalled? Guess agin, Molly. Give
yer three more, and *then* yer won't."

"You's tell," said Molly, with her sharp cough.

"Well," said Jemmy Lucas, slowly loosening his jacket,
mother pinned it, Molly, 'cause father took a notion he
wanted the buttons on his 'n. And I'd found a pin somewheres. Yer see the snow's a-meltin' and runnin',—and I
kinder thought mebbe it 'ud git wet, or old Limp might
s'picion it, worse luck. And so I jest fetched it here." And
Jemmy took from his breast Molly's little Bible, so long hid
away in the old well.

With a quick cry of gladness, Molly took the Book into
her own hands, holding it fast.

"You's real good, Jemmy," she said; "now's we read
some more."

"I was jest as near bein' ketched, Book and all, as ever I
could be," said Jemmy Lucas, his face shining with a reflection of Molly's pleasure; "and by old Limp, too. Don't
yer think he took ter walkin' round this mornin', of all
days, and what should he see but me a-pokin' about the
well? So I run, and he took arter. And ef he didn't holler
out the worst names! My! but the Book warn't hurt, nor
me nuther."

Molly handed him back the little Bible, and Jemmy
Lucas turned the leaves over, trying to find out where to
begin.

"S'posen' I try it 'way back, Molly?" he said. "We's never read there a bit."

"I likes it," said Molly.

And Jemmy Lucas opened at almost the middle of the Book, and began to read. Marvellous words!—too hard to understand some of them, and some of them too hard to read,—Jemmy went stumbling on through some places, while in others he stopped short, all dazzled with the heavenly light which seemed to radiate from the very lines of the Book upon the two little waifs from Vinegar Hill.

"O Lord, thou art my God,"—so the chapter began. Molly raised herself eagerly, leaning on her elbow.

"That's us, Jemmy," she cried. "And that's the King."

"It's the King, sure enough," said Jemmy Lucas, "but I doesn't see where we comes in, Molly?"

"Why, it says so," said the child, stretching her hand out to lay it on the Book. "Read it agin, Jemmy."

Jemmy read the words over, and pondered.

"As ef He sorter b'longed t' us, like, someways?" he said, inquiringly.

"He 's—my," said Molly, sinking down again upon her pillow. "What's next, Jemmy?"

"'I will exalt Thee, I will praise Thy Name.'"

"That's it as makes the music," explained Molly, with a happy look.

"You's allers so understandin'!" said Jemmy Lucas, in admiration. He toiled on through the next two verses—then came out into the "open."

"For Thou hast been a strength to the poor, a strength to the needy in his distress."

"Now *them's* us, and no mistake," said Jemmy Lucas, pausing to consider the passage. "Jest put down for you'n me special, that was. Wonder how the Book ever knowed! Why, ain't the King sorter heartened us up lots o' times?"

"You's 'member the milk?" said Molly.

"And the tin pail," said Jemmy Lucas. "Come ter think, Molly, I does guess the King must 'ha helped yer consid'rable the day we come ter fetch it back, 'cause yer ain't been good for a single speck o' nothin' since. And, yer see, it 's so handy for him ter look arter yer here, with folks ter do jest what he tells 'em."

"And when I's all ached up, too," said Molly.

"Does yer ache very often, Molly?" said Jemmy Lucas, tenderly.

"Yes, I aches," said little Molly, with her patient face. "And then I hears the music, and it 'freshes me. Read on, Jemmy."

For several verses Jemmy read on, through a very thicket of hard words and unknown thoughts; but what a burst of light came then!

"He will swallow up death in victory; and the Lord God will wipe away tears from off all faces; and the rebuke of His people shall He take away from off all the earth; for the Lord hath spoken it."

Molly heard, and then clasping her hands over her face she broke into a fit of sobbing, that brought Mrs Bingham in haste from her work at the distant table.

"Oh, I wish we was there," the child said, for all answer to her earnest questions; "but it 's so fur."

Mrs Bingham glanced at the open page where Jemmy's finger still marked the place, then sat down and took Molly in her arms.

"Listen, dear," she said; "listen, and let Jemmy read the next verse, and see what that says."

"It shall be said in that day, Lo, this is our God; we have waited for Him, and He will save us; this is the Lord; we have waited for Him; we will be glad and rejoice in His salvation."

Little Molly caught the old watchword, and her tears stopped.

"Yes, we 's wait," she said, patiently.

"'Cause He knows. We 's waited a good deal, Jemmy, and bimeby we 's be there. We 's be glad," she murmured to herself, sinking away again to sleep. "We 's wait—we 's 'joice—bimeby. Yes, Lord Jesus."

T

CHAPTER XII.

It had been an unsuccessful week at Vinegar Hill. Whether farmers had grown careful, and housewives had grown wary, or whether all extra stock had been disposed of and put away, certain it is that the depredation returns were light. Neither barnyards nor clothes lines had yielded much.

As a natural consequence of this state of things, the whole boy and man population of Vinegar Hill was in a frame of mind that might be termed growly. Shorn of their profits, stinted in their drams, the boys avenged themselves upon the village windows, and the men upon their wives at home. Many a lost garment that could own the name, many a poor remaining bit of furniture, passed in those hard days into the all-devouring den of James Dodd.

Not last among the spoilers of hearth and home, was Walter Limp ; and there is no doubt that poor Mrs Limp and the pale baby would have followed the old stove, if anybody could have been found to take them off his hands. Failing that, Limp did what he could ; making such a raid upon the premises, that Peter thought best to absent himself altogether, lest his own private personal stock of rags should follow the rest. All these supplies, however, gave but a scanty income, and between whiles Walter Limp roved round in a semi-sober and all barbarous state, seeking what he might pick up.

It was in one of these quests, when the bright thought had struck him that water was a useless luxury in a family like his, and that the old rope and bucket might fetch something better, that Limp had caught sight of Jemmy Lucas. Ten minutes more, and the boy would have been too late to secure Molly's treasure ; but as it was, Limp only saw him from a distance, and thought he had taken something, and could not tell what. Two or three stones aimed full at Jemmy Lucas, fell harmlessly wide of the mark ; and Walter Limp stumbled on to the side of the well, and looked in. Rope and bucket were there safe enough, but Limp soon spied the little nest among the stones, lined even yet with a bit of the old quilt, which Jemmy Lucas had left, caught there in his hurry. Walter Limp swore a deep oath, and lurching away with some difficulty from the dangerous edge of the well, he started off at once in pursuit. But the trail was not easy to strike, and if Limp had not stumbled upon Peter, and put him in a corner of bodily fear, he would maybe never have found out where Jemmy Lucas had taken his prize nor what it was.

Meantime, the little Bible was safe at Mrs Bingham's; and Molly, having fallen asleep in that good woman's arms, and been thence gently transferred to the old couch, was resting there peacefully in the watch and ward of Jemmy Lucas, while Mrs Bingham gave attention to her oven and her bread.

It was a true spring afternoon, with a late snow yet filling the hollows and capping the hills, but with a soft, persuasive wind blowing, that promised to soon breathe it all away. The window was open, letting in all the spring freshness of grass, and song, and cock-crow; and peace hushed everything within and without. Jemmy Lucas himself grew slumberous; and again and again his head went nearly down upon the broad knee-patches of his trousers, only seeming always in doubt between the blue patch and the brown.

Suddenly a huge ball of hard snow broke upon his head, drenching Molly and the floor with its white fragments, and Walter Limp's own head and shoulders leaned far into the room through the open window.

"Hi!" he said. "*Here's* where yer be! Now I's got yer. You, Molly, come out o' that. I want yer home."

"She couldn't go, ef she was ter try ever so," said Jemmy Lucas, who had jumped to his feet, and now stood before Molly, making himself as tall as he possibly could, and trying to screen her frightened eyes. "She's sick."

"Sick, is she?" said Walter Limp, with an oath. "I'll warrant she'll go with me arter her. How'd yer like t' be drug back by the ears? you and her both? I say, Moll, d'ye hear?"

"She's got the lady's things on, too," said Jemmy Lucas, prolonging the defence.

"The lady's things, is they?" said Limp, peering into the room with increased eagerness. "Where's the good clothes she come in? S'pose the lady's took them in 'change. Hurry up, Moll; I's got business pertic'lar. Ef I has ter come in arter yer, yer'll wish I hadn't. Come along, I say; take yer right through the winder and save time."

With the old habit of terrified obedience to all Walter Limp's demands, little Molly raised herself, all white and shaking, from the couch, and, putting her feet slowly down, tried to stand up and walk. But with the first step her power failed, and she fell to the floor in a dead faint.

If the window had been but a trifle larger, Walter Limp would have scrambled in, and seized the child just as she was; but after several vain struggles to force himself through, Limp caught up a handful of snow from the pile that still banked the house, and by way of restorative began to pelt Molly as she lay on the floor. And Mrs Graves and Mrs Bingham, running in, alarmed by a shout from Jemmy Lucas, found the attack still going on, and Jemmy gallantly making of himself the largest barricade that was possible in the circumstances.

Women never know how they do things in such a crisis, and so Mrs Graves never could tell how it was that the big, brutal form of Walter Limp disappeared from the window, and went to print its ugly shape in the snow bank below. She had a pleased recollection of seeing him lie there, for one swift instant, as she swung to the heavy wooden shutter and closed the window; and then running hastily to draw every other bolt and bar on the ground floor, the two women hurried back to the sitting room again, where Molly lay still in her faint, and Jemmy Lucas sat on the floor beside her, crying bitterly.

They lifted the child up, and bore her away to the kitchen, where the windows were higher from the ground, and so beyond attack, and there tried all sorts of reviving measures. But Molly was slow in coming to; and when at last she

stirred a little, and half opened her eyes, still they could get
from her neither word nor sign. It seemed as if the fright
had frozen her very life. There was nothing to do but to
lay her gently down in her old place on the couch, and to
sit by her there in the darkened room, and watch. They
could hear Walter Limp storming round the outside of the
house, and did not dare open a window nor a door; so Mrs
Bingham lighted her lamp, and the three sat there in deep
stillness, broken only by the distant oaths beyond the window, and the long-drawn sobs that came yet, now and then,
from the very heart of Jemmy Lucas.

"If the doctor was only here," said Mrs Bingham at last;
"maybe he could do something."

"I's fetch him," cried Jemmy Lucas, starting up and
rubbing his eyes very hard to clear their sight; "I'll run
every step o' the way."

"You, you midget!" said Mrs Graves, kindly; "why, that
man would eat you up before you'd gone ten steps."

"He'll find I ain't 'xactly a spring chicken, ef he tries it,"
said Jemmy Lucas, stoutly; "I's go, ma'am."

"No, no, you shan't go," said Mrs Graves; "you must
stay here and watch Molly; I'll go myself. Let me out on
this side, while he's on the other—that's all."

She was ready in a minute; and watching her chance, Mrs
Bingham opened the front door softly, and again closed and
locked it. The light was fading a little, with lingering sunbeams still, but with creeping shadows that said it would be
dark very soon; and Mrs Graves went off at her utmost
speed. First, for Molly's sake; but then an angry, half tipsy
man, is not a pleasant enemy to leave in the rear, and Mrs
Graves sped over the ground at a great rate. Nor without
cause; for Walter Limp's watchful ears had caught the
sound of the closing door, and he at once gave chase, firing
a snowball now and then, as he ran, by way of summons.
But Mrs Graves had the start, and was all herself, while her
pursuer went lumbering along, with here and there a heavy
tumble. Still, it was a long way to the village street, and
the brave little woman remembered with a shiver two or

three turns in the road, where a skilful short cut might head
her off. She fancied, too, that the last snowball had come
nearer than usual—and—oh, were those her own home sleigh
bells jingling up to meet her?

Sure enough, there came Farmer Graves dashing along in
his little cutter, most utterly and totally astonished to see
his wife running at that pace along the road.

"Why, 'Lizy!" he said, "why, 'Lizy"——

"O Ahab, drive fast!" cried his wife, tumbling herself
into the sleigh, she didn't know how. "I want the doctor
—and he's after me!" And Mrs Graves broke down in a
genuine fit of hysterics.

"Well, I vow, if I know which way to drive!" said the
astonished farmer, giving his horse however a stroke, which
—in the mystified state of Mr Graves's mind—was probably
meant for the absent doctor.

"Yes—that's it," said Mrs Graves, catching her voice for
a minute; "and, O Ahab, I do believe I pushed him out of
the window!"

"Reckon you don't want me to go and pick him up," said
Mr Graves, grimly. And then, as in broken words his wife
explained, the farmer chuckled and scolded by turns.

"There ain't a doubt on my mind but what that 'ere crow's
nest'll be the death o' me yet," he said. "Well done, 'Lizy!
but dont you never have the first thing to do with none of
'em again."

He drove on, however, at a great pace, to the doctor's, and
then equally fast with him to Mrs Bingham's far-away little
home. But he would not go in.

They threw open the window of the little sitting room,
and the last long sunset rays streamed in, and lay softly
upon the child's white face, sealing it with the King's own
signet of peace. But the old doctor shook his head as he
looked.

"Better so," he said, kindly, laying down the wasted hand
which he had taken in his own. "There's no spring-time
here for such little seedlings. She's winter-killed."

A great cry broke from the lips of Jemmy Lucas, looking

in terror from the old doctor to that other face so bright and still. Mrs Graves stooped down, and put her arms about him, weeping.

" Don't, Jemmy," she whispered. "Hush, dear, she's there ! "

  .   .   "   .   .   .   .

"And other fell on good ground, and did yield fruit that sprang up and increased ; and brought forth, some thirty, and some sixty, and some an hundred."

SPRING WORK.

SPRING WORK.

———◆———

CHAPTER I.

"He that observeth the wind shall not sow."

AGAIN the village Sowing Circle met at Mrs Bingham's, but this time not to make aprons. There were rents in society they found, that needed closing; and other things to mend besides cast-off clothes; and stuff to be wrought that lay mile deep below the reach of needles. With sober faces the members came in, one by one; thinking much of their last meeting; and giving each a kindly, tender word to Jemmy Lucas, who played the part of door-opener on this occasion. Mrs Bingham had kept him with her for the fortnight, partly to soothe his grief if she could, and partly for fear of what Walter Limp might do to the boy, if once he were back in the lawless haunts of Vinegar Hill. That fear was over now; for Farmer Graves, always ready enough to work in one direction, had exerted himself to such purpose, that Walter Limp was provided with safe lodgings in the next town for some months to come. So that if poor Mrs Limp and the baby starved, they would at least have the comfort of starving in quiet. Still, the man's term would wear by, after a while; and besides, Jemmy's own father was another of the same sort; and if anything was to be done for the boy, if he was ever to be anything worth anything, the work should be taken in hand now. If no better might be, Mrs Bingham resolved to keep him herself; but then, as she truly said, the child *ought* to be with some one who would teach him farm-work, or a trade,—some business by which he could grow and thrive, and be an honest man. Merely fussing about her house and garden was not enough. It was better than nothing.

Poor little Jemmy! not all Mrs Bingham's tender care could hinder his being a very pale, sad little boy in those days. He grieved and grieved, till she thought he would grieve himself sick; and now as the pitiful little face appeared at Mrs Bingham's door this afternoon, not one of the ruddy village dames could pass it by without a kiss or an apple or a cookie,—something or other from their hearts or pockets. Mrs Graves stooped down and put her arms about him, and Jemmy Lucas cried upon her shoulder, getting much comfort therefrom. For Mrs Graves and he had mutually set their hearts upon each other,—but there the matter came to a dead lock.

The Society drew round Mrs Bingham's fire, resolving itself into a Committee of the Whole. What should be done for Vinegar Hill?

If you have a set of really willing hearts, a very few business heads will be enough in such a matter; and so it was not long before the hearts and heads had worked their way to three conclusions. If they came in somewhat inverted order of precedence, it was because the heads let the hearts arrange that as they would.

First, then, every child that could be got away from Vinegar Hill, was to be placed in a first-rate village home.

"Or to put it more practically," suggested Mrs Bingham, "we'll say that every first-rate home that *will*, shall be supplied with one of these forlorn children."

"Well," said Mrs Coon. "I like t'other way best. You'll have to push 'em with the sight of the children. Then the doors *has* to open."

Second in order, the happy mothers and wives of the village were to visit, often, their wretched sisters of the hamlet, giving such aid and comfort as might be possible; whether it were work or food, or counsel or a kind word.

"Have some of 'em down to tea now and then," suggested Mrs Coon.

Have them to tea !—the tidy housewives stood aghast.

"'Twon't hurt ye—not a speck," said Mrs Coon, looking amused. "Why, Mrs Kensett had a lot o' the little ones down last summer, and her room never smelt a bit the worse next day. Fact is, *I* thought it was sweeter. Give us a little chance to clear up, maybe, but you know we all like that."

There was a stir and laugh at this sally, and then the meeting passed on to its third point.

The men of the village were to talk to the men of the hill, as they could ; persuading them, encouraging them, finding them work.

"Ahem !" said Mrs Bingham.

> " ' He would if he could, and he couldn't ;
> He could if he would, and he wouldn't.'

Who's going to bring that about ?"

"Why *we*," said the schoolmaster's new wife. "We've just got to coax 'em into it. It all comes round to the women, after all."

Ah, if it all did !—Little Mrs Graves, sitting silent in her corner (she had spoken scarce a word) wished most devoutly that that were true. To which of all this work might she put her hand ? Perhaps to none ! Yes, she could pray; Mrs Kensett had said so. But Mrs Graves drew a deep sigh, nevertheless. Hard to sit there, not able to say she was ready to take everybody and do everything ; and worse still, not able to say why she said nothing. But the little woman was true as steel, and loyal to the very depths of her heart. The blame should all fall upon her head ; they might call her close and hard-hearted, if they liked, but they never should say that of Ahab. So Mrs Graves smothered her longings as best she could, and sat listening and smiling, and feeling every minute as if she should fly.

"Well, I don't know as we can better anything," said Mrs Bingham, when plans had been discussed and turned over and picked to pieces. "I've set the table for 'em all, and I've got 'em a first-rate supper And after that we'll see."

Mrs Bingham's "them," it may be said, referred to the absent lords of creation, who had been specially invited to come and "see their wives home." And when by and by one after another drove up, Mrs Bingham's little parlour gained such an infusion of the stronger material, that business ought to have been in a most prosperous way.

Supper was the first thing; and the wily womankind never even hinted at what they had been about, till coffee and cakes and ham and preserves had done their part towards mollifying the stern hearts of the assembled farmers. Never were farmers so waited on, so deferred to, so plied with dainties!—and it is safe to say that never were farmers more unsuspecting. Sugar was on every man's tongue, but Vinegar Hill was in every woman's heart.

"Well!—I do s'pose we've done about all that could be expected of us," said old Squire Peasely at last, leaning back in his chair with a laugh. "And if that's so, guess it's about time to tackle up."

"That's so!" said another farmer, emphatically. "Mis' Bingham's got her ground well cleared, anyway."

"Squire Peasely," said Mrs Bingham, "what shall we do with Vinegar Hill?"

"Do with it!"

"Vinegar Hill!" echoed half the men present. Squire Peasely sat open-mouthed and dumb.

"Hope ye ain't waitin' for me t' tell ye, Mis' Bingham," he said at length.

"Plough it under—if I had my way," said young Comstock.

"Pity the earth couldn't open and swaller it up, in old-time fashion," said young Skillet.

"Mind you, I didn't find out that something ought to be done," said Mrs Bingham; "Mrs Kensett began it. But it's got to be carried on. If we've slumbered and slept all our lives, that's no reason we should any longer."

"Don' know as I am awake," said Farmer Smith, "hearin such things stated. Vinegar Hill!—I'd like t' see the man

as would take that up. What d'ye want done? Some
more o' them fellers sent off to jail?"

"I want you to keep them out of jail," said Mrs Bingham.
"Visit them, talk to them, set them to work. That's what
we want you men to do."

"Tight little job, that, I reckon," said Farmer Smith,
raising his brows expressively.

"And a handy time o' year to begin," said young Comstock.
"Ain't much else wants doing in April."

"Guess it'll have to wait a spell yet," said old Squire
Peasely. "What ails it to go on as usual, Mis' Bingham?"

"What ails us that we've let it go on so long?" said Mrs
Bingham, with spirit. "Vinegar Hill is a disgrace to the
neighbourhood,—and to the church,—and to us!" After
the firing of which loaded shell, Mrs Bingham subsided,
and looked round to see the execution.

"But what ye goin' to do?" said Squire Peasely, looking
extremely puzzled.

"We're going to give 'em t'other end of Job's wish,'
said little Mrs Coon, colouring up very much at the sound
of her own voice. "We're going to make wheat grow
instead of thistles."

"Ah!" said the farmers, in extreme derision.

"Tight little job—very!" repeated Farmer Smith.

"Well, it *has* grown there," said Mrs Bingham. "So it will
again."

"Like t' see some o' that 'ere Vinegar Hill wheat," said
Farmer Graves, drily. "Got a sample, ma'am?"

"Yes, I've got a sample," said Mrs Bingham, promptly.
"But the Lord's gathered the first ripe into His garner. The
thing is just here, Farmer Graves. *We* are going into that
thistle patch to work."

"You'll get all tore up!" said Farmer Peasely.

"Well, then, we *will*," said the schoolmaster's wife; "but
we're going, all the same. And if you men with your strong
corderoys won't clear the way for our calicoes—then we'll
do it ourselves!"

And every brisk little feminine boot under the table gave a tap of lively assent.

"Now did ye ever?" said Farmer Graves, looking round at his peers, with also a vain attempt to catch his wife's eye.

"She's right, though," said young Peasely. "That thistle patch is a cryin' shame."

"It's a prickin' one," said Farmer Graves. "How many chickens d'ye s'pose me and 'Lizy was lightened of at one haul last June?"

"Can't tell you nothin' about chickens," said another.

"Guess I kin come up t'ye in sheep," said a third.

"Three new buffaloes I've bought, this blessed winter;" chimed in Squire Peasely.

"That's just where it is," said his son. "That 'ere hill is foulin' the country. But what's your plan, Mrs Bingham? Which way d'ye count to run your furrows?"

"Help the children, help the women, help the men," said Mrs Bingham, keeping to the first order. "We'll do the two first, and the last we leave for you."

"That's it, exactly!" said Farmer Graves, chuckling. "Fits like a shoe. Ef we'll tend to the prickles, you'll see arter the downs."

"Downs!" Mrs Bingham repeated. "Ah! there's not much of that about seeing a blessed little child die of starvation and cold and fear, just because one of us hadn't taken her in long before! I tell you, *that* pricks."

"Jes' so!" said old Squire Peasely. "Dessay it may. But what ye goin' to do?"

"I'm going to take the first girl I can find, that wants a home," said Mrs Bingham.

"And I'm goin' to see the poor things once a week," said Mrs Peasely. "I'm goin to teach 'em and help 'em and lift 'em up,—the Lord helpin' me."

"I too," said little Mrs Coon. "And if I can squeeze my six so's to hold another, I will."

"Guess I can find 'em in work pretty often," said Mrs Comstock.

But at that there was a masculine outcry.

"They'll steal your eyes!" said Farmer Skillet.

"They'll run off with your dinner and come back for the dishes!" said Squire King.

"They won't leave a thing about the place they can lay hands on," said young Comstock.

"Holler on me when it comes to you," said his mother, composedly.

"It's hirin' folks to do nothin', at double wages,—guess that's about the figur'," said Farmer Smith, slowly, when the laugh at young Comstock had subsided.

"Don't you worry," said Mrs Comstock. "I'll see to that."

"Pity if we can't," said old Mrs Peasely. "I'll have the poor souls to work every chance I get, Squire; if I *am* out o' pocket. Tell you what, I felt sick o' my pocket last week! Mean old money that couldn't help and *might* have helped! —It burnt me pretty bad, if it didn't the pocket."

Young Peasely clapped hands joyously over this outburst from his mother, and the applause went round the table—there was no helping it.

CHAPTER II.

FARMER GRAVES looked curiously at his wife all this while, wondering much at her extreme silence. She never looked at him, she never opened her lips. Was she trying to come over him that way? thought Mr Graves. But watching her closely while the laugh and clap for Mrs Peasely went round, Mr Graves saw her hand go to her eyes with a quick, secret, impatient motion,—first one hand and then the other, —as if she were in a fight with something and well nigh getting the worst. But she never gave so much as a glance his way, to turn other eyes in that direction. The farmer read it all pretty clearly, and at first it touched him, and then he got out of patience. Why didn't she speak up, and take her place among the other devisers of kind things?—and

U

not sit there making him feel that it was all his fault?
Farmer Graves drew his brows together and looked—
until others began to look too.

"What's Mrs Graves going to do?" said young Comstock,
with his mocking air. "We's lookin' to see her in the very
thick of the patch. The farmer takes to thistles."

Mrs Graves started, and the pink spots in her cheeks
deepened into roses that were more than bright; but she
answered with quick, seeming carelessness—

"Make your mind easy, Joe, I'll see."

"See how the thistles feel first,—that's wise," said the
young farmer, laughing. Whereupon Farmer Graves fired
up.

"Ef there's a woman in this hull town that *ain't* afeard
o' thistles—nor o' nothin' else," he said, "she's the one.
Speak up, 'Lizy; let's hear. Tell 'em what ye'll do. I'll
back ye through the worst thistle patch that ever grew."

"More to the purpose if you went afore, farmer," said
Squire Peasely; and again the laugh went round.

"Well, well—never was good at words, in all my life,"
said Farmer Graves, good-humouredly. "Get at the sense,
can't ye? I say she shall do what she likes, and I'll stand
by her—or afore her, ef ye like it so. Speak up, 'Lizy!"

Ah, venturesome Farmer Graves! For one swift moment
his wife caught her breath,—flushing deeper, growing white;
then answered, low and steadily—

"I think I will take Jemmy Lucas."

It was a bold step. Mrs Graves could not tell the next
minute how she had ever dared take it. She only knew that in
that moment's pause her heart had sent up a mute unwonted
cry for direction—and then the words were out, of themselves as it were. Yet there sat her husband, who had vowed
he would have no Vinegar Hill infusion in his household,
and here sat she, declaring that she would take Jemmy Lucas.
Not a look passed from one to the other, the farmer on his
part being all dumb with astonishment, as his wife on her
part was silent with fright. But he had asked her, she repeated to herself,—he had bade her say what she would do.

Didn't he mean that she should take him at his word? No, he didn't, she reflected now in her cooler moments. It's a way men have sometimes.

Meanwhile other tongues were busy.

"Well done! well done!" said old Squire Peasely, tapping the table, and much relieved that this little job at least was off his hands. "Couldn't be beat! That's the very boy Mis' Bingham wants learned farmin',—and there ain't a man in town could do it better 'n Ahab Graves."

Mr Graves gave a twist in his chair which was very nearly a bounce out of it, but he only took a large slice of cake and disposed of himself in that way.

"*Your* summer's work 's cut out, sir," said young Comstock.

"Gen'ally is by this time o' year," said Mr Graves, who had his own private share of pride. "Me and 'Lizy 's been cuttin' out all winter. I ain't the sort of man as likes to hev t' make up, first."

Now young Comstock was.

"I wish Jemmy was here this minute," said the delighted Mrs Bingham, "but I didn't want him to hear our plans tonight, and so I let him go home. I can have him back tomorrow, Mrs Graves."

"Reckon she kin wait as long as that," said Farmer Graves, gathering himself up. "And ef she kin, I kin. Now, 'Lizy, ef you 're through eatin' cake, we 'll go."

And with this double-barrelled shot, Mr Graves stalked out to the barn to fetch his horse.

Now Mrs Graves, brave little woman as she was, would rather have taken another chase from Walter Limp, than to face that pretty drive home in the spring twilight.

"Whatever *will* he say," she thought to herself. But at first he said nothing. Walking into a trap is not always the pleasanter for having set the trap yourself, and Farmer Graves fretted and chafed inwardly, back and forth, at himself and his wife, without in the least bit seeing his way out.

"'Twarn't hardly fair, 'Lizy!" he said at last.

His wife started, and asked, "What?"

"'Twarn't the place, neither," Farmer Graves went on, in an aggrieved voice. "Gettin' the advice o' the hull town upon your business, 'stead o' talkin' it over quiet at home. And it warn't the time. And you warn't 'xactly the one t' come a trippin' me up like that. Steady there!—Mind what ye're about!" and Mr Graves reined in his frolicksome young horse, with a certain new appreciation of the benefits of bit and bridle. "No, 'twarn't fair," he said again, returning to the charge.

"But Ahab, you said"—began his wife.

"Land sakes!" broke in the farmer, testily, "what's the odds what I said? What's that to do? Folks can't always tell what they're sayin', no more'n you kin tell where breachy cattle gits over a fence. Nor *how* they got over," said Mr Graves, with an air of reflection; "nor what they'll do when they're there. 'Cept mischief. All ye know is, they're over."

"Well, that was just the way with my words, too," said Mrs Graves, with a cheering-up little laugh. When her husband came to illustrations, things were always mending.

"Ay, ay—I daresay," said the farmer; "but I could ha' druv mine back—headed 'em off like. Yours has got t' stay in, eatin' the corn. And treadin' down more'n they eat," Mr Graves added with a doleful shake of the head.

"Then you'll let him come!" cried Mrs Graves, giving a little scream of joy, to which the farmer's young horse danced as if it had been music.

"Whoa!—both on ye," said Mr Graves, with some asperity. "Let him come?—like t' see how I'd set out to help it!"

"Why it's for you to say, Ahab," said Mrs Graves, softly.

"It is, is it?" said Mr Graves. "Very good to hear of,—last piece o' news as come out, I guess,—of a man jest knowed what to do with it. Ef you ain't found out that you always has your own way, 'Lizy, first or last, *I* have. So there's an end."

"Then you'll really make this beginning, Ahab?" said Mrs Graves, joyfully.

"Beginnin' o' what?" said the farmer.

"Why, beginning of trying to see what we can do," said his wife.

"Love her!" said Mr Graves. "Did ever any soul, *but* a woman, talk so afore, I wonder? *I* know what I kin do, now, 'Lizy,—you don't. There's jest the difference."

"But I mean, you'll let the boy come," said Mrs Graves.

"Tell ye I can't help myself," said the farmer. "He's bound t' come. Mind ye, I don't say how long I'll stand it, though. Come?—yes, and all Vinegar Hill arter him. You kin jest chuck your pickles out o' the winder, 'Lizy," said Mr Graves, as he turned up towards his own door. "*I* shan't want no more this some time."

For all answer to which, Mrs Graves involved herself and the farmer and the buffalo robes and the reins, in such a complicated tangle, that Mr Graves gave it as his opinion, that "a woman couldn't be easy ten minutes 'thout gettin' into a mess o' some kind."

"Ef you're agoin' t' drive, 'Lizy," he said, "why, drive! and be done with it. Mebbe 'twould suit ye best to be run away with, and throwed out,—and ef it would, don't use no ceremony with me. The mare's all ready. Whoa, there! So! —There's a pair on ye, I do vow!"

It did seem a little that way; for Mrs Graves danced out of the waggon and into the house, and black Jet danced all the way down to the stable and into it.

CHAPTER III.

JEMMY LUCAS did not present himself next day at Mrs Bingham's. He had gone home that night a neatly mended-up little boy, with pockets full of comforts for himself and his mother, enough to last a day or two if he should want to stay so long. Mrs Lucas took note of the improvement, but shook her head.

"'Twon't stay," she said. "Look out for the rags again to-morrow, Jemmy. Nothing stays, in this hole—except rags, and dirt, and wickedness. And you needn't to cry for Molly. My! wouldn't I like to be her!"

But it was hard for Jemmy Lucas, after that fortnight of wonders in a clean village house, to believe that even Vinegar Hill could be just the same. He hung his jacket and trousers on the chair with no misgiving, and went to bed, and dreamed of Molly.

But when dreaming was really ended, he thought it had just begun. In the first place, the chair was empty. In the second place, there lay on him, not only the ragged covers under which he had gone to sleep, but also a heap of other rags,—dirty, dingy, undistinguishable at first, but then showing sleeves and legs and fronts and bands which seemed to belong to each other, and yet were held by slight and unreliable connections. Jemmy looked—stretched his eyes wide open with his fingers—then shouted.

"I say!—mother!"—

"Well?" said Mrs Lucas, putting her head in at the door.

"Where's my things?—I's got ter be right straight off."

"They couldn't wait, and walked off afore ye," said the woman in her cold jarring tones. "Don't ye cry now, dear!" she said more gently, watching the flash of dismayed comprehension that came to the boy's face. "'Tain't nothing new—if it *don't* never get old."

But Jemmy did cry long and loud, and could not be comforted.

"They's not *my* rags, anyhow," he sobbed, flinging off the tattered heap with extreme disgust. "They's some other dirty feller's. And he's took breakfast and all!"

"Took that first of all," said Mrs Lucas, coolly. "Couldn't expect it wouldn't make him thirsty."

"I's been all clean down there!" sobbed Jemmy. "Like the King's children."

Mrs Lucas raised her eyebrows with a strange look, that was half mockery and half despair.

"There! there!" she said,—"I'll wash 'em out for you, if that's all. And you can wear my t'other frock round till they dry. I'll tie it up."

So the other frock, which *was* clean, though short and scant and patched all over, was put on Jemmy Lucas; and his mother turned up the bottom of the skirt, and tied it round his waist.

"Looks 'most like a dressing-gown," she said,—"if one could only think so."

"What's a dressing-gown?" asked Jemmy Lucas.

"Somethin' I used to see—and shan't never again," said the woman. "Great folks wears 'em, Jemmy,—they ain't nothin' to you. Keep out o' the sight o' the boys, now, or they'll tear it off ye, sure."

Jemmy knew that. He had a wholesome fear of being seen wearing his mother's gown; so he curled himself down in the furthest corner of the room, ready to hide at a minute's warning, and from thence watched Mrs Lucas as she washed out the tattered garments which were to replace her dress.

"I'm afraid to hang 'em out," she said, arraying the fluttering strips upon an old chair behind the stove. "If Lucas come by, and was to see 'em, that would be the last. There's no keeping your clothes here if they ain't on your back, and not always then. Are ye starved, child?"

"Oh, I had *ever* so much supper, 'fore I come last night," said Jemmy Lucas, calling up his courage. "All them things was for you, mother."

"'Tain't no use fetchin' nothing to me," said the woman, hardly. "That's done. Lucas would take the skin off my face if he could get it. I'm most afeared to wash it sometimes, fear he will as it is."

"But the King knows," said Jemmy, with a deep-drawn sigh as he remembered Molly.

"Does He?" said Mrs Lucas. "Well, get all the comfort ye can, child,—'tain't much. I shan't hinder ye." And she took up her pail to go for water, and dropped the subject.

Jemmy Lucas on his part sat still and thought. What was he to do now? As to going back to the village, even to see Mrs Bingham and explain matters, that was out of the question. Once he had thought no more of tatters than of dirt, but Jemmy had grown into an excellent dislike of both, and having for one short fortnight tasted the sweets of civilised life, the plunge back into barbarism was very, very hard. Couldn't his mother maybe mend the clothes?— Jemmy shuffled across the room and examined. Mend them!—they were not good enough to make patches for something else. There was no patching *them*—the very stitches wouldn't hold. No, his knees must poke out here and his elbows there, and his ankles try the spring winds without any sign of shelter, and buttons must be a forgotten thing. However should he hold the rags together, Jemmy thought, with his new views of what garments were meant to do! Really the easiest way would be for his mother to sew them on him, and no more about it. Jemmy Lucas returned to his corner with a very decided loss of interest in the speedy drying of the things by the fire. No, he could never go back to the village again; and so day after day went by, and Jemmy moped about the house, hiding his rags, shunning his father, and losing daily the little colour and roundness which had begun to come back to his cheeks. For it was about as hard to keep soul and body together, those days, as it was the rags. Only one little ray of comfort gleamed down upon the house, and that Jemmy Lucas had all to himself. It was the old watchword, "The King knows."

"He knows—we's wait," little Molly had said, and now the words were like daily bread to Jemmy Lucas, what though with that "waiting" he often cried himself to sleep. But oh! blessed waiting that is sure!

"Blessed are all they that wait for Him!"

"They shall not be ashamed."

The Lord had not forgotten, He was not slow to hear: the answer was at hand.

As the days passed, and still no sign of Jemmy Lucas, Mrs Bingham was much surprised; and at last she volunteered to go in search of him herself, and perhaps bring him back with her to his new home. For Mr Graves had set his foot down upon one square inch of ground—his wife should not go near Vinegar Hill.

"Shan't do it, 'Lizy," he said,—"not with nobody, and not 'thout nobody. They kin find enough ugly folks about the village that 'll answer.'

"Ugly folks ain't always the best for the purpose," ventured Mrs Graves.

"Mebbe not," said the farmer, "but the one partic'lar pretty cretur as belongs t' me, I 'll *keep*. So that 's settled. And when it *is*, there ain't no use talkin'."

Mrs Graves knew that, by old experience! With a sigh she took her name from the visiting band of workers, and with another gave up the pleasant thought of seeing Jemmy's first glow of delight; and then set herself to making as many preparations for him as if he had been a young prince. Skilful in contrivance, handy in work, swift and dexterous in everything of which her fingers took hold, what did not the farmer's wife do in that week! Old pantaloons were brought out and cut down and made over; neat jackets emerged from the skirts of old coats; and little checked shirts, and little white collars, grew and multiplied, and kept pace with the socks that were knit in the twilight and the odd minutes of waiting. Mrs Graves had hardly been so happy in her life. But like a wise little woman she kept it all to herself; wrought at her manufactures when her husband was a-field, and hid her work-basket in the closet, and her scraps of song in her heart, when he was coming home. But you can't hide everything, always.

"Have done runnin' up-stairs, will ye, 'Lizy?" said Farmer Graves one night. "What 's to pay? Didn't smell fire, did ye?"

"No," said Mrs Graves, with slight hesitation. "Oh no, Ahab!—of course I didn't smell fire!"

"What, then?" said Mr Graves, helping himself to butter. "Somebody give ye a new pair o' feet, and you 're a-tryin' of 'em on?"

Mrs Graves laughed a little nervously, but answered no.

"Like to want 'em, at this rate," said the farmer. "What ye got up-stairs? Let 's hear."

"Nothing,—no," said Mrs Graves, again hesitating a little.

"I only—I just thought, Ahab—I'd run up, you know, and see how the room felt."

"See how the room felt!" repeated Mr Graves. "'Tain't took sick, is it? Which room, of all things? Used t' have more 'n one in the house."

"I mean—Jemmy's room," said Mrs Graves. "That is —the room where we 're going to put Jemmy."

Mr Graves returned to his supper with an air.

"Might ha' knowed it," he said. "A boy as has slep' out o' doors half his life, likely, and she's been up a matter o' three times this livin' night to see how the room felt. And him not even there."

"Twice, Ahab, only twice," said Mrs Graves, with a blush.

"Twice too often," said Mr Graves, drowning part of his disapproval in his tea.

"Well now, Ahab," began Mrs Graves.

"What's up?" said the farmer, handing his cup to be re-filled. "Out with it, 'Lizy! take 'em in order. What comes next?"

But instead of other reply, Mrs Graves set down the empty cup, and darting away to her closet brought thence the basket—not of unfinished but of finished things. This she held up before her husband, kneeling then at his side, without a word.

"In the name o' wonder!" ejaculated the astonished farmer. "Why, 'Lizy!"

The truth began to dawn upon him. Glancing at his wife's face, so full and trembling and glad, Mr Graves turned over the contents of the basket with bewildered fingers. The pretty shirts and collar and socks, the neat little outfit for Jemmy Lucas, which yet had cost nothing but her own work, and which had plainly been such a labour of joy as well as love ;—if, as Ruskin says, the *thought* is the thing in a picture, then was that basket a masterpiece! The farmer's face changed.

"Run away with 'em—there's a girl," he said, huskily "And give us the tea, 'Lizy ; my throat's in an astonishin'ly queer state o' mind."

"Not sore, is it?" said Mrs Graves, with her demurest face, as she poured out the tea.

Mr Graves drained his cup before answering.

"Nothin' to worry about, 'Lizy," he said. "Tea sets it all straight. Guess I'll have another."

CHAPTER IV.

SPRING was everywhere in the village, and in the brown belts of forest, and on the outlying farms. There wasn't a cow that didn't know it, there wasn't a cock that didn't tell it, there wasn't a squirrel that didn't dance for joy. Up and down the broad fields, where the winter wheat put on its vivid green; in wild wet places, where the cowslips blossomed and the frogs held forth; in the woodland, where the birch trees shook out their newly-arranged tresses and the maples donned their scarlet and yellow; everywhere went the spring. Hiding under leaves with the squirrel-cups, sunning herself on the rocks with the saxifrage, laughing with the robins, rejoicing with the bluebirds, frisking with the young lambs upon the hillside, humming busily with the bees,—there was Spring. You need not go ten steps to find her.

Of course, such being the case, Spring was also inside the village houses,—people opened their windows and doors on purpose; but why Spring within and Spring without should be so very different, always will remain somewhat of a mystery. Outdoors, Spring trailed her flowing robes over every sort of a floor; but within, she tucked up her garments and fell to cleaning house—scolded the maids, tired the mistress, disturbed the master, played unheard of pranks with the children. Here she stirred up the dust with no gentle wind, there she dispensed the fumes of soapsuds, instead of the perfume of violets and the smell of the new grass and the strange scent of the fresh-ploughed field. Outside she was in her tip-top decorations; but within, the oldest, most faded, most forlorn garments that could be found, served her turn; very nearly transforming the fair young Spring into an Afrite of giant proportions. Outside, she went touching things here and there, stroking them into order by sweet degrees; but in the house everything must be begun, carried on, and finished at once. First raise a pile of general confusion, and then pull out order from underneath.

Well, of course, such being the state of things, Mrs Bingham and her house could not escape. Chaos had reigned there comfortably for some days; and as a consequence, Mrs Bingham had not yet been to Vinegar Hill. She could not go "looking a sight;" and as to bringing out and putting on respectable things in such a general muss, of course that was out of the question. So early and late, bright spring morning and sweet spring night, the work went on.

At last came a day of grand climax. It was plain that something must happen and that pretty soon. Either order must win the field in the hand-to-hand fight, or else everything would be resolved into its first principles, and Mrs Bingham and her household disappear together in a cloud of dust.

Things were in this state and the fight as yet uncertain, when somebody knocked at Mrs Bingham's door. Once, twice, thrice, and this time so loudly, that the knock rose even above the din of battle. Mrs Bingham paused.

"Come in, Jemmy," she called. But no one answered. Mrs Bingham laid down her weapons and went to the door.

"It was all that was wanting! I do suppose," she said as she went, extending no mental welcome to the visitor. But there—all tidy and clean and smiling—stood old Mrs Peasely and little Mrs Coon.

"You blessed people," said Mrs Bingham, frankly. "I haven't a place to ask you to!"

"Oh, we don't want to come in," said Mrs Coon, smiling; "we want you to come out."

"Come out!" echoed Mrs Bingham. "Why, I'm up to my eyes!"

' Oh yes, so was she," said Mrs Peasely, nodding towards

Mrs Coon; "but I giv' her a hand, and here she is. We're going to Vinegar Hill, so don't ye be long."

"But I can't possibly go to-day," said Mrs Bingham. "If you could just look into the house once, you'd see."

"Dear heart! haven't I seen my own?" said Mrs Peasely. "There I was, up to my eyes, as you say, and down to my elbows, when in comes Richard after his seed package o' new spring wheat. And says he, 'Mother,' says he, 'how about those other houses on Vinegar Hill. When are you goin' to take *them* in hand?' 'Why, Richard,' says I, 'you don't s'pose I'm agoin' to turn things upside down *there?*' 'They want it bad enough,' says he, walkin' off with his wheat. 'Or settin' right side up. What do you think of houses that ain't *never* cleaned?'"

Mrs Peasely paused, waiting for a response; but Mrs Bingham, leaning back against the doorway, studied the matter in silence.

"Well," the good woman went on. "I goes back to my work, and I couldn't do it. Couldn't get on a bit! Scrub, scrub, and wash, wash, and all the time the brush kept saying—'Never cleaned,—never cleaned!'—and thinks I they never *will* be, unless somebody takes it up. So I just tidied myself a little, and ran over to Mrs Coon, and then we came round for you."

"Coon said we'd better muster strong the first time we went," said the quiet little woman who bore his name.

"Well, I'm just astonished at myself!" said Mrs Bingham, starting up. "D'ye know I really *didn't* know I was so selfish? Now I'll be ready in just two minutes. Walk on slow, and I'll catch ye."

It might have been more than two minutes, but it was certainly very few, before Mrs Bingham's brisk step overtook her two neighbours.

"I'm downright ashamed of myself!" she said. "I can tell you, one needs look sharp to find out how *many* Bible words he's workin' out at once. Now I knew I was 'not slothful in business'—and forgot all about that other verse: 'All men seek their own, and not the things which are

Jesus Christ's.' I'd like to know what business my soapsuds has to come between those poor starvin', sufferin' folks and help? But I've locked it up now, to look after itself,"— and Mrs Bingham stepped off at a rate that made it not too easy to keep pace with her.

Spring had ventured even within the bounds of Vinegar Hill, but you could see that there she worked without heart. It is hard to beautify a place where so very much else wants doing first. And so the grass grew rank and tangled by the brookside, with no gentle cropping to keep it down; and on the hill, and by the road, it was worn and trodden and chafed away, in spots and streaks and whole patches. The wildflowers that will come up and try everywhere, looked pinched and care-worn; the graceful bending stems of the bushes and saplings were broken and jagged and split; and the trees of larger growth, which had somehow striven above their hard childhood, were still dwarfed and crooked and gnarled, and would never be anything else.

"For pity's sake!" said Mrs Peasely, as they fairly entered the hamlet and passed the first small house, "what a lookin' place!"

"Just *see* the children once!" said Mrs Coon, as a swarm of half-naked urchins came out and clustered upon the doorstep.

"Where does Jemmy Lucas live?" asked Mrs Bingham, pausing before the house.

But an indescribable hubbub arose at that, making the answer (if there was one) quite unheard. Such cries of "Hi!"—"Look at 'em!"—"What yer want?"—"None o' yer business!"—"Give us a penny!"—Mrs Bingham felt like stopping her ears and running away. Then a tall slatternly woman came out of the house, and with a handful of well-directed cuffs enforced silence.

"Lucas lives down t' the foot o' the hill," she said. "Ain't like t' crawl up, nuther. Wish yer joy o' yer friends!"

"Are these all your children?" said little Mrs Coon, stepping nearer.

"They ain't none on 'em yours, anyhow," said the woman, briskly.

"No—certainly," said Mrs Coon, somewhat taken aback. "I only meant"——

"Like t' have some ?" said the woman, with a sneer. "Let ye have 'em cheap if ye'll take the whole lot. Won't have t' change their clothes, for they ain't got none,—won't have t' teach 'em tricks, for they's got plenty. Needn't t' mind robbin' me,—I've got enough more."

And such a din as broke forth at that !—The three friends beat a quick retreat, followed by pebbles, clam shells, old bones, and clots of mud ; and whatever else that could be used for such a purpose came to hand.

"And I've been cleaning my house this whole week," said Mrs Bingham, "and making this place *wait !*"

"But what's to be done ?" said old Mrs Peasely, much cast down.

"Oh, try again," said cheery Mrs Coon, "just as you do with a spot on the floor,—rub and rub, and by and by it ain't there."

"She said at the foot of the hill," said Mrs Bingham. "Which way, I wonder ? Well, we'll go down and walk along the edge."

So down,— through narrow ways and tangled bushes and muddy spots, till the foot of the hill was reached, and they struck a little foot-path which wound round the edge of the level ground, in front of a fringe of small dark houses. At the first of these they made another pause, but not a head showed itself. So with the next, and the next. Vinegar Hill seemed to withdraw out of sight at the first warning of strange eyes.

"Well, I shall knock and ask," said Mrs Bingham, boldly. So at the fourth house she knocked, but still nobody appeared. Mrs Bingham went on to the next, and tried there. A noise inside, albeit not of the encouraging sort, made her wait longer here ; and after a little delay, the upper half of the old door was opened far enough to show the head and face of Jem Crook.

"Mornin', ladies," said Jem. "Sorry as I can't ask yer in, but two o' the family 's down with the pox, and the rest is powerful bad with the fever."

"Where does Jemmy Lucas live?" said Mrs Bingham, standing her ground well through this broadside.

"The sweet little feller ain't to home now," said Jem Crook, in a drawling voice. "He's out o' town, on a wisit to his nuncle. When he *is* home, he lives up top o' the hill commonly."

"At the top!" said Mrs Bingham; "they told us at the bottom."

Jem Crook nodded.

"Only failin' Jemmy as I knows on," he said; "he allers *does* think things is jest the 'tother way from what they ain't."

"Your *sure* he's away?" said Mrs Bingham, hesitating.

"Nuncle come for him last night," said Jem Crook,—"went off in style, he did. 'Tain't somethin' as us poor fellers is like ter be mistook concernin'. Nuncle's rich as two sticks," Jem added, with a confidential air that was quite bewildering.

Mrs Bingham stood in doubt.

"Wantin' to see him partic'lar?" said Jem Crook. "Thinkin' ter settle here, likely? Now ef I could help.—There's all them," said Jem, with a sweep of his arm towards the first four mansions in the row. "Likely houses, every one on 'em. Speak for yer ter the folks when they comes back from their work. Farms is so henderin'," Jem added, with an air of innocent good faith.

"Thank you," said Mrs Bingham, hastily, "I won't trouble you." And as she stepped out into the road again, she was followed by a peal of laughter that well nigh set the three friends off on a run.

"There wasn't a word of it true—and I *knew* it," said Mrs Bingham, indignantly. "But what shall we do now? One says at the bottom, and the other says at the top. I can't go knocking at all the doors in turn."

"There's a man coming, ask him," said Mrs Coon. "Boys will be boys, I s'pose, always."

The man came on,—a rather young fellow, bright-checked, black-haired.

"Do you know where Jemmy Lucas lives?" said Mrs Bingham, accosting him. The man stopped, taking off his hat with a swing.

"Jemmy Lucas?" he said. "Old Lucas's boy?"

"I suppose so," said Mrs Bingham. "Does he live at the bottom or the top of the hill?"

"That's accordin' to circumstances, in my experience," said the man, coolly. "Old Lucas lives just next door to the devil, and if you happen to know where that is you can't do better than to go straight there. Likely you'll find 'em both in."

And having so said, the man put on his hat with another extreme flourish, and walked away. Poor Mrs Peasely burst out crying.

"I'm just frightened to death!" she said.

"Oh, come, come!" said Mrs Coon, cheerily. "'The Lord on high is mightier than the noise of many waters;' we'll try again."

CHAPTER V.

SLOWLY now, for they were tired, the three friends climbed the hill again; keeping from the houses as far as possible, till they should decide what to do. Then suddenly came upon two little children sitting under the bushes, and filling the air with their lamentations.

"Dear! dear!—what's the matter now!" said Mrs Peasely, accosting the children. "Who are ye? and what ails ye?"

"He's Joe Wiggins," said the little girl, between her sobs. "And I's Kate. And Tim's been a poundin' of us both."

"He didn't get it, though,—for all," said the boy, with an air of triumph.

"He throwed it inter the brook," explained the girl.

"And it was jest sposh afore he could get it out," whimpered the boy, but still exulting.

Y

"And Tim rubbed him in it, and pounded him too." said the girl. "And he pounded me, 'cause mine was all eat up."

Traces on the boy's face and head of what might have been yellow mud—or dissolved gingerbread—or possibly both, were easy to see.

"Tim dropped it—and we run—and he ketched us," said the children. "Boohoo!"

"Where did Tim get the gingerbread?" inquired Mrs Bingham, with a comical look.

"Dunno; him had hull lots!"

"*I* know," Mrs Bingham said softly to her companions. "It must be the same that walked out of my pantry this morning while I was up-stairs, and the house all open. Fresh baked last night."

"Poor children! poor creatures!" said Mrs Coon.

"See here," said Mrs Peasely, taking two extra-sized cookies from her pocket, "that's as good as gingerbread, any day. Now, don't you want to go to school and learn?"

"I knows now," said the boy, devouring his cookie in hot haste. "Daddy says I'm lik'lier 'n Tim. He's big, and I creeps inter the holes."

"Why him 'll hide right afore yer eyes, and yer won't see him," said the girl, admiringly. "Him 'll quack! quack! and fetch the ducks right out. Won't yer, Joe?"

Joe nodded, and looked up for commendation, or possibly another cookie.

"Her's smart, too," he said. "Fetched in three hull hanks yesterday."

"Three hanks of blue yarn?" said Mrs Peasely.

"Warn't it, though!" said the children. "Blue as huckleberries. And soft!"

"Mine, as I'm a living woman!" said Mrs Peasely, with a groan, turning to her companions. "I missed it off the fence. The little!—Now ain't this whole thing gone too far to be mended?"

"Not a bit" said bright Mrs Coon. "Nothing is, I guess.

See here, children, would you like to have a cookie like that every day?"

"You go bail!" was the expressive answer.

"Well, I'll give you one every day, if you'll come for it," said Mrs Coon. "You ask for Mrs Coon's house, and anybody'll tell ye where it is."

"Don't want no tellin'," said the boy. "Apples in front, pears ahint,—I knows it. Gate squeaks."

Mrs Coon shook her head with a half laugh, but then her eyes filled full.

"You poor, forsaken, little souls!" she said, stooping down by the children, and taking something from her pocket. "See here—here's a picture. That's the Lord Jesus blessing little children like you. Did you never hear of the Lord Jesus?"

"No," said the girl, looking at the picture.

"Yer have, too," said the boy. "It's Him as Jemmy Lucas tells about. Daddy says Jemmy's all spiled and busted up."

"My, don't him look nice, Joe?" said the girl.

"There, you may keep it for your own," said Mrs Coon, "and then you can look at it as much as you like. The Lord Jesus loves little children."

"What fur?" said the boy, eyeing the picture askance with some suspicion.

"Because they're so little and He's so great," said Mrs Coon. "Because they're so weak and He's so strong. Because they need so very much that He can give them."

"Like ter know what," said the boy, with his finger in his mouth.

"Why, a new heart," said Mrs Coon, "and a sweet temper, and a happy life. Just think! He can help them always to be good, and never to do a single bad thing. The Lord Jesus doesn't like to have little children do bad things, —it displeases Him very much."

The children nudged each other, looking covertly out of the corners of their eyes, but they said not a word.

"There," Mrs Coon said, "I must go now. But rememher, the Lord Jesus loves little children, and wants them to be good; and when you come to my house, I'll tell you some more about Him. Good by."

No answer came; but looking back from some way further up the hill, the happy women of the village saw the two little mites of forlorn humanity still side by side in the dust, and studying the picture.

The day was ebbing fast now, even that long spring afternoon could not last much longer; the friends quickened their steps.

"I must give it up for this time," said Mrs Bingham.

"Yes, I must be home to get supper," said Mrs Coon.

"Tell ye what I'll do," said Mrs Peasely. "I'll just send Richard to hunt the boy up. He's achin' all over for a job, to judge by the way he talks. Oh dear! Oh dear!—did ever mortal eyes see such a baby afore, I wonder?"

A baby like a white shadow; a woman as white, as thin, but on whom the dark shadow of life showed too, wearily trotting the baby up and down at the door of a miserable house,—such was the picture.

"Is the baby sick?" cried Mrs Coon, stepping up to the woman.

"Don' know as you'd call him nothin' special," said the woman, drearily. "Been like that along o' two year."

"Two years!—didn't he *never* grow?" said Mrs Peasely, breathless.

"Can't grow 'thout nothin' t' grow on," said the woman. "Folks used t' say as babies had oughter be fed reg'lar, and o' course he can't expect that, no more'n the rest."

"Do you mean to tell me you can't find food enough for such a little child?" said Mrs Peasely, in horror.

The woman's face never changed.

"Like t' see where it's t' come from," she said, coldly. 'Peter, he fetches in by spells, and sometimes it's a crust as can be sopped; but when it's nuts they doesn't go fur."

"But if you can get milk to soak the crust," said Mrs Bingham, "he might take that sometimes alone."

"We uses water down here," said the woman. "'Tain't so

heartnin' as milk, likely, but it grows round. Ain't much else as does, 'cept badness."

"And does all this place full of children live without bread and milk?" said Mrs Peasely, folding her hands in despair.

"'Cept when they dies," said the woman, "that's pretty often. And 'cept when they helps themselves, and that's pretty often. Yes, they lives, if so you call it."

There was something so inexpressibly forlorn in all this, —the hopeless, dull wearing of sorrow and want and care like an accustomed thing—that there seemed no words to answer. The three from the village stood silent, watching the poor mother and child.

"He must have bread and milk every single day!" Mrs Peasely broke out at last, in a tone of authority, "and he shall, too. Just you send down to Mrs Peasely—at the squire's—about milkin' time. *I'll* make him grow."

"Ain't no one to send 'thout he goes hisself," said the woman, with unconscious irony.

"Who's that you spoke of a while ago?" said Mrs Coon. "Peter? Why can't Peter come?"

"Likely he wouldn't choose," said the woman. "Molly could ha' went—but she's took, like all the rest."

"Molly!" cried Mrs Bingham; "you're never Molly Limp's mother?"

"I's Walter Limp's wife, worse luck," said the woman, trotting her baby. "Molly's took."

"But you never came to see her all the time she was sick!" said Mrs Bingham. "Nor after," she added, softly.

"How's I t' go 'mong you rich folks?" said the woman with something of bitterness now, and holding up her ragged sleeve. "Go t' see her? I'd ha' fell t' pieces by the way, likely. And he'd ha' took my head when I comed home. 'Twouldn't ha' made much difference," she added, in her old tone, and beginning to trot the baby again in the old monotonous way.

"I tell you what," said Mrs Coon, with decision, "you must come for the milk yourself, and bring baby. It'll do

him more good than anything else.   And we'll find a gown
that *won't* fall to pieces."

"And if you'll come and wash Mondays," said Mrs
Peasely, "or stay half a day at a time and help me clean,
why you'd have five dollars in your pocket in no time."

"Five dollars!" repeated poor Mrs Limp, a strange gleam
lighting up her face.   "It's many a long day since I seen
the colour o' one!"

"Well, you come down to the village to-morrow for
the milk," said Mrs Peasely, "and we'll soon set things
straight."

The three friends turned away from the poor little house
towards their own happy homes, and Mrs Limp and the pale
baby sat and watched them.

"I do declare," said Mrs Peasely, stopping short as they
reached the high road, "I never once thought to ask if
they'd got anything to keep 'em alive *till* to-morrow!   Now
ain't that too bad?   Let's go back."

But even little Mrs Coon doubted whether that would do.

"Too late," she said.   "The bushes are getting just full
of men and boys.   I saw 'em peep out as we come by.   Best
hurry home."

And a smart stroke of a small pebble on her shoulder,
while another hit Mrs Bingham on the ear, confirmed this
prudent resolution, and made the party quite forget that
they were tired.

CHAPTER VI.

"RICHARD," said Mrs Peasely next morning, as they sat at
breakfast, "I want you to drop everything to-day and go
hunt up that Jemmy Lucas.   It'll take a man to find him, I
reckon."

"Shouldn't wonder," said young Peasely, giving close attention to his breakfast.

"So you must go," pursued Mrs Peasely.

"Dick's bespoke to-day, mother, 'fore you took it up," said the old Squire. "He's seedin' down that 'ere hilltop next to Joe Comstock's. Likely job, ain't it, Dick?"

"First-rate, sir."

"Seedin', is he?" said Mrs Peasely; "then his hand'll be in to scatter somethin' round Vinegar Hill."

"Guess *that* job'll hev' t' wait a spell," said the Squire. "Finish the hilltop to-day, Dick."

Young Peasely laughed.

"Which of 'em?" he said. "Don't see ever in the world how I'm to manage both."

"I mean the seedin'," said Squire Peasely.

"So do I," said his wife. "Think of a hill that *never* gets planted, Dick,—as you telled me yesterday about my cleanin'."

"That's fair, mother," said the young man, growing grave. "But just look out once!"

Yes, it was a day of farming perfection. Clear, bright, with cool sunbeams that came streaming down into the world with a promise to warm it up by and by. The air still and fragrant, the birds in full song.

"Everything's just on the jump, mother," said Richard Peasely, with a deprecating look.

"It don't stand still down *there*, I tell ye," said Mrs Peasely.

"It's more'n time the seed was in!"

"With the children growin' up and dyin' off so fast," said his mother.

"There—there," said young Peasely, quitting the table,— "you've got the best of it. I'll have to give in. But it might rain to-morrow,—and *then* I could go just as well as not."

"And you might sprain your ankle and then you couldn't," said Mrs Peasely, beginning to put the dishes together. "I guess it's gen'rally safe to see to the Lord's work first."

"So it is, so it is," said the old Squire, while Richard went off without another word. "Still, mother, the hilltop's pressin'."

"You'd think so, if you'd been there once," said his wife. "I declare, Squire, *I* don't know what we've been thinkin' of, all these years. It's a wonder to me that every prayer for the world didn't stick in our throats and choke us right then and there, for sayin' what we didn't mean."

"Why, my dear!" said Squire Peasely, "we did mean it, sure."

"We meant it should be done without much of our help, then," said Mrs Peasely, bustling about. "Tell ye, Squire, if I was to sit all day hopin' the rooms was clean, you'd have a house worth lookin' at."

"'Tain't exactly your way, mother," said Squire Peasely, with a laugh, "and I never heered no one charge it agin ye."

"It isn't going to be, any longer," said Mrs Peasely, dousing her cups in the scalding water. "And I don't want it should be Dick's. He's *most* a first-class farmer, now," she went on, with glistening eyes, "and I want to see him tip-top." And Mrs Peasely stopped talking and gave all heed to her work, and the old Squire filled his pipe with sundry reflections, apparently, and soberly smoked them out, one by one.

As for Richard himself, he went off with an air that said he had more on his mind than he could manage. What a day it was! what a press of spring work hailed him on every side! Things on the jump, as he had said, and all seeming to need attention at once. How could he take half a day—and of such a day—to work on the waste lands outside his own neat premises! Couldn't Vinegar Hill wait, as his father had said? *Could* it?—"Children dying and growing up,"—yes, that was all true: and young Peasely had not forgotten his adventure in the barnyard when the snow lay deep. Yet still—. The young farmer strode back and forth his beautiful hilltop, scattering the grain with an even hand, but with strange thoughts and words doing their own work the while.

"White already to the harvest,"—could *that* be true of Vinegar Hill? His own fields were not in a hurry like that.

Vinegar Hill,—that nest of thistles! Then came back his mother's story of what the Lord himself had gathered there, —how could such things "wait?" How could his own? "Well, I don't see but one of 'em's *got* to!" said Richard Peasely aloud to himself, pausing a moment and emphasising his words with a blow on the bar post. "And if one of 'em *has*," he went on slowly, "after what I've promised, I don't see but it's got to be mine. Guess I didn't just say I'd give the Lord all the time I could spare. And if I meant what I said—and I did mean it, too—stands to reason His work comes first. There's no doubt but I wish He hadn't set me about it to-day, though!"—with which frank confession, Richard went down the field with steady steps, his mind in the ease of a right determination.

Walking briskly on, full of thoughts and cogitations, Richard Peasely's quick eye suddenly caught sight of something near the fence,—as if something had appeared for but a second from behind it. A flourishing clump of wild plums which grew just there, hindered his seeing very distinctly, but that something had started out and darted in, he felt sure. Was it a bird? a snake? Perhaps,—no, he thought not. Walking on his brisk way, which brought him nearer and nearer to the fence, and still sowing his grain with the same even, steady cast, young Peasely noticed how near his coat and lunch pail were to the fence. The coat hanging on an outstanding plum bush, which per favour of a rocky bit of ground had been allowed a place within the field, and the little bright tin lunch pail standing close beneath it. Looking closer from under his broad straw hat, and advancing nearer every minute, the young farmer saw a bit of rag fluttering among the bushes on the outside. Not fluttering as if fast on one of the twigs, but as if some moving, breathing thing helped on its motion.

"Best move my traps further off, I guess," was Richard's first thought.

"Then he'll go right on and steal from somebody else," was the second.

Richard was generally quick in determination. Lithe

agile, light of foot, he was at the fence, and had thrown himself over it, before the rag owner had time to even guess what was coming, and had him fast—not by the collar, for there was none—but by the shoulder, beyond all hope of escape. A tall, loosely built boy; his dress ragged in the extreme, his face all white with fear under the shadow of his long tangled hair.

"Let me be!" he cried, fiercely. "I aint teched nothin'. Let go, I say!"

"Who are you?" said young Peasely, holding fast his prize.

"None o' yer business," said the boy, in the same tone.

"And what were you doing here, watching me?" pursued Richard.

"Warn't,"—said the boy. "Ain't so handsome as yer think."

"Look here," said Richard Peasely, giving the boy a little shake, "this won't do. Speak up like a man, and answer."

"Tell ye I warn't adoin' nothin'," said the boy, beginning to whimper; "jest alookin'—that was all."

"Looking at my lunch pail," said the young farmer.

"Didn't hurt ye none, did it?—ef I *was*," said the boy.

"Are you hungry?" said Richard, eyeing the boy's gaunt cheeks.

"How's you?" inquired the boy,—"when yer's ain't had breakfast and don't expect supper?"

"Like a bear!" said Richard, throwing his mind into the case for the sake of the argument.

"Jest,"—the boy answered concisely.

"Now, what's your name?" said the young man. "You've got to tell, boy, so you'd as good be about it."

The boy twisted and whimpered.

"Let me be!" he said. "I's Wily Poll. And I ain't done nothin' to yer nor teched yer. Didn't see yer for a spell."

"Ah! I daresay," said Richard. "Now, Wily Poll, if you'll come in and sit down and be quiet, I'll give you some of my lunch ; but just as sure as you start to run away, I'll take you home and lock you up. D'ye hear ?"

Wily Poll gave sullen assent, looking up defiantly at his captor.

"Come in, then," said Richard, seating himself on the fence so as to keep hold of the boy until he was well in the field. "Now, we'll go off to that tree and eat our lunch there."

"Bushes is good enough," said Wily Poll, with a longing glance towards his late shelter.

"They ain't good enough for me," said young Peasely,—"come on."

And on they went, to the very centre of the field, where a tall hickory cast a soft spring shadow from its young leaves.

"Know how to run ?" he inquired, as he seated the boy on a broad flat stone beneath the tree.

"Mebbe I does—and mebbe I don't," said the boy, cautiously.

"Well, I do," said Richard. "Faster'n anybody you ever saw. I'll try a race with you any time you like, but we'll have something to eat first."

And as he opened the bright pail, the savoury mingling of sweet bread and butter, and pie, and cheese, and cake, which floated out, quite mastered Wily Poll, and banished all thoughts of running for the present.

"I say !"—he ejaculated. "Hi !"

"Doesn't your mother make such things ?" inquired Richard Peasely, handing the boy a great piece of pie and a "quirl cake."

"Ain't got none,—nary one o' the six," answered Wily Poll, taking the pie and cake in alternate bites.

"Who does your father have to take care of the house ?" said Richard, leaning back against the tree, pie in hand, and surveying his charge.

"Ain't got none o' them neither," returned the boy.

"Neither father nor house !" said his questioner. "Where do you live, Wily Poll ?"

"Round,"—was Wily Poll's reply.

"What do you do all day?"

"Goes huntin',"—said the boy, with a sly gleam of the eyes.

"Oh! that's it," said Richard. "And at night?—what do you do *then?* where do you sleep?"

"Ain't noways partic'lar," said Wily Poll, finishing his pie. "If it's hay, it's hay; and if it's a waggin, it's a waggin."

"And if it's neither one?"

"Then it ain't," said Wily Poll, composedly.

"Have some more pie?" said Richard Peasely, handing forth another huge triangle. "The fact is, Wily, I want to get a boy to come and live here for a while. Easy work, and good livin'—so if you hear of such a chap, send him along."

"What's the job?" inquired Wily Poll, with great promptness.

"Oh, light work," said young Peasely. "He'd have to eat flapjacks in the morning, and pie at noon; and help feed the cattle, and drive the cows afield. I should want him to turn right in and take hold of what was up, till supper time, you know. Then he could go straight to bed after that."

"I rather guess I'm yer man," said Wily Poll, with an air of deep consideration. "Don't jest know,—but sounds plaguey like it. Nothin' else?"

"Nothing much," said Richard. "I'd want him to wait till he was helped, you know, so as not to make mistakes through helping himself. And to speak out straight—so we'd know what we were talking about."

The boy's eyes twinkled.

"Guess I could do that too," he said, "for a spell."

"I meant to have Jemmy Lucas," said Richard, with a thoughtful air, "but Farmer Graves has got him."

"Jest yer let him!" said Wily Poll, leaning forward in his earnestness and laying a hand on Richard's knee, "Jemmy's no more'n a shaver t' me. Can't do half a hand's turn o' nothin', he can't. Ain't the fust thing t' what I be."

"But then suppose you wouldn't come?" said Richard.

"Tell yer I *will*," said Wily Poll, earnestly. "Jest yer keep the pies ready, and I'll be on hand."

"All right," said Richard; "when will you come?"

"What's the use o' comin'?" said the boy. "Ain't I here?"

"Oh, very good," said the young farmer, getting up. "If you'll eat that other quirl cake then, Wily, we'll go work."

CHAPTER VII.

GREAT was Mrs Peasely's astonishment, to see her son walk in at noon with Wily Poll following him.

"O Dick! Dick!" she cried, "you've fetched the wrong boy!"

"I's all right now, please 'm'," said Wily Poll, bobbing his head. "And I's ready for dinner."

"Yes, it's all right, mother," said Richard, with a laugh. "This is my boy—Wily Poll. He's had a good splash in the brook, and so of course he's more hungry than ever."

It is astonishing how different our thoughts and wishes look, if they are suddenly personified and set before us. Mrs Peasely was for a minute more dismayed than she would have believed possible. Of course it was the first resolution of the Society that every needy child should be furnished with a home, and of course it was a delightful thing to have Mrs Graves take Jemmy Lucas; but for her —in her neat household, with her many cares!—whatever could Richard be thinking of? She stood speechless,—then glancing at him, saw his face lit up with a merry smile, and felt her own grow red.

"Fairly caught, mother!" said her son, breaking into a laugh. "Now, can't we have some dinner? I've had a morning's work of it, and am hungry too."

Mrs Peasely bustled about without a word, setting on the dinner, but eyeing Wily Poll between whiles much as if he were a young monkey or a tame bear, suddenly brought home to amuse the family. Looking round once, she found that Richard had whisked the boy up-stairs, bringing him down again shortly with the rags replaced by old garments of his own; so that Wily Poll looked now a tolerably decent fellow. And by this time Mrs Peasely had recovered herself a little by dint of a hearty scolding.

"What's Dick at?" said old Squire Peasely, looking on from his corner. "Be that the boy he was to fetch home for Graves?"

"He's fetched this one for himself, father," said Mrs Peasely, trying to laugh.

"We don't want a boy," said Squire Peasely, disapprovingly.

"I guess Dick does, father," said Mrs Peasely. "And he gen'rally knows what he wants."

"That's so," said the old man, looking perplexed. "But he's clean out this time."

"Oh, well, we'll see," said Mrs Peasely, soothingly. "Dick'll manage it right, I daresay. Dinner's ready now, and of course the poor child must have his dinner. Dick says *he's* hungry—so doubtless the boy is too."

But speak as cheerfully as she might, the good woman was—as she confessed afterwards—sorely "put about." Richard kept his new charge down at his end of the table, and attended to him in a way that left no one else anything to do in that line. Yet in spite of all, Mrs Peasely found herself watching Wily Poll to a degree that quite interfered with her own dinner. Hungry? why if he eat at that rate, he would need a chicken pie baked for himself alone, with a special pot of potatoes, and another of apple sauce. How often would she have to make bread now?—Every day? How long would her pickles stand such an onslaught? As for buck-wheat cakes and molasses, Mrs Peasely trembled to think of them; and coffee must now be boiled by the gallon.

Then what if he should (so to speak) swallow his spoon, by slipping it into his pocket? Mrs Peasely's thoughts ran on, and she just was counting her spoons next day, and missing one, when she caught Richard's eye and heard him laugh.

"Maybe not, mother," he said. "I guess not!"

"I didn't speak to you, child!" said the good woman, again much put about.

"Goin' to plough this arternoon, Dick?" said his father.

"No, sir—I'm going to Vinegar Hill."

"Why, I thought you went this morning!" said Mrs Peasely.

"No, I didn't," said Richard. "Vinegar Hill came to me."

Wily Poll listened, and laid down his knife and fork for the first time.

"Don't yer go!" he said, earnestly. "They's a bad set, and they's jest come all sort o' dodges over yer. Don't yer go!"

"You shall go along, and take care of me." said Richard.

But Wily Poll knew when he was well off.

"*I* ain't agoin'," he said, evidently suspecting a trap. "I likes it better here."

"You must stay in the house, then, till I come back," said the young man, getting up from the table. "Mother, can't you set him to churning or something?—I daresay I shan't be gone long."

"Churning! at this time o' day!" said Mrs Peasely, with some sharpness. "Bless the boy!—whatever's become o' your sense, Richard?"

"Safe, I hope," said the young man, laughing.

"But stop—just look here!" said Mrs Peasely, following her son to the door. "Whatever *are* you thinkin' of, Dick?" she added in a whisper, with her hand on his shoulder. "I'd sooner take charge of—of a ring-tailed monkey, at once," said the good woman, in straits for a comparison. "What *could* you be thinkin' of?"

"Why, I was thinking of the first of your resolutions, mother," he said, with a look half laughing and half grave

"If he's *less* than 'the least of these,' I'm sorry. Good by—I'll be back soon."

And Richard Peasely strode off, followed by Wily Poll, and Mrs Peasely stood watching them both. The first of the resolutions!—what was that? Mrs Peasely thought it over again. "Every one of those forlorn children that needed a home should have one." So it stood. And "the least of these!"—who were they? "Hungry, and thirsty, and naked, and sick, and in prison"—that was the list. Was Wily Poll "less" than these?—nay, he was just one of them. Mrs Peasely looked again, following the two figures as they passed down to the barn, with eyes that had found a new point of view. The strong, elastic, well-made form of the young farmer, with health and activity and truth in every motion,—that was God's free gift to her,—her joy and her pride. And that shambling, creeping boy that followed, brought up hitherto upon want and craft, was not he also God's gift? Had not the Lord just brought him to her, saying in the words of old time : "Rear this child for me, and I will give thee wages ?"

Mrs Peasely laid her head against the door-post with a gush of tears, vowing in her heart a vow that was half a prayer ; she would be a mother to Wily Poll.

Richard saw the change as he rattled by in his waggon, and gave her a sunny smile that made her heart leap ; and Wily Poll saw it too, for he crept close to her, and looked up in her face.

"*Ain't* him handsome,—jest !" he ventured at last, as the waggon wheeled out of sight.

"If he ain't, I don't know who is !" Mrs Peasely answered with energy.

"Guess he'll notion some o' the other fellers 'stead o' me ?" Wily asked, doubtfully.

"No, indeed," said Mrs Peasely ; "he's not gone for that. Now, Wily, you and I'll set to work, and have the house all nice by the time he comes back. I'll show you how to wash the dishes, and then you shall sweep out the kitchen, and I'll make some cake."

" 'Twon't be for supper, will it?" inquired Wily Poll with interest. But being much heartened by the assurance that it would, he set to work in earnest over the dishes, proving himself quick to learn and to do. New ways came easy—how far would old ways crop out? Mrs Peasely tried hard not to watch the boy—and found herself watching him all the time !

Wily Poll was not slow to find this out, but took it as too much a matter of course to be offended. Indeed, he undertook to set Mrs Peasely's mind at rest on the subject of his own proclivities.

"I ain't ter tech nothin' 'fore he comes back," he explained. "I telled him so, and he telled me so,—so it's a bargain."

And Wily kept his word.

Richard Peasely, meanwhile, amused, comforted, full of many thoughts, went swiftly along towards Vinegar Hill. Suddenly came a hail—

"Say !—Dick !"

Joe Comstock stood by the fence of his own ploughed field, looking over. Richard Peasely pulled up.

"Nobody sick, is there?" said young Comstock.

"Not down our way," said Richard. "What's the matter with you?"

"Where on earth are you going, this time o' day," said young Comstock. "'Tain't the middle of the afternoon yet."

"And what on earth are you resting your team for, if it ain't?" said Richard, laughing. "They won't know night from day, nor Sunday from week days, Joe, if you don't look out."

"Never you mind," said young Comstock, giving his arms a more easy position on the fence. "I'm resting myself. Wherever are you going, Dick?"

"Why, I'm going to Vinegar Hill," said Richard, bravely.

Joe Comstock laughed long and loud.

"They've broke you to harness, sure as ever the world !" he said. "Goin' to take a boy, Dick?"

Y

"Thank you—I've got one," said young Peasely. "I'm after one for Ahab Graves."

"Ahab Graves'll thank you," said Joe Comstock. "I saw through him t'other night. That pretty wife o' his does rule the roast. And by the way, Dick, if I was you, I'd go round by Squire King's, and get company. Vinegar Hill's such a nice drive,—and gives ye so much to talk about."

"If you was me, you'd mind your own business," said Richard, something hotly. "I must be about it too. Hope you'll get rested 'fore I get back, Joe."

And away went the young farmer at the double quick of his good horse, and lazy Joe Comstock stood still and looked after him.

A mile or so of that pace cooled Richard down, scattering both the flush on his face and the annoyance in his heart.

"There,"—he said to himself, "of course some folks'll make fun. But I'm going, for all. And this shan't be the last time, if it is the first. What was that the old stranger minister said now?—

"'Ye must take the wind on your face, if ye would fetch Christ.'"

Richard Peasely bared his head to the fresh spring breeze that came sweeping and rustling through the woods, accepting it both in the reality and the figure.

A little further on, quite near the confines of Vinegar Hill, he met Mrs Coon, or rather he overtook her.

"Mrs Coon!—so far away from 'all the six,'" called out the young farmer, cheerily.

"Yes, I'm after the seventh," said Mrs Coon, smiling.

"Oh, that explains it," said Richard, reining up. "Then we're both going the same way. Jump in, Mrs Coon, and I'll give you a lift. Now you shall tell me where to find Jemmy Lucas, and what I'm to do with the people here generally. I'd sooner plough up half my farm—and I'd about as leave hem a pocket-handkerchief! How do you get hold of 'em, Mrs Coon?—and what do you do *then ?*"

"Why, it's the Lord must take hold of 'em," said Mrs Coon, with a shy glance at her questioner.

"But we first ?" queried Richard.

"No, not a bit," said Mrs Coon. "We *with* the Lord—that's all. Just think o' Peter tugging away at the man that couldn't stand,—tryin' to get him on his feet and hold him there by main strength for a spell, and then askin' the Lord to cure him !"

"Is that my way, I wonder ?" said Richard, half to himself.

"Peter just gave him his hand 'in the name of Jesus,' and it was all done in a minute," Mrs Coon said softly.

"And you mean ?"—questioned the young farmer.

"I mean," said Mrs Coon, colouring, "that folks should pray their work. Feelin' just like a hand through which the Lord's comin'."

"I know he *may* come," said Richard. "I can't be sure of it."

"Well, when all your expectation is only from the Lord," said Mrs Coon, "you'll find yourself expectin' a great deal."

"Even at Vinegar Hill," said Richard, as the mountain which only faith could touch came in sight.

"Ay !" said Mrs Coon. "'Whatsoever the Lord pleased, that did He in heaven, and in earth, and in the sea, and in all deep places !'"

"Mrs Coon," said Richard, suddenly, "however came it that you—— No, that's none of my business," he said, checking himself.

"I guess it is," said Mrs Coon, with a smile. "However came it that I didn't come here long afore ? Was that it ? Well, I s'pose I thought I had my hands full a'ready. It's a mistake we're all liable to, but it besets me."

And with that Mrs Coon got out of the waggon, and went to search for a "seventh" child to foster and bring up.

CHAPTER VIII.

RICHARD PEASELY found no difficulty in his new undertaking, so far as it concerned Jemmy Lucas, except, indeed, to persuade the boy to get into the waggon, all rags as he was, and so present himself before the eyes of his new friends at the village. And even that was not a very hard matter, by dint of Richard's handsome face and bright way of putting things. Mrs Lucas hurried them off.

"I ain't glad to be rid of ye, child," she said, "but I'm first-rate glad ye're goin'! It's the best thing I've seen this ten year. And don't you never come back,—d'ye hear?"

"I's comin' to see you every day," said Jemmy, with a little tremble of his mouth.

"No, you ain't," said the woman, firmly; "if you come back, Lucas'll find some way to keep ye; so don't you never come *near* comin' back."

"She'll come and see you," said the young farmer, kindly.

"No, I won't," said the woman. "Much they'd thank me where he's goin'! I'll get sight o' him somehow, maybe, now and then; but there'll be no 'comin to see' between us."

"I's get sight o' you too!" said Jemmy Lucas, brightening up. "Down to the cross roads, mother, Saturday. Will it be afore supper?—or arter?"

"It'll be afore my supper, if it's ever," said the woman, bitterly. "Lucas fetches that, most days, and I ain't apt to go out after it. You's safe, child,—I'm glad! Jemmy," she whispered, stooping by him, "don't ye never walk crooked—d'ye hear? Or you won't never get where Molly is. Now mind!"—

She wrapped him in her arms with a choked sob that was almost a cry,—the pitifullest thing, Richard declared afterwards, that he had ever heard; and then she unlocked the boy's arms from around her neck, and herself carried him out and put him in the waggon, but shedding no tear then.

Poor Jemmy, on his part, certainly shed enough for both when they first drove away; but Richard Peasely had a natural gift of comfort and help in all sorts of contingencies, and he drew such delightful bright pictures of Mrs Graves, and the farm, and Jemmy's learning to be "a man"—that acme of attainable perfection—that the child forgot both his rags and his tears, and listened in a state of enchantment. It was late in the afternoon now, and the busy fields were all deserted; while wide open barn doors told of the evening feeding and milking and rubbing down that were in full progress.

"Ever see Mr Graves, Jemmy?" Richard asked, as they drew near the house.

"Oh, I's seed him often enough," said Jemmy Lucas; "he ain't never saw me."

"I guess he ain't in yet," said Richard, looking towards the distant barn, its doors flung open like the rest, "so you'll only see Mrs Graves first."

"I knows *her!*" said Jemmy Lucas, warmly. "Ain't she jest a beauty, though!"

"Well, when Mr Graves comes in," said Richard, smiling, "you must get right up out of your chair and make him a bow, and then wait till he speaks to you. Know how to make a bow, Jemmy?"

"Guess I does!" said Jemmy Lucas, ducking his head with much more ease than ceremony.

"Well, make it a little slower than that to Mr Graves, and say, 'Yes, sir,' and 'No, sir,' to him." Richard went on, driving slow that his instructions might have the more force. "And, Jemmy, remember—everything here belongs to Mr and Mrs Graves. If you want something, ask 'em for it,—but don't touch a thing without leave, as they do at Vinegar Hill."

Jemmy Lucas looked up with full intelligence.

"I knows," he said, "I used. But we's set out."

"Set out!" said Richard, looking down at the little fellow by his side.

"Molly and me," explained Jemmy, with the quiver that always came over his face at any mention of his little companion. "We's set out ter find the King, 'cause He's asked us, yer know. And she's got there fust—and I's follerin's hard as I can."

Richard Peasely thought unutterable thoughts as he drew up before the farm-house.

"I'll see you through thick and thin, Jemmy," he said, as he put the boy down. "If ever you want help, come to me. Ah, here she is!—Mrs Graves, I've brought Mr Graves his 'sample o' wheat.' Tell him to give it the best chance he's got! It'll pay." And the young farmer rattled off, leaving Mrs Graves and Jemmy Lucas to their mutual rejoicing and explanation, and general exchange of sentiments. Then Mrs Graves hurried Jemmy into the house and up-stairs.

"We must be all ready for supper, dear!" she said, bringing the child into his little paradise of a room, which was certainly warm enough on that occasion, and helping him to get rid of every vestige of Vinegar Hill. Then while Jemmy stood wonderingly before the little glass to get acquainted with himself over again, Mrs Graves hurried down to her dairy, bidding Jemmy follow to the kitchen fire as soon as he was ready.

And so it happened, that when Farmer Graves came in with his milk pails the kitchen was empty,—and when after a few minutes he came back there, with changed dress and improved hands and hair, there sat in the chimney corner a small, pale, neatly clad boy, with terribly thin cheeks and a strangely wistful little face. He was all alone, for Mrs Graves, with her dairy work all finished, yet stood still in the sweet-scented pantry-like place; leaning her head against the doorpost, and quite unable to come out till she heard how things were going.

Just at the time when Mr Graves came in, Jemmy Lucas sat eyeing the fire, and at that very moment was making it the profoundest bow that he could get off. But he was on his feet in a second, and favoured Mr Graves with the twin bow to that bestowed on the fire. Then he stood still and

waited. Whereupon Mr Graves made the only remark that
occurred to him, and said—

"Hullo!"—

"Yes, sir," said Jemmy Lucas, true to his lesson.

"Where the dickens do *you* come from?" said the farmer
in some confusion of mind. "Boys seem to be plenty!
Ain't the second cousin o' my grandmother's niece, are
ye?"

"No, sir," said the child, glancing up at the tall strong
man before him. "I's Jemmy Lucas, sir."

"You ain't never from Vinegar Hill?" said Mr Graves.

"Yes, sir," said Jemmy Lucas. "I comed this arternoon."

"Don't look like it. Oh, you did!" said Farmer Graves.
"And so you belong to Vinegar Hill?"

"Please, sir, I b'longs here now," said the child, simply.
"Mother said I warn't never to come back no more."

Whereat Mr Graves, being then and there at the end of
his tether, stood still in the middle of the floor and shouted—

"'Lizy!"—

There's no denying it,—Mrs Graves did look a little bit
"Huldy" when she came out—

> "All kind o' trembly round the mouth,
> And teary round the lashes,"—

but she controlled herself bravely.

"You want me, Ahab?" she said.

"Always want ye!" said Mr Graves, with an indescribable
mixture in his voice. "Always did, and always shall."

"For what in particular just now?" said Mrs Graves, with
a tiny bit of a laugh that was also just a wee bit hysterical.

"Supper comin' off any time 'fore mornin'?" inquired Mr
Graves. "Or is we to live by lookin' at each other? 'Tain't
hardly hearty enough fare for me,—and one o' the party's
fed on it too long a'ready."

"Supper'll be on the table in just two seconds!" cried
Mrs Graves, taking heart from these last words, and flying
round like a small locomotive at play. "Come help me,
Jemmy!—quick!"

Now that was one thing Jemmy could be. He could be
soft in his motions too, poor child, having learned that good
art in a very bad school. But it all was in place now, and
he darted back and forth after Mrs Graves so readily, and
brought dishes and set them down so quietly, that Farmer
Graves approved in spite of himself.

"Well done, little chap!" he said. "You've earned *your*
supper, there's not a doubt. I say, 'Lizy—got that 'ere big
pitcher o' milk handy?"

Of course she had!—and a harder man than Abab Graves
would have been touched, to see that shadow of a child
taking in health and strength from a little of its overflowing
abundance. The farmer found himself watching the opera-
tion with curious interest, almost to the neglect of his own
supper; for well as he knew what "hungry" meant, "fam-
ished" was a word unknown. Mr Graves gave a groan of
an extremely mixed description.

"'Lizy," he said, "it'll be just the best thing for him to
run out to the field now and then, where they're ploughin',
and get the smell o' the earth. Ain't nothin' up to that, in
my experience."

Mrs Graves gave sign of assent, but her voice couldn't be
trusted.

"Times when he ain't wanted here, ye know," Mr Graves
went on. "Send him along a spell afore dinner—case I
forget," the farmer added with a laugh. "Father livin'?"
—this suddenly to Jemmy Lucas.

Jemmy flushed very much, answering, "Yes, sir."

"How comes it you ain't helpin' *him*, then?" said Mr
Graves.

"Ain't nothin' I can do—'cept—'cept"—Jemmy hesitated,
—"'Cept what's crooked," he said at last.

"Crooked!" Farmer Graves repeated. "Ay!—I see.
What 'nd he set ye at now?"

"Liftin',"—Jemmy Lucas spoke very slowly and unwill-
ingly,—"and runnin' off—and fetchin' in. 'Most all sorts,
sir."

"And he learned ye t' do 'em all, I warrant," said Mr

Graves, with something of the old suspicious look coming back.

"Yes, sir," the child said in his quiet voice. Mr Graves felt puzzled.

"How about your mother?" he said. "What did *she* teach ye?"

Jemmy considered.

"She told us we wouldn't never get there ef we went crooked," he said, with a deep sigh as he thought of Molly.

"Get where?" Farmer Graves inquired, not unnaturally.

"King's house," Jemmy answered. "Arter we'd set out, yer know."

"The King's house!" Mr Graves repeated in high astonishment. "Now, 'Lizy, did ye ever! Who learned ye *that*, child?"

"White lady up to the meetin' house," said Jemmy Lucas.

And Mrs Graves added—

"Mrs Kensett."

"Ay, ay?" said Farmer Graves, certain uneasy recollections stealing over him. "Ay, ay? It's o' her sowin', is it? 'How many church members'—that's what she said, sure enough. Well, she's done her share, I guess."

"She telled us a heap," said Jemmy Lucas, feeling himself called upon to explain yet further. "And she giv' us the books, and Molly'n me read. And Molly'd 'splain wonderful!"

The bright look faded suddenly from the boy's face; he set down his half-finished cup of milk, and sitting back in his chair with lips tight pressed together, Jemmy Lucas touched nothing more that night.

CHAPTER IX.

NEXT morning everything sang,—Mrs Graves over her work, and Jemmy Lucas over his, and the birds in the bushes.

Only Mr Graves whistled slowly, as he drove his team along the dreary road to the potato field : could it be possible that "that 'ere boy" was going to turn out a comfort after all ?

No doubts on the subject troubled his little wife at home. As the days went on, Mrs Graves worked over butter and made pies, with a fulness of content that was only equalled by the spring flush of joy outside. And in much the same mood, Jemmy Lucas washed dishes, and swept the floor, and tended the fire, saying very little the while, but thinking a whole world ; breaking forth into snatches of song, and checking himself before they were well out of his mouth. Only when he was fairly away in the stoop setting that to rights, all alone by himself, did the words and tune flow on without interruption. What was he singing ? Mrs Graves listened, but could not tell. One tune she recognised as sometimes sung in the church, but the next was wild and new. She crept softly round to a little window in an angle of the house, where she could both see and hear ; listening then with all her heart, though soon her head went down on the window seat.

Jemmy Lucas had done his sweeping, and stood in the open doorway gazing up at the bright sky. Half leaning upon his broom, speaking the words with a clear distinctness that was more like talking than singing, so he told his hymn. Well Mrs Graves remembered the refrain, as one which had been on the lips of little Molly Limp,—the rest she had never heard.

> " 'Little child, I call thee to me ;
>   I will take thee for my own.
> Art thou ready ? Wilt be steady ?
>   Choose me for thy King alone.'
>   'Yes, Lord Jesus.'

> " 'Little child, I bid thee listen
>   Every time I speak to thee :
> Do my pleasure—then the treasure
>   Of my love I 'll give to thee.'
>   'Yes, Lord Jesus.'

" ' Little child, I bid thee follow
　　Everywhere that I may lead,—
Always cheerful, never fearful,
　　Trusting me in every need.'
　　　' Yes, Lord Jesus.'

" ' Little child, remember always
　　That the Lord hates every sin ;
Then be careful, and be prayerful,
　　Watch and pray lest wrong begin.'
　　　' Yes, Lord Jesus.' "

The hymn ended, and Jemmy Lucas put away his broom
in the corner of the old stoop, and was hastening in to see
what more there was for him to do, when at the open door
appeared a most unwelcome sight,—even the face of Jem
Crook peering round from behind the doorpost. Jemmy
Lucas stopped short, in some doubt as to what was best to
do.

"Why, *'tis* him," cried Jem Crook then, with affected surprise. "Here I's been a sayin' to myself, 'tain't never
Jemmy Lucas, as I was so fond of."

"No, I guess it ain't," said Jemmy Lucas, rather coolly.
"Not if you *was* fond of him."

"Come now, don't yer be hard on a feller," said Jem
Crook. "I say, Jemmy !—good pickin's and sich ? "

" I's done with pickin's," said Jemmy Lucas, stoutly.

"O' course yer has !" said Jem Crook,—" but you's a
smart boy, Jemmy, and knows what's round. Supposin' yer
hadn't done with 'em, yer know ? "

"Tell yer I *has*," said Jemmy Lucas. "And the sooner
you is, Jem Crook, the better.'

"Me ?" said Jem Crook, with extreme innocence,—" there
ain't the fust pickin' o' a wishbone about *me*. What with
Peter's bein' took serious, and Sam's takin' ter one foot, and
your's goin' out t' service, and my gettin' up feelin's—Dear !
dear !" said Jem Crook, affectingly, "t' think o' how times
was, and how they ain't."

"Take care o' yer feelin's, or they'll catch ye," said Jemmy
Lucas, with some scorn.

"Fact!" said Jem Crook, looking more melancholy than ever. "There's Wily too—*he's* run aground,—take more 'n a freshet ter float *him*."

"Don't you try to do it," said Jemmy Lucas, earnestly. "Now, Jem Crook, jest you let him alone."

"Beats me ter tech him!" said Jem Crook. "That 'ere young Peasely don't never let him out o' his sight for two seconds. No more 'n old Graves don't you."

"They don't watch me, neither," said Jemmy Lucas.

"Saw *her* head a-lookin' out arter you, as I come along," said Jem Crook. "I say, Jemmy! this here thing's about played out now. Yer's got all smarted up, and yer's found where things be, and yer's tired on playin' pretty,—now jest yer give 'em the slip, like a man. Other folks' heels ain't hardly the place for a chap o' spirit. Why, yer's growed as meek as skim milk!—ain't one o' yer friends as would ha' know'd yer but me."

"Well, *you* needn't ter, next time," said Jemmy Lucas. "Not unless you's got new ways."

"Seen yer mammy last night," said Jem Crook, eyeing the boy with no kind look.

"Oh, did yer?" cried Jemmy Lucas,—"what'd she say, Jem?"

"Her's most sick abed for yer," said Jem Crook. "Would be quite, I guess, only she ain't got much o' one ter be sick on. Kinder spirits are down, it does, jest ter think how yer's forgot her and took up with other folks."

"But she wanted me to," said Jemmy Lucas. "And I haven't, neither."

"Can't tell nothin' 'bout that," said Jem Crook. "'Taint no business o' mine, anyway. I can tell her yer's most forgot yer own name—so 'taint no wonder if yer has her. Mornin' ter yer."

And Jem Crook turned and walked away with an air of deep grief and disappointment.

"Jem! Jem Crook!" called Jemmy Lucas, in much distress; but Jem Crook gave no heed, and walked away faster than ever.

Jemmy Lucas leaned his head against the doorpost again, greatly troubled.

"But she *telled* me not ter come back," he said at last. "So I *couldn't*, anyhow. And I's learnin'—and when I's a big man' then we'll see! The King said I was ter come here, sure."

And Jemmy Lucas hummed softly to himself again—

> " 'Little child, I bid thee follow
> Everywhere that I may lead,
> Always cheerful, never fearful,
> Trusting me in every need.'

"There it is now!" said the boy to himself, much comforted. "Yes, Lord Jesus,—so I will! The King knows,—and my! why, He can do everything! 'Course He can look arter mother 'n me too. I's jest got ter trust Him—that's all." And a radiant little face presently appeared before Mrs Graves, and a happy little voice asked for—

"More work, ma'am?"

"Why, Jemmy," said Mrs Graves, "I thought maybe you were tired—you staid out in the stoop so long."

"I ain't, though," said Jemmy Lucas. "Not by a long jump, ma'am."

"But you were leaning your head against the doorway for ever so long," said Mrs Graves.

"Yes 'm," said the child, simply, "but I was only tellin' the King."

"Telling the King!" Mrs Graves repeated. "What did you have to tell Him then, Jemmy, in the midst of your work?"

"Midst o' work's a like enough time," said Jemmy Lucas. "Yer see, ma'am, one o' the old boys had been round, botherin' me. And when I's bothered, I always does have ter stop and tell the King, 'cause He knows," the boy added with a sigh of relief—then turning to Mrs Graves eagerly for orders. "Now, ma'am, what's next?"

Mrs Graves gave her directions, but as Jemmy Lucas went off to his work, singing his favourite refrain, she thought to herself that he was like to teach as much as he would learn, and she to learn more important things than she could teach.

CHAPTER X.

"Good morning, Mr Graves," said the gay voice of Richard Peasely, some days after this. Mr Graves was in the field, and Richard on horseback at the fence. "How's your new seed wheat coming on?"

"Well, pretty fair," said the farmer, checking his sturdy team. "Don't quite know what to think of it yet. Seems to be sproutin' out consid'rable. How's your'n?"

"Rather more of a mixture than I could wish," said Richard, with a laugh; "but I'm in hopes of a crop by and by."

"Somewheres along two bushels t' the acre, I guess," said Mr Graves, dryly. "And they says you're tryin' to plough up the old hill itself!—heard ye was down there last Sunday a preachin'."

"Not preaching exactly," said Richard,—"only Bible reading. Mrs Coon has her days, and I have mine."

"Like t' know where ye get spare time?" said Mr Graves, somewhat severely. "*I* don't find none in the market, at no price."

"Make it as we go along," said Richard, smiling. "But, Mr Graves, there's a lot o' those fellows hangin' round the village this morning,—so look after your boy a little. I'm going home to see to mine." And Richard Peasely galloped off, leaving Mr Graves in no pleasant state of mind.

"Allers the way!" he said to himself,—"jest you go stirrin' up a hornet's nest, and o' *course* next minute they're swarmin' all round the country. Look arter my boy!—that's what comes o' *havin'* a boy! Hain't I telled 'Lizy so, a matter o' twenty times? Like t' know who'll look arter this 'ere plough while I'm gone? No, no,—he's jest got to see to himself. Gee-up!"—

The patient oxen moved on, with impatient Mr Graves at their heels; the bright ploughshare cut its straight course through the stubble. Farmer Graves made extra time to the top of the field and back. But then he paused, and looked down along the road.

"Supposin' they should be round, now?" he said,-- "skeerin' 'Lizy t' death."

Mr Graves shut one eye, and peered up cautiously at the sun.

"'Tain't noon yet, by a long sight," he said,—"wants a good hour 'n a half. Don't see what ever I kin do. Haw, there!—come about, I tell ye!"—

Again the oxen trudged on, laying open another straight clean furrow to the top of the hill, and once more down to the bottom again. But this time Mr Graves found something to look at. A boy of some sixteen years old, respectably dressed, and of a very proper behaved presence, stood leaning over the bar place.

"Now he's come down the road, likely," thought Farmer Graves. "Reckon I'll ask him."

"Act as though ye was tired," he said, addressing the boy. "Come far this mornin'?"

"T'other end o' the village," said the boy. "Been workin' for Squire King a spell back."

"Oh, you come along that way," said Mr Graves. "Met many folks out?"

"Didn't see a livin' soul, 'cept one little shaver," answered the boy.

"Where was he goin'?" said Farmer Graves, pretending to busy himself with the ox yoke.

"Store," said the boy. "Got a lot o' the handsomest eggs ever I see. We's been short o' eggs down to our place and I'd ha' took the hull lot, but he jest set off t' run, soon as ever I mentioned it. So as he comed from down this way, I thought I'd jest step round and see if there warn't some more to be had. Mis' King's got a matter o' six hens all aching t' set."

"Well, ye can't get no eggs o' me," said Farmer Graves, something shortly. "We're scant too. What sort of a lookin' boy was it now?"

"Mighty fixed up," said the stranger. "Looked 'most

like a pictur', he did. Blue check shirt, and jacket and
trowsers o' butternut, and necktie and pocket handkercher'.
Smart as sixty. So you ain't got no spare eggs?—couldn't
let Mis' King have jest a settin'?"

"Ain't a spare egg about the place," said Farmer Graves,
contracting his brows. "Not as I knows on," he added,
half to himself. "Good day t' ye—sorry I can't oblige ye.
Haw, there! g' long!"—

"Now that's the very boy," said Mr Graves to himself,
as he mounted the hill. "And if them warn't my eggs, I'm
a Dutchman, and no more about it. *Thought* 'twas kind o'
queer the hens didn't lay. Reckoned they'd stole their
nests,—and 'stead o' that 'twas the eggs was stole. What'll
'Lizy say now?" quoth the farmer, with a chuckle. "Gee
up, now!—come about!"—

"Won't never believe it," he went on. "*That's* what
she'll say. Only way'll be t' go straight home and catch
him comin' back with the basket. Comes o' havin' boys!"
said Farmer Graves, with a groan. "I kin look arter myself, easy. Here I've got t' unhitch and go streakin' home
an hour afore noon!"

It was part of Mr Graves' plan to go quietly, so no sound
or warning of his approach reached the house, and Mrs
Graves was in blessful unconsciousness that her dinner
might be called for an hour too soon. Very quietly the farmer drove his team into the barn field, very quietly he came
stepping along through the chip-yard to the house. All was
quiet there too, only he heard his wife singing, as she was
wont, over her work.

"Poor thing, poor 'Lizy," said Mr Graves, with a stir of
compunction. "Now she'll just cry her eyes out over this,
as if it hadn't t' be looked for and expected; and it'll be—
'Oh give him another chance, Ahab'—and—'Don't be hard
on him, Ahab!'—as if I was a sort o' a stone chisel!" con-
cluded Mr Graves, with some natural indignation at the
comparison. "Can't be helped,—he's got t' walk. Feed
him up well, and let him go."

With which benevolent sentiment, Mr Graves entered the

kitchen, nearly making his wife drop the pan of potatoes she was just putting into the pot.

"Why, Ahab," she cried, "whatever's the matter? 'Tisn't a minute more than half-past."

"Guess I know the time o' day—commonly," said Mr Graves. "'*Most* as well as you do. No objection t' my comin' home at half-past, is there?"

"Why, no—of course not," said his wife, gazing at him. "Not if you like it, and if you're well."

"Ef I'm sick, s'pose I'd better stay in the lot," said Mr Graves.

"But *are* you sick, Ahab?" persisted his wife, setting down her pan and coming towards him.

"Tell ye no," said Mr Graves, placing himself so as to conveniently watch the high road. "Had some business t' attend to—that's all."

Mrs Graves was too much of a woman not to see through this, but she was also enough of a woman to ask no further questions. So silently, and with some undefined forebodings of evil, she took up her pan again, put the potatoes on to boil, and began to fetch out bread and butter and pickles and salt; setting them all on the table in a mechanical sort of way, with her mind full of other things.

"Love ye?—I ain't a mouse," said Mr Graves, something sharply, when her quick glance had come his way for about the twentieth time.

"I hope I'm not a cat!" said his wife, trying to laugh. "But whatever *are* you sitting there for, Ahab?"

"Like it better ef I'd stand up?" said Mr Graves. "Want to be as accommodatin' as I kin."

"But you're so queer," Mrs Graves broke out.

"Oh, well, if that's all," said Mr Graves, "jist make your mind easy. I ain't the only one. We all has turns on it by spells. How come you t' be settin tables?—Thought that ere boy was a goin t' save ye all kinds o' trouble."

"There," said Mrs Graves, "*that's* it. I *knew* it was something about Jemmy!"

And with all the briskness of success, the little woman finished her preparations, and putting the spider on the fire, began to fry great slices of juicy ham.

"Don't believe she never thinks o' nothin' else but him," said Farmer Graves, in a tone which the fizzing and sputtering of the ham turned into an indistinguishable murmur.

"What did you say, Ahab?" cried his wife.

"I say, what about Jemmy?" said Mr Graves. "Ain't gone back to Vinegar Hill, is he?"

"Oh dear no!" said Mrs Graves. "Jemmy and I have been hard at work in the cellar all the morning, and then I sent him up-stairs to make himself decent."

"How long's it take him?" inquired Mr Graves. "Had about since ten o'clock, hasn't he?"

"He's had about since ten minutes before you came in," said Mrs Graves with another glance, as she dished up her ham, and went off to the pantry.

"Got any o' that 'ere apple butter left, 'Lizy?" Mr Graves called after her. "Ham's kind o' dry eatin' 'thout eggs or some sort o' sass."

"You don't want eggs, then?" said Mrs Graves, pausing in the pantry door, basket in hand. "Yes, I've got plenty of apple butter, and plenty of butter not made out of apples, and plenty of apples not made into butter You can have which you like."

"'Sakes!—ain't she spunky now," said Mr Graves, admiringly. "Firin' up like an old seventy-six muskit!"

"Yes, they've always got a charge in 'em nobody counts on," said Mrs Graves, with some spirit.

"What on airth are ye standin' there for, lookin' at me?" said the farmer. "Ain't crocked my face, have I?"

"Thought maybe you'd come home to get dinner," said Mrs Graves; "so I'm waiting to hear what it's to be, that's all."

"Well I *haven't*," said the farmer, "so *that's* all. Go ahead, and get what ye like. I don't care a red cent."

With an indescribable little air of the head, Mrs Graves came forward to the fire, and setting down her basket, began to take out the large snow-white eggs, and break them into the pan.

"What does eggs cost ye, down to the store?" said Mr Graves, raising his voice above the sputtering chorus that the eggs set up.

"More than they do at the barn—that's all I know," said his wife, carefully handling her slice.

"I'll go bail for that," said the farmer, coming towards the fire in his turn, and taking up the basket. "Why, here's a matter o' eighteen left! Needn't ha' bought so many at once, 'Lizy; mebbe we'll find some way o' gettin' our own."

"Well I do believe you're crazy!" said the little woman, standing back once more to look at him. "You haven't been drinking, because you never do. For pity's sake, Ahab, sit down and eat you're dinner, and don't speak another word as long as there's an egg left on the table, or I shall think it ain't you."

Mr Graves obeyed in silence, yet seeming not much more like himself than he had in speech; and his wife, with really an anxious look on her brow, gave for the present her chief attention to Jemmy Lucas. Her own dinner did not amount to much.

"Very fair eggs," said Mr Graves at last, when the dish was empty, and pushing back his plate which was in like condition. "Never did think much o' store eggs, but these is fair o' the sort. What d'ye s'pose ails our hens now, 'Lizy?" he went on, eyeing Jemmy Lucas furtively the while.

"Haven't heard them complain," said Mrs Graves, trying to laugh. "Unless because they can't lay twice a day. They seem to enjoy the first time so much."

"Pity they wouldn't do it more days then, if they *does*," said Mr Graves, still eyeing Jemmy Lucas, who went on finishing his dinner with extreme composure. "How does the eggs taste t' you, Jemmy? Ain't nothing bitter about 'em?"

"No, sir—mine's sweet as anythin'," said Jemmy Lucas, looking up in surprise.

"Ain't, hey?" said Farmer Graves.   "Now I kind o
notioned there was."

Mrs Graves gave a little impatient sigh.

"Ahab," she said, "I wish you'd stay home this afternoon.
Now do! I don't think this hot sun's good for you. It'll
give you a headache, as sure as the world."

"Sun ain't hot," said Mr Graves; "and you ain't so dreadful lively down here that I kin afford t' give the arternoon
for it."

"Oh, I'll be as lively as a cricket," said Mrs Graves, rousing up.   "I've got a grand story to tell you."

"Tell ahead, then," said Mr Graves, helping himself to
another quarter of dried apple pie.   "No time like the pressin'.   Maybe by and by I mightn't want to hear it—or you
mightn't want to tell, which comes to the same thing."

Poor Mrs Graves drew another long breath—then got herself in hand.

"Well," she began, "Jemmy, and I were busy over the
dishes, and planning what we'd do in the cellar, when all of
a sudden I heard a hen cackle,—that Dorking, Ahab,—you
know she always lays early."

"Used to," said Mr Graves.

"Well, she *does*," said his wife.   "But we've been short
of eggs lately."

"So I said," put in the farmer again.

"And I thought maybe some of the hens had hid their
nests," Mrs Graves went on, fighting her anxiety as best she
could.   "So I told Jemmy to drop the towel, and run as fast
as he could, and see where she was. And I waited and waited,
and he didn't come back."

"Ah,—didn't come back?" said the farmer.

"No," said his wife.   "So then I ran out too. And there
was Jemmy, all beset with another boy. Jemmy had his
arms round the egg basket, and the other boy had his arms
round *him*, and I really thought he'd scratch the child's
eyes out—or kick his feet off, before I could get there. You
can see the mark yet."

"Yes, he's tore up considerable," said Mr Graves, whose

own face was undergoing sundry changes. "Didn't know, but he'd been in the bushes."

"No, it was that boy's claws," said Mrs Graves. "He might as well have been a cat, at once. He didn't see me at first, and I almost got hold of him,—but then he let go and ran, faster than anything I ever saw in my life!"

"Don't he, though!" said Jemmy Lucas, who had listened with intense enjoyment. "Even his foot can't stop him."

"What come o' the eggs?" said Mr Graves.

"Oh, we brought them down to the house," said Mrs Graves, —"a whole nest-full: just a little cracked, some of them were."

"They'd ha' been all smash, only the basket was so packed," said Jemmy Lucas.

"And Jemmy rolled himself round it like a ball," said Mrs Graves. "I never saw anything quite so funny."

"'Cause yer know if Sam 'd once got a hold of it," explained Jemmy, "that 'ud ha' been the end. He's so strong."

"Oh, then you knowed who it was?" said Mr Graves, studying the boy's face.

"Guess I did!" said Jemmy Lucas. "Ain't a boy down our way as don't know Sam Dodd—and wish he didn't."

"What sort of a lookin' chap is he, now?" said Mr Graves, the light of a new idea beginning to dawn upon his face.

"Big chap," said Jemmy Lucas,—"yaller hair, red face."

"Clothes all rags?" inquired Farmer Graves.

"No, sir," said Jemmy Lucas. "Sam don't *never* wear rags. Old Dodd's rich as fun, and Sam allers fixes up tip-top."

"Sort o' cast in his eye?" said Mr Graves, the light of the idea growing stronger.

"Sees right round the corner all the time he's lookin' straight ahead," said Jemmy Lucas. "Limps, too, since he fell down-stairs."

Mr Graves left the table.

"Thought I'd seen him!" he said. "*Next* time guess I'll know it. 'Lizy, don't ye worry 'bout o' me,—I'm all right, thank ye. Come down t' the lot along towards supper-time, you 'n the little chap, and I 'll give ye a ride home in the cart, and learn him how t' drive the team."

"If I ain't sold out *this* day," said Mr Graves, as he tramped off at the heels of his oxen, "then it 's jest because there warn't nothin' o' me to sell,—that 's all !"

CHAPTER XI.

It was a pretty thing, that afternoon, to see the little procession from the field to the house. Up in the great ox-cart sat Mrs Graves, her face all April sunshine, and not a bit troubled by the company of the plough and harrow that reposed in the cart behind her. Had she not the distinguishing dignity of a bundle-of-straw cushion ?

The team, in splendid order, as Mr Graves' cattle always were, stepped briskly along to their rest and supper ; and by their side marched Jemmy Lucas—half bewildered with pleasure, brandishing the long whip, and giving his whole soul to the mastery of "Gee" and "Haw" and "Come about." Farmer Graves himself, walking a few steps in the rear, was scarcely the least pleased of the party,—the very tone of his instructions told that, not to speak of various nods and glances that went to Mrs Graves in the cart. The spring breeze blew softly, the sun dipped slowly towards the west, and the little birds sang vespers on every bush and tree.

Richard Peasely on horseback met the cavalcade, and laughed for pleasure,—Mrs Bingham saw it afar off from her little waggon, and clapped her hands for joy. And hidden in the bushes by the wayside, cold, hard Mrs Lucas bent down her head among the young leaves, and cried the first warm, real tears that had wet her eyes for many a day.

"It 's about the best ride I ever had in my life," said Mrs Graves, as she sprang out of the ox-cart at her own door.

"First-rate teamster the little chap 'll make," said Mr Graves, approvingly. "Cool, ye see, and steady. Knows what he's about—and so the team know what *they*'re about. Pictur'—ain't it?" added the farmer, in a half aside to his wife, and nodding his head towards Jemmy Lucas, whose little hand was making loving acquaintance with the dark red coat of the ox by which he stood. "Now, 'Lizy—want him t' help ye get supper?—or shall he go with me and turn out the team?"

"Oh, let him go with you!" Mrs Graves said, eagerly, then standing in the door to watch them, the tall figure and the little one; catching every sound of either voice; her eyes shining with a very rainbow of promise.

"Ahab!" she called out, as the oxen went down the slope towards the barn,—"will you have some more eggs for supper?"

But the farmer shook his head.

"Guess not," he answered, without looking round. "Fact is, 'Lizy, I've had as many eggs this day as is good for me. Reckon I'll let 'em alone a spell."

Whereupon Mrs Graves went to work, and tossed up marvellous biscuits. And the night came down in utter peace upon the fair outlying fields, and the ploughed ridges and the springing grain, and the bright old farmhouse with its cheery supper table and happy faces.

So let Vinegar Hill rest. But down there as well as elsewhere now, spring work is gaining ground. Slowly but surely, faintly yet steadily, the work goes on; with not much leaf and blade as yet, but with a true living tiny root here and there, which will by and by show blade and ear and full corn in the ear.

Mrs Bingham has found her girl, and is well nigh as much wrapped up in her as is Mrs Graves in Jemmy Lucas. And *he* is growing up into quite a sturdy boy, under the sweet influences of sunshine; helpful within doors and without,—till it's a matter of question often now with Mr and Mrs Graves, who shall have him for the day. And the farmer will say—

"Ef you *kin* spare him, 'Lizy, why, I'll take him along,—that's all."

If you could be at the "cross-roads" on Saturday afternoon sometimes, you would see, too, how light will spread through the darkest places if once it has a chance. Jemmy Lucas is always there, and in those few minutes his mother gathers up and takes in her week's supply of sunshine ; she never will come to the farm ; but the hardness and the coldness are fast giving way. It gives Mrs Graves a twinge sometimes, thus to keep up Jemmy's hold upon his mother or rather hers upon him ; but there is no need : "legitimate affections never clash ;" and the boy loves her with a depth of love which she could hardly measure, save by her own for him.

Wily Poll is growing too. Not with so regular and swift a growth ; "the mixed seed" shows itself more in his case, and there are times of waywardness and trial. But he holds fast to Richard, and Richard to him.

Mrs Coon has her "seventh" well tucked in among the rest ; and is visitor, and Bible reader, and nurse, at Vinegar Hill, by turns. The women have learned to watch for her now, and to hail her coming.

Richard Peasely, too, does much of the same work, and is in hard treaty with two or three of the men to give up drinking,—promising to find them work and food and coffee.

Mrs Limp and the baby come regularly to Mrs Peasely's every week to wash, and both are thriving wonderfully. And Walter Limp has died in jail, before his term was out, and can make no one wretched any more. But nobody as yet can get hold of Peter, in any line of help or improvement. Nor does Sam Dodd's lame foot hinder his being first in all manner of mischief.

Old Mrs Peaseley goes down to Vinegar Hill once a week, and coaxes the children round her with gingerbread and pictures, and tells them Bible stories to take home and act out.

And Mrs Graves can do none of these things,—the farmer is as determined on that point as ever. But she is praying for Vinegar Hill ; and when she looks at Jemmy Lucas she gives thanks and is silent.

"How beautiful upon the mountains are the feet of him that bringeth good tidings, that publisheth peace; that bringeth good tidings of good, that publisheth salvation; that saith unto Zion, Thy God reigneth!"

THE END.

PRINTED BY BALLANTYNE, HANSON AND CO.
EDINBURGH AND LONDON

www.ingramcontent.com/pod-product-compliance
Lightning Source LLC
Chambersburg PA
CBHW021711110726
47902CB00005B/1149